Praise for *Cwen*:

'A clever, strange and wonderful book, which brims with mystery. A group of women recount their past and present stories, revealing their visions of the future. *Cwen* by Alice Albinia is a rare book, bold and powerful' Xiaolu Guo

'A wild, original, sure-footed feminist reimagining of the present and the past that brushes up against the mythical. It reminds us, eloquently and passionately, what is or can be possible, and in its depiction of a revolution becomes a revolutionary book itself. Beautiful work' Neel Mukherjee

'From the very first page, Alice Albinia's *Cwen* draws you into a world that is glittering with beauty and aching with promise. A portrait of the British Isles, *Cwen* is also an absorbing saga of women's lives drawn from different parts of the world, skilfully weaving in strands from Bosnia, Pakistan, France. This is a book that speaks of the persistent human need for freedom and community, and of the as-persistent clash of these impulses with power and authority. A story for our times, and a book that will endure' Taran Khan, author of *Shadow City: A Woman Walks Kabul*

'A phenomenal novel showing us that learning to love our female selves is essential for survival. Alice Albinia's diverse cast, from ancient Britain to contemporary Pakistan, step up to support each other, take down patriarchy and create a new collective story' Farhana Yamin, Environmental Lawyer, Woman's Hour Power List: Our Planet

'An unforgettable story with a dazzling cast of characters that will stay with me for a long, long time. As Albinia inverts and recreates our man-made world layer by layer, the novel reminds us of the epic range of human possibility, of who we might have been, and of who we still could be. A breathtaking, beautifully told, profound novel for our times and beyond. I loved it' Mirza Waheed, author of *The Collaborator*

'Swept on the current of so many centuries, this transporting tale lands powerfully at the point where vision and errancy combine in pursuit of what one wants most: a place to truly belong' Sharifa Rhodes-Pitts, author of *Harlem is Nowhere: A Journey to the Mecca of Black America*

'Alice Albinia's *Cwen* is a skilful counter-history, a disruptive and compelling reimagining in microcosm of a society designed and controlled by women. Albinia brilliantly weaves together historical material and a narrative of life in contemporary Britain to demonstrate how our history might play out if women took charge. The book leaves me disoriented in the best possible way – a superb achievement' Daniyal Mueenuddin, author of *In Other Rooms, Other Wonders*

'A superb book: original, fierce, elegant and full of surprises from beginning to end' Sonia Faleiro, author of *The Good Girls*

Also by Alice Albinia

Empires of the Indus: The Story of a River
Leela's Book

Cwen

Alice Albinia

—

SERPENT'S TAIL

First published in Great Britain in 2021 by
Serpent's Tail,
an imprint of PROFILE BOOKS LTD
29 Cloth Fair
London
EC1A 7JQ
www.serpentstail.com

Mountain motif: Image Detail from Boreray & Dun Hirta (diptych). © Jason Hicklin.
Courtesy of Eames Fine Art

While every effort has been made to contact copyright-holders of reproduced material,
the author and publisher would be grateful for information where they have been unable
to contact them, and would be glad to make amendments in further editions.

1 3 5 7 9 10 8 6 4 2

Printed and bound in Great Britain by
Clays Ltd, Elcograf S.p.A.

The moral right of the author has been asserted.

A CIP catalogue record for this book is available from the British Library.

ISBN 978 1 78816 660 7
eISBN 978 1 78283 771 8

FSC
www.fsc.org
MIX
Paper from
responsible sources
FSC® C018072

For Adi & Aphra

cwēn

Woman, wife, female ruler of a state.

cwēn *old English*

queynte *middle English*

cunt *modern English*

Cwen is a thing with a womb and two breasts. A brain and two far-seeing eyes. A clever nose and nimble fingers. The clouds are her children, and the waves, and the shells which the waves spit on to the sand. The islanders opposite, they are her children, too; and the sheep up on her island's high bank; and her chickens, down by the shore. The birds crouch under her stroking hand; she raised them from chicks. Now, if they have a mother, it is her.

There were people here before her, she knows that, for they left a cairn on the hillside just up from the shore. An ancient mound, grass-covered, it is three paces from her spring, bigger than her hut, and shaped like a breast, or a belly-full-of-child. There is a large stone, blocking the way in. Cwen sits there in the early morning, her back against the stone, her body full of spring water, as she waits for the islanders opposite to arrive in their boats, with their offerings of grain, and slices of dried meat, and their questions, all quite predictable, about their harvests and wombs, their neighbours and the gods. In winter, the stone receives the glare of the rising sun. In summer, when the sunrays touch the top of the mound, Cwen sits up there instead, looking out over the other islands, all twelve of them. In this way, she bathes in gold.

Inside the cairn are the histories that remain to guard this island, her spring, and her. Every morning, every evening, she stands on the cliff and looks down at the tide; how the sea rustles in, and is sucked back out. Twice a month, when Moon is at its thinnest and its fullest, its birth and its death, the bay below her cliff empties completely of water, and on those days she walks right out, in her long dress and leather boots, to ease sea creatures from the sand.

She calls herself *Cwen*, and *Cwen* is what the island will be called after she is gone; after her bones and her hair have been dispersed to the sea, and her thoughts to the winds, and the sea creatures whose relatives she ate are eating her. *Cwen*, call the tides; *Cwen*, say

3

the bubbles of her spring; *Cwen* says the Moon, as the sea aligns and realigns her island's bounds.

———

There is an island beside Britain where sacrifices and rites are performed like those at Samothrace in honour of the goddesses Demeter and her daughter Persephone.

Strabo, *Geography* (Greek), 7 BC

Judge

The night Eva went out in her boat, the storm came in off the sea. It span across the islands in a great wailing tumult, blowing chickens into the air in Astrid; pulling washing off the lines in Tarn; darkening and deepening the sea in the harbour; causing the beech trees in the wood to rend their clothes and tear their hair. It lashed the shore with water, great sheets of it, grabbing at the earth, sucking at sand and rock.

Within hours of her leaving, there was little hope. But they went on looking: early in the morning, islanders were out, walking up and down the coast on both sides of the channel, as two creel fishermen searched the island of Cwen. Texts and emails flew back and forth. *Have you heard? Such a tragedy. They tried – the coastguard was out all night.*

When the storm abated, and the deserted main street in Ayrness filled again with people, opinions flared. 'There's still no sign of her boat.' 'What did she think she was doing? What possessed her?' 'It's awful, not knowing.' 'We went to that Christmas party once, at the big house.' 'Do you remember her late husband, the minister?' 'She became a different person after his death.' 'She was flamboyant, wasn't she.' 'She was a bit too much; everything she did was over the top.' 'I liked her. She taught my daughter.' 'What will happen now, to the Islands of Women Study Centre?' 'Not just that – the Archipelago Women's Club. Wasn't she the one supporting Inga at the council?'

To some islanders, Eva's disappearance proved what they had always known; that despite her efforts, she wasn't local. Nobody who'd grown up in the islands would have gone out in that storm. It was a north-easterly; the wind was at forty knots—

Not when she went out; the wind got up suddenly, out of nowhere.

—it could only have been an incomer doing something so stupid. She did other stupid things, too. The sort of people she'd been consorting with recently. Even before she disappeared, there had been murmurings. The nonsense they were feeding the young boys and girls at Ayrness High. The preferential treatment of female entrepreneurs. The secret symbolism of the island flag; how wicked it was, when you really looked at it. The money that became available for the museum to rewrite its exhibits – *Neolithic female what?!* – destabilising millennia of good solid island history. Not to mention the books in the library. They'd even installed women's urinals; behind the abbey, of all places. Somebody must have encouraged Eva in these insane schemes and untenable positions.

In the days after Eva disappeared, women were seen going down to the Islands of Women Study Centre, one by one, and in groups. Not just incomers; islanders, too. They walked there, heads down, coats tight around their bodies, cowrie shells in hand. People love honouring the departed with flowers. But these women left a flotsam of seashells outside Eva's office in the harbour. Shells, being aerodynamic, survive the wind's scouring better than sunset-pink supermarket tulips, or fragile white lilies in crackly plastic.

Eva had set out from England; but who knows where she ended up. Scotland; Norway; Thule. Despite everything, there were women who continued to say that Eva would return to them. *Cwen had taken her; Cwen would give her back.*

Others were less sanguine, given the circumstances.

Some – men – found the sight of all those women with their seashells difficult to take. At the supermarket checkout, in the harbour, on the gangway of the ferries, they began calling one another out. *Did you . . . ? Had you . . . ?* Some of them had known; might just've gleaned it in passing from their daughters or wives. Others denied it. Online, lists of offences were exchanged, magnified. *They were changing the street names! The hospital too. And the library. They tried to promote women in fishing, in the fire service, as farmers. Did you hear about Pregnancy Celebration Day? It would've wiped out Chri—*

The English coroner made her judgement: 'presumption of death'. Nobody could have survived, out in those seas, for more than a few hours.

The law had recently changed in England, making it possible, in the case of the missing, to settle their estate without waiting the customary seven years. So the will was read, and Eva's sons, the Harcourt-Vane boys, found out about the house, and the money. In Ayrness, there were public denunciations; inflamed meetings in the town hall. Eva's solicitor threw up his hands – he'd done everything by the book. Newspapers printed photographs of Zoe, Eva's granddaughter, fleeing Harcourt House with a cardigan over her head. There were calls for certain community leaders to be fired. A top London immigration lawyer offered to represent Mariam, the Pakistani woman Eva had taken in, pro bono. A crowdfunding page was set up, to have Mariam's quilt returned to her. There were angry interviews on television. It became libellous to suggest to journalists that Sister Lucija from All Our Holy Mothers Convent might have stolen Eva's rare photographic print by the late Bosnian photographer Mevludin. In Westminster, in private, special advisers began looking it up on their phones: the archipelago's whereabouts and relationship to the United Kingdom. As the price of Mevludins went up ninefold on the global art market, questions were put to the prime minister on a succession of Wednesdays. Eventually, the Minister for Women announced she was asserting her power under the Inquiries Act, by sending up a judge to arbitrate between the islands' now-irreconcilable positions.

A public inquiry is not a legal entity, nor is it a court of law. But it is full disclosure: a dissection, in public, of society's function. It can be embarrassing. It can vilify or redeem. It can drag on for weeks, sometimes months or years. It can be random, personal, and imprecise. Few on the islands liked the sound of it; but by then they had no choice.

When Colin Grieves, acting press adviser to the Archipelago Council, made the announcement, his forehead broke into a sweat, his freshly ironed shirt developed damp patches, his arms flew up and down: his body unable to contain his excitement at having finally caught and pinned to a board the archipelago's most famous butterfly, *Eva insula* (turquoise, iridescent, insouciant), sole cause of his late-life discontent. He spoke at length about Eva. Within a decade of moving to the islands, she had 'become enthused with the zeal of a convert'. Over the ensuing fifteen years, 'everybody who lives in our beautiful archipelago was to suffer, unknowingly, the effects of her social experiment. She set out to promote women in every one of the islands' major institutions, businesses, the very education system itself. She did this with every resource available to her: her late husband's money, her children's inheritance, and by raising funds from unwitting public bodies in the name of the All Islands' College, of which she was deputy principal until her presumed death by drowning, late last year. Over the next several weeks we will be conducting a far-reaching inquiry into her activities, bringing together church leaders, past and present council members, and other pillars of our community, as well as Mrs Harcourt-Vane's own sons. Details of the appointment of the judge to head the inquiry will become available within the—'

The official title was An Inquiry into Unfair Female Advantage in the Islands.

But Eva's women called it *the Grievance*.

Most of Eva's women refused to speak to the press, saying they didn't want to prejudice due process. This was true, because most of them – almost all of them – had been called as witnesses. Also, they were scared. The women whom Eva helped elect to positions of island power; those like Barbara and Lucette who took grants or loans from the Foundation; staff at the museum, college, council – they were all under suspicion. Mx Thompson at Ayrness High was put on unpaid leave. Inga Stenbridge, head of the council, was suspended pending investigation. The Archipelago Women's Club stayed open – female-only private members' clubs are mere historical tit for tat – but any other women working in positions of traditional male power, from the three ferrywomen to the director of the museum, editor of the paper, and Jen, head of the Islands of Women Study Centre, were visited by a solicitor from the inquiry.

As if to call her back, the schoolchildren, with their disgraced teacher, painted a huge mural of Eva: smiling, arms outstretched, rainbows in her hair, a garland of flowers around her neck. After it was defaced (dick in mouth), some women began backsliding. Late at night, hurt by the shocked whispers – the even more shocking online comments – there were women who felt ashamed for stepping out of line. They wondered whether Inga's female takeover of the council had been necessary, actually; felt guilty about the many good solid male start-ups that must've suffered because of Eva's rampant ideology. Maybe Eva had gone too far? Maybe *they* had? But all they'd done was act on instructions from Eva. Not even instructions. More like hints. Because, whatever Eva intended always remained a bit inscrutable. Plus, she never did understand the island way, coming as she did from outside. Typical incomer's error. Islanders never rock the boat. Some things have been this way forever.

And so it might have ended, had it not been for Cwen.

Cwen is a tiny speck of an island. At the time of the inquiry, it was uninhabited save for a flock of hardy black sheep. But it has always been alive and resplendent with its years of use as a sacred site. The island's skyline was permanently altered by a grass mound, constructed four and a half thousand years ago with untold hours of human labour. Cwen's iconic swollen belly catches the eye almost every day, if you live in Ayrness, or drive that way along the coast. Perhaps because it is so very near the mainland – only five minutes by outboard-motor dinghy; twenty minutes or so, if you row – islanders see Cwen all the time, in all its phases. How the island changes with the passing clouds and coming storms. The obscene lightning. The multitude of rainbows.

By the time the inquiry was announced, threatening everything, Inga had been convening regular women's meetings on Cwen for at least a year. After the judge opened proceedings, Inga put out an open call to all women of the archipelago. Together, the assembled women came up with a strategy for *community healing*. They decided that whatever the conclusions of the inquiry, on the day that judgement was handed down, the schools and college would empty of women, the female-run businesses and leaders whom Eva had supported would put down their tools, and all would meet to give each other succour. In the hour before the judge began summing up, the women would set out from Harcourt House, to march on Ayrness. Island women. The nuns from Papa Astrid. Tara, Inga, Jen. Stella with her fiddle. The women would walk across the public footpath, over the field, and along the coast road, as the sun rose higher over the sea. Zoe, with her Eva-hair, would march in front. The women would smile and laugh, singing one of the ancient epics Eva loved. There would be energetic squalls of rain but the sun would come out through the clouds, filling the air, and the fields, and the sea, with its gold. When they arrived on the outskirts of Ayrness, armed with nothing but their chant, other women would join them, and island men, too. Waiting for them in town would be women's groups from all over Britain and beyond – Lerwick, Lyon, Lima. As the numbers swelled, they would march on the library, on the inquiry, to show those people, the television crews, the judge, the men, the force they were. Zoe would take the microphone from Inga and speak directly to the crowds of everything her grandmother had taught her, of the sacred women-shaped spaces that ancient people built – the regenerative principles they were steeped in. She would ask them if they could imagine a world like this. And the crowd would roar its approval.

That was Inga's plan.

Of course, everybody knows how hard it is to countenance the idea of women-only gatherings, women-only groups. The mere sight of women assembling en masse makes certain people, women as well as men, feel uneasy. *Queasy*. Everyone's felt this way, at some point. There's something deeply disgusting about female gatherings. Women just shouldn't express solidarity with each other.

The first people to express that sick feeling were the men from over the water, who came for the inquiry. They gathered on the streets of the islands, calling Eva's women names. When it came on the evening news, Eva's women found it funny. They were even a little bit pleased with the attention. But in the wake of the angry men came more television cameras, and journalists, taking pictures and asking questions. Interviews with island men were published. *Poor Jim's going to have an aneurysm*, Jen texted Inga after seeing James Mills, the geography teacher from Ayrness High, complaining to the BBC of 'covert and extreme deviations from the national curriculum'. The all-male rallies got bigger. By week three of the inquiry, the national dailies were covering it. There were headlines such as FEMALE TAKEOVER OF ISLANDS' LEADERSHIP; or UNFAIR FEMALE BIAS IN BRITAIN'S FORGOTTEN ISLANDS; and even, FEMALE EDUCATORS CAVORT TOGETHER NAKED. Then the protests turned violent. Janice Handsworth, fifty-two, mother of three, came home with a bruised face and bloody nose. Barbara Anderson, seventy-seven years old, grandmother of six, was shoved against the wall of the abbey as hands grabbed her breasts and crotch. Things might have ended for the worse had the police not arrived in the form of DCI Ruth Brock.

The official line was that the violent men were incomers, ferrylubbers, over on the boat for some opportunistic women-bashing; but the women knew they were also being turned on by their own kith and kin. Some of the men who waved banners and shouted slogans were their neighbours, colleagues, brothers; expressing very well, on the whole, their indignation at having been hoodwinked into accepting, even lapping up, those well-ordered years of female rule. Euan F—, who had fainted in biology when Mx Thompson dissected a mouse (and was then made to stand on a chair as the girls circled around him, chanting, *Gender stereotypes are social constructs*), was holding up a banner with the words WOMEN ARE SEXIST TOO blocked out in fluorescent yellow. James Mills himself, who had won Ayrness High's anonymous online poll for Creepiest Male, was caught on camera with fist thrust in air. The television reporter from BBC Scotland called it 'an unprecedented scene of public male fury'.

And still the women didn't know what had happened to Eva.

The archipelago where Eva staged her coup is shaped like the constellation Cassiopeia. Together, the islands make up a wave-crest reflection of that starry Ethiopian queen who was punished for boasting of her beauty by being spreadeagled in the sky: a nightly reminder of the barbaric status quo. Eva liked to look upon the islands as places where myths assume new meanings, where Cassiopeia's feet are unshackled from their stocks, where she is free to run and dance in the heavens.

Of course, it is natural for islanders, with their clean air, to love the stars. In the islands, stars hustle, demand attention, are noisy in their beauty. Sometimes they cascade down like women's hair.

Eva liked to hint how, if the moon and sun draw the tides through the seas, an equally epic – if distinct – force draws the blood down through women's wombs. That, in the islands, everything is connected: sky, water, blood, land. She boasted openly of the islands' beauty, the historic fierceness of their storms, the salt toughness of their kith. She saw these things as female, intrinsically. She seemed never to have been concerned that those who boast, often end up, Cassiopeia-like, upended. Nor that almost everyone finds womb-blood disgusting.

Until the inquiry, the archipelago was barely known south of Berwick, north of the A1. Off the east coast, beyond the mainland, beyond your ken. To travel there across the water is actually to have an illusory mental fog descend. To arrive by sea is literally to be cast into a spume of bluey-grey: out of which, after the passing of one hour, some jagged shapes of land emerge. *This is the main island, with the harbour towns of Lerston and Ayrness, the capital.* The smoother, smaller sugar lump to the right is Astrid, the speck to its right is Papay, and well beyond that is the crab cake which is Tarn. The serrations to the left are Dounsay, Skellar, and the skerries. Straight ahead, at the dead centre of the main island, is a Neolithic stone circle. To the east, on a spit of land with the harbour of Ayrness on one side, and woods and sea on the other, is Harcourt House. And just across from the Harcourt woods and beach, is Cwen.

The inquiry was held in Ayrness, at the All Islands' College, in the Harcourt Memorial Library, a monument to Eva's husband's family's largesse. It was there that the judge sat, beneath the large windows overlooking Ayrness Bay. Every day, Eva's women waited at the back of the courtroom created by the council, listening as islanders stood up to defend or attack her work. They watched the changing expressions of the sea beyond: the water, hurrying in its businesslike way across the bay; the luscious streams of darkened silk that moved across the sixteen leaded panes behind the judge's august head, where the archipelago's forebears are depicted in a kaleidoscope of coloured glass, beginning with Saint Victus, including a Viking warlord, and ending with Zoe's great-great-great-grandfather, Henry Harcourt, the kelp, soap and glass baron himself. They grew accustomed to counting off the ferries, noting the promptness of the Astrid–Ayrness service, skippered by Joanna Havant (taught by Eva), and the tardiness of the 4.10, which, in the care of old Sid Cobb, carried schoolchildren back to Tarn. They listened nervously as the inquiry examined various claims and counter-claims: how and why council rules were changed to stipulate fifty-one per cent female representation; who was responsible for the blatant feminist slant to the island paper; whether any of the hundred other female-friendly projects amounted to illegal discrimination or corruption.

Silence, said the judge, more than once. But that solemn place of learning was changed forever by angry voices and innumerable images of the seated judge, the solicitors, the witness in question – giving evidence beneath the soon-to-be decommissioned portrait of Eva Levi's late husband, the islands' former political representative, Harry Harcourt-Vane.

1: *Why did Eva do it?*
&
2: *Who knew what and when?*

These are the questions the inquiry circled back to, again and again.

STELLA: She detested her husband's politics? And what his party was doing to Britain, especially to the north? She wanted a place where things could happen differently? Like, *outside the patriarchal frame?*
JEN: Although personal frustrations contributed, I hope you will see that her motivations were wider. Although she didn't set out a blueprint at the beginning of what she intended, the implication is clear in her various pronouncements, and if you'll let me finish I just want to stress that—
CAMILLE: She felt she had failed as a mother. Her sons, you understand, grew up to become their father.
MARIAM: Very nice lady, very good, very kind.
LUCIJA: Bosnia was more important than you think. She was formed by her work there, by her love affair. It was in my own Yugoslavia that Eva realised – as she had not done growing up in England – how much the politics of a country affects its people.

NINA: I wasn't ever comfortable with who she was and what she stood for, OK.

RUTH: I had no idea, the whole time. We never discussed it. We never discussed anything, except Zoe.

INGA: In her mitigation, she was granted this privilege suddenly; she didn't grow up expecting it, as men have done for centuries. Therefore, I am pleased to say, that when privilege came her way, she didn't waste it.

ALICE: She discovered her mission midway through her life, and it drove her. I don't think she stopped to question the notion, once it became apparent. That was always how she spoke of it, each time I interviewed her. She knew we were running out of time.

TARA: When she was younger, she went to hear Greer speak. That was before she left London. She saw herself as one of those canaries Greer writes about. She wrote in her notebook that it made her feel guilty and pathetic and weak, listening to a catalogue of all the mistakes she had made as a woman.

A canary. Poor Eva.

ZOE: It had always been difficult between my two families. My grandmother, Eva, in the big house. My mother didn't like it. But even she came round to Eva in the end. After Eva disappeared, unfortunately.

In the evenings, or early mornings, when Zoe and Eva lay together in her big airy bedroom, reading picture books, then chapter books, then the morning papers and weekly magazines, the love flowed between them, swirling and unstoppable. It was the calmest and strongest of loves, grandmother–granddaughter, no worries, none of that deep anxiety of mothers, creative, happy, trusting. Eva would talk, Zoe would listen, occasionally turning her eyes to the black-and-white photograph of the Sarajevo women which hung there – *Jewish women*, Eva would say, *like you and me*. Zoe listened to everything her grandmother told her, about what had always been, and what had been suppressed, about what should happen, and what might come in the way. Eva wanted her to see for herself how high the stakes, how wide the scope, how tiny the chance.

Then Zoe would take her time answering back.

Cwen thought she was going to be left alone, for a thousand years. Now she knows this isn't so, and mostly she is interested in having her isolation ended. She has lain very still. She has let the birds make their nests in her hollows. She has felt the lobsters burrow into her thighs, and crabs scuttle landward between her fingers and toes. She has waited through rain and hailstorms, snow and sun, and those effervescent love-children of the weather, called *rainbows*. She has felt Sun warm her skin, and her touch dry seawater saltwhite in her hair. She has lain here, alone, for absolutely fucking aeons.

Now, though, people are coming. She knows there are things she can give them. There is still so much they do not know.

When called upon to speak, Cwen always said things as they came to her. Even for her, it was sometimes hard to tell whether they were utterings from her own mind or direct dictation by the goddess. She absorbed things through her skin, out there on her island. She saw what the birds were up to, watched the fish beneath the water, and when the northern geese arrived too soon, or the gorse flowered late, or lobsters were thrown up on to the shore, she warned the islanders opposite; reminded them what to do.

The goddess has many names now: Bridgit, Mary, Freya. In Cwen's day, she was *Anu*. Nowadays, when they are wrapped up together in the warm black womb of the mound, Cwen and the histories are Anu. Before, when the islanders opposite brought offerings, the flowers were for Anu, and the metal was for Spring. But Cwen got the food, and the sheepskin to sleep on. It was only wise to keep the goddess's mouthpiece warm through the winter.

It was Cwen's father who taught her how to snare animals and catch birds with a string – the rabbit-breathing, fox-walking, bird-weaving. He taught her the best way to dig a furrow for potatoes, and the only way to make a poultice for milk-fever. How to extract medicines and poisons, which are often the same thing, differently administered. What would grow on the island, and what could be scooped out of its waters. The blue fallen stars, with their long stinging tentacles.

She asked to be taught, along with her brothers, but he would have shown her anyway.

Later, he said, of the islanders opposite, When they come over, you must always give them something. Even if you know they don't need it. If you aren't sure which thing, give them both; and never forget the prayers.

He put his new metal divining rods into her hands, before he died, and his piece of amber the size of a hen egg, and all the herbs and roots he had collected for three times as long as she had been alive. He had been taught by his father, who had been taught by his mother, and so on. It was still not clear whom Cwen was to teach. This was the last thing on his mind as he died.

Cwen blows on the water, making the waves erase a bit of her island. The waters creep higher. She feels them. She feels this too: that she is waiting. She is waiting for someone.

———

This small island in the Britannic Ocean, called Sena, is inhabited by nine virgin prophetesses . . . who stir up the seas and the winds by their magic charms . . . and know and predict the future.

Pomponius Mela, *Description of the World* (Latin), AD 43

1

Alice

The first person to give evidence at the inquiry will be Alice. As she walks out, into the library, to take her place beneath the portrait, she will notice the ghost of some breast milk on the lapel of her black jacket, deposited there that morning. *Shit.* She is frowning as she is asked to confirm her witness statement, which runs to forty-two pages.

JUDGE: Is this your evidence?
ALICE: It is.

The judge will ask her to summarise, for the inquiry, how she first met Eva, and then, having met her, what her role was in Eva's mission, and what Eva's was in hers. Alice will hesitate before speaking, searching for the right words. Trying not to be intimidated by the sea of tense faces before her. *Choppy.* Her face will prickle with fear. *This is it; judgement.* What she says here, what her mind utters, matters.

She will catch Zoe's eye, at the back of the courtroom.
Zoe smiles.
Alice clears her throat. She starts to speak.

ALICE: I didn't meet her the first time I came here. I arrived in such a rush.

JUDGE: When was this?

ALICE: Just over a year ago. Or rather [*blushes*] exactly thirteen Celtic
moons? I was researching my book on British—

JUDGE: Can we please move to paragraph 3 of your witness statement.

Only when the women question her that evening, on Cwen, will
Alice feel free to explain, without any interruption: *You see, I had
been on a research trip in Shetland. But because it was early days, and my
daughter was young, I didn't feel I could be away for long. I fitted in a trip to
the islands as an afterthought only, on the way home to London.*

And they will sigh, and hold hands, and *listen.* (Eva taught them
to try and do that; even if it's sometimes *really fucking annoying.*)

As Alice said, the first ferry had deposited her in Aberdeen at
five o'clock that morning, and so, as she took the coast road south,
through Edinburgh, it was with the tremor of the night's journey
still in her bones. She crossed into England and waited in her car
next to the small ferry terminal for the east coast archipelago –
the office was barely more than a hut – scanning the water for the
boat, feeling nothing but impatience for her journey's end. After
ten days on the road, she wanted to be back in London with her
child. She wanted to be home for bath, and story, and the brushing
of that always-sticky, tangled hair. Just this one last journey. And
then, back home. By the next day's nightfall.

Alice didn't notice the nuns on the boat. But they saw her,
because, as Sister Lucija has testified, *hovering over her head as she
slept* – Alice slept the whole way, curled into a reclining seat –
was the Virgin Mary. Our Lady buzzed and crackled, flickering
in and out of focus, as if she was being transmitted over a dial-
up modem. One minute she was dark-skinned, in a billowing
turquoise sari – 'Our Lady of the Sea,' said Sister Geraldine, who
was born in Goa – the next she was white plaster, head bowed,
flowing white robes, toe to brow. 'The Catholic burqa,' said Sister
Lucija. As the archipelago came into view in the distance, the
transmission stopped entirely. When it returned, twenty seconds
later, all the nuns gasped. 'Who is *that?*' asked Sister Brigid,
from County Wexford; she had not been keen on joining the
archipelago mission in the beginning. 'The Goddess Kali,' said
Sister Geraldine, 'Hindu.' Sister Lucija asked, 'And ... all that red,

around her mouth?' There was a pause. Then Sister Geraldine said, 'Oh, that'll be nothing but a bit of blood.'

They watched Alice warily for the rest of the journey. When, after the passing of a further half hour, the boat arrived at Lerston, the archipelago's second-largest town (small and maritime and generally eighteenth century), she was still fast asleep. One of them shook her gently by the shoulder, and the transmission, which by that time was buzzing promiscuously between goddesses and virgins of all hues, stopped dead. There was a last flicker – Parvati, mother of Ganesh, wife of Lord Shiva. Sister Geraldine sighed with relief. Now the only thing above the woman's head was a poster screwed to the wall in a plastic frame, advertising the museum café in Lerston. Sister Geraldine felt in the pocket of her heavy green habit and pulled out a cough-sweet, which she unwound from its paper and put in her mouth. Also, one of their new green business cards, which she dropped into the open patch pocket of the woman's coat.

The woman they had woken sat up and gazed around her. She picked her bag off the seat, and felt in it for her car keys. She had meant to have a tea on the boat; her travels had tired her out, which was bad, because the moment she got back home, her sleep deprivation would be redoubled by her daughter. She always intended to top up her sleep supplies when away from home. This rarely happened. Hostel curtains, tent coversheets, hotel blinds, B&B ruched creations, they were all too thin. They let the light in. Either a knife in the eye at 5 a.m.; or a gradual saturation: so you woke at six, dead in the water.

Alice glimpsed what were clearly nuns, as she drove off the boat: seven or eight of them, dressed in long green habits, topped by tartan headscarves. They processed in their comedic puffin way, up the same ramp as the cars, into the drizzle. She laughed. She wouldn't mind a green habit like that, and a headscarf. She had been taught by nuns as a girl, jolly ones, with toffees up their sleeves; it seemed that you never lost it, the impression of female sexlessness as a virtue. She shuddered as she passed them, wondering briefly where they were off to, before accelerating up the hill.

There was a sign at the first junction: smartly painted by hand in black and red, advertising that same museum café. Since it actually seemed to give off the aroma of city-strength coffee – you could smell the crunch of beans, see the swirl of milk, feel your ensuing caffeine throb – Alice parked, and grabbed her bag, and went inside.

JUDGE: In paragraph 14 you state—
ALICE: Oh yes, my female epiphany. [*Sighs*]

Because of her tiredness, and the coffee, and the rain, she was unprepared for being picked up, and shaken, and set down again, by the things she read. *But so it was.* Beyond the café, in the museum's light-filled atrium overlooking the harbour, was a display called 'Island Women'. There were biographical vitrines containing black-and-white photos, articles of clothing and trade, recordings of voices: speech and song. But the part which grabbed her attention – fingers to the throat – was older than all that. Some other age entirely.

Eva made sure that all the women of the islands knew about *passage graves* (as they call them in England; in Scotland they are *chambered cairns*; in Wales, *burial chambers*; in Ireland, *passage tombs*). Nobody knows what Neolithic people called these exquisite corbelled-stone edifices, but they built them in their most sacred places across the British Isles, most often on islands. The ones Eva liked are dramatic structures: grassy mounds, with an overlay of turf to keep out the rain, and an entrance passage so long and low it forces you to crawl on your hands and knees; until you reach a large central chamber, where, at certain times of year, the solstice for example, or the equinox, the sun penetrates in a shaft of golden light.

Almost always the signboards outside these places – nicely produced, to withstand all weathers – describe them as burial chambers; acoustic sound-rooms for the transmission of chanting at lower resonances; ritual spaces for Druid-like high priests. Pictorial reconstructions might show young, usually old, white men with short, usually long, beards. But the display in the Lerston Museum makes other claims. It asserts that these *womb-shaped sacred spaces*, complete with *birth passage and fallopian-tube side chambers*, are *architectural representations of the female body*, built to accommodate

24

not just annual solar celebrations, but year-round female rites of passage, such as *menstruation and birth*.

ALICE: I felt a jolt. *Oh my God! Really?* I'd spent the past two years visiting islands, and island shrines, from Orkney to Jersey. I'd never noticed the breast shape, the womb. And so, the shame rushed in: *Why hadn't I thought of that?*

Two museum guides, young women smartly dressed in black, were conversing quietly by the large windows over the water. Their accents showed that they were local—

ALICE: I felt transported by the realisation. Those amazing, mysterious Neolithic people had put women into their most important artistic creations. There women were, emblazoned upon the landscape in sacred monuments. There they still were! It was breathtaking.

—soft, as the accent of the archipelago is: distinct, different, neither Scottish nor English, southern nor northern. Alice approached them and asked, 'Excuse me, who wrote the section on the Neolithic?'

ALICE: You have to understand that the island histories I'd been researching until then were so overwhelmingly male, apparently – Neolithic builders, Druid priests, Roman soldiers, Christian monks, Vikings, raiding and fishing. Plus, in the islands themselves it was always men I found myself interviewing – fishermen, politicians, monks. My cousin pointed it out to me: she said, women rarely put themselves forward to be heard. They are too modest, or too busy. Or they just aren't used to having people listen.

The guides glanced at one other.
'Felicity, I would think?' said one; 'Felicity Davidson? The museum's director?'
'Wasn't Eva involved?' said the other. 'And Jen?'
The first shrugged. 'Felicity's away at the moment but I can give you her card.'
'Eva's the important one, though, isn't she?' the other woman insisted.

Alice sensed a wordless struggle taking place. Then the first woman reached out and took the other's hand.

'Eva's who you need to speak to.'

'Eva Harcourt-Vane.'

'Eva Levi.'

'We'll write the name down for you, so you don't forget.'

'We'll give you her number, she always calls back.'

In a kind of daze, Alice took the piece of paper, with the name *EVA* written on it in slanting black capitals. She walked back to her car. The rest of the day passed in a haze, as she tried to rationalise the information she had absorbed in the museum, while continuing her tour of the islands, as planned: north to the stone circle, where the signboard detailed how, *in these islands, the adoration of the mother goddess was a controlling principle of life in the Neolithic*; east to a nearby ruined convent where you pressed a button on the interpretative panel to hear a young woman's voice describe how *this remote outpost, with the abbey as motherhouse, was a cult centre for women from early Christian times*; back to Ayrness, where a leaflet claimed that *many early saints took male names but were really women, including the islands' early medieval anchorite in the harbour* – a merry-go-round, in short, to get a general sense of the place, before returning at a later date. She wanted to visit the chambered cairn on the island of Cwen, with its V-symbol carved on the back wall, but it required a special boat trip, booked through a skipper called Gemma, and there wasn't time.

During the ferry ride home to England, Alice stood on deck, watching the islands recede into the distance. A juggernaut of fog rose and covered them completely. She blinked; and as she unfolded and looked at the piece of paper with the number, and the name, *EVA*, her mind misted with uncertainty. She only partially enjoyed the CD of female folk voices which she had picked up in the ferry shop and listened to, dutifully, all the way south, as rain hit her windscreen: vengeful needles, thrown by fairy-tale spinsters, tired of being typecast.

As it was, the very moment she pushed her way through her front door, family life swamped any nascent thoughts about the islands. *Ma-ma!* Little arms clasped around her neck; a snotty kiss on her cheek; a bottom asking to be wiped; a burgeoning spirit, demanding, demanding, demanding her full attention.

God knows when she would have found time to return to the islands, thereafter, were it not for the newspaper article: which she read, quite by chance, a few weeks later. She's a *Guardian* reader, obviously, when she buys newspapers at all, but on this occasion it was a discarded copy of the *Standard* which changed everything. September, London, the optimistic half of the autumn term. She was travelling out to Barking, where she taught creative writing in a school. The article was a gossipy diary piece about the coalition's new junior minister at Defra, a post entirely uninteresting to her – except that the incumbent and she had been at university together. She only knew him in passing, he was two years above her, but they were in the same college, and as a student he had been a visible presence, out and about, canvassing for his party, the now much-derided Lib Dems. Sebastian Vane had grown handsomer during the ensuing fifteen years: the spit and buff of power. The article was a puff piece about public figures and the places they grew up in:

Vane was partly raised in the North Sea archipelago where his mother Eva, author of a book on the former Yugoslavia, still lives in the beautiful family home.

Alice looked up from the newspaper. *Eva.* She knew that name now. Where had she put the number? And: *Yugoslavia.* She herself had visited that country, just as it broke apart. During her first week at university she signed up to a student aid convoy to the Bosnian mining town of Tuzla. They left after Christmas, travelling south through Croatia in three battered lorries, along the coast to Split, and north into Bosnia, the very month the war there finally came to an end. She continued to feel upset by her memories. The bullet holes, principally. The soldiers. The checkpoints. Her feet, picking their way through Mostar's silence and rubble, treading where her brain dared not, into the holes punched in the skyline.

The next morning, in the British Library, Alice ordered Eva's book. Eva had published *Beyond Illyria* in 1969, under her maiden name, *Eva Levi* – indeed, she wrote it before getting married to the Rt Hon Harry Harcourt-Vane – and Alice read it in one sitting, at one of the library's green-leather-covered desks, with its view over Euston Road and Judd Street, as four things struck her.

First, it was excellently written.

Second, she never remembered Eva's son, Sebastian, mentioning the war in Yugoslavia, which was going on while he was at university, in any of his student political addresses or literature, nor at parties, nor in the student bar, ever.

The third thing – which seemed irrelevant in the moment, a glitch of the brain, and only later came to be revealed as the key – was that, while an undergraduate, Sebastian fathered a child with an island girl. Nobody at Alice's college ever met the baby, or her mother, but for a while they all talked about them. Back then, at university, parenting seemed a completely outlandish thing for anyone to do. Alice searched for the child's name, sitting there at her desk. *Sebastian Vane announces* ... *Sebastian Vane opens* ... *Sebastian Vane argues* ... There was nothing about Seb's daughter, nor her mother, on the entire World Wide Web.

The fourth thing, was that Eva Levi made reference, in passing, to some excavations then taking place in the north of Yugoslavia, in the vanguard of a new hydroelectric dam about to flood the Danube Gorge. The archaeologists were examining a series of Neolithic temples along the banks of the river. At one of these sites, Eva described meeting a Slovenian archaeologist from an American university who told her that the temples were shaped like the female pubic triangle. On one of the altars, the archaeologist said, they had found a stone carved with a vulva.

ALICE: That was it. Electric. The same feeling I got in the museum. So, the following weekend, I flew north again.

It was a stupid time to have gone north – crazy, in fact. Her husband was on a work trip abroad. To go away, herself, for three nights, necessitated meticulous planning, of the kind that pushed out all other thoughts. But she called on her mother, her siblings, and two different childminders, and in this way concocted a three-day, twenty-four-hour roundabout of care. She left instructions about bedtime and breakfast; food in the fridge; money on the table for Friday dance class, Saturday bakery, Sunday market. Her daughter seemed oblivious to the drama. Alice kissed her goodnight, hugged her mother goodbye, and pulled the front door shut behind her. She was getting a night flight up to Edinburgh, out of Stansted; and

28

on to the islands early the next day.

Throughout the journey north, Alice exchanged texts with the childminders and her mother. But the moment she checked in for her flight to the islands, it was all about Eva.

'Oh yes, you must meet Eva,' the besuited woman beside her in the airport departure lounge said. 'She's involved in so many things.'

In Ayrness, the taxi driver said, 'Have you been to see Eva Harcourt-Vane? She teaches my daughter gender studies.'

'Good?' Alice asked, glancing at her in the mirror: brown eyes lined end to end in black, a pink bindi between the brows.

The woman laughed. 'Vulvas and tits. Wisdom of the womb.'

That afternoon, Alice rang the college where Eva taught. A young woman's voice informed her that Eva had left for a function in the college library – a talk from a Swedish diplomat about feminist foreign policy. But by the time Alice arrived, Eva was already at a meeting of the Archipelago Women's Club, which was located on an off-island, and the last public ferry had departed twenty minutes before. Alice was standing, disconsolate, before the table of white wine and crisps, when somebody came to her rescue.

'I'll tell Eva that we've met and to expect you tomorrow morning,' said a rosy-cheeked woman with a strong accent (from the Isle of Lewis), who turned out to be Dr Jen Mackae. 'She rises early. If you turn up by half past seven, you can talk over coffee, before her phone starts to—'

To the outsider, this kind of friendly-hectic encounter can seem serendipitous, which is obviously true. On an archipelago the size of Eva's, coincidence is commonplace; a function of geographical self-sufficiency. Before Alice left that evening, she had received detailed instructions about how to get to Eva's home. She was to catch the Lerston bus out of Ayrness, alight at the stop by the church and, with the sea to her right, walk up the hill to the house at the top of the track. *Really, it's hard to miss.* So it was. Alice was unprepared, however, for the sheer glory of Eva's home, built in warm honey-coloured stone, with its stupendous views out across the sea. The dew was still on the grass as she crossed the lawn, and her feet left prints behind her. She rang the doorbell. Eva came to answer it wearing an apron dappled with flour. Her hair stood out from her head, curly and grey, a cloud filled with sunlight, in a way that was beautiful but also suggested chaos, as if she was Daphne, being transformed into a tree. For a moment their eyes locked and Alice felt a twang of something deep inside her.

JUDGE: When you say, 'twang' ...?
ALICE: [*Clears throat*] ... I mean, *twang*. She was the woman I'd been looking for, without knowing it ... for my book. For my life, really.

Alice followed Eva through the house, past a suit of armour, under the aquatint gaze of an eighteenth-century woman with almost-entirely-bared breast and enormous piled-up hair, into a room in which one swam through a shoal of shimmering ceramics and silverware, as she tried to explain who she was, her book, her project.

'Albina,' Eva said, interrupting, as she pulled out a chair in the kitchen. 'What does she mean to you?'

'Oh well,' Alice began. She knew the story of Albina, concocted, or adapted as it was, during the Middle Ages as a national founding myth for Albion. In Syria (some versions said Greece), the princess Albina was punished, along with her sisters, for her anti-patriarchal rebellion – together, they had killed their abusive husbands. They were tried by a council of men, who set them adrift from their country in a rudderless boat. 'I suppose it means their migration,' Alice said; 'how they navigated their way across the Mediterranean, north to the uninhabited islands of Britain. It's such an unexpected story of female power, coming out of Norman England. With a chilling modern echo of migrants into Europe—'

'I'll tell you,' Eva broke in. 'She was also an ancient goddess of death and art. The name means radiance, rather than white.'

'It must also mean white,' said Alice.

Eva wrinkled her nose. 'How quickly the colour bleached out of these islands,' she remarked. 'All those rain clouds. All those lost goddesses. Yes, I particularly like Anu.'

'Anu?'

'Irish ancestral mother-goddess.'

'I know nothing about Albina's ancient avatar,' Alice said. 'But I did notice how the medieval story is still so misunderstood—'

'All these nation-building myths are made up,' Eva said, 'but it's how we tell stories which is at stake here. Of course authors like Holinshed and Milton find the Albina epic offensive – they prefer a story which starts with a man. But isn't that unnatural? It's women who give birth, after all. It's women who begin things. And whoever wrote down that story about Albina knew that people want to hear women's stories. Some subversive person dreamt up a group of women taking charge of their destiny.'

'They kill their husbands,' Alice said.

'Of course they do, in self-defence probably,' Eva replied. 'They also enjoy having sex; they hunt and fish to fill their own bellies, and grow fat from the creatures they trap.'

'Yes,' Alice said, frowning, 'I guess it's the bit about them growing fat that stops modern women from embracing the epic. I read in one book something about how the failure of Albina's attempt at a self-sustaining matriarchy is inscribed on her expanding flesh.'

'As if Henry VIII's expanding flesh ever stopped his self-sufficient patriarchy in its tracks,' said Eva. 'You know that the medieval Albina story was probably inspired by *The Suppliants*? Aeschylus? *The Suppliant Women*? You don't?'

Alice shook her head.

'The only Greek tragedy with the chorus – a group of exiled women – as protagonist.'

'Oh wow,' Alice said. She shivered. 'Women speaking together. I really like the idea of that. As far as women are concerned, everything in our culture is so oppositional—'

'But the point is,' Eva went on, 'these stories existed. Somebody made them, in their imagination. If they were made once, they can be made again.'

'I love the Irish poem about the voyage of Bran—' Alice began, and again Eva interrupted:

There is an island far away; a lovely land, through all the ages of the world. Begin a voyage across the clear sea, to see if you may reach the Islands of Women.'

'Yes,' Alice said. 'Seventh century, isn't it? The islands of women! When I was writing my first book, I kept reading about a northern land of women in ancient Greek and Sanskrit texts. It was somewhere in the Himalayas. And eventually I went there and found it to be true: a place where women were freer and more powerful than anywhere else.'

'Probably all early worship was nature-based, shamanic,' Eva said, 'and it left no trace. The goddess was the hills and the river and the sun. Pregnancy was sacred. Fertility was as mysterious then, before the age of forty, as it has become now, after it, don't you think? I am sure we are in the midst of a sacred recalibration of society. A rebirth. A metamorphosis. People who weren't born women, becoming them. Women freeing themselves from their gender. It's really very holy. More and more, I think that it's at the point in history when womanhood stopped being a sacred act, a superpower, and just became an encumbrance, that everything went wrong for our culture.'

For a moment there was silence between them. Alice thought, disloyally, that womanhood had been an encumbrance to her, periodically. Probably that was one of the reasons she couldn't call herself truly emancipated, as a woman. She listened to the boom of the sea in her head, and to the cries of the seabirds circling over the house; circling and circling; female souls reaching back, beyond the grandmother you loved, and the great-grandmother whose name you barely knew, and the other countless, unknown, faceless, voiceless women who had nevertheless given birth to your mothers and whose very being you carried in your genes, your spine. She glanced at Eva. Alice never normally revealed to the islanders she met the specific thing she had begun to look for, while visiting for research. But Eva was drawing it out of her; and so Alice found herself saying, a bit too quickly, 'You see, I've come across so many ancient references to British islands ruled by women, that I've begun to think, *They must have existed.* In recorded history, or the recent past, if not now? But I've been looking, and I've found no such—'

'You have,' Eva said. 'They're right here.'

After that, Alice could only listen, and watch, as Eva – tall, bold in her movements – became a zoetrope of all the women she was describing. Their thoughts, words, arms, legs, mouths, vulvas, filled the kitchen with their clamour, a singing of brightly coloured birds in the apple tree outside; and as Eva talked, she prepared the coffee, tapping one finger urgently to her cheek and looking out at the morning, which by now was lashing its magnificence against the glass. She talked of things Alice had only imagined; until she remembered the bread: laughed when she opened the door of the oven; removed the loaves, tenderly as a midwife, holding up the glistening blackened bricks, so that Alice, too, could share in the glory: those trophies to the all-eclipsing importance of their mandate and their mission.

Before Alice left, Eva took her outside again. Her footprints had disappeared from the grass. In the distance the archipelago's islands floated in the sunlight.

'You see,' Eva said. 'This is what we have. This place. This chance.'

JUDGE: What did you see?
ALICE: I saw for the first time how...
JUDGE: Well?
ALICE: I saw the possibility of that ancient female power, resurrected. It's there in the Neolithic, with the female symbolism of islands. We know from Roman report that there were female Druids on Anglesey. The Greeks and Romans write repeatedly about British islands where female mystery rites were performed. And it persists into Anglo-Saxon times, in medieval Irish legends, in Arthurian romances. The Lady of the Lake, you know? Eva thought so too, and when I got back to London, she wrote and offered me some work. She wanted me to help her collect those lost female epics. It seemed logical to me. Men have always collected epics for their own advancement. Why not women?

Alice didn't tell her editor, but her husband knew. He disapproved. It's such a distraction, he said; you haven't got time. He was right that Eva took up a lot of her time. He was also right, annoyingly, that what Eva was doing in the islands could not be contained (as Alice had argued to him at first that it could) within her current book. It would not fold neatly into a convenient vignette. No, it was a thing unto itself. A monster. A ghost. A mermaid.

JUDGE: A monster?
ALICE: A *mermaid*.

Alice had already travelled that year to many islands, and it was always the same, whenever she got back home. Tell someone in

London you've just been in Shetland, and they will, very likely, furrow their brow; mention Anglesey or Alderney at a dinner party in Dorset and a blankness overtakes the room; say that you've lived in *Orkney* and people hear: *Auckland*. Often, English people – or their grandparents – have an island in their history, a favourite Hebridean hideaway, the childhood memory of an endless Scilly summer. Before cheap flights abroad, Londoners took the train to Thanet, and Liverpudlians summered on the Isle of Man. But this is for sure: in England, acquaintance with one island does not translate into geographical knowledge of the rest. (Plus, there persists an extreme vagueness with regard to Scotland.)

It was no different with Eva's archipelago. As soon as she began going there regularly, Alice got used to explaining, in the face of repeated perplexity: *North Sea, north of Lindisfarne, English–Scottish border*. Placing it for people, with slightly patronising glibness. *Between the two Berwicks? Well, due east of the mouth of the Tweed.* And then, making a geopolitical point: *You see, while the land border is fixed, the sea border keeps shifting.*

Her daughter refined it further: *Mummy boat, Mummy sea, Mummy-pelago.*

Mummy-Wonderland, said the child's father, just a little too wryly.

Now, of course, Alice can see that Eva sacrificed too much. She risked her life – and left them all alone. *She left Zoe alone.* Sometimes, Alice wakes in the night, fearing Eva's ire, if she ever returns. She hopes (but isn't sure) that Eva would have understood her decision to collect, not just lost female epics, but also, where appropriate, accounts of Eva's work, with diverging opinion from family and friends. Although she is glad that Eva acted as she did, when she stops to think about it, it sometimes takes away her breath. She herself wouldn't dare. What to make of Eva's sons, for example, who are now claiming that by giving away all their money, she was acting in the least motherly of ways?

JUDGE: What do you have to say on this point?

ALICE: What can I say? Yes, arguably this is so. She did not act in the way society expected in their regard.

Alice's official line on how she got involved in Eva's work was the islands and their epics. But in truth there was another, deeper, more mysterious connection, which drew her back there again and again. That very first night, for example, when she returned home to London, her legs stiff from driving, she stood on her doorstep feeling in her pocket for her house keys. What she pulled out instead was a small green business card. She looked at it, in the dim yellow glow of a street lamp. It was a picture of Mary, Mother of God, dressed in a green tartan sari, standing in a seashell, and holding in her hands a grey, vulva-carved stone. *All Our Holy Mothers Convent, Papa Astrid.* Alice felt her memory stir and stretch. She recognised what it was: a kitsch hotchpotch of cultural appropriation, such as her own Catholic childhood was full of. But she also saw, reaching back through the centuries, the reassuring spiritual devotion she had known once and lost.

Suddenly she remembered the dream she had had on the ferry: Mary, Kali, and women's vanished prehistoric wisdom, all entwined.

Cwen's father had seen what she could see. They had sung the same songs. Sometimes he is there still, when she sweeps her mind up and searches for the words she needs above the clouds, or beneath the seaweed, or under the rocks with the squid. She can find him if she listens very carefully to the seashells she brings back from the beach. She sometimes hears him when she crouches through night vigils in the mound. She knows that she still owes him an answer to the question that concerned him. She has failed to pass her knowledge on.

After Cwen died, they buried her, exactly as she asked, with her dagger and divining rods, inside the ancient mound on her island, wrapped in flax cloth. Just in case, they stationed one of their daughters to sit by the spring; and that was clever, for when the visitors started coming, the girl took payment. She picked up Cwen's cowries from the beach and sold them; she extracted coins for a sip of Cwen's waters or one of her apples. At first they came from all over the islands. Then they began coming from Bernicia, Deira, Mercia. By the time they were visiting from England as a whole, and Scotland, and even France, Cwen's spring had a little chapel built over it and a piece of the true cross embedded in the altar. Cwen's own flax-cloth shroud was exhibited twice a year, around the solstices.

The true cross was there for show. It was Cwen's healing powers that grew, year by year, despite her, better than her, such that soon Cwen began to wonder if she had been mistaken. Perhaps it was she – not Anu or Freya or Mary – who was the goddess. That kind of thinking is dangerous, she knows that.

Then, for a long time, everything went silent, and Cwen slept undisturbed.

Once, during this long time alone, she had a dream that the sea tasted different. It uncovered her; it covered her back up; it dragged stones along her thighs; it sucked sand and grit out of her vulva. It submerged her up to her armpits, and left her lying adrift, wet sand beneath her, like a dying whale. It tumbled her through the seaweed; and pushed her down down down to where her island joined the seabed. It was definitely trying to tell her something.

So she was already awake by the time she heard men knocking on the outside of the mound with shovels, pulling away turf and earth and stone, and eventually stepping fully shod, uncleansed, into her sanctum.

She opened first one eye, then the other, as they lifted her out of the mound, bone by bone. She heard the ancient histories shriek as her body was carried off the island.

It made no difference to Cwen. Her body had gone; but she wasn't going anywhere.

Every visitor who has come to her island since then, she watches. She waits until the right moment – and then she holds her breath, and blows, very carefully, over their faces. *Pray to Anu and Freya and Bride and Mary, that this time they will listen.*

People used to pay for this.

Nobody reacts. Not one. Cwen swirls her fingers through the water and makes the weather turn.

She hears a human cry. A boat is coming over. *Careful, Cwen.*

She watches, and holds her breath, as the woman approaches.

———

The Britons make no distinction of sex in their royal successions.

Tacitus, *Agricola* (Latin), AD 98

He prepared to attack the island of Mona [Anglesey], which had a considerable population of its own, while serving as a haven for refugees . . . On the beach stood . . . a serried mass . . . with women flitting between the ranks. In the style of Furies, in robes of deathly black and with dishevelled hair, they brandished their torches . . .

Tacitus, *Annals* (Latin), c. AD 117

2

Eva

Eva was the absent witness.

Hours and hours at the inquiry were dedicated to working out what she thought, what she wanted. But as soon became clear, there was no theory, other than the obvious one, propping up her vision. She was a private woman, who never justified her project, ideologically to anyone. She read books – they are there on her shelves – but there was nobody in particular she quoted, no single thinker whose theories she borrowed as a shield. Perhaps all the glory and faults of the system she created lie exactly there: in her unformed sense; her preference for instinct over dogma.

What Eva did do was fill forty-three notebooks. Recently, Zoe and Alice counted and numbered them, from first to last. They begin with Yugoslavia, which is where her note-taking habit was formed. The twelve Yugoslav notebooks comprise transcriptions of interviews, jottings during conversations, thoughts scribbled on buses and trains, pages sometimes marked by the coffee cup she placed there as she sat in Sarajevo cafés, thinking through her journey as she waited for a friend. A book, *Beyond Illyria*, grew out of them. They themselves have been lodged for posterity in the Islands of Women Foundation Archive.

There are also seven London notebooks, which Eva kept during the early years of marriage. Later, she went over them heavily in thick black felt-tip, crossing out anything tragic, demeaning or offensive. Even so, the London notebooks make distressing reading in the main. Stylistically, moreover, they sometimes resemble diaries or journals in the hurried quality of the prose – the clarity of her thought marred by the internal chaos she was experiencing. Zoe, in particular, hates dwelling at any length on Eva's marriage. Of course it was important to Eva's formation as a thinker; but Zoe, at least, insists that it is best to see Eva's reflections on marriage and motherhood as nothing more than a painful prelude to the project that gave such shape and satisfaction to the second half of her life.

It is impossible to tell how long Eva spent thinking before acting; the notebooks do not say. What is clear, however, is that the moment she committed herself, everything changed for the better within her. The final twenty-four notebooks, unlike those which went before, are identical. She bought them in bulk from the stationery shop in Ayrness, nothing fancy: the cheap, spiral-bound type, a brand called Black n' Red. She wrote in black fountain pen, and from the moment she put pen to paper (in that record-breaking cold October, the day after Zoe's christening), her recovery seems assured.

JUDGE: You were the pivot?
ZOE: Yes, well, clearly the personal heavily influenced the political.

Unlike Zoe, Eva was not island-born. She remained an outsider, in her own perception as much as anyone else's, even after living in the archipelago for some forty years, running its higher-education college and nurturing its political identity. During the inquiry, the soundness of Eva's political opinions was repeatedly called into question with the rhetorical device of questioning her credentials as an islander. Man after man (many of whom had lived in the archipelago for less time than her) stood up to emphasise her comparatively short residence in the islands, remarks that were then used to justify dismissing what she thought, and had stated publicly, about the islands' need for change. It didn't matter that Eva was right.

Eva grew up in Hampstead, London, in a light-filled flat where she lived alone with her father, an architect. Her mother had died when she was a baby; her father had fallen out with her relatives, and his, on account of having no time for organised religion. He brought Eva up with a sense of her own freedom; but it turned out to be a fragile plant. Her formative intellectual years were among clever Jewish girls at school; she was taught by female tutors at university; and found her voice thanks to the outspoken Yugoslav women whom socialism had empowered. She was thus completely unprepared for Harry Harcourt-Vane and his ilk; for the adamantine seam of male dominance which runs through Britain like a geological fact.

ALICE: She had been planning to move back to Sarajevo after her book was published; she was in love with a man there – Daris. Her desire to return was written into the structure of her book.
JUDGE: How did she meet her husband?
ALICE: Her father did some work for him on a flat he owned in Aldwych.
JUDGE: What was her husband's connection to these islands?
ALICE: In 1703, one of his ancestors bought a decrepit medieval mansion with a good sea view.

During her travels, Eva had become so used to being taken by young men of Harry's age to flat-roofed cottages by lakes, or small stone dwellings on the Dalmatian coast – where the most extravagant features were hot-water cylinders and the most important cupboards the ones containing jars of preserved peppers, and bottles of plum brandy – that she expected to find a one-storey summerhouse at the end of the long stony drive, set in an orchard with a lean-to shed for chickens. The building her Yugoslav-delimited imagination conjured, as Harry and she flew north one Friday evening, was about twenty times smaller than the house Harry had inherited.

INGA: Inherited over the head of his elder sister; out of the hands of his younger brother. Inequality and inequity were there from the start.

The house was built in a style which she immediately guessed, architect's daughter that she was, to be early or mid-Georgian. As

Harry unpacked the car, he nodded dismissively and explained what a mishmash it was: medieval, some late-Tudor improvements, if you could call them that, a complete Adamesque remodelling of the façade; internally, some belated Victorian gestures towards comfort and proper sanitation. I'm afraid we'll really be camping, he said. But first, I will show you the view.

They stepped together across the front lawn. It was almost midsummer and the islands barely get dark at that time of year; summer solstice nights are dreamy and strange. The field at the front of the house led down in a slope to the churchyard. On the edge of the lawn was a crab-apple tree, and a bench. The house, with its back against a hill, was flanked by fields below, and behind, by a wood. In the distance, all was grey. But as Eva looked, a ray of sunlight fell suddenly from the clouds, piercing the sea: a thunderbolt from heaven. *The sea.* Not the calm Illyrian blue through which boats drifted at the periphery of one's concentration but a grey, all-encompassing expanse, the very mass of which suggested peril.

INGA: An entitled house.
STELLA: Isolated and aloof, in a clearing on a wooded hill—
TARA: —the sea spilt at its feet like a moat.
STELLA: Nothing modest about it.
JEN: Having been owned by nine generations of Harcourt-Vanes, it was a building that weighed upon her emotionally.
HENRY: Of course, the family goes much further back than that.
ALICE: Eva Levi's tribe goes all the way back to Adam.

The house is large, and was well stocked, in those days, with treasures from these islands and beyond. It had been empty for some years when Eva first saw it – Harry's grandfather having spent his dotage in France. The housekeeper, Mrs Rendall, did her best to air the bedrooms and keep the upholstery from damp, but the place had the musty stillness of abandonment, the tins in the pantry bore pre-war prices in shillings and pence, and water from the taps ran brown with peat, as well as setting up a singing and moaning throughout the house which made Eva gasp as she lay that first night in the huge cast-iron bathtub, watching her legs looming towards her through the bathwater like pallid sea monsters rising from a loch. Of course, the plumbing was almost impossible to improve. Over time, Eva made many other changes, slowly bending the will of the place to her own. But even now the house sings its own indecipherable, echoing song, like a chorus of seals, out in the bay.

That first morning, Eva awoke in the high four-poster bed. She slid out to stand in her bare feet on the worn rug by the window, gazing on the misty layers of island green. Despite the cloudiness she felt in her head, she thought how exactly the house was circumscribed by the fields, the fields by the bounds of the island, and all this, by the sea. It gave her a feeling of calm but also trepidation.

Start with the house, and the husband, and all the rest unfurls like a fistful of gravel – male-to-male inheritance, entitlement, belittlement. Eva's study was full of it, folders and notes, shelves of books, historical clippings and photocopies. She knew exactly where the Harcourt name, initials and crest (a handsome prancing stag) were printed and stamped and moulded in features and furnishings all over the house. She knew about the Harcourt-Vane fathers, and the Harcourt-Vane wives. She knew about the black maid, Darcy, introduced from Jamaica along with the architectural renovations of 1720; and the Indian valet, Babu, imported to these shores in 1850 with a large consignment of Darjeeling tea. She felt their presence. They suffocated her, at first, with their unhappiness and mistreatment.

JEN: You see, she always intended Harcourt House to become a female sanctuary after she'd gone. She wished to invert centuries of male domination. For it's true, when you think about it: men had always owned it, a male architect redesigned it, the masons and carpenters and builders who cut wood and dressed blocks of stone, they were male too. Crazy, isn't it.

JUDGE: There must have been women who cleaned it.

JEN: No one remembers them.

Painful though it was, the house was part of what made her. And certainly, even now she is gone, Eva Levi remains in this building:

all along its passages, through its rooms, up and down its stairs: the momentum of her body. Harcourt House: Eva's house. *Her House.*

Later, when one of the women dropped in to visit, or Zoe got in from school, Eva would be sitting on the front lawn, if it was summer, with her account book or pile of correspondence on her knee, her telephone lying on her papers. She would glance up at the house, sometimes in silent admiration at its resilience, sometimes with resentment. It was a scar she touched to remind herself of everything that impinged upon her as a woman.

JUDGE: As for her husband – you never met him, of course?

ALICE: No, not me. But I read about him in her notebooks. It shocked me.

JUDGE: What did?

ALICE: How meek she is with him, by her own admission. She cooks his supper, arranges his clothes, organises his diary – this was when she was living in London.

JUDGE: He was still her husband, after all.

ALICE: But she didn't want to, and yet she did. He pressed a button and she acted differently all of a sudden. She was exuberant and free when she met him. And he sucked it all out of her like meat from a whelk.

INGA: Yes, I met Harry once. He came to open a new building at school. He was attractive, of course. Never ran to fat, kept his hair, into his fifties. Handsome throughout his life, if high cheekbones and a little bit of cruelty in the eyes are the kind of thing you like. I remember thinking, even then, *A bit of a dick.* I was sixteen years old.

STELLA: When there was a motion at the council to drop the patriarchal name of the Harcourt Hospital, I pulled up the clippings they have on Harry Harcourt-Vane at the newspaper archives. Posh is the first thing. A charming man, an effective communicator. Not reliable, I would have said. That's probably why women liked him.

JEN: Of course, many women have asked the question: Why did Eva make herself his wife? Why? Because women do that. She is not the only long-suffering wife, is she?

ZOE: She never spoke to me about Harry, even though he was my grandfather. Not once. Nobody did.

JUDGE: [*Pause*] So that's it? The case against Harry? No abuse, no neglect?

ALICE: They had an unhappy relationship. All the power was his from the start.

JUDGE: But the situation was not unusual ... It is all well within the range of typical marital relations in this country.

ALICE: As I say, I think we should be careful when discussing Eva's marriage. Yes, it was a motivating factor in her desire for change, but it would be prurient and unnecessary to reduce this to a story about a power struggle between a woman and her better-equipped opponent. Don't you think? She told me once that when you are young, you see life naively, as something endless, full of optimism and luck, as fresh as a bunch of mint. It doesn't occur to you to mourn the lost lives and mislaid chances. You don't understand that your life is already marked by scars and stumps, and all the bright, blighted aspects of yourself that never came to be. When you are old, you look back, and it is the mistakes you made that stand out.

JUDGE: What were her mistakes?

ALICE: She read too many books from a bygone age. They set up in her an expectation that the most important thing in life is love between a man and a woman, romantic love; that love is bitter, and that bitterness must be borne. The books, her upbringing, society – she acquired the kind of temperament which accepted suffering, and grew adept at hiding it. It created a pathway and she walked right down it. It took a monumental effort of will to take a different way.

He married his architect's daughter, she heard it said in the years after Harry and she were wed, as if in certain homes in Bath, Brighton or Berwick, architects and their progeny lined up, set squares in hand, along with those other village trades: the gamekeeper's daughter, the goose-plucker's, the miller's scion.

Levi's daughter married out, was what her father might have heard them say of her in Hampstead, had he cared for public opinion. But he didn't care. He cared only for Eva and the mistake she made.

ALICE: In her notebook of this time, Eva describes a dream. There is a storm. It is raining so hard that she can't see anything out at sea. But she knows the man she loves is out there, on a boat, and as the rain falls harder and harder—

JUDGE: Another man, not her husband, clearly?

ALICE: No, the man from Sarajevo. She dreamt of him all her life. The rain falls, blurring her vision. She repeatedly calls his name. She wakes herself up by shouting. But by then it is too late. She has married Harry, of her own volition.

They got married in St Margaret's, Westminster; Harry was already a young politician for the Conservative Party. She wondered often, in the months that followed, what was usual in marriage, and what was unconventional; but as an only child with no mother it seemed she had little experience to go on. In Yugoslavia, marriage customs were changing. Perhaps marriage customs were changing in England, too.

For at least the first ten years of her marriage, Eva lived in London, where Harry represented the constituency of Kensington and Chelsea. She began having children, and neglected her writing. The first book had come to her so effortlessly, she took it for granted that she would write another. But Harry didn't want her to go abroad again while their son was young. There was absolutely no question of the baby going with her. If she minded that the writer part of herself was hung up, alongside the children's coats, its pockets full of mothballs, she did not say so. When her baby woke in the night, and her toddler had flu, and her five-year-old was being bullied at school, and her husband was so busy – and apparently so understanding about the lack of sexual contact with his exhausted wife – that she didn't want to bother him with the comparatively insignificant complaint of her writing spirit leaching slowly away. It became easy to dispense with words: which are little more, after all, than a self-indulgent assembly of ideas and ambitions grouped together on the page, and meant next to nothing to Eva's family, nor to Mrs Rendall in the islands, nor to Susan (who cleaned the London house every Tuesday). At least – unlike other writers – Eva never pinned her failures on her publisher or husband or children or the world. It was she who had failed to nurture the literary wraith inside her. She continued to write in her notebooks. But she published nothing further.

ALICE: Her marriage was even lonelier than her writing. Her ensuing life's work should be understood as the antidote.

Eva moved to the islands around the time that Sebastian, her youngest, was sent away to school. He was eleven; she had kept him at home until then; at least she had managed that. Politics was the reason given for her move. Harry, ever-ambitious, had been promoted to cabinet, as Secretary of State for the Environment. He needed a rural hinterland, which Eva would incarnate.

ALICE: Eva was desperate for something different. She didn't know what.

She found the islands immediately absorbing; both vital and remote. The shops stocked tinned things only, dusty packets. No olive oil or dark chocolate. Rare sightings of wizened tomatoes and apples tinged with the taste of the soap powder with which they had been brought over on the boat; robust local turnips, sturdy local carrots. Eva's doctor was a drunkard; and although the abbey hosted occasional concerts, and the Selkie Café in Ayrness held regular ceilidhs, all the theatre and exhibited art which Eva had taken for granted, her entire life, in London – a high-culture which now seemed sickeningly rich, from a distance – was almost entirely missing.

Vital because there were literary conversations; and wild conversations, not just about books, but about history and colonialism, independence and creation. Through the minds of those islanders she admired, she felt her sense of the world shifting around her, regardless of her will, as if she was a stone the sea was moving up and down the beach.

It was true that some months in the islands it was hell, seeing the same faces, and enduring the same conversations, and watching what was probably the same bird as yesterday turning mindlessly in the sky above your head. But there was always the sunshine to look forward to, to feel upon your back. It was the sunshine that saved her, and the shoreline, the land below the high-tide mark which her husband didn't own, where she went to tramp out her frustration.

At first she felt unable to shift the immobilising aura of the islands; the waves pounding like a headache on the sand; the still, unchanging inland copses, the sinister spinneys, the forbidding manses, all reaching out to bind her in subtle chains of habit and expectation.

Then she began to notice something.

One could sometimes go for days without seeing any men. By midwinter, it was women who drove tractors through darkening fields, who picked up children from the school gates, who handed over packets of sausages and chops in the grocer's and butcher's. The doctor was not the only man who was drunk. Men had long been absent from these islands, away at sea after whale and fish. The women of the islands had long coped alone, despite being poorly represented at the council and in the college. It was a complete anomaly, when you thought about it, that men took all the paid leadership roles.

ALICE: That was the first glimmer.

The islands themselves spoke to her differently after that – their physical properties of stone and green and soil. She took it upon herself to discover them as if for the first time. Until then, she had thoughtlessly followed Harcourt-Vane summer holiday tradition and only ever haunted certain places. The beach called the North Strand, on the less-frequented side of the island; the hermit's island in Ayrness Bay (in the days before Health & Safety you could climb the medieval tower where a monk – or was it a nun? – had lived, and throw stones at the gannets). Family celebrations were held at the Royal Hotel in Ayrness, which was the only place during the entire 1970s that served a decent dinner, so Harry used to claim, as he sat over a plate of island lobster, 'like a tribal chief'. Eva heard the comment – one of her sons – and afterwards imagined how scathingly she might have replied, mentioning Boudicca, quoting Tacitus. But of course she said nothing.

So when she began visiting the outlying islands on the Scottish side (which didn't consider themselves outlying at all), and the English ones, with their population of eccentrics, in self-imposed exile from the mainland, it was with determination to pull the various phases of island history out of their shell. Hunter-gatherer, Pictish builder, Viking raider, pagan farmer, Christian hermit, sacred to secular, island independence to mainland subordination. History's unpredictability, its dizzying instability, led her to believe that change was imminent, inevitable, the good part of being human.

ALICE: Nothing was fixed, after all. Nothing needed to be how it was.

In particular, Eva liked to walk out – not just down through the churchyard, and across the public footpath into Ayrness; but east, up through the wood, over the top of the hill to the edge of the cliffs. It was very windy there and exposed and the path down to the shingle beach was narrow and could be slippery in wet weather. But Eva loved this beach. The only signs of the outside world came in by sea; a lobster pot, a tangle of fishing rope, some plastic. The prettiest sea fetishes, Eva carried away up the steep cliff path – the skull of a bird, a stripy shell, a once-red plastic fork, now pebble-smoothed into a piece of pink coral. Often, she would stand on the beach and look out at Cwen, the small, uninhabited island which her husband's family owned. It had been a place of pilgrimage in medieval times, the sanctuary of a prophetess, or saint. The journey to the island cured broken hearts. Until the Reformation, people from all over the north-east came to drink the waters of Cwen's spring.

JUDGE: Cwen is the island where the meetings happen?
ALICE: The island had significance for Eva long before her women started holding their female gatherings there. I think Eva sometimes dreamt of doing a Cwen herself – you know, disappearing to her island fastness. But it wasn't possible for her in life. She often took friends there in her dinghy. She took me. She took Zoe.

They would walk in sunshine, or rain, over the close-cropped grass; the Harcourt-Vanes rented the island out for grazing. Whether in the long summer evenings, or the softer midday light of winter, the place seemed watchful and alive. Just imagine, Eva would say, she lived out here, all by herself. Overhead, the clouds began to thicken; the sun would disappear. What spirit, Eva would continue, ignoring the weather. Her hand: crumbling the calcareous soils of the shoreline. Her face: awed but happy.

The culmination of the trip was always to the chambered cairn: the grassy mound, aligned with the rising winter solstice sun. It had been sealed closed during the Neolithic, broken into at several points during medieval times, and then abandoned completely until Robert B. Turnbull, the Oxford archaeologist, reopened it again in 1933. He led two summers of excavations with a team of students. Eva, talking fast now – about how Turnbull, like the others, had misunderstood almost everything about this site, there are really interesting Neolithic carvings which he interpreted as arrowheads but which are clearly vulvas; he became obsessed by the medieval depositions, a dagger and rare leather gospel book, even though the pre-Christian female spirituality was far more ancient and important – would push open the stone door. It still turned perfectly on its Neolithic pivot. Eva would crawl in, urging her guest to follow. There was no light; she carried no torch. The guest would crawl after her along the tunnel into the darkness of the central chamber. There, Eva would seize her friend's hands and move them to the huge stones of the back wall, to feel the V-shape carvings—

JUDGE: You dispute the submission made in the joint witness statement by Henry and George Harcourt-Vane, Eva's elder two sons, that she was coerced into leaving the island of Cwen to the Foundation?

ALICE: Cwen was always part of her plan. She said so herself. You can see this is true from what happened with the short-lived women's commune on the island of Skellar.

During the archipelago's long history, only three or four of its thirteen islands have ever been privately owned. One of these is Cwen. Another, originally called Skellar, and of similar size, changed hands around the time that Eva began teaching literature at the All Islands' College. Barely three miles long, with only two houses, and at the time, no shops or ferry connection, Skellar had been for some decades in the possession of an absentee owner. Some said he (always a 'he') was from Denmark, others that he lived in London. One fine June day, new owners came over on the boat, their possessions bound up behind them in an array of trunks, suitcases and boxes. The ferryman, Fred, told Eva that evening, when she met him on the pier, that the ladies in question had insisted that he could bring things to the island, on his boat, but never set foot there himself. They had come to the archipelago, you see, because of its ancient female sacred history.

'Its what?' said Eva.

TARA: She knew nothing!

One of the women, Gayatri, whom some islanders were overheard calling 'the Paki one' – her family was from India, though she had a degree from a university in Britain – opted to do the weekly shop. Every Thursday afternoon at two o'clock, Fred waited for Gayatri at the Skellar landing stage, and ferried her over to Lerston. He reported that she always bought milk (the commune didn't yet have electricity or a fridge), packaged bread, fresh vegetables and fruit. He watched her munching on an apple as she prowled the aisles; purchasing candles, porridge oats, biscuits and pasta; a bottle of whisky. She disliked any foodstuff with an explicitly male name or history – Uncle Ben's, McVitie's, Cadbury's.

The commune soon declared its intention to hire only work-women. The first female plumber, from Edinburgh, left in a huff, and was replaced by another from North Berwick, tutored from the boat by her brother. Fantastic-looking bathroom fittings were carried over by the sceptical ferryman. These were followed by an expensive gas stove with cast-iron hobs, many gas bottles, and a kitchen table which the commune had persuaded the joiner from one of the Scottish skerries to help his daughter make from timber imported from the mainland.

At the beginning of September, a notice went up on the pinboard in the post offices in Lerston and Ayrness. It addressed itself to the Women of the Archipelago, and offered a trial evening class that Wednesday in 'Cleansing Thought'. Those interested in the workshop were to wait at the pier for Fred at six o'clock. The boat would return to Lerston at eight, but a night's accommodation on Skellar was offered; sleeping bags were recommended.

Eva was the only woman from the islands who showed up at the commune that Wednesday. In her notebook she records that she enjoyed the diatribe (as she put it) and liked the women who gave it. They were on Skellar to live out the principles of the Women's Liberation Movement. All nine women took their turn to speak about this. The 'blonde one', Gloria, started by talking of culturally-ingrained patriarchies. She began with the church, the male god of Christianity, the male god's male son, the death of the pagan matriarchal goddess; went on to speak of the modern political system (no mention was made of Margaret Thatcher), the unjust judiciary, the dominance of men in banking, media and manufacturing. After that, Gayatri spoke about words and their meanings, and possibly about colonialism, although by then Eva felt her brain aching as never before with the effort to keep up. She followed the argument of the third woman, Mary, a little better. Mary wore a black hat and white dress, and soliloquised on the oppression of beauty. Simone interrupted, to be brusque about the tyranny of the female body. Audre, whom Eva had assumed was French, too, until she began speaking, reminded Simone about the useful directions in which Gayatri had taken the conversation on race and oppression. Before things got too heated, a sixth woman, Betty, made an announcement: they were changing the name of the island to Gyno or Vagina or *Bean* (the Gaelic word for woman); voting would take place that evening, after refreshment. Eva couldn't help laughing. 'You think it's so funny?' said Gloria. 'Is it funny to call a tiny island after women? I don't hear anyone laughing at the Isle of Man.' Eva, chastened, sat quietly after that. She listened as Christine discussed myths and legends, especially the Amazons. Donna provoked a lively discussion of how women had become conditioned to imbibe the violence of their menfolk through the horrific deaths meted out to cows, chickens, pigs and sheep; and the state of things on the islands was worse, for gun-blasted fauna were offered up as dinner. (Eva shuddered; the Harcourt-Vanes owned a whole moor which was rented out for stalking.) Finally, Judy spoke. She was the sternest. Her speech concerned the nature of the commune, and its wider purpose. She exhorted Eva to return with other women of the archipelago, so that they could all learn, hand in hand, how to insert themselves and their achievements into the course of history, retrospectively. She wanted women of the future to grow up under a just dispensation, and she was sure Eva wanted this too; plus, it was worth bearing in mind that no woman could consider herself truly free until she had rid herself completely of reliance, however trivial or loving, on husbands, brothers, male authority figures, and all types of tradesmen.

When the talking was over, Gayatri came forward with plates of refreshment, which consisted of onion pakora accompanied by island-grown rhubarb chutney (made by Mrs Anderson from Upper Braeside Farm), and the name of the island went to a vote. *Bean* was chosen by a narrow margin.

On Thursday morning, when Eva stepped off Fred's boat again, she was still telling herself that everything the women had said was just *a little too much*. Then she drove back to Ayrness, and she saw it as if for the first time: men everywhere she looked: in the political structures of the islands and the country, running the council and the college, in the names of the streets, the churches, on lamp posts, road names, even drain covers. Overhead, underfoot, men were predominant without even trying. She parked her car, and walked up the road towards the college; she felt as if the women had inseminated her with ideas, and that her life up to that point had been a big joke. She shouted up at the birds wheeling overhead, and shouted out at the milkman (Billy, whom she had known for about ten years), and shouted hello to a male student coming down the hill the other way. The shouting made her breathless, removed from her body. She felt elated. Her attitudes, her thoughts, her demeanour – she wanted to change it all.

During the autumn, Eva visited Bean as often as she could. She took along a new friend she had made through her book group, Lucette, who had begun becoming a woman only after moving to the islands – she said she found them 'freeing'.

❦

LUCETTE: Eva found our friendship freeing, I think. There was always a frisson in the air, between us. The whisper of love. We were subversive, the two of us.

On Saturdays, the commune served a hot lunch from the main-house kitchen (Gayatri's lentils and rice served with Patak's mango chutney – the condiment a rare, tangy dollop of female business initiative). Lucette and Eva would eat their lunch sitting at one end of the huge kitchen table, listening to the bold-faced talk. Sometimes, Gayatri or Donna or Gloria would walk with the visitors around the island, pointing out the new, all-important female-features of the commune's design. They told Eva and Lucette that they shared tasks non-hierarchically; were especially proud of the re-Neo breast-mound they had built of earth from their septic tank, scattered with grass seed—

More nipple than breast, Eva wrote in her notebook.

One Saturday, Eva came home from Bean, after dropping Lucette in Ayrness, to find Harry's car in the driveway.

ALICE: It was horrible.

Her husband, it turned out, had come to the islands, not to see Eva, but for a week of shooting. He had three friends arriving the following morning. Eva met him in the kitchen, where he was frying himself an egg. She was glad that Lucette hadn't taken up her offer to come in for some lunch; Harry would have taken it badly but worse, Lucette would have thought less of her. There was a bottle of gin on the table and a cigarette in one of her painted Breton porridge bowls. They immediately began to row: about where she had been, what she was up to, whether or not she had been warned about Harry's visit and should have got the house ready. He, as always, remained aloof, and that in itself was a form of hatred; for in doing so he chased her down as inexorably as one of the hinds he had come up here to shoot, until, cornered by his logic, she shot herself in the heart by reaching out for something to throw across the kitchen, in this case the trusty bowl in which she kneaded bread every night – she was too cowardly or sensible to grab at his mother's teapot or the gold-rimmed ancestral plates – and Harry watched, detached, as she wept, sweeping up little shards of cream-coloured ceramic. It would not be a straightforward bowl to replace. It would require a day trip by ferry to the mainland; and even then the bowl would be new, and thus bereft of its history with her, all the loaves she had carefully nurtured in its cavern.

Harry profited from Eva's state of mortification for the rest of the week. Each evening that his friends were in the islands, she provided a well-appointed supper. His friends at first took Harry's lead in treating her politely, as if she was little more than housekeeper, little less than spouse. What was she then? Eva did her best to keep out of the way. As the mother of three sons, she was used to being surrounded and outnumbered by maleness. But they flirted with her as she made their coffee in the morning, leapt towards her as she carried a saucepan of water from the sink to the stove (*Let me help, Eva*), followed her down to the cellar as she went to fetch more wine and offered, with a hand on her back, to steer her through the darkness. Eva felt that her Jewishness was a factor. In their eyes, she was not of their class. Were all the men of Harry's ilk sexually ostentatious, socially assured? Would her sons be? She had begun to suspect so.

ALICE: You see? Something was happening inside her, a rebellion. And then the commune ended – she was distressed by that.

As autumn turned to winter, the women of the commune were still boasting to friends in the city about the exhilaration of the elements, the goddess-like feeling of the wind as it prodded and pummelled. But island winters are long: five incessant months of rain, random hailstorms, episodic deep snow. In spring, a storm washed out the paltry beginnings of their kitchen garden; a gust mockingly lifted the roof off the chicken shed. Nobody fixed the shed for three days, and the fowl got ill; one of the pullets was found with its face chewed off by rats. When the weather cleared, Betty took their rowing boat across to Lerston to buy some whisky. The currents that flow between the islands funnelled her out to sea; luckily, some creel fishermen saw her, and dragged her on board. She was so cold, she had to be helped out of her wet clothes and taken to the hospital in Ayrness, naked, wrapped in one of their coats.

The scare repatriated Betty. Gayatri and Judy's visits to the city became longer and longer. Gloria, having fallen for the plumber's brother, moved to North Berwick. Mary moved in with

57

her girlfriend in Edinburgh, Audre moved back to the continent, Simone got a job in New York, and Christine became a nun. Soon only Donna was left. She sold the island to a surgeon from Glasgow before the summer was out.

Eva was upset; but the commune's failure didn't diminish her admiration. The nine women had offended and alienated other islanders – hostile columns appeared in the local press, hostile things were overheard by Eva at dinner parties, in the shops. The women had failed; but each failure is also a small advance, an exploration.

ALICE: She understood, suddenly, how it should be done. Keep it quiet. Don't tell anybody.

JUDGE: Isn't that dishonest?

ALICE: Maybe. [*Shrugs*] No, I don't think so. She began tentatively mapping out a possible future. We found a note scribbled on the back of a bill from her garage.

JUDGE: We?

ALICE: Zoe and I. It was stuffed into one of her recipe books in the kitchen. Elizabeth David. Five acres of land to be given to every island-born girl at birth. Mandatory re-education for men aged seven to seventy-seven. Christmas pub quiz, question number 1: *Why is 'gynotopia' not listed as a word in either the* OED *or Merriam-Webster?* Answer: *Because men have erased such places from our memories.*

JUDGE: She had radical ideas.

ALICE: I'm not sure if radical is the right word. She wanted to change things without any of the usual associated conflict. Her ideas were practical, secretive . . . but she could never have put them into place, I don't think, if she hadn't been widowed.

JUDGE: The money?

ALICE: The money. But also, to be fair, the headspace.

Cwen only metamorphosed thrice, in her life. Once, she ran out of food in winter, and the storms cut off her island for weeks. She'd finished the mutton, the sheep were off the island already, and it was too rough for fishing. She had fasted before, but not to the extent that her head grew a beak and her arms became wings. When she dived, she fell out of the air direct as a bolt of lightning, dark through the water to where she saw the silver glint. The fish didn't stand a chance. Oh, that piece of smoked venison was good, when they put it between her lips three days later.

The second time, she flew as well, but upwards. Whatever it was had been mingled with the mushrooms the traveller-girl brought with her, as payment for the prophecy. If the girl knew, she said nothing. That night, Cwen made her usual stew. They ate it sitting in the doorway of her hut, looking out to sea. Soon she felt the beginnings of a lifting in her body, which hitherto she had known only through starvation; and when she held out her hands to the spirits, it was Wind who came and carried her upwards, and she felt it all over her body, and between her thighs, and pressing her feathers so they fitted together like the scallops of a newly-hatched pine cone. The feathers, when she looked around her, were iridescent, the colour of that traveller-girl's hair, and with the door closed behind them, and the girl's many tongues in her hollows, and three of her fingers, five, four, ten, no, as many as the stars, searching and finding, she felt herself pushed through the seas, into one star chamber and out through another, and then it was Wind again; Wind, turning her around and around in a cyclone. Which meant that the next day, when she woke, and sat before her usual audience, with her mouth only slightly dry and a swaying in her head, she was able to tell them to be quick in gathering in their harvest this year, for there was trouble coming.

The only other time was in the cairn itself, not in the passage this time, her back pushed up against the huge rough stone of the floor, but in the central chamber, with eight other women and the door closed for darkness. The drums were beating. It was the year that only girl-children had been born, and the island men were troubled. In the beat of the mound's darkness, with the women swaying around her, Cwen became neither she-bear, wolf, nor raven. She became herself. Her limbs were strong, her mind was clear, she guided the women. They enjoyed themselves so much that, were it not for the advent of boy babies, Cwen might have got in trouble with the menfolk.

Since then, in her hibernation, Cwen has thought it over. She's had long enough to come to certain conclusions. What she thinks is that everyone should be offered at least one chance for the necessary transformation. She has had time to practise. But even so, it's not as easy as it was.

Cwen shuts her eyes again. The island sleeps.

The men took it out on her later, anyway.

The next metamorphosis

—will take all the strength she has.

———

Near to Britain are some islands where the women . . .
Perform sacred rites for Bacchus,
Wreathed with clusters of dark-leaved ivy.

Dionysius Periegetes, *Description of the Known World* (Greek),
second century AD

3

Jen

The judge stated:

The remit of this inquiry is fourfold: to determine whether, as has been claimed, Eva Harcourt-Vane was exploited by the politically-motivated women around her; to establish whether the charity she set up was properly constituted and governed; to determine whether crimes were committed; and to ascertain whether there were conflicts of interest between Eva's, and her colleagues', charitable, social, political and business roles in this island community.

At the beginning, Inga counted up the witnesses they could rely on: Alice, Zoe, Jen, Camille, Mariam, Lucija, Stella, Nina?, Tara, Ruth?, Inga herself. Twelve women, including Eva, some angrier than others. Plus grateful supporters, such as Sister Geraldine, Edna Reynolds and Lucette Smith.

In the middle were women like Felicity, from the museum, and Ursula, from the paper, who refused to come to Cwen or acknowledge any links with Eva's operation.

On the anti-side were Colin Grieves and the men from the council, Eva's sons, and various men in entrenched positions of island power, such as the Methodist minister, the lord lieutenant, men from the Masons, the head of the Young Farmers, and the entire board of Archipelago Fisheries.

ANNE: It's absolutely appalling how Eva has treated my poor nephews.
My dear Harry would be turning in his grave.

During the Cwen sessions, Inga counselled the women on appearing in public. She was used to it – had been coached by Eva in the early days – but she knew how devastating it could be for those women who weren't used to having their every action and appearance scrutinised for imperfections. 'For example,' she said, 'they rarely if ever mention men's hair colour. But they'll describe me as blonde, they always do. They can't help it. Even I think of myself as blonde. You young ones won't care,' she said, nodding to Stella and Tara. 'But how about you, Lucette? And Jen?'

Lucette, who was proud of her appearance, was also used to opprobrium. At the inquiry she relished the opportunity to speak in defence of her friend. She told the judge that Eva's support for her 'never once wavered'. Jen, too, was a forceful presence. As she told Inga and the others, 'I'm not classically beautiful by any means, thank God. Breasts too large, voice too loud, for the Classics.'

'But you're photogenic,' said Inga. Not everyone has that photo-telly thing. Jen does.

Where Eva was elegant, neat, precise, Jen is rowdy, energetic, fun. She always wears impractical high-heeled boots, and scarves as bright as sweeties; her earrings jangle as she speaks. She wafts the same perfume wherever she goes, depositing it on hand towels, hands and cheeks. She usually arrived at Eva's house, where they held all their early meetings, bearing a funny story of some incompetent student, or man – she was indiscreet like that. She let herself be intimidated by no one.

Jen was also sociable; popular in the islands. Although she didn't care for cooking, she frequently invited friends over for pasta – she bought, in bulk, the Lerston delicatessen's mediocre pesto – and her very nice husband Alan could normally be prevailed upon to produce a roast chicken dinner, or a reasonable summer barbeque of sausages and burgers. She always had ice cream in the large chest freezer, always bags of ice for drinks, always wine and lager, always a bottle of archipelago whisky. With the work she was doing, it was important that nothing should be wanting.

As soon as the inquiry began, both Inga and Jen were offered police protection. Both have had death threats and rape proposals; had rotten eggs thrown at their cars. A child put a dead rat in Jen's daughter's school locker. Jen's husband had a pint of *Eilean-nam-Ban* tipped over him in the Hope and Anchor. On the days she gave evidence, Jen was met by protesters holding up SAVE SÌNE posters.

JUDGE: You first met Eva Harcourt-Vane when she offered you a job.
JEN: That's right.

By the time Zoe was born, Eva had been teaching for some years at the archipelago's college. By the time Harry died, she had been given the job of deputy principal. The promotion meant that her place of work changed from the modern (1970s) purpose-built campus halfway up the hill out of town, to an austere Victorian building which had once been a brewery and loomed over the seafront in Ayrness.

After Harry sold the huge family house in Chelsea, dispersing some money to his sons so that they, too, could enter the housing market, he purchased a bachelor pad for himself in Westminster. All the good paintings, furniture and effects were shipped to Harcourt House; insurance was cheaper in the islands. Harry didn't think any further than that. He didn't need to: Eva was looking after Harcourt House; he was looking after Britain; his sons were, in all ways, well endowed. It seems never to have occurred to him – reasonably slim fifty-eight-year-old that he was – that his life might end. He had a stroke while taking a shortcut to the House of Commons through Westminster Abbey gardens.

Eva inherited his entire estate.

By that stage, Eva and Harry's relationship was tolerably polite and remote. If Harry thought of Eva at all, it was as a custodian of Harcourt House for their sons. She wasn't going to have any more children by then – she was in her fifties. It was tax-efficient for Harry's sons to have their mother inherit the house and its chattels.

To pass it on to their sons. That was the clear expectation. Harry was thinking of his bloodline.

JEN: As soon as she got her hands on the money, she created an anonymous endowment for a Chair of Archipelago Women's Studies, with herself named as overseer of the appointment.

JUDGE: Was she explicit with any of you about her financial arrangements?

JEN: Eva was an intensely private woman. You've got to understand that. She didn't have time to go into minutiae with me. She was busy trying to end the vicious circle of the past [waves hand] four thousand years.

The core endowment was for £400,000, which was to pay for an extra salary at the college for five years. Eva's boss at the college – one of the men dragged out of retirement to condemn her – was a mild-mannered man, island-born. He was an island success story in his way; the first person from his island (Dounsay) to attend university. He had a degree in engineering, and Eva always credited him with pioneering the successful development of wind-power technology in the islands – a big thing, for it made them self-sufficient in energy, and thus independent, in this way at least, of the mainland. The college itself put up one of the first community wind turbines, and Dr Finlay negotiated the very favourable contract with Scottish and Southern.

Dr Finlay was surprised when Eva told him of the offer she had received from an anonymous donor. He didn't quite see the point, didn't believe a *Chair of Women* had any internal logic, thought it a waste of good money, but since the money wasn't his, and he couldn't see what harm it could do, he raised no objections. Eva advertised the post widely and there were applications from all over Britain. Dr Finlay agreed that the Chair of Archipelago Women's Studies ought to be a woman; but until it transpired that the anonymous donor had stipulated it as a condition, he insisted somewhat doggedly on interviewing at least one male. In the end, all three candidates who presented for interview were women: a reader in literature at Bristol, a post-doc in philosophy from Durham, and Dr Jen Mackae, whose specialism was gender studies.

ALICE: Eva writes in her notebooks about the thrill she felt, on reading Jen's application. The list of publications included a paper on American nineteenth-century gynotopias. As a schoolgirl in the island of Lewis, Jen had started the island's first and last Feminist Support & Action Group. Since then she had written a much-trolled blog about the difficulties her mother faced as a single parent, navigating the male-dominated island culture; the deference to the Free Church hierarchy, et cetera. Also, because Jen had grown up on an island, one more conservative in many ways than these, she was unlikely to flee home suffering from bright-lights withdrawal. She wouldn't colonise college meetings with complaints about the insane amount of meat in the island diet, or the insane-inane speed at which islanders drove. She was the one Eva wanted.

Dr Finlay's preferred candidate from the outset was the woman from Bristol, whose application, instead of harping upon inequality, summarised her PhD (soon to be published as a book) – a study of eighteenth-century female education, with particular reference to the novels of Jane Austen. (Dr Finlay was in love with Emma Woodhouse.) The candidate's partner had work that tied the family to the South West, where the children attended an excellent and over-subscribed church school. She wanted to commute to the islands: up on Monday morning, away on Thursday night, one day working from home. During the morning interview, Eva got through a whole packet of wine gums. As she sucked she said, by the by, 'The ferry service is very competent. One of the best. During all the time I've been here there hasn't been a single accident, despite the storms – we aren't the Western Isles!' She turned her head to gaze out the window at the fog which still hadn't lifted. 'You were all right getting in, weren't you? Over the winter, the cancellation rate is only twenty per cent. Figures are similar for flights, of course. My guess is that for about eight months of the year you should be able to fly home every weekend. No problem.'

By the following Monday, the Bristolian had withdrawn her candidacy.

Then there was the philosophy post-doc from Durham. Eva guessed, as soon as she met her, that the woman – wan, thin, pinched mouth – was newly pregnant. She refused a drink, that night, in the

Royal Hotel, and when Eva ordered oysters – they're local, she said, holding up a paprika-dusted specimen – the woman held up an almost translucent hand in opposition. During the interview the following afternoon, when Eva's assistant, Susanna, came in with a strong coffee, Eva may have asked after Susanna's sister, who had just been transferred to Edinburgh at forty-one weeks because Harcourt Hospital was unable to deal with anything other than routine deliveries; she may have lamented that Berwick-upon-Tweed's maternity unit, which was nearer, had reported 'serious safety concerns'—

JUDGE: Dr Finlay, given what you know now, is it your opinion that she fixed the appointment?
MICHAEL: It seems that way, but I couldn't prove it.
JUDGE: And at the time, did you have any idea that was going on?
MICHAEL: None at all, no.
JUDGE: Your impression was that all proper protocol had been adhered to?
MICHAEL: Absolutely. Nobody suggested otherwise.
JUDGE: And the suggestions now are mere surmise only?
MICHAEL: That is correct. I wouldn't like to comment further.
JUDGE: What was your opinion of Eva Levi?
MICHAEL: I admired her. I didn't always find her easy to work with but she had huge energy. She did great things for our islands.

The third candidate was Jen.

Jen Mackae was thirty-three when she came to the islands to work with Eva – just the right age, as she joked at the inquiry, to start a mission. She, too, had a young family, and a partner who couldn't move out to the islands just like that, but none of it put her off. From the start, and almost to the end, Jen and Eva faced the troubles and excitements of their work with exhilaration. Every time you saw them together, you could sense it: the delight which fluttered out from their fingertips, rippled through their voices, emanated from somewhere deep inside them, from the place that must have been their souls.

JEN: She was an imposing presence, you know? Without being overwhelming. I got the impression of a woman who had things to do

and accomplish. I liked that. It inspired me. And later, as the project grew, she flourished—
JUDGE: You liked her.
JEN: I absolutely loved her.

At college, Eva and Jen immediately subjected the entire teaching programme to scrutiny. Where individual lecturers were amenable, suggestions were put to them for updates to standard reading lists and teaching schedules. Where lecturers showed themselves unwilling to be swayed, Jen and Eva went ahead and gave out alternative reading lists at the office of the Islands of Women Study Centre. They advertised for candidates to write a theology PhD on the sacred feminine. They hired the young archaeologist (Susie Wells, now at Birkbeck) who had written a paper inspired by Professor Marija Gimbutas's work on prehistoric matriarchies, and whose consequent reinterpretation of Britain's Neolithic chambered cairn culture was promoted in the museum, the college and the paper. Susie also received a grant from the Wellcome Trust to re-examine nineteenth- and early-twentieth-century excavations of medieval burials, to verify with modern techniques whether the skeletons were in fact male, as often claimed; and duly discovered that the skeleton removed from Cwen by Professor Turnbull, labelled *monk or hermit*, and placed in a box deep within the Ashmolean, was in fact easily identified as a woman.

Eva and Jen also set up Archipelago Women in Work, to support female entrepreneurs. By the time Eva disappeared, the fund had helped thirty-seven female-run businesses and organisations get off the ground – such as the women's community shop on Astrid; the Archipelago Women's Whisky Distillery (they now make gin as well); Mrs Edna Reynolds's support network for women in late-life retraining; and, after some heated discussion, the Archipelago Chocolate Factory, set up by Eva's friend, the trans woman, Lucette Smith. One of the stipulations of the fund was that the newly-created bodies should be fifty-one per cent controlled by women. The rules were very strict on this point.

JUDGE: Had she already decided, at this point, to spend all the family money?

JEN: I think it was on her mind to. Money was always a big concern for us. To secure more money you need to prove impact, but how can you ask for money for impact that isn't supposed to be happening? Of course, we did a lot, just the two of us, from our base at college. But we needed more leverage than that. Thank God for Inga.

Inga Stenbridge's glorious ascent happened after Jen, newly installed as Chair of Archipelago Women's Studies, began giving free evening lectures in gender politics. Inga, island-born, was working in the council's sustainability department. She signed up, came along, they became friends. Or rather, Jen took her up. Inga – young, pretty, clever, local – had just the right profile.

At the inquiry, when Colin Grieves described the meetings that took place at Harcourt House as 'nothing less than a witches' coven', all the women present – those who knew Eva, and witnessed her at work with Jen and Inga – will have recalled for themselves the pleasure and excitement writ across the faces of those women: their optimism, palpable as the flick of a dolphin's fin, as they glimpsed their collective potential.

The first time Zoe met Inga it was a summer evening at Harcourt House. Zoe was sitting upstairs in the library, at the new grown-up desk that Eva had prepared for her, under the window, among the leather-bound books with golden writing on the spines, amid the mushroom-smell of venerable texts that nobody ever opened, when she heard voices from the kitchen.

The door opened: it was Eva, coming in to tell her that she had a guest, and wouldn't be able to drop her home.

'Can you walk,' she said, 'or shall I ask Ruth to stop by and collect you?'

'I'll walk,' Zoe said.

'Come and meet my new friend,' Eva said, and led her downstairs.

Jen and Inga were already halfway through a bottle of red wine. Jen's cheeks were pink; voices were raised in drunken excitement; even the mutton-stew-scented steam rising from the Aga seemed to wreathe the room in collusion. Zoe stopped in the doorway. Inga was leaning against the kitchen sink, glass in hand, and wearing such high-heeled shoes that it occurred to Zoe to ask what they were for, exactly. She was too shy to say anything. But she knew who Inga was. Inga was Mx Thompson's girlfriend.

ZOE: I didn't need to speak. The three of them were always talking.

Despite the wine, several decisions were taken that night. In order to win a seat as councillor in the upcoming elections, Inga needed to pull off something magnificent; the election was only six months away. Since she already worked in sustainability, Eva suggested that Inga introduce hydrogen-fuelled public transport. At first, Inga argued that this was too expensive. So Jen mooted the introduction of a free bike scheme: but everyone drove, so uptake was unlikely. How about gifting a compost bin to each household? *Boring.* We're going to do it anyway.

'I want to do things that haven't been done before,' Eva said. 'We need rules around sustainable harvesting from the seas. It's so male to take out everything and leave nothing behind—'

JUDGE: She thought it was *male* to over-exploit natural resources?
JEN: [*Smiles*] That's right: the theory of human evolution which puts the male hunter at the centre. Rising up on two feet, walking across the world exterminating species; which may indeed be why seventy-five percent of large mammals disappeared from Australia and the Americas soon after humans arrived. However, there is a competing theory of how humans learnt to walk across the globe, which Eva loved: that bipedalism evolved as people foraged, sustainably, along beaches and rivers. Water providing buoyancy, for women especially, with their breasts and subcutaneous fat. Humans share this with dolphins. The only other mammals humans share menopause with, interestingly, are toothed whales. It's all about transmission of grandmother-knowledge. Post-reproductive female humans and post-reproductive female, er, killer whales and narwhals, I think, being key to the survival of their species.
JUDGE: [*Pause*] So, you got your hydrogen bus.
JEN: Yes. Then we implemented a marine reserve around the islands. That was a bit triggering for some people, of course. But Eva didn't care – the year before, a fisherman on Astrid had wiped out the razor clam population of that island by going in with electrodes.

Anyway, it was fine because we distracted everyone with our vote-winner in perpetuity: free fuel for the masses. Free electric-charging points, subsidies on buying an electric car, and above all, subsidised heating from wind power. We've got loads of free wind here. We needed to use it up— After that, nobody could stop us. We banned plastic packaging. And the sale of chemically-polluting detergents, and pesticides and fertiliser. None of the farmers minded. The hotels complained at first. But then we rebranded the islands, through the tourist office, and visittheislands.com, as *Britain's oldest and most sacred site of female worship*. They liked that. It had cachet.

Inga became a councillor but it wasn't until the election four years later that she was elected leader by her colleagues. By this stage the shy young feminist with her lilting archipelago accent had metamorphosed into a *power-suited harridan*, as somebody recently tweeted. Jen's self-confidence, Eva's optimism, rubbed off on her; but it took a social campaign of its own to persuade a majority of the twenty other councillors to vote for an island girl with only four years' experience. By then Jen and Eva, armed with bottles from Harry's cellar, were experts in this kind of action.

Once in power, the first thing Inga did was to change the rules of the council's constitution, so that it stipulated:

(1) *Fifty per cent of the councillors on the council's board must be women;*
(2) *Over any ten-year period the convenor should be a woman fifty per cent of the time.*

Of all the changes introduced by the troika (as the press termed Eva, Jen and Inga), it was this – the council's quota system – which caused most outrage later.

JUDGE: Meanwhile, you went into politics. You have written that it was 'an unhappy time'?
JEN: It was a big mistake. I thought it would change things. We wasted five years that way, Eva and I.

Eva had supported Jen when she stood as the SNP's candidate in Dounsay. She'd won easily, after the incumbent, an island man who had once been in Lucette and Eva's book group, was arrested for sleeping with two of his pupils. The girls, in his English class for their Highers, reported the crime only after the Edinburgh pop group V's song, 'Tarn', became a hit. The lead singer, Verity, had grown up on Tarn and more or less rewrote a council leaflet on child sexual exploitation that Inga had been distributing to schools throughout the islands. Jen, who had to move her family to Dounsay after being elected, gave interviews standing on the pier, the wind whipping one of the colourful scarves she always wore around her face, as she asked for 'peace for our island community at this difficult time'. She hated the ensuing five years; the sense of treading on some other person's political territory, even if he was a criminal; the closed-in nature of island life, the exclusion; the unhappiness of her children and husband; but worst of all was the interaction with Westminster. 'Nothing's ever going to change there, in a hundred years,' she told Eva. It was a setback, being in politics; achieved nothing, other than frustration.

JUDGE: It has been suggested that Eva decided to take control of the local paper, almost in reaction to that era?

JEN: To me it would have been the obvious next step but I can't say what Eva's views on the subject were.

JUDGE: How did she go about taking control of the paper?

JEN: I don't know if she did anything.

JUDGE: Did she buy it?

JEN: I don't think so.

JUDGE: Do we have any clarity on the management structure at the paper?

SOLICITOR: [*Whisper*] *Archipelago Now* is owned by a company called Bean Offshore Holdings, registered to the British Virgin Islands.

JUDGE: Is there any link to Eva?

SOLICITOR: Her sons submit that it was around this time that she sold her mother-in-law's diamond ... choker for ... [*rustle of paper*] £250,000, and in this way bought a controlling share.

JUDGE: Is that it? Did you know about this ... necklace?

JEN: I'm afraid she never discussed family jewellery with me.

JUDGE: Were you involved in the appointment of the new editor at *Archipelago Now*?

JEN: Not directly, no.

JUDGE: Not directly?

JEN: Eva may have shown me her CV, discussed one or two points. I met the editor, of course, after the appointment. But I had no direct involvement.

JUDGE: And why was Eva involved?

JEN: The new ownership structure was in the form of a trust, and Eva was the chair.

The new editor of *Archipelago Now*, Ursula King (whose evidence to the inquiry, like that of the curator, Felicity Davidson, has been curt not to say uncooperative), claimed recently that it was her own idea to launch a weekly column with a covert feminist slant, written anonymously by one of Eva's ex-students. Nor has the question of whether or not Eva held a controlling share in *Archipelago Now* been conclusively proved or disproved at the inquiry. But most women concur that Eva was deeply committed to supporting Ursula King's work at the paper (despite, as she liked to joke, her unfortunate surname).

Archipelago Now, which is published weekly (on a Monday), had for some decades been edited and printed in a modern, purpose-built, squat concrete structure which sits like a grumpy toad on the waterfront across the bay from college.

Ursula King grew up on Tarn. Her parents moved up from Manchester when she was a little girl, and all her childhood memories are of the islands. She did well at school (clever children almost always do well in the islands; there is never, island people like to say to each other, the tragic waste of talent you find elsewhere) and she eventually went across the water to university. A little time and training outside can be an excellent thing in the making of an island stalwart; it isn't always a brain drain. So it proved with Ms King.

Jen and Eva both spoke very highly of Ursula King – and so, during the two weeks in late August that Zoe spent in the newspaper office doing work experience: shadowing journalists who covered the health beat, crime, arts, finance and immigration (something the islands generally encouraged) – she was shocked by how nobody had a good word to say about their boss. She grew accustomed to the raised eyebrows and shrugs that followed Ms King through the open-plan office, to the disparaging comments over midday coffee concerning her *aloof management style*, her *lack of editorial experience*, the *piss-poor* features she had churned out in Glasgow, where she had worked before returning home, her *over-the-water* dress sense (she wore short fitted dresses), even the marriage she had failed to hold down (she had sole custody of a son, aged five). To Zoe, who had grown up around women, Ursula's direct style of speaking seemed normal; but in the office, with its historic macho culture, Ursula was called *overly aggressive*. Despite her university degree, and her time on the Glasgow daily, she was spoken of as *under-qualified*.

Zoe was sent out with Colin Grieves, an old-time journalist who covered finance, to a GreenFuel press conference on its latest tidal-power developments. Instead of getting the W8 to Lerston, as Zoe expected, they got into his battered Mazda, a proper rusted island car, and drove at something over the generally observed speed limit of 60 mph along the straight road which linked the archipelago's largest towns, overtaking three tractors, several geriatrics and the W8 itself, happily puffing out water.

Colin hated green energy, doughnuts with holes in, and feminists. He also hated the W8, Inga at the council, and everything that the evil alliance between the two represented. Environmentalism took the piss, it encouraged sensible individuals to speak as if they were away with the fairies, and the numbers didn't add up. The infrastructure was exceedingly expensive, with very poor and unreliable returns, and hydrogen buses were the worst of it. We're a fairly big archipelago at eighteen thousand, he said, barely glancing in his rear-view mirror as he swung off the roundabout into the Lerston industrial estate, larger than Berwick, and even though the council doesn't receive revenue from the oil industry we rely on it for jobs. The fact that the council is in league with GreenFuel makes me suspicious; I'm not going to stand up cheering as our money is pissed away on cash-gobbling vanity projects. The council's getting a subsidy from somewhere; and I smell unfair business advantage. He braked hard to avoid hitting a GreenFuel minibus, then sat for a moment behind the wheel, taking several deep puffs on his e-cigarette.

Zoe reported this conversation to Eva later that afternoon, and her grandmother barely flinched—

COLIN: That's totally disingenuous, not to say dishonest. I checked the archives at the Women's Foundation. Eva Harcourt-Vane records in her notebook that she rang both Jen and Inga that night. And a few months later, Ursula King conducted a purge of old-timers, me included.

—but Zoe needed clarity, she wouldn't be put off.

'It's a really really strange situation,' she said.

'What's strange about it?' asked Eva, glancing round at her.

They were driving up to the ruined convent in the north-east. Eva liked to go there every now and then, when she couldn't get across to Cwen.

'Well, shouldn't they be fired for talking like that?'

Eva scared her by thumping the steering wheel and shouting, 'Zoe! They are dinosaur men.'

'The women in the office say things like that,' said Zoe, unhappily. 'I don't think it's an emancipated place. I don't think I should be there.'

'It's good for you to learn what needs to change,' said Eva, perhaps a little too glibly. She brought the car to a halt outside the convent. 'When I first came here,' she said, 'I used to hear people talking about the monks in the abbey. Can you believe it? And yet, until the Normans banned double monasteries – convents inhabited by monks and nuns, and run by abbesses – and, in their place, imposed celibate Benedictine rule, these islands were one of Britain's most important centres for early Christian female worship. I didn't know that for years. But it's really not surprising at all because, for centuries, every single aspect of female history that is important or inconvenient has been either suppressed or ignored or stolen from under our noses.'

'Yes, I know that,' said Zoe.

'Here,' Eva said, 'have a wine gum.'

They got out of the car. 'So you have to be constantly on guard, that's all,' Eva went on. She led Zoe through the kissing gate that kept out the sheep. They walked in the sunshine over the close-cropped grass, into the refectory and on to the dormitories, and then to the church itself. Its cruciform shape was still evident in the tracery of stones in the grass. The ruin was deserted; very few people came out this far during the week, only birdwatchers; there weren't any houses because this side of the island was too exposed, the cliffs too steep. Somebody had recently mown the grass between the walls of the convent, however, and in that lovely long-shadowed evening, the convent seemed alive, and watchful, its well-maintained lawns and jagged walls suggestive both of domestic propriety as well as the violence of its end.

'It was big, wasn't it?' Zoe said, as they strode the length of the church together.

'Ninety nuns, they think,' said Eva. 'They lived out here, all by themselves.'

Overhead the clouds began to thicken and the sun disappeared. Against the jagged back wall of the church, in what looked like a fire pit, somebody had laid a bouquet of dried flowers, or herbs. Zoe picked it up.

'They had real independence,' Eva said. She reached out to take the flowers. 'Imagine the freedom,' she went on, as her foot prodded the fire pit. 'In that age, the seventh, eighth centuries. They had their own community, with its own rules. They had a library, they collected books. They wrote books, illustrated them. They grew vegetables, kept bees. Some of the women were high-born, some not. I imagine them as a community with a wellspring of values, a sisterhood.'

'But they were controlled by the Pope, or bishops, or someone,' Zoe said.

'They did their own things on these islands. I don't think anyone would have bothered them much. The motherhouse was the abbey in Ayrness.'

'Where did the nuns go? What happened to them?' Zoe asked.

'When the abbey in Ayrness became Benedictine,' Eva said, 'the nuns were evicted, and were sent here. They hung on for a few more centuries. But then the bubonic plague happened. At first, the islands were protected from the plague by the sea. They didn't need anything from outside. Until a monk from one of the mainland monasteries came to the convent library, looking for ancient manuscripts. He was probably a merchant of some kind. Almost all the nuns died.'

Eva's face, framed by its wild hair, had seemed almost youthful, moments earlier; now Zoe saw how tired she was.

They walked towards the clifftop. Out at sea, a green and yellow sailing boat was cutting slowly through the water. Zoe took Eva's binoculars and looked across the horizon, up at the storm petrels and Arctic terns, and down at the boat.

'It's Inga,' she said after a moment. 'It's Inga in the boat, with Mx Thompson.'

'Well now,' said Eva, taking the binoculars from her. She watched the boat. Then she said, sounding pleased, 'She's done it. She's got really good at sailing.'

Zoe slipped her hand into Eva's pocket and took out the wine gums.

'When are we going over to Cwen next? It's our time. I know it.'

The first time the girl is brought over to her island, she is only a child.

She is brought over by the woman at the summer solstice, when the skies are suffused with light. Cwen watches them, and knows they are grandmother and granddaughter. Too old to be her mother, even for these times. She watches the love flow between them, back and forth, meeting and turning and overturning, like tides around her island.

The woman is familiar. She has come over before: at the spring equinox, for example, when the fish are on the move, and there are squalls in the heavens. Sometimes, around the autumn quarter-year, she might spend a day reverently picking Cwen's apples, or her ear mushrooms, or sheep-girl's supper. Even shaman's dream. The woman has come over often, with friends. But never before with the child.

The woman shows the little girl everything. They begin with the mound itself. She pushes open the stone door, and crawls in first, in case the child is scared. The child is scared, and has to be coaxed inside. But they spend a long time in there, singing and chanting. When they emerge into the sunlight again, they look dazed, as if they might actually have heard the histories. Cwen can believe it. They walk down the long eastern beach, and the woman shows the little girl where the cowrie shells are to be found. They find three of Cwen's cowries, and a Druid stone with a hole clean through the middle, and a piece of dried bladderwrack with the holdfast still attached. Then, from the beach, they walk up towards the spring. *At last,* Cwen thinks, *they are coming for my water.* They approach quietly, whispering to each other. Cwen is pleased by that. She watches. She waits. She has been waiting for so long now. She holds her breath, not wanting to do anything to disturb them. She shushes the waves, shushes the currents of Wind that swirl above them. Patiently, she waits, hoping. For the purpose of drinking they have brought a metal cup. *I would have liked a metal cup back then,* Cwen hears herself thinking; and maybe they can hear her thoughts, maybe she is inside their heads already: for they tie some string around the cup's handle, and tie the string to a rock. Then they drink. They do not strip, nor step into the stone-lined tank and bathe, as women once used to. But they have taken Cwen's waters, and that makes them hers.

Then an amazing thing happens.

When Cwen blows on her, the child opens her eyes. Brown eyes, with light glinting in them like fish in a rock pool. They look straight into each other. Cwen will never forget it. Everybody else so far has remained impervious. One small child. It is a beginning.

It is right, Cwen tells the birds above her, and the mackerel that swoop past in their seriously single-minded silver groups. *It is right,* she tells the mushrooms growing out of the burrows of the puffins. *It is right,* she tells the cowries themselves, and the Druid stone that the waves have pummelled into meaning. *It is right,* she tells the flock of black sheep, so loudly that they look up in surprise. *It is right,* she tells anything that will listen.

———

At about the time of the winter solstice, the sun is never seen on this island for forty days . . . when they bring back word that the sun will shine upon them . . . this is the greatest festival which the natives of Thule have. Among the barbarians who are settled in Thule . . . the Scrithiphini . . . do not till the land themselves, nor do their women do it for them . . . The women join the men in hunting, which is their only pursuit . . . For they do everything in common.

Procopius, 'Thule', *History of the Wars* (Byzantine Greek), sixth century AD

4

Zoe

Zoe cannot see Cwen from where she stands at the podium that is the witness box. The sea is a mere shimmer through the stained-glass window behind the judge's head. But she half-shuts her eyes, and she knows Cwen is out there. Eva has gone but Cwen is still there, talking to her, encouraging her onward.

ZOE: She took me over to that island every year. It was our safe space.

One thing became abundantly clear at the inquiry:
Eva's project tracks Zoe through the years.
Cassiopeia-like, they reflect each other, exactly. Zoe's conception was the beginning of Eva's re-education. Her genesis was all.
Throughout Zoe's life, Eva watched her granddaughter with utmost care, as if she was an organism in a laboratory experiment, which, in a way, she was. She asked leading questions, she noted Zoe's reactions to the leading women of the isles, she moulded her, and watched as she was moulded from afar. In a way, because of her other grandmother, Granny Ruth, the cards were stacked in Eva's favour, where Zoe's development was concerned; but reading through Eva's notebooks, recalling the incidents she observed, the things Zoe said about her schoolfriends, the attitudes she displayed, some of which were absorbed from prevailing island culture, Eva

evidently did manage to change the world she ruled. She banished, she upended, she demanded, and the world responded to her touch.

ZOE: I dream of my grandmother. The feeling of her. Or we are going
    somewhere together, in a hurry. These dreams are the ones I like. I
    like remembering her when she's happy and busy. But more often she
    is trying to tell me something, and then I can't hear what she is saying.
    Then I wake up struggling, and sweating. My mum says I shout in my
    sleep. These are more like nightmares. [*Pause*] I hate not knowing.
JUDGE: It must be hard, the absence of her body.
ZOE: [*Weeps*]

Eva Harcourt-Vane was one of three people who brought Zoe up. Her father, Eva's son, absented himself from Zoe's life the moment he spilled his seed inside her mum (in the pub playground, after closing time). Zoe tries not to think of it too often:

—a young man, barely nineteen, is humping the barmaid under the climbing frame. Nina, barely sixteen, is still at school. Her skirt is pushed up around her hips, her tights and pants pulled off (she has kept on her new Wonderbra, too good to be true). *Sebastian Harcourt-Vane, from the big house.* How she will boast at breaktime on Monday morning.

Sebastian Harcourt-Vane. The scent of over-the-water privilege and opportunity rises from him as surely as archipelagic limitations and Impulse rise from her.

Sebastian was in the islands for Christmas after his first term at Cambridge. Eva complained that she had never seen him so pumped up with his own importance: sleek, buoyant, irrepressible. (That's why they called those round bobbing plastic things out in the harbour, buoys. They were insufferable. That's what she wrote in her notebook.)

Eva also wrote about Nina, the girl. Her exact words were: *A typical island teenager with a blonde perm and no ambition.* Harsh.

It is true that almost everyone thought Nina was *dopey*. It was what her friends said; what the whole Harcourt-Vane family said about her; they'd written something only a little politer on her school reports. Ruth, Nina's mother, didn't mind. Nina had always been quiet but she had a good heart. It didn't matter that she wasn't wordy; she liked to save them up. Occasionally she'd say something illuminating. Ruth felt grateful on these occasions; illumined.

As for the pregnancy, it was easy from the start. Nina's periods began when she was eleven. For five years she had endured the upwelling of melancholy each month; all that blood only made her quieter. So it was a relief to think of something permanent growing in there. She listened intently to the midwife; imagined those little fingernails pushing themselves outwards, and the little beating heart; stared for ages at the alien scan shot they printed off for her. The baby was so tranquil. It was lying on its back. It had a lovely nose. It was peaceful. It made Nina feel peaceful too.

Her mother Ruth shielded her from the Harcourt-Vane family. Ruth herself would never have countenanced an abortion; it was nothing to do with the fact that she was Catholic. She simply became more and more implacable in the face of Harcourt-Vane persuasion, which soon assumed the character of coercion. All the islands knew what a demeaning time it was for the people in the big house. Harry Harcourt-Vane, having kicked his heels at the Ministry of Agriculture, had recently been promoted to the MoD, the brute parameters of which he loved. But since he was due for re-election in a year, by these same island constituents, naturally he was incandescent. Sebastian acted abashed in front of his parents, was boastful with his friends, and smug with his two elder brothers. Eva was exasperated. She realised how little her son thought of, or feared for, the future. Rather, he was taking away the valuable lesson that one made mistakes – and the women in one's life cleared them up. Also, that his family could afford a mistake of this nature. Even so, they baulked at the cost of a baby.

By now Eva was used to being shocked by her sons' lack of self-doubt – it was the entire point of their expensive education – but she was incapable of understanding how this generous-hearted youngest boy of hers could fool himself so readily. He was pretending that Nina Brock was some kind of earthy free-spirit when actually she was – so Harry kept repeating – an ill-educated, Papist, benefit-scrounging hussy.

'She won't be living on benefits,' said Eva. The more pregnant Nina grew, the more intolerable Eva found her husband's politics. 'Sebastian will support her.'

'He's a bloody student!'

'We will have to support her.'

'Damn stupid boy.'

Eva's eyes narrowed as she poured more water than was necessary into her basil plant in the kitchen.

'At least it's not the other way round,' she said, and thought, as she watched muddy water seep over the base of the tray, how hard it would have been had a daughter of theirs got herself pregnant by one of the local lads. Luckily they didn't have a daughter. She condemned them both for this thought.

INGA: Eva had only recently moved to the islands; it was a difficult time for her. She hadn't yet found her life's work; her marriage was, let's face it, a disaster.

ZOE: But I was her lucky charm. Not everybody finds their second chance, do they?

Eva would see Nina, in town, walking along the sea wall, in her hunched but steady way, dressed in a tracksuit. By month five, Nina dropped out of school, and spent the early summer days sitting with her bump on a bench against the sea wall, reading lurid teenage magazines, and allowing the entire archipelago to witness her steady inflation outwards. 'Like some perverted pregnant sex doll,' said Eva's elder son, Henry. Eva was shocked at his viciousness; but secretly it hurt how Nina paraded herself as visual proof of Sebàstian's lack of judgement.

Soon enough, to her surprise, Eva found herself looking out for her daughter-in-law – she thought of her as that, even though no one else did. She grew immune to the island gossip; the voices that stopped speaking when she entered the bakery, the greengrocer's, the post office. The bigger the bump, the more exciting it was. She once caught sight of Nina through the window of her office. She was swimming out from the little beach beyond the bay, moving slowly through the water. Eva was alarmed; there were unpredictable island currents. She walked down to the beach and stood there, waiting, her heart thumping. At last, after many solemn strokes, Nina turned round and swam back. As she came closer, Eva could see her smooth child's face, furrowed in concentration. She watched, straining her eyes. When Nina emerged from the sea, walking up the shingle to the grass where her towel was spread out in the sunshine, Eva felt with a jolt to her heart how, inside that belly, a new thing was growing, with its own spirit, irrespective of the feelings of its forebears.

They looked at each other across the shingle.

Eva wished Nina and she could have been friends. But some borders are impossible to cross.

Sebastian, father of the bump, spent most of his first long vacation, Nina's third trimester, out of the country. He returned home a week before the baby was due, talking with exasperating confidence about communal theories of child-rearing, his skin still hot from the Mediterranean sun, his hair blonder and curlier than before. As he stood in the kitchen talking non-stop while Eva prepared one of the dishes she had been cooking throughout his childhood and adolescence, she didn't ask how many Israeli, Italian or Greek girls he had slept with; how many other babies he had spawned across the ancient world. As he lounged in the garden, she felt angry. In Bosnia, a war was breaking out. She wrote in her notebook:

In 1245, as the south wall of Harcourt House was being built from local stone, Islamic learning and culture was flourishing in Sarajevo.

During the construction of the Victorian tower in the orchard, the Austro-Hungarian empire was sending its troops into Bosnia.

As Zoe was created in her mother's womb, Sarajevo's library was set on fire. In the weeks that followed, the citizens of that city came out into their gardens to find pages of books floating down from the sky, landing in plum trees, fluttering along streets, the fortune of a culture blown apart by their neighbours' guns—

JUDGE: What does this mean? She felt, what, that her priorities had narrowed?

ALICE: She'd been very prudent as a young woman. Too prudent to get pregnant without thinking and planning. There'd been a man she had loved in the city the Serbs were laying siege to. And here she was, in England of all places, *gardening*, caught up in a petty domestic drama. The house, those sons: parasites on her time and energy. She wanted to be full of something new, like Nina; absorbed; without caution. [*Pause*] During the war in Bosnia she didn't do anything, beyond giving money. She didn't offer refuge. It astonished her later.

87

Zoe was born in Harcourt Hospital; a straightforward birth, a ten-hour labour, during a night of heavy rain. Nina's exertions were almost rhythmic, in the way they chimed with the crashing of the thunder and the crack of lightning across the labour-room wall.

Sebastian missed the birth entirely. He had been in the islands in the week leading up to the due date, so Eva was completely dumbfounded when he arrived in the kitchen one morning and asked if she could drive him to the airport. She gathered from Henry that there was a *totally delicious* girl he was seeing from college; she lived in a castle in Northumberland; it was her twenty-first. Fatboy Slim, whoever he was, had been booked to play.

JUDGE: Your mother stood in for you, as it were, in your daughter's life, from the beginning?
SEBASTIAN: [*Clears throat*] I believe she did, yes.

When Nina went into labour, Eva left a terse message for Sebastian on his expensive new portable phone. *Mobiles.* They gobbled up money when you rang them. Then she drove to the hospital, and sat downstairs in the reception, reading, or thumbing through the already-thumbed magazines, under the terrible lighting. She was there all night. After she'd read every magazine, she sat in a reverie, remembering her own births, part ominous biblical hat-trick, part sinister fairy tale. Henry, her firstborn, had been pulled out by forceps, Eva with her legs up in stirrups. They'd taken him away for feeding with all the other babies in the hospital nursery. With George, they'd given her anaesthetics again, but at least let her push him out all by herself. Only with Sebastian did Eva really feel like she knew what she was doing. She'd been given a book by a friend: grainy black-and-white photos of naked women, their legs spread, their faces set in what was probably agony but might also have been ecstasy. Stubbornly, she'd paced the hospital corridors, grunting. It had been hard. Where was Harry? Elsewhere.

She'd breastfed George and Seb, at least. It had fallen out of fashion in Britain, so none of the midwives encouraged it. But she remembered how in Bosnia, under socialism, nursing mothers who worked in factories, and needed to breastfeed their babies, were allowed two hours off during the day, without having their pay docked.

Nina's midwife called her in at eight forty-five in the morning. Outside, rain was hammering down through gutters and pouring along pavements. Puddles were reflecting the undersides of trees and patches of previously unnoticeable sky; fields were turning silver. Nina was lying on the hospital bed, the nails on her fingers and toes lacquered in an ever-changing configuration of stripes and dots and colours. She looked exhausted but serene, like Eva herself, back in Sarajevo, nonchalant but high, after a three-day trek across the forests of eastern Bosnia. Ruth, Nina's mother, was clasping the baby's tiny hand in her own. Her usually-severe face was suffused with relief. *The baby.* Eva gasped. She, too, felt giddy.

Outside, the rain kept falling. Zoe's birth: the year of the floods.

JUDGE: In your submission to this inquiry, in paragraph 2, you have suggested that the arrival of Zoe caused friction in the family.
GEORGE: I was sitting my finals and wasn't present for most of the family summits. But there was uproar. Typical Sebastian. My brother was always completely impulsive and irresponsible.

JUDGE: Zoe's existence seems to have changed everything for Eva.
HENRY: Utter tosh. Completely untrue. My mother seemed to take the crisis in her stride. We all did.

JUDGE: Did you have much contact with your niece?
GEORGE: Look, she lived in the islands, I live in London, and whenever I visited she was ... No, not much.

Sebastian phoned from Cambridge a week later, by which time nothing had been sorted out between the grandmothers except an agreed monthly payment, proposed by Eva's solicitor and, judging by raised eyebrows, far more than Nina's mother had been expecting. After some months, the child was christened *Zoe Kylie Brock* in a ceremony in the Catholic church in Lerston – a perfectly hideous building, whispered Harry (who insisted on coming, for appearances' sake), so that the people in the pew in front turned and shushed them. Eva felt embarrassed by Harry. Until now, she had felt like his inferior. Now she merely despised him. She was relieved that Nina Brock had given the child her own strong rustic island surname. She didn't like the dreary church and the toneless modern hymns either. But she admired Nina and her mother from afar. As for the baby—

The beautiful baby bawled and cooed at number 9, Oaklands Close, and each time Eva looked into her eyes she saw not Sebastian, nor Harry, but herself and Nina and Ruth, the exact mixture of them, the female line, triumphant in soft skin and pale curling hair. Eyes that followed her round the room and smiled when she leant over the cot. Zoe was her Jewish grandmother; she was Silvana, the singer she'd heard play in Sarajevo; she was Virginia Woolf and Aphra Behn.

In Zoe's early years, Eva made several faux pas, despite or because of her eagerness to please. During a trip to London she bought several very expensive cashmere cardigans, gloves, trousers even, from a shop in Hampstead near her father's old flat. She knew immediately, upon getting back to the islands, that the extravagance was an offence. She persisted in buying the baby picture books, fairy-tale collections, story anthologies – coming round every week that she was in the islands, with a new book, ordered from Hatchards; she would have come round every day if she could. The baby was very friendly but Eva knew that she was too much for Ruth and Nina. They found her patronising. She found it impossible to strike the right tone.

Things were awkward for a while between the families. Until Nina started work, and the child went to school, Zoe rotated solely in her mother's orbit. Conversation, stilted at the best of times with babies themselves, was almost non-existent with Nina. The television was always on; and there were other habits concerning food and physical activity which Eva instinctively shrank from. But she understood that her inability to win a place in their affections was Sebastian's fault, and Harry's, and hers. Not Nina's. Not Zoe's.

Luckily, Eva was humble enough to make herself indispensable. Ruth was busy at work. Nina was young, and wanted to go out sometimes. Eva and Zoe struck up a friendship.

ALICE: The fact is, Zoe healed her.

One of Zoe's earliest memories is being picked up by Eva for the first time, from infant school in Ayrness.

ZOE: A tall, angular woman with big grey hair – a whole bush of it coming out of her head. [*Laughs*] She may as well have been dressed in a cape and carrying a broomstick, the way the other children stared.

Although Zoe lived – still lives – with her mum and Granny Ruth, in the 1950s estate in Ayrness, as a child she was often up at Eva's. Ruth, a police detective, has always worked long hours; and when Zoe was a schoolgirl her mother, too, didn't get home from working at the bakery in Lerston until long after the school day ended. So it was Eva who picked Zoe up from school, or, once she was old enough, was waiting for her as she walked home to Harcourt House. Even as Eva's schedule at the college grew more intense, and her days filled with excitement and strategy, she would put down the telephone, or turn away a visitor, or conclude a meeting early, if Zoe needed her attention.

LUCETTE: She brought Zoe with her on a tour of the chocolate factory once. I just *loved* seeing the two of them together. [*Wipes eyes*] I always thought, that of the two of us, I would be the first to go. I'm the smoker, the drinker, the one always falling in love with unsuitable suitors. Eva was so sensible. She was always there for me. It's unbearable, being left here without her.

Throughout her childhood, for at least half the year, at least once a day, Zoe would walk from Harcourt House, two miles or more home, across the island in the dark. The dark was warmth, lit by the moon and singing friendly noises.

STELLA: If ever she moves off island, to one of those mainland cities where stars are obscured by street lights, and permanently-lit offices, and car headlights, she will miss our islands' night-times most. Mainland lights: insect apocalypse.

She was used to waves crackling like fire; to the island smells of rotting seaweed and peatsmoke; to the way lights appeared across the water as boats passed. The way other islands came nonchalantly in and out of view.

Sometimes, when she reached the coastpath, Zoe liked to imagine she was somewhere huge (*rather than really tiny*), the American prairie perhaps. Often, her journey home from Harcourt coincided with the departure of the last ferry, when the islands' connection with the mainland was severed. Sometimes, she reached the road into Ayrness as the ferry pulled out, and then she was almost close enough to hear its rattles, smell the diesel, see returnees to Berwick or London, sitting in the bar, hunched over their laptops. Sometimes it was by ferry that her father came to visit.

In the summer, the walk was quicker, because she didn't have to be careful of her footing. Purple rock-cress grew over the stones at the O'Reillys' farm. From the top of the lane she could see for miles out to sea. There was the abbey, and the island of Cwen, with its breast-mound, in the distance. She passed the oak trees by the playing fields, stooped in the wind; ran her hand through the exuberant yellow toadflax, a little crazy and bouffant, like her mum's hair with a punk-cut blow-dry. Beyond the playing fields was the path to Oaklands Close. The eighteen houses were built in a circle with a fenced-in bit of green in the middle. Number 9 was on the far side. This was all it took to get from Zoe's father's side of Ayrness to her mother's.

For much of the year, Zoe had Eva to herself – relatively speaking, for she always had to share Eva with other island women, with Eva's programme of reform, with her mission. Nor is she Eva's only grandchild. Her father, Sebastian, has two subsequent children, born to his wife Camille. His two brothers have three children between them, and although all five are younger than Zoe, the demands of legitimacy are strong, and on the rare occasions when the sons arrived at Her House with wives and babes in tow, Zoe soon learnt to absent herself from the strange pull they exerted over Eva. The turmoil they created – the love and the poison.

But mostly, it was just Eva and her.

Zoe, as she has proved since, by drawing detailed plans, and lists of contents, knew the house inside out; better than her father or his brothers (she liked to think – they grew up in London), better than her cousins. She knew its smells – coffee grounds in the kitchen, orange flower water uncorked from an old glass bottle on Eva's bedside table, lavender and cloves when you opened a drawer in her boudoir, the smell of bread when she embraced you—

She often lingered in Eva's bedroom. Eva's dressing table was a fine Jacobean piece (Eva said) but it was the photographs on top which drew the eye. Forbidding Uncle Henry, mounted on a horse, aged six. Taciturn Uncle George as a dragon, aged nine, with curly green gilt tail and red paper tongue. Sebastian, Eva's baby, sitting in the bath upstairs, hair slick, clutching a rubber duck. There was Eva's wedding photograph: Harry, elite-neat; Eva, in a narrow dress of lace and silk, stitched by her aunt. There was a newspaper clipping – from *The Times* – of the day Harry joined Thatcher's cabinet. On the wall between the windows was a photographic print, black and white, evidently taken decades ago, of two foreign women and a child, standing in a cobbled street. All the other pictures in the room were Harry's, bought by and inherited from, his parents – the eighteenth-century painted-glass portrait from France of a couple on a donkey, the woodcut of peasants cutting wheat, the dark charcoal sketch of the island of Cwen; the furniture was Harry's, too. But it was Eva who washed saddlebags clean of dirt, darned silk curtains, had enormous saggy chairs reupholstered. She who bought silver polish and beeswax for her cleaner, her daily-man.

MARCIN [PRZYBYLSKI]: She was always very respectful.

Zoe knew her grandmother's gait: the way she clicked her fingers as she walked. The way she walked fast below but dreamily above, her head tilted as if the two parts of her were not quite connected. Zoe loved Eva's low, emphatic voice; it purred inside her. From the library window, as she did her homework, Zoe would watch Eva: crossing the lawn, holding a trug, bending down in the border, weeding. She was tall until the end. Her eyes: peaty, modulated, quick-moving. (Zoe has those eyes.) She was an ebullient grandmother, a good mother, an ideal host, a forgiving friend. She was interested in other people. She tried not to let her frustrations show.

When Zoe was a little girl, Eva often spoke to her of the islands' history, and of the Islands of Women. The story was very old, Eva said, so old that it had almost been forgotten, but she hadn't forgotten it, and she didn't want Zoe to forget it either. Once upon a time, over a thousand years ago, a group of women took a boat, and all their possessions, and set sail from Britain or Ireland, to make a new life. They sailed to some islands very much like ours – *perhaps they were ours* – where they could live life on their own terms.

ZOE: That is how I remember her retelling the story of the Islands of Women. We spoke of it often: imagining how it would be to live in such a place, what roles we would perform, how it would feel, and (when I got older) whether we would miss our male authority figures or whether for me, being brought up by three women, it would seem quite natural. She spoke of the things that our Islands of Women would banish, like excessive phallic symbols and uncapped air travel—

JUDGE: She inculcated you.

ZOE: [*Nods*]

ALICE: Eva used to say that the really frustrating thing about the myth of the Islands of Women is the historical fog that surrounds it.

JUDGE: By which I understand you to mean, there is no established corpus of work, no academic monograph?

ALICE: Exactly.

JUDGE: Wasn't that the point?

ALICE: Yes, the ease with which rebel histories can be wiped out. What I came to understand, through her, was how we are all collectively responsible for our epics – as we are for our gods and goddesses. They are made by us, over time, together. It's an ongoing process. It doesn't stop. What we do with them matters.

The first active role Zoe played in Eva's mission was at the museum. Daytime meeting places like tea shops and cafés are a big part of life in the islands; of women's lives especially. But until Eva joined the board, revamped the displays, and hired Dr Felicity Davidson, the pink-haired, seashell-tattooed curator, the museum café was a typical old-fashioned island place. It served only two types of coffee (black or white), often in styrofoam cups; offered a choice of three robust home-made cakes, and at lunchtime, either shepherd's pie or fish'n'chips. There were embarrassing posters on the walls of yellow chicks peeping out of, or trying to climb into, variously-shaped pink plant pots.

For a year or so after she arrived, Felicity Davidson never ate in the museum café; she brought a kettle and fiddly little AeroPress thing into her office. The other staff watched her coming and going, the tattoo (on her wrist) sometimes obscured by the high tide of her leather jacket, at other times exposed, and felt disappointed at her distance. Having finally recognised it as coolness towards themselves, they then felt offended.

The museum café was run by an island-born woman, Barbara Anderson, who had a white fluffed coiffure, soft, papery face, and a matronly air. For some three or four decades she had opened the doors of the place six days a week, 9.45 a.m. to 6 p.m., took only three days' holiday a year, and all over Christmas, when the museum was closed anyway. Her husband had only recently died. A gentle, undemonstrative man, he had looked after her with love, and she missed him. Oh yes, she had been deeply loved; you could sense that in her. That the lover in question was a man, a very manly man, was possibly essential to the love that made her glow. She had done all the laundry and all the cooking, all her life. He had done the DIY. Barbara had been happy.

Now that he was dead, it was simply unthinkable to upset Barbara in any way. Barbara was true island stock; all her children and their spawn still lived in the islands; a feat considered by some the very-highest-level qualification in island living. Unfortunately, Barbara also disliked Felicity. She missed the old days when the museum was run by Dr Denis Morris, whose enthusiasm for the excavation of which he had been part, as a young man, of an Iron Age roundhouse on Tarn, had not dimmed as he advanced through life. He had been enthusiastic, always, in his praise of Barbara's pink-iced banana cake and her strongly-stewed tea, which he took white with two sugars. He always asked after her grandchildren, and always paused long enough, over his tea, to exchange important island gossip. He never failed to leave tips that, though not extravagant, were like little jolts of happiness, for Barbara, in the form of fifty or twenty pence.

'Why don't you get a job in the museum café?' Eva said to Zoe one afternoon when she was in her thirteenth year; and Zoe looked up, surprised, from her homework. *What glamour:* to work as a waitress.

Was Zoe exploited as emissary and spy? It is possible. Did she know? Even she can't really say. There was the evening when

Barbara and she stood together in the kitchen, doing the final wash-up and wipe-down, amidst the dim flickering striplight and the hum of the old refrigerator, and got talking about Barbara's late husband, who had farmed the family croft in addition to working as a security guard at the fish factory in Lerston. The old lady told Zoe how she had recently found among her late husband's effects a recipe book kept by his mother, who grew up on Dounsay. Zoe spoke to Eva about it, who spoke to Inga, who spoke to Felicity Davidson. Since the comprehension gap between Felicity and Barbara was as difficult to navigate as the Eastray crossing, Zoe was instructed to offer to type the recipes up – they could sell the most promising ones as leaflets – and Barbara was pleased, even touched, by the proposal. One mid-November afternoon, as Zoe sat by the window overlooking the beach, peering at Barbara's mother-in-law's thin copperplate handwriting (describing the method for skinning turbot), Wendy, who ran the museum shop, came in, all flowery prints, powdered cheeks and disquiet, to propose in her high nervous voice that if the recipes proved popular with clientele, couldn't they be edited up as a book? We could even collect other recipes, from across the islands – it would be *lovely*. Maybe a display in the museum? Zoe put in. And how about selling some archetypal island dishes in the café?

Barbara was so pleased with the support that the notion of a *Book of Recipes from the Islands* received that she got to work on it right away. She experimented with dishes such as battered scallops, from Dounsay, and bobbit, a spicy Tarn teabread, which soon began to make regular appearances on the café menu. A notice was posted in *Archipelago Now*, and put up in the museum foyer, calling for recipe submissions. Zoe was employed as typist and copy-editor, and although she didn't believe everything she was sent – was Inga Stenbridge's recipe for 'Poor Woman's Pot' authentic, or had she made it up? – such was the good feeling generated in the museum (Barbara, on the front page of *Archipelago Now*, grinning as she held up a spatula) that Felicity Davidson dropped by one morning. She ordered an Eastray kale and potato scone, declared it *delicious* (it was not), and made an important announcement: she had managed to free up a Café-Redec Budget (she called it that) to coincide with the book's launch in January. Barbara Anderson took the itemised budget, studied it carefully, and ticked those items she approved of, which included: *Professional espresso machine with grinder* - - - - - - £8,000. She also approved the large-format printing of the island photographer Elise Vallor's 1960s photographs of locations mentioned in the book, which were to be hung on the repainted walls in place of the chicks. The bakery at Lerston was to supply the café with pastries and cakes, including an exclusive Tarn bobbit.

JUDGE: Do you recognise the description painted during this inquiry of the changes at the museum?

FELICITY: It's completely spurious and defamatory to suggest that my management of the museum had any gender-motivation whatsoever. What happened in the café is a prime example. No man got fired. The woman who was running the place stayed in her job. All we did was redecorate. I don't understand what all the fuss is about. Eva tried to persuade me to go for a Neolithic V as a motif but we decided against it.

JUDGE: What about the new displays you put in?

FELICITY: We consulted with a wide spectrum of experts, from the islands and beyond.

JUDGE: Dr Weissbluth, within your own work and teaching – you teach at the University of Oxford – are you saying that you would never promote, advertise or alert students to ideas such as those here in the museum?

IAN: I'm not saying that the display boards are wrong, per se, but the kind of claims they make would not be tenable outside that forum, say, in peer-reviewed academic journals. I would never promote or advertise those ideas, no. I might alert, with caveats.

ZOE: Does the patriarchal view of history come with caveats?

JUDGE: You were part of it from the start.

ZOE: I guess so.

JUDGE: You didn't mind?

ZOE: I liked it. Nobody else in my family was discussing these important women questions with me, were they?

Zoe's mum?

Her dad barely spoke to her at all, and only, Zoe suspected/ absolutely knew, on Eva or Camille's urging. (*Hello Zoe* – awkward shoulder punch – *How you've grown!* – then a series of questions about her progress in school, *Do you really only take eight GCSES in the islands?*)

All the reliable/un-sad things Zoe knew about her parents, in fact, she gleaned from Granny Ruth. Eva had nothing reliable to say on the subject, according to Ruth. Regarding her mum in particular, Zoe knew that people in general were guilty of something like a patronising attitude. *Is Nina depressed?* Zoe overheard the women saying to each other at Harcourt House. It was only when Zoe reached her eleventh year – by which time she was going to secondary school in Ayrness – that she came to understand that what Eva and her friends might consider as 'being depressed' just meant watching television every evening. The television was on from the moment her mother came home from work, it was on through teatime, and it was the only noise in the house as Zoe did her homework. It stayed on when Granny R arrived back home from the pub, although at this point the channel was switched to the News at Ten. Watching the news was the one thing Granny R insisted they do together every evening as a family. It was more important than family meals. It was *knowledge*. It was *being informed*. It was *not labouring under popular misconceptions*. Granny R would comment on the news loudly, as it happened, item by item. She liked Tony Benn, she hated Tony Blair, she loved Red Ken. Everything that had happened since then turned her stomach. She wouldn't even utter the names of D/G/N.

As a matter of policy, Ruth didn't criticise Zoe's mainland father ever; never tutted when birthday presents arrived a day late, or voicemails about school went unanswered. She was unreserved in her scorn of his party, however.

AS WICKED AS THE TORIES

Because the archipelago had once been a Tory safe seat, and was now held by Zoe's father's party, Ruth often stressed to Zoe that they were living among the *clearly apathetic*, the *morally wicked*, the *straight deluded*. The sea couldn't keep out the worst things – politicians such as Zoe's father – but it did pretty well. Those stupid films with their muscly male heroes doing unlikely stunts – James Bond, Batman, Spider-Man; people had to go to Berwick to see them, ha. Or, the annoying kids' craze for Go Go Hamsters – that only came in with Juliette Thomas, who was given one by her cousin in Dundee; it never caught on. The archipelago kept its old music, fiddle sessions in the pub, regular ceilidhs. Its love of whisky; its predominantly salt-fish diet.

It's why we're all so clever, Ruth liked to say. The fish; not the whisky.

Ruth was proud of having joined the police service at the age of just nineteen. She named her own daughter, Nina, after the suffragette who founded the first Women's Police Service. Nina was proud of very little. She had spent her entire working life to date – bar the significant short stint in the Hope and Anchor pub which gave rise to Zoe – in the bakery at Lerston. It was a family business, Nina Brock the only outsider. Sometimes she worked in the bakery shop, sometimes in the bakery itself, and sometimes in an adjacent room, armed with a big syringe, with which she injected strawberry jam into row upon row of sugared doughnuts. In the bakery, her mother wore a white buttoned coat, like a nurse, and this had given six-year-old Zoe the impression that Nina was engaged in work of critical, clinical importance. She was disabused of this notion as a matter of course; it ceased to exist as naturally as a hymen breaking.

Zoe was well used to the whispers as she crouched down by the penny-sweet counter in the post office, calculating how to divide her weekend quota. *Opaque, sugar-covered babies.* 'Harry Harcourt-Vane, such a good constituency MP, always answers letters, always drops in when he comes to the islands; must be a bit of an embarrassment, the connection with Nina Brock.' *Yellow flying saucers.* 'She's never wanted for anything, if she hadn't got pregnant what would she have done?' *Sherbet-coated snakes.* But then the island gossip changed. *Strawberry bootlaces.* 'An absolute travesty in this day and age, leaving Nina and Ruth to raise that girl alone, in that draughty police accommodation, he should have married her, look at him with his foreign black wife—' *White and yellow fried eggs.* Ruth would have none of it. *Pink and white mushrooms.* 'We have no need of a man around. God save us.' *Fizzy cola bottles.*

Zoe developed her own opinions. Her father and she were definitely to blame for her mother's physical decline/departed beauty. Nina Brock had only briefly been pretty: Zoe was able to judge this for herself from the photographs her mother stashed away haphazardly in a box behind the TV. The photos divided into three: Nina the chubby, lost-looking child; Nina the teenager, pretty as a peach; Nina the mother: overweight/bit stressed/could-be-happier.

REPORTER: Today at the inquiry, the issue of your mother's weight was discussed. Isn't body positivity what feminists are working to promote?
ZOE: The tyranny of the female gaze; one of our blindspots.

The pretty phase ended about three years after Zoe's birth. Zoe raised this subject only once with Ruth. Her grandparent turned stern; explained that if you added up the hours which the average woman spent obsessing with her appearance, you understood why men had all the power.

Zoe's mother, on the other hand, sporadically tried her best. It was with her mother that Zoe went shopping, the only place they went together. In Ayrness town centre, at the weekends, Zoe's mum tried on heavily-scented gloop and overly-tight Lycra. None of her efforts achieved what she wanted. Zoe, finding lipsticks and mascara wands discarded in the bathroom bin, felt angry/upset with these unassailable commodities. But she was relieved, when exploring her aunts' bedrooms one Christmas at Eva's, to find evidence, there too, of inhuman female effort. She touched her finger to the lid of a glass perfume bottle; put that finger to her nostrils. She ran her hands over a smooth leather handbag with a shiny metal clasp. In the wardrobe hung printed dresses, big-bowed blouses, brightly coloured slacks. They, too, stank of womanhood's conflicted/yukky odour.

Once, when Eva was still adhering to the Harcourt-Vane tradition of the Christmas party, and Zoe, aged about eleven, was handing out trays of vol-au-vent, she made her way through the crowded sitting room and into the hall, to find her Aunt Octavia coming downstairs. Zoe saw her taking out her cigarettes, and her lighter. She saw her pick up a coat from the stand in the hall, and open the front door. By the time Zoe had got through the burst of people, Octavia was sitting in the porch, hunched into her coat, staring out gloomily into the blackness and the rain, cigarette smoke wreathing itself around her head like a pack of whining dogs.

'Would you like an Island Puff?' Zoe said to Octavia's back. 'I think they're the nicest. It's squash from the Tarbert Veg Scheme and soft cheese made by the Lerston Dairy. It's an almost entirely indigenous product.'

Octavia turned to look at her, refused the puffs with an upturned hand, and Zoe thought that was going to be it, except that her aunt, putting her cigarette-free hand up to Zoe's ponytail, said, 'Why don't you wear it down?'

This was such an unexpected piece of attention that Zoe stared. Octavia, who, up-close, had wrinkles of worry across her forehead, looked incredible from afar. With her expensive clothes and upright posture, she looked like something from a magazine, Zoe thought. Which possibly she was. (In some magazine, somewhere; in somebody's far-off world.)

Zoe placed the tray of vol-au-vent carefully on the bench so that Octavia could pull her hair out from its band and consider her chances. 'There's a product for this problem,' Octavia said, musingly, as she felt the texture of Zoe's hair, between thumb and forefinger. 'Sit,' she said, indicating the bench.

Over the next half hour, Zoe, sitting very still with the tray of vol-au-vent on her knees, learnt several melancholy/unholy things: that Octavia had never counted the numbers of shoes she owned; nor had she admitted to George the number of handbags in her possession. The three most expensive, made of animal skins so rare it was a form of bad luck even to utter their names, she kept in the safe in her office in London. So tiny and beautiful, they rarely saw the light of day, and yet even in the office, the feeling one got – fingertips running over something scaly, cheek pressed to predator flank, nose inhaling rainforest interstitched with savannah – was, in some months, the most sensual pleasure that Octavia derived from her life as a thirty-seven-year-old PR executive, wife, and mother of children aged eight and five. The handbags smelt and felt like impeccable taste, elegance, comportment, success, and all the other things which it was impossible to teach, and which Octavia, upon regarding her grubby-faced daughter Polly, who at eight favoured Gap sweatshirts over smocked dresses, despaired of passing on. Also, with two mucky children, and a husband into countryside pursuits, it made sense to keep spoilable purchases away from jam-smeared fingers, muddy gumboots, bottles of gun-cleaning fluid and leaking felt-tips. The pieces she chose to expose to the coarse environment of home were made from cows, lamb and other animals so common the islands were full of them; in fact, now that one thought about it, fields themselves were nothing more than shopfronts of little mobile handbags. Octavia laughed. The other items were too expensive for everyday life: which gave rise to the existential issue of there not being enough days left in Octavia's life to do their exquisite workmanship justice. The thing she dreaded most was them falling, one by one, out of fashion.

TARA: It saddens me how Eva allowed frivolous people, such as her daughters-in-law, into her house, and said nothing about their conspicuous consumption—

JUDGE: Eva couldn't outlaw frivolity.

TARA: It's not just frivolity. It's the insidious way in which women are held down. At the college Eva actually ran a campaign *against* handbags, *pro* pockets in women's clothing. She wanted the students to learn to see something seemingly innocuous and irrelevant like a handbag, as part of something larger and much more sinister: the way women are prevented from having their hands free to defend themselves, or make things. Men's clothing always has loads of pockets. Men don't carry handbags, because handbags are annoying. So men reap the benefits of two million years of evolution. That was why *Homo sapiens* learnt to stand up: to have their hands free. It's just one example of women's fetters. And Eva knew all this, and had a handbag obsessive to stay, and said nothing.

JUDGE: This seems excessive to me. What could she have said?

TARA: I guess she could have been bolder about articulating how women are hampered by society, by being valued for the wrong things? It is frustrating, because in other areas of her life she fought for female solidarity. When it came to her own family, she was really inconsistent.

If Ruth was hurt or annoyed by the outlandish things Zoe talked of when she returned from Harcourt House – *Virginia Woolf, again; the ice-cream parlour called Egipat in Sarajevo; vagina carvings on Neolithic rocks* – there was little she could do. The mother and father had ceded all control, and thus did the child learn to interpret the world: through the eighteenth-century window glass of Harcourt House, with its slight green tinge and ripple, its elevated vista; through the dense black mirror of the Oaklands Close television, the coloured-glass front door, the windscreen of a police vehicle.

RUTH: It could've been worse.

Ruth: the first island girl to make DCI.

By the time she got to secondary school, Zoe had begun to wonder: How is it that Granny R got emancipated? How is it that my mother appears not to care? She asked nobody directly. She made discreet enquiries. She came to these conclusions:

i) My mum has no island-pride because of the way I was conceived.
ii) Granny R is so fiery due to a teacher at her Astrid school, who, in the early 1970s, thought she saw in her fourteen-year-old pupil a candidate for university. (Except that Ruth Brock had set her heart on joining the police force.) And also to a nameless lover from over the water, about whom nothing further shall be spoken. (Except to say that he fathered Nina, was encouraged to disappear, and made Ruth appreciate the impudence of men.)

Absent grandfathers were one thing. Entering her middle-teens, embarking on her GCSEs, the thing most on Zoe's mind was her own f—

WOEFULLY NOT THERE

Not having sufficient access to one of her own, Zoe spent her mid-childhood in deep study of other people's. Her friend Kath's dad, who worked as a 'traditional island builder', and took off his tool-belt only as he approached the table for tea, lectured

Kath and Zoe on the importance of trying hard at science, and seemed a figure of impossible kindness and compassion. (Her own father never suggested that she try hard at anything at all.) Staying over at Kath's, she watched their family rituals as if she was David Attenborough and they a pride of lions. She observed their feeding times, their argumentative-playful conversation, their attitude to schoolwork, weekends, and school-night television. Kath's dad, for example, took no part in the preparation of food but always praised it, and was always on washing-up duty after. Pauline Parker's, by contrast, was tall, with spiky blonde hair and an earring, and cooked one of his four special dishes every Tuesday, Friday, Saturday: macaroni cheese, cauliflower cheese with cherry tomatoes, feta and spinach filo pastry pie, spaghetti bolognese made from island beef. Zoe had tried them all. The bolognese was most complicated and required most swearing.

What Zoe's father failed to provide in terms of presence/attention (forget meal-cooking), he made up for (in other people's eyes) by his appearance on national media. I heard your dad on Radio 4 this morning, Pauline's mum would say approvingly, as she stepped through the back door with Pauline, in time for macaroni cheese. Or: Your father does come across so well on telly, doesn't he? Or: Hey guys! Zoe, Zoe, quick! Your dad's being interviewed again! (Kath's younger sister). And so Zoe would enter the front room sheepishly, squeezing on to the settee between Kath and her mum and sister, and watch with a mixture of pride, shyness and fear: as her father argued with a member of the opposition about fisheries policy. That was the nearest she got to having a real father mostly.

Zoe would've died for the story Pauline told: of locking herself in the bathroom when she first got her period, of her father standing in the passage, banging on the door, and shouting, Get on with it, child! Do you want me to come in and wipe your bottom? Of her coming out, and telling him what had happened; of him immediately hugging her to him, and saying, Run and tell your mother. Of them having his special spaghetti for dinner that evening. What would it be like to have a dad like that? A dad you could talk to, one to one, in person? Her periods hadn't started yet. But when they did, she would ring Sebastian up and tell him. And he would be so—

Friends: often mean, sometimes hateful.

At school, during one of her regular week-long periods of being un-friended by her friends, Zoe walked into the toilets in the library, to find two older girls sitting on the floor under the hand towels, stamping a pile of leaflets with green stars and stickers. She knew exactly who they were: Stella Armitage and Tara Gill. They looked up at her and grinned.

'Here, take this,' said Tara, handing her a leaflet. With her shaved head she could've been a boy. It was rumoured she had a triangular tattoo on her ankle. 'We're having a gathering this afternoon.'

'You'll come, yes?' said Stella, who wore green nail polish, had a nose ring and played the fiddle.

Zoe took the leaflet and retreated to a cubicle. As she peed, she read, *The polar ice sheets are melting. The time for inaction is over. See you@5, Library Meeting Room.*

When she came out again, the girls had gone, but she could smell something of them in the air still, through the air freshener, a smoky woodiness. *The Green Club.* That would be something to tell her father, the man on the telly, the next time he ever stopped to ask her anything about herself. That she, like him, was an environmentalist.

It turned out that the Green Club met to consider, not the environment as such, but *environmental actions.* Zoe had never heard of an *action* before the afternoon she watched the video that Mx Thompson played, with its high-octane television footage of scruffy people shouting at policemen. Afterwards, Mx Thompson (they/them/theirs), skinny as a razor clam, pale, silent, with freckles the colour of their gold-red hair, one of those teachers who liked the sound of their own voice much less than normal, explained that it was a *road protest*; that the protesters were protecting trees; got them to think about the *sacred oak* in Celtic culture; how the human love and veneration of trees was *deep in our psyche*; which is why we all put up fir trees in our homes at Christmas; which was why these young people had camped out to protect *ancient woodlands from being decimated by careless governments.*

When the two older girls proposed that the group should continue their meeting outside school, without the teacher, Zoe was so intoxicated – *she, Zoe Brock, hanging out with Tara Gill* (who had sewn a green thread all the way down the leg of her grey school trousers, and the teachers said nothing about it), *Stella Armitage* (who said that yes, *obviously* idolising footballers and film stars was brain-dead), *and a boy from the lower sixth* (they called him Ravi, to match them, a bilingual false etymology – his given name was Raymond) – that she barely noted the focus of discussions. They went to the tea shop on the high street, where Tara proposed motions, Stella sewed banners with emotive messages about climate change and decimated forests, and Ravi took minutes. It was a while before Zoe had the courage to mention the nature of her father's job, but when she did, nobody seemed to think badly of her for it, despite all the criticism of the government which went on at these meetings. By then, of course, she was used to people in her everyday life being in awe of her father and his out-of-the-ordinary circle. Ravi's dad worked on the fish farm. His mum, who was from Turkey, didn't have a job yet; but was managing the family's construction, at the weekends, of a wooden kit-home they'd ordered online. In the meantime, they lived in a caravan on the outskirts of Ayrness.

'My mum just got a grant from Women Entrepreneurs in Work to put on a green roof,' said Ravi, out of the hearing of Tara and Stella. 'You should come round and see it, it's really cool.'

The environment: totally fucked.

By now Zoe knew, of course, how past-life/patriarchal the world beyond the islands was, with its male-dominated throb of tyres on roads, testosterone-fuelled engines broadcasting their smoke into the air, doors slamming through endless streets, planes shrieking overhead. Island living was superior. But during the autumn half-term, when Kath was off to London, Pauline to her cousins' in Edinburgh, Tara taking the boat to Berwick, and Stella's family driving to Wales, Zoe (along with a not-inconsiderable proportion of her peers, but still, she felt abandoned) stayed in Ayrness. In the summer, her island-prison was at least enlivened by the tourists, with their unstinting jollity, their interesting-looking beach novels and awe-inspiring dresses. Few were the visitors to the islands in the autumn, however.

Her Uncle George came up to see them. Sitting in the library at her homework desk, she overheard him talking on the phone in a heated way about the woods above the house. She knew he was arguing with Sebastian, her father. (Zoe, the silent ghost of Harcourt House, avidly absorbing grown-up conversation.)

Our islands: boring boring boring

As George ranted about the bottom line, Zoe stood in the library at Harcourt House looking at the old map of the islands which hung there. The map was in black and white, with old-fashioned spellings. This was what the islands felt like to her:

`black and white`

OLD-FASHIONED

spotted with marks of age and usage.

JUDGE: She took you to Cwen, the island?
ZOE: Cwen? Yes. Many times.
JUDGE: Did you like going there with her?
ZOE: I did. [*Laughs*] I only sometimes wished she wouldn't talk to me so much about women.

BOYS

Yes, them. Zoe has begun to notice the few men around her as if the spotlight of her brain has picked them out of a generalised darkness: her uncles, brusque, false-friendly. That boy, *Euan*, from biology, taller than her only by a fraction, who smells so familiar (laundry powder, school dinners). At night, or worse, when she is sitting at her desk, doing her homework, she feels a cavernous warm space open up within her; *it is waiting for something.* She thinks of Mr Mills, who teaches their class about renewables. Even though his eyes move over the classroom of pupils in annoyance – *teenage girls are so stupid* – she bestows on him her thoughts. She doesn't think of him naked – she doesn't know how to think such a thing

– but she thinks of him so often, his clothes become superfluous; he is the sum of the words he speaks to her and they are thrilling.

BOY/FRIENDS

Kath Kidman and Pauline Parker, Zoe's once best-friends, become quite jealous when Zoe joins the Green Club. It is all because of Ravi, that boy from the lower sixth. Not having boyfriends either, they are bottomless pits of vicarious sexual appetite. As they blow bubbles with their gum, or squint at their hair for split ends, or retwist their rainbow cotton bracelets, or scroll through posts on their phones, all they talk about is *who they can go out with* and *how soon they will have sex*. The three girls have chosen each other as 'supports' for the *female bonding mornings*, introduced that term by Mx Thompson, to free female pupils from the infamous mainland-fetter of *objectification in the service of male sexuality*. The girls meet in small self-directed groups every Monday morning at ten to nine, while boys assemble en masse for lectures called things like Deconstructing the Masculine. But as soon as Pauline, Kath and Zoe have signed themselves in with Mx Thompson, they go off to their own corner of the playing field, to sit under the oak tree, and Zoe knows that absolutely everything that comes out of Kath and Pauline's mouths will be completely forbidden. Kath and Pauline do not care. During those *rare and precious, life-skill-building minutes*, when they should be giving each other *space and support* to discuss their menstrual cycles, or undesirable male attentions, or *how to truly realise their ambitions as women*, instead Pauline will try to imagine where his hands go when you get to *second base*, or what you do when you feel it *hard* against you. Then they will pester Zoe for photographic evidence of her with Ravi. Or they'll try to scare her with horror stories of the perverted things those older girls, Stella and Tara, get up to. Like, *are they lesbians?* Like, *what is she doing hanging out with them?* And Ravi, maybe he's gay?! Is that why he likes you?

There are two women by her mound. They've undressed – their clothes, in eye-watering gorse yellows, and the kind of blues that must require entire fields of woad – are piled neatly on the ground. But Cwen isn't looking at their clothes now. She's looking at them. She sees a mouth close down thirstily on the other one's nipple. She sees that one's finger slide inside the other. She sees the arch of a back, and the nipple-mouth replaced by fingers, and the mouth sucking belly skin, and vulva hair and now – a, a, a, a – it's sucking where it should be, and Cwen, too, is sucking, and licking, and her fingers are sliding in and out, and she hasn't felt like this for so long, was it when that traveller-girl came over for a night? The year 725. *Fuck.* Her mouth opens, she howls.

The island shudders.

———

Then she sang these fifty verses: 'There is an island far away, around which sea-horses glisten . . . a lovely land through all the ages of the world . . . Begin a voyage across the clear sea, to see if you may find the land of women.' Then the woman went from them, and they did not know where she went.

Anon, *Voyage of Bran* (Irish), seventh century AD

But as the woman departed . . . she threw Connla an apple . . . The woman said: 'There is yet another land . . . which rejoices the heart of everyone who wanders there; No one lives there, except women.' Then Connla gave a leap into the woman's crystal boat.

Anon, *The Adventures of Connla the Fair* (Irish), eighth century AD

5

Inga

When Inga first took a girlfriend to Cwen, she got the epiphany she needed. The island showed her what she needed to do.

She hadn't been planning a tryst, or anything. It was just that she was stuck, vision-wise. They borrowed Jen's husband's dinghy, which had an outboard motor, and took a picnic, and were on the island in what seemed like seconds. Inga pretended she knew what she was doing. She pulled the boat up beyond the high-tide mark, and plonked a rock in the bottom.

They had sex on the east side of the island, with their backs against the mound. The creel boats occasionally came this way. But they wouldn't be able to see anything from that distance. Except through their binoculars. Anyway, all Inga and her girlfriend could see was each other, which was the important thing. Their skin, and the sky, which was vast. And the sea. Eastwards, it was nothing but sea between Cwen and Norway.

Darkness.

After she came, she opened her eyes. She watched a bird in the sky for a while, without speaking. Its wings made a V and she traced this in the grass with her finger. It had its eye on something.

When it plunged down like an arrow, Inga sat up. The bird emerged from the sea with a fish. Inga pulled on her knickers. The orgasm had been instructive. As had the bird and the island. She said, 'I'm going to bring women over here, to be educated. We need to build a community, in a new way. Also, I need to learn to sail. It's rubbish relying on the ferry service.'

She got Eva involved. Eva didn't know anything about those archaic male arts of rowing and sailing, either. Not that Inga wanted to be out on the water; she didn't like it at all really, but she knew it was necessary for what she wanted to do. She looked for a female teacher nearby, but couldn't find one. In the end, Eva and she went on a training weekend off the west coast of Scotland. They returned with a boat.

They timed each other, sailing back and forth to Cwen. Eva preferred rowing. It was simpler. But they both became quite good at sailing. They kept the boat and its dinghy in a noost on the eastern beach, behind the house. They would go out on a Sunday afternoon, and return that evening wet through, despite the oilskins, hair splattered on to their foreheads, determination on their faces. They laughed at each other.

'Awful, isn't it,' Inga said to Eva.

'Awful but necessary,' said Eva.

Each time, Inga liked it more. The inversion of the usual paradigm of things. Being in another element; manipulating that other element with forethought and skill. According to the internet, humans are mostly water. That's how it felt, anyway, out there in the cove: *going home*. And she liked the slightly rocky feeling that stayed with her on dry land, sometimes for days afterwards; unstable, as after an orgasm or two. By this time Inga had been leader of the council for five years. She knew she didn't have long.

INGA: That's why I just don't believe it – she knew what she was doing on the water. She would never have gone out in that weather. There's something we're not seeing.

After becoming convenor, Inga moved to a new-build flat in Ayrness, overlooking the abbey. She liked clean, simple lines. (A small logistics company in Berwick shipped IKEA to the islands.) The only colour was provided by her growing wardrobe – the splosh of a claret winter coat over the sofa, the shudder of an oak-green shift dress hanging in the bathroom. Her aged parents lived on Astrid and seldom came to visit, partly because she went out to see them once a week.

Her current lover was Rowan Thompson, who taught at Ayrness High. They lived together but couldn't walk along the street hand in hand. Not really. The archipelago wasn't the kind of place you could do that. Not if Inga wanted to remain in charge at the council. As a result, things weren't that great between them at the moment. They hardly ever made love any more. But at least they were aligned, politically.

COLIN: Inga Stenbridge did not hide the fact that she was a lesbian. But then she began living with a woman, a teacher at the high school, and that upset some islanders and their councillors. It's one thing in the city, where nobody knows each other. But here in the islands, it's very unwise for a professional person in the public eye to disrespect the views of the people they represent.

JUDGE: [*Pause*] Mr Grieves, you moved from the paper, edited by Ursula King, to the council, run by Inga Stenbridge. Would you say that you began to resent the proliferation of women in positions of power?

COLIN: I would say that, yes, the working places of the islands were taken over by women with axes to grind, who failed to acknowledge us because we were men.

After Colin Grieves moved to the council, Inga invited him to a thought-speak meeting with Jen and others – their growing collective of island women. She wanted to give it a go; to give him a chance. All the women had heard, and seen, and read, about the frayed tempers, the brutal or bombastic posts; they knew the position that he, and others in the council, had adopted towards Inga. She had begun to attract negative attention – first, she was pretty, young and blonde; second, she had stopped being diplomatic and started saying what she thought; third, what she said was often critical. Any criticism of island culture and the way things had always been done was taboo. As the island saying went, 'the nail that sticks out gets hammered'.

The women suggested meeting at the museum café, seeing as it was a space open to all islanders, innocuous and neutral. Colin didn't see it like that, at all. For a start, there were nine women, and only one of him. He walked into the café, where they were sitting at three tables pushed together along the harbour window.

'I'm recording this,' he shouted. 'I'm photographing it, and I'm posting it on social media.'

The women looked at each other. Some of them smiled – bad idea. Others shrugged. Stella tugged down the back of her mint-green T-shirt to better expose her new tattoo. She reapplied lipstick.

'This is a completely compromised choice of location,' Colin said.

'Where would you like to meet?' Tara asked politely. She was only seventeen.

'I'm not here to meet you,' he said, causing Barbara Anderson to look up in alarm from the till, where she was putting through their very large coffee order, 'I wanted a record of who you all are. And now I've got it.'

The women laughed. They weren't that scared. Not back then. That was before the inquiry was announced.

COLIN: They put women in the fire service, for example – forced them to join, when actually women aren't good at this job, not at all. They don't have the upper-body strength; they don't understand knots, or how pumps work. And then, after women began signing up, something else was lost, too. A kind of camaraderie. Men working alongside men, in complete confidence? That's how fires are put out, and wars are fought, and the country is defended. It's been like that for centuries. Since the beginning, probably. And then the flag – we were all really upset by that.

JUDGE: The flag seems to be everywhere. On cars, on flagpoles, in gardens.

COLIN: They came up with it during Inga Stenbridge's time at the council. It was sold to us as an island-patriot emblem and the take-up was huge. Islanders like to support each other. The original press release said red for England, blue for Scotland, a scallop shell for our nautical economy, and a W for the shape of the archipelago's islands. What does that say to you?

JUDGE: The W is symbolic of the islands' geography, and inclusive of—

COLIN: Not inclusive. *Subversive.* Look at it another way and all you see is a triangle of red on a background of blue.
JUDGE: By which you mean?
COLIN: A white W for women. A red V for ...

Inga had also wanted to meet Colin in the museum café because by then it, too, had experienced a renaissance. Things were changing, was her point.

JUDGE: How exactly did Eva change things at the museum? I haven't quite followed the process.
INGA: She was on the Board of Trustees. She pushed for the appointment of Felicity, and everything else flowed from there. She really enjoyed rewriting all the exhibits. It's amazing how much had been missed out, under the previous guy, Denis Morris.
JUDGE: But the museum was a publicly-funded body.
INGA: Yes, exactly, so Eva had to proceed with caution. Everything she couldn't do there, she did on Skellar instead, with the Archipelago Women's Club.

The idea of a women's club or retreat had been part of Eva's thinking from the start. But it was hard to make it work. Inga, Jen and she tried operating it in an informal and unstructured way from an empty farmhouse on the outskirts of Ayrness, next to the distillery. But in the winter, heating proved a problem – the whole of the downstairs was flagged in stone. Also, the house was a fifteen-minute walk from the nearest bus route.

'It's nothing better than a chilly version of the Islands of Women Study Centre,' Jen complained.

'The Athenaeum has leather armchairs and green velvet curtains,' Eva said. 'And an art collection. I went there once with Harry.'

'For fuck's sake, that's unfair,' said Inga.

INGA: We met Queenie Miller, wife of the Glaswegian surgeon who had bought the island of Skellar, at a fundraising event for the Islands of Women Study Centre. Eva was really clever how she brought Queenie onside, and also the nuns of Papa Astrid – the two islands are only ten minutes apart, by motorboat. Her main investor was a female-run group of Icelandic venture capitalists, Aud Deep Mind. Queenie provided the island; the female entrepreneurs' fund, Archipelago Women in Work, offered further money and guidance; and the nuns were the workforce. Eva was co-financier. Theirs were the names which went down on all the business papers, and eventually on AWC's letterhead and branding: *Queenie Miller, the nuns of Papa Astrid & Eva Levi.* It was an excellent money-making venture.

JUDGE: Why didn't Eva do this on Cwen?

INGA: [*Pause*] Cwen is a holy island. It has a long and sacred female history. AWC is a business. The whisky distillery women tried to persuade Eva to let them use Cwen spring water for their products, but she refused. Anyhow, getting the nuns to manage it was the master stroke. Sister Brigid and Sister Geraldine, principally; Lucija is now in charge of the new retreat at the convent.

Most of the clientele of the Archipelago Women's Club were well-to-do mainlanders, and the spa-hotel acquired quite a name in Edinburgh, Durham, and Glasgow. The rules were that island women could buy discounted membership; that any man was welcome to stay during the week as long as he was accompanied by a woman; but each weekend, from Friday at five until Monday at ten, the house was reserved for women only.

Queenie's daughter, a graphic designer, provided the branding. She adapted one of the Neolithic carvings from the chambered cairn on Cwen, an elongated V; and the colour scheme (Precambrian grey, seal brown, gorse yellow). Queenie herself hired the chef – a Spaniard who had trained under someone famous in California. 'Vagina tart' is the kitchen's popular hit: a bisected plum or fig lapped by an eggy bay-leaf custard.

Eva conceived the events and classes (Yoga, Dance, Massage: Tantric, Vedic, Celtic) partly as a joke, but patrons loved them.

INGA: I found it depressing, to be honest. A capitalist version of the original Bean commune.

JUDGE: Are there any profits?

INGA: Oh yes. Queenie and Eva receive salaries as directors but all profits go straight to the Islands of Women Foundation.

During the early women-only weekends, Eva sent all her women to stay there. Their only penalty was to fill in 'Satisfaction Surveys'. *The sheets are like cream*, one of them wrote; *I lay naked in bed feeling the wind-dried cotton lap at my epidermis*, wrote another. *Ooooh*, wrote a third.

Eva took Zoe, too, to witness female solidarity.

ZOE: Solidarity? Female triumph. Female sheer enjoyment of luxury.

That night in the pool there were nine or ten women, all naked, and Zoe. She was probably twelve by then; quiet. Self-consciousness had dawned even if puberty hadn't.

ZOE: The sight of those women was a shock. I had no idea that women were so different from each other, under their island uniform of jeans and jacket.

Naked breasts. Dimply, hairy, smooth, taut, saggy; vast brown patches around the nipples, pink points, freckly. A whole new landscape.

ZOE: One of them was pregnant. The skin on her stomach was stretched so tight I thought I might be able to see the baby.

We women. For the first time, the words sounded good; sensuous in the mouth. The women ran from the pool down to the sea. It was cold; the water glimmered green and silver with phosphorescence. It was thrilling; feet sunk in sand, toes barely gripping on to the island's edge. Eva and Zoe went with them, hand in hand – the almost-teenage girl, the almost-old woman—

JUDGE: How did you feel about your work, at this point?
INGA: By the time AWC was set up I was burnt-out, really. I had begun to suspect that we were just tinkering; imitating. After all we'd achieved, I was like, *Is this it? Is this how power feels?* It felt empty. Something about it wasn't going to the essence of what really mattered to me, as a woman. I didn't even know what it was, that essence.
JUDGE: So what changed?

INGA: Jen was absorbed in her documentation project – she wanted every single thing to be replicable elsewhere. Like a franchise. Eva had Zoe to bring up, and the female epics collection work she was doing with Alice. That was her spiritual outlet. But what did I have? It was Eva who suggested I go to Cwen. I had always known she liked the island, but thanks to her, I saw how, for the sake of the future, we need to use the past. That healer saint is still with us. We forgot her, neglected her, along with the others. But she is part of our collective wisdom, if only we let ourselves remember. She is in the landscape, our soul. It was startling to me, coming to that realisation.

JUDGE: [*Pause*] One of the allegations levelled against you is that you encouraged Eva to leave her house and wealth to the Islands of Women Foundation—

INGA: We were of course delighted that she did.

JUDGE: —by representing her sons to her in a bad light.

INGA: [*Smiles*] We didn't need to do that. They did it for themselves. Of course, they also live in London, a man's world; the kind of place where it's difficult to effect the necessary paradigm shift. That's why we now encourage men, as well as women, to come up here for a time of thinking and retreat, to order an Nth wave, AWC's iconic whisky sour, made with island whisky, eggs and a coulis of berries, and to learn what it feels like to live in a place where we have redesigned our lives not by and around the lives of men but for everyone, regardless of gender—

Interruption as court officials remove spectators from the public gallery.

120

Back in the day, when the men came for her, Cwen was ready. It was the price she paid for her isolation. There was only so much Anu could do to protect her.

It helped that she did exactly what her father had advised. He was dead a year by then already. When she saw the boat coming across, and saw who disembarked, she drank a tincture of nightshade root against the pain. It was two men. They were unknown to her but she knew what they were there for, and who had sent them.

They smelt of expensive oils and incense, and the fresh heat of their excitement. Thanks to the nightshade, she was easily able to make her eyes roll back in her head. They took their fill of her limp body, almost completely unaware of the little nick in the soft skin of a neck, and wrist, which she made with her thorn, tipped with juice from the shiny dark berries. Father had never done it himself. But he had kept the thorns ready, for that purpose.

Once the poison was in their blood, she was able to watch beneath her eyelids as they got to their feet, and stumbled, dressed only in their shirts, down to the shore. By the time they got to their boats they were puking. But they cast off anyway, and after that there was no hope for them.

Cwen had no control over the weather during her life, but maybe the seas were already answering her thoughts, for the boat was swept quickly around the north side of the island and out towards the skerries.

Cwen went through the belongings they had left behind. She burnt their clothes on the east beach, so that the islanders opposite wouldn't get wind of it, but not before feeling in all the pockets and removing three coins, which she stored in the cairn. She ate the cheese and bread, and sharpened the knife. The metal brooch which she unpinned from one of the jerkins was the most cleverly worked thing in metal she had ever seen. She looked at it for a long time, tracing the pictures engraved there with her finger. Around the edge were dogs, interlaced, and in the centre was a man, looking out, with big wide eyes. Framed on four sides of him were four further men, one holding his nose, the second with his hand cupped to his ear, the third licking his finger, the fourth stroking his cheek. Cwen laughed out loud when she realised: the five human senses.

There was also a bag, containing a book, bound in soft red leather. She had never held a book before. All her knowledge was held in her head, and her hands. There were pages of dense marks which she recognised as writing – but Cwen could not read. She looked carefully at the pictures. There were four portraits, also of men. They had yellow, brown, black and greyish hair, bare feet, and were wearing robes of lush colours, green trimmed with red, blue lined with pink. Each of them was holding a book. One of them was accompanied by an animal, like a large cat. She noticed again that there were no women there. So even though the object was worth a lot of silver, many winters of grain, she put it aside. She would store it in the cairn, with the coins, for the histories to deal with.

Only then did she wash herself in the soap she made from clean ash and animal fat, in water from her spring, heated. She felt herself all over. There was blood, and many bruises. It had hurt, despite the tincture. She smoothed on ointment. Finally, she drank a purgative, and after she had been sick, cheese and bread and man, she crawled under the sheepskins in her hut, and slept. That was the first time.

The second and third times were easier because she disregarded her father's advice and fought back. The man who entered her hut at night smelt of beer and dirt. She cut him under his chin with the long dagger the two previous men had left her. She almost killed him but he got away. She knew he wouldn't come back. She had tipped that blade, too.

The third time, the man spoke no language she knew. He carried an axe with which he intended to break into the mound. He hadn't come for her, he had come for the gold which he believed she kept there. But she could see that he would kill her if she stood in the way and, if not, then rape her when he found there was nothing worth stealing.

Cwen had left out some henbane wine, but he didn't drink that. So she made a trick-knot in two loops of rope and, as he heaved at the cairn's door, she flicked one loop over his neck and, with the other, took his axe. Then she tied him to the branch of her apple tree that had come down in the storms, poured the henbane wine over his face, so that it ran into his ears, and dragged him to his boat. She dislodged the rudder, and pushed the boat out into the stream. The tide was on the turn. Cassiopeia's current took him.

The fifth man killed her. She was old by then, and the islanders opposite had been advertising her skills, even as far as the mainland. This man, stupid as he was, had come over to eclipse her fame. He was a monk, as she saw from his tonsure. There should be only one healing hermit in this stretch of sea. He bludgeoned her to death. She saw it all, but felt nothing. Since he had dispatched her as she dreamt, he set her free, and she sent him mad with her screaming.

———

The island of apples which men call 'The Fortunate Isle' gets its name from the fact that it produces all things of itself . . . There, nine sisters rule by a pleasing set of laws, those who come to them from our country.

Geoffrey of Monmouth, *The Life of Merlin* (Latin), c.1140

6

Mariam

JUDGE: Before I call my next witness, I would like to address the public directly. Mariam Maher cannot be here in person. She will give evidence by video-link. While she does so, *there will be no calling out*. I am aware that during the press coverage of this inquiry, and the events directly preceding it, Mariam Maher's story has been bandied this way and that. I will not tolerate name-calling or misbehaviour. I hope this has been properly understood.

MARIAM: Should I speak?

JUDGE: Please, in your own language. We have a translator here.

TRANSLATOR: Not her mother tongue, excuse me. We will speak in our national language, which is Urdu.

MARIAM: I came to England with my marriage. My husband was a businessman. The centrepiece of his collection was an alarm clock which played the call to prayer. He had a very wide range of burqas – all the usual black tents, and some Afghan shuttlecocks in several lovely colours – though these were more for show. He stocked a wide range of moralising pamphlets, green cloths and wooden stands for the holy book; as well as prayerbeads, amulets, and other such superstitious items. I liked but was surprised by the things blessed by association with saints; and not that he kept them hidden from most of his customers. The last thing he wanted was for Faisal Enterprises to be tainted by accusations of *shirk*. 'False worship', that dreaded slur. [*Waits for translator.*]

TRANSLATOR: She was married to a travelling salesman.

How did Mariam come to be married? It happened like this. Her father was a Sheedi – 'one of the original Muslims', he liked to say (the first *muezzin* of Islam was an Ethiopian); 'a caste of African-Pakistani labourers', said the others. He was clever, got an education, and entered the army. *At the time, Pakistan's only Sheedi private.* As a result, he made a good marriage, with a fair-skinned, narrow-nosed mixed Sheedi-Sindhi girl with long straight hair from Thatta. Mariam, however, came out just like her father, as her aunt kept repeating. While Mariam's father was alive, what her aunt thought meant nothing. But when he died, Mariam's chances would have been severely jeopardised, after all, had not a soft-hearted general from Lahore stepped in – army largesse – to raise a good dowry.

JUDGE: [*To Solicitor*] Am I correct in thinking that it was the witness who was the catalyst for Eva Harcourt-Vane setting up the women's refuge on the island of Papa Astrid?

SOLICITOR: That's right. The financial side is contained in her accountant's witness statement.

JUDGE: Are we to talk to the accountant?

SOLICITOR: Sigrid Henderson is due to give evidence later this week.

In Mirpur Khas, Sindh, Mariam's aunt narrowed things down: three respectable suitors. She frowned as she handed the three photographs across the table to her niece.

Mariam, too, frowned as she laid these men out, shoulder to shoulder. Then she divided herself in three – *Ma, Ri, Am* – and sat back to survey her three-way prospects.

Ma was to be married to the bureaucrat from Hyderabad, who was chubby with a pleasant smile. But Mariam wished to escape her native state, so that ruled him out.

Ri chose the Sindhi cloth merchant who had settled in Lahore – but though he was rich, he had a wife already, and two young children. Could she live as a second wife under one roof with the first? No, she could not. All her romance film watching had taught her that.

So a lot came down to *Am*, who was partnered with the youngest. His age was given as thirty. In the photo he was wearing a baggy Western suit.

TRANSLATOR: Her parents are dead. She lives with her aunt. You can see she is dark. But she is pretty. She will find a good husband, if she is modest enough. But in this case she makes the choice herself. It is her African blood. Very bold. Also, she talks to herself. A bit too much wordy woman.

While he didn't look reliable, he at least looked modern in outlook. But that wasn't it. He had one clear advantage over the rest. *He lived in England.*

His was the photograph which she pushed back across the table to her aunt.

'He lives in England,' said her aunt, as though this was a death sentence – rather than the passport to freedom that Mariam knew it was.

TRANSLATOR: A rather too-independent lady.
JUDGE: This is all very interesting but could you please ask the witness about the refuge on Papa Astrid?

Three days after the wedding, Mariam and her husband took a flight out of Karachi, Sindh, Pakistan, Asia, to Heathrow, London, England, Europe, from where he took her right across the city, to Wood Green, and into McDonald's for a celebratory treat of chips and milkshake. Already, she was stunned by England's whiteness, greyness, blackness. People, weather, clothing. As he led her inside the restaurant she could tell from his swagger that he thought she was being offered every Pakistani village girl's dream. To dine at McDonald's in London, to eat hot thin chips in your fingers dipped in tomato ketchup – wasn't that something to tell the people back home? Well, he was partly wrong, partly right. Her aunt, who never spoke about her father's family's African roots, would have frowned at the dirty, tacky street, the poor, grubby clients – mostly Sheedi type people. Mariam remembered Father reminding her that England was a melting pot, so he had heard, a good place for someone from their community, even if the food was very bland. But yes, the girls at her school would have been excited by McDonald's, which wasn't available in Mirpur Khas – but was spoken of as existing in Hyderabad and Karachi.

TRANSLATOR: She isn't saying anything about refuge. She is saying she got married to a decent fellow.
JUDGE: I believe she went there just before Eva's disappearance? Rather, Mariam was the first to disappear.

Back at the flat, he turned on all the lights, and she saw what her home was. It was not really a home at all but a zone of stockpiled produce. The bedroom was stacked high with bags. There were boxes of books and pamphlets all the way down the hallway to the kitchen (which, she saw with a shudder, was next to the toilet). There was no space to sit down in the front room. Boxes, boxes, boxes.

TRANSLATOR: She is complaining only about the home her husband has brought her to.

He showed her everything she needed to know about the business on her second day in England. He made her try on every female garment, so that she would understand the ties and Velcro patches. (Why else, she wondered, did he think she left her homeland?) She would apprentice herself to him, learning the patter and the trade, *and* how to drive, and once she had done these things to his satisfaction, he would let her loose in a van of her own, kitted out with stuff just for ladies. It was her task to take notes, on everywhere they went, so that she could remember how to get there.

He said she could choose something for herself, so she did. She picked out an oblong plastic model of the Kaaba in Mecca, and the Prophet's Mosque in Medina, made in China. It was glamorous yet pious, raining shiny pink and purple plastic balls over Islam's most holy places, when you shook it.

What she didn't tell him about was the amulet of her father's that she had carried with her from Pakistan. A symbol carved in white stone. A very ancient stone, her father thought. It fitted into the palm of her hand. Discreet. *Haram*, her aunt said. But to Mariam, its V-shape was birds, flying home along the valley.

TRANSLATOR: Auntie is right, such things are forbidden in Islam.
JUDGE: My specific question is, was it Eva Harcourt-Vane who offered Mariam Maher refuge in the islands? Did Mariam approach Eva, out of the blue as it were?
TRANSLATOR: Blue? [*Pause as translator speaks to witness on screen*]
MARIAM: Yes, yes. Blue.

The first time they went travelling in the van, she was in shock. Not just because of all the ghostly white faces. Nor because they were driving outside London. But because of the p—g farms which stretched in a great muddy patch outwards from the highway. The p—gs themselves were impossible to mistake, lolling naked and pink outside their huts, snouts in the air.

Her silence extended as far as the turning off the motorway (they were on the way to Southampton). She asked the question which was pressing on her brain – Do they *really* eat it? He didn't answer at first. Then he said, as he fiddled with the van's radio: They say we share forty per cent of our DNA with onions. We Muslims? she asked. He laughed at that: No, we humans.

TRANSLATOR: He spends time educating her.
JUDGE: Please could you translate, and not merely summarise what the witness is saying?
TRANSLATOR: Excuse me but I have told you already, she is talking too much. I am powerless to stop her.

The second or third time, they drove to Dover. He parked the van on a quiet street lined with brick houses. There were hedges in front and, behind them, large windows with net curtains. Behind one of these curtains was an Islamic school for ladies. The appointment was for 4 p.m. He couldn't go in; so he left her at the door with six boxes, and said he would drive around for a while. And off he went, and didn't return for the next two hours. Since there weren't many students – twenty, maybe – it didn't take her long to show them the burqas and headscarves and pamphlets on issues close to

131

their hearts, such as purdah and family planning (why not to). She sat in the front room of the Islamic school as the students examined her wares, and she stared through the white net curtain at the high green hedge on the road outside, at the British people walking by. *It is easy to forget how exotic normal-British people once seemed to Mariam Maher.* The smell of the place – thick, cloying, warm – was the smell of female bodies in close proximity to each other. She knew that smell. It was the smell of home, the smell of her school, the smell of the madrasa she had gone to in the evenings, after her aunt discovered that she shared her father's love for Sufi poetry, the smell of every cousin and aunt and all the women she had grown up with. The smell made her think of her cousin, Aliya. You be brave for us, Mariam, Aliya had told her as she left for the airport. These were the last words Aliya spoke before Mariam did her vanishing act to England. So Mariam tried to be brave. She wiped away tears, and by the end of the day she had sold one burqa, three headscarves, two books and a small woven carpet of the Kaaba.

JUDGE: What is she saying?
TRANSLATOR: She is not good at her job at all.
JUDGE: [*to Solicitor*] This is hopeless.

All these transactions were recorded in her tidy script (which had won prizes at the Oxford Buttercup Model School in Mirpur Khas). The cash was collected in a small plastic bag. When her husband arrived, he seemed in a very great rush. He made her wait in the hallway, while he loaded the boxes into the van. Then he called through the gate for her to hurry. The van was a Ford Transit with a hatch dividing the cabin (where they sat) from the loading space at the back. It was there that their mattress was, and her aunt's handsewn quilt. As they drove out of Dover town, back towards London, he turned on the radio, and the cabin was filled with strange new voices, singing and talking. She listened, not understanding, but knowing that what they sang was definitely haram. She wished Aliya was with her. It would be easier, in England, if she had just one friend. But there weren't any other Sheedis from Pakistan in the whole of London, England, Europe. England was her country now and she was all alone.

TRANSLATOR: She is an anti-national.
JUDGE [*to Solicitor*]: Who hired the translator?
SOLICITOR: Apparently, he was hired by the Islands' Council.

Over the next two years in London, Mariam tried to remember the advice her aunt had given her as she left – not just any advice, but a nugget chosen for her in particular – *Don't ask too many questions, Mariam Sheedi.* Which was the opposite of what her father had told her when she was little: *Intellectual curiosity is an escape from drudgery; never forget this, my little pumpkin flower.* So it was in her father's memory, rather than her aunt's, that she began to keep her *Notes on English Cities.*

Dover: There are several Afghan refugees in this historic town on the English Channel. All of them are men. None of them wish to buy authentic Muslim clothing. They wear jeans, gold chains and spike their hair with gel.

JUDGE: Yes, but is he a professional?
SOLICITOR: I believe he [*pause*] normally works in the tandoori house in—
JUDGE: Unbelievable.
TRANSLATOR: She educates herself now.

She found, when she passed English women in the streets, close enough to touch, or saw them from afar when she was driving with her husband, that she did not feel the horror she had expected. It was true that their hair was often unbrushed, or brashly multicoloured; that their bottoms and breasts were visible through their clothing. But after the day she saw a woman of her own age wearing a transparent green raincoat, her hair dyed a light aubergine purple, her eyes dark and yet her lips unpainted, Mariam began to look forward to glimpsing more of these surprising creatures. She knew that to them she was a blank, a black sheet, a *nothing* that their eyes passed over as quickly and fearfully as if she was naked. Driving out of London, along smooth black roads and into the provinces, her glance travelled downwards, from their heads to the skin exposed on their arms and chests. She watched the breeze pass over the plucked and puckered skin of these women's legs, and as her husband parked the van at their destination, and it was time to pull a cloak over her own legs in their cotton trousers, Mariam felt a pang of pity for *Am*. She knew what *Ma* and *Ri* would say. They would say that she was becoming corrupted—

TRANSLATOR: She is becoming corrupted by her exposure to England.

—by her exposure to England.

JUDGE: How quickly can this situation be rectified?
SOLICITOR: By tomorrow at the earliest—

He had complained about her skin, the first time she took off her headscarf. There was a line where the make-up ended, and her real, dark skin began. For her wedding photos she had been made-up even paler. Mariam minded that he minded. She had not expected this cool feeling from the man she married. She was nineteen years old now, and aware of the potential for loving passion.

TRANSLATOR: He is a modern husband.
JUDGE: I'm going to need this testimony as a full transcript in word-for-word translation.

She waited for a baby, but no baby came.

SOLICITOR: There's a translator in Berwick but he won't make the evening flight from Edinburgh today and unfortunately the last ferry leaves before—
JUDGE: What a travesty.

Aliya got married, to a teacher from Mirpur Khas. She posted Mariam the wedding photos: the pale make-up, the glittery gold, the red silk. Mariam saw the faces of her cousins and aunts. There was her Cousin Fatima, with a new baby; it lay, immobile in her arms, bundled in a scarf. Fatima's face was radiant with happiness, like a kid with a sweet. The happiness of home cut Mariam like a knife.

She reminded herself, at least once a day, that because of her father having been an army man, she could have married any number of respectable husbands. The bureaucrat from Hyderabad, for example; and she thought of her lost lives sometimes, as the van pulled into a pub car park of an evening, and her husband trotted inside to buy some cigarettes and make a quick call from the coin phone next to the bar, and she found herself shocked yet again by the parade of drunken English ladies in the road outside. She hadn't wanted to stay within spitting distance of home, she reminded herself of that. She had wanted adventure. Sitting in the van, waiting for her husband to return, Mariam reminded herself that her father had made her watch *Only Fools and Horses* for a reason. She herself preferred the Britain of *Kabhi Khushi Kabhie Gham*; not to mention *Kuch Kuch Hota Hai*; the point being that she, Mariam, formerly Sheedi, now Mrs Maher, was the brave one.

SOLICITOR: He will be here first thing tomorrow.
TRANSLATOR: These are not good television programmes. She should be watching our Islamiat channel.
SOLICITOR: And we should have a transcription tonight, with any luck.

—*It is England, not him*, she thinks, *that I have pinned my hopes on.*

JUDGE: So I have to endure this for now?
SOLICITOR: I'm afraid so.

Driving to Bradford, the hills brought her to tears again, as she thought of the trip up to the Kirthar Mountains with her father during his annual leave.
    She sent her aunt a text:
    England is so clean and tidy!
    Her aunt wrote back:
    Still no baby?
    Mariam wrote up the entry on Bradford in her *Notes on English Cities*:

One hundred years ago this town was very rich. Rich men built large buildings out of pale local stone. Today, in those tall old houses, live families from Bangladesh and Pakistan. It is the Bangladeshi women who grow gourds and pumpkins in their long backyards. Or if there is no garden, and space is short, plants sprout from bathtubs on the terrace, green tendrils wind up broom handles.

JUDGE: I cannot honestly recall such an egregious example.

Aliya sent more photos. There she was, lying on her marital bed, beneath her a lovely new quilt the fresh green of henna paste, with all-over red-gold stitching – and popping up in the corner of the frame, little Cousin Faiz, wearing a big mirrored cap that was probably his brother's. It was the sight of that cheeky smiling face which broke Mariam's heart – little Cousin Faiz. His smell of fenugreek and warmth. He must be eight already.

She wrote to her aunt:

No baby! I am a career woman!

Her aunt wrote back:

Are you doing your prayers? Remember not to over-salt the daal like you do at home.

In her notebook Mariam wrote:

Bristol: On the map this city is almost at the sea. The river takes boats containing manufactured goods out of the country, and at the port vessels dock with cinnamon and cotton from the lands I come from. There are many shops selling halal meat in Bristol but Muslims there laugh because an Orthodox Jew wishing to eat lamb killed and bled in the kosher way has to get supplies from London.

TRANSLATOR: Muslims are so great in number, even in this ungodly land.

In November, when her husband went to China on a stock trip, the sensation of glimpsing the lives she could have had became so intense that Mariam thought she could hear them, *Ma* and *Ri*, as she walked back to the flat, or climbed the steps to the library, or as the bus stopped and from high up through the window she saw a woman, far below her, step out on to the street. She thought of *Ma* and *Ri* with something like a sob. She began to wonder, Are the lives they're leading better than mine? Are they?

She knew now that she had made the wrong decision. She should never have left home to come to this faraway place where nobody loved her. What had she been thinking?

She sent her aunt a text:

It rains in the winter season here!

TRANSLATOR: She is a complaining kind of lady.

Ten days after he left, two things happened. First, she found out from her doctor that she was six weeks pregnant. Since her husband was not due back for another four days, and since it was too early to tell him, she kept this news inside herself. In an emergency, she had been told to ring his aunt in Bradford. But this was not an emergency. This was usually a cause for rejoicing. Second, while her baby was no bigger than a little green lentil inside her, she took the overground train to a hospital clinic on account of some sores which had developed on her body.

Her aunt replied:

Remember to keep your hair covered and not to eat snacks unless it is written HALAL.

TRANSLATOR: Excuse me! [*Gestures at screen*] You should have gone to stay
     with your aunt in Bradford. That would have been the correct thing.
JUDGE: Please! *Do not lecture the witness.*

That night, after visiting the clinic, Mariam slept very little. She thought about Pakistan; children crying from hunger, floods sweeping away bridges and homes. She thought of England with its dirty men and diseased mothers with their diseased children, and the sex-minded single men walking their unholy dirty dogs. She thought about her dirty diseased husband. She rested her hand on her belly and talked to her lentil. This action calmed her.

TRANSLATOR: She is blessed with a child.

In the morning, when the light came, she prayed for the well-being of Pakistan. She prayed that the army would continue to govern the country fairly; that the urs at Bhitshah, going on right now, would happen without any hitch. She prayed that *Ma* and *Ri* were safe and happy; that the bureaucrat in Hyderabad loved *Ma*; that the first wife in Lahore had made things easy for *Ri*, supporting her and comforting her in this lonely time of leaving her parents' home and making a new life in her husband's. She remembered what her aunt had quoted: *Therefore righteous women are devoutly obedient—*

TRANSLATOR: At last, she reads our holy book.

JUDGE: Do not interrupt!

—and in times of absence guard what Allah would have them guard.

She stood at the window in the kitchen looking out on the tarmac courtyard where the rain fell and a boy as lonely as she was sat under a shelter listening to his music. Mariam stopped looking at the boy and looked at the glass she had polished to make their home nice. The glass which got dirty so fast, the paintwork which was impossible to keep white. When the tears fell, she put her hand on her belly and whispered to her lentil, and her lentil whispered back that she always got morose in the mornings before her first cup of tea, and that she had better go down and buy some milk from the shop on the corner.

TRANSLATOR: She is missing home again.

JUDGE: [*To Solicitor*] One of the witness statements mentions the role Mariam Maher played in the Foundation's programme of female re-education. Could you find it for me, please?

SOLICITOR: One of the schoolgirls?

JUDGE: That's right. Tara Gill.

Mariam barely noticed the girl on her way out to the shop. There were often white girls, sitting on the steps of the block, smoking and playing with their hair, and what did they care about her? But when she returned with the milk, the girl was still sitting there, and as Mariam pushed past, she spoke his name. Mariam stopped. The white girl's awful hair was scraped back from her head. When Mariam didn't answer, the girl took a blob of gum from her mouth and stuck it to the step; a very dirty habit. Are you his sister? the girl said. He told me his sister had come from Pakistan. I haven't seen any other Pakistan types, the girl went on, so you must be her. And slowly this time, rudely, the girl repeated Mariam's husband's name. There could be no mistaking. But you don't look much like him. Different father?

Mariam chose not to answer. Who was this girl? She was nothing to her. She put her key in the lock, stepped through the door, pulled it to. The first thing she did when she got upstairs was to send her aunt a text:

I cooked lamb korma and it tasted just like yours!

Then she made herself some tea. After she had drunk two cups, she sat for a very long time at the table in the kitchen. She looked at the picture of Aliya that she had pinned up next to the stove while her husband was away: new green headscarf, pinkish lipstick, in a kitchen Mariam didn't recognise – so it must be the man's place. Aliya's happy eyes. Suddenly, she remembered the stockcheck she had been tasked with, while he was away.

TRANSLATOR: There is some culture shock. This is natural.

She began in the bedroom. She opened every cupboard, every box, every envelope, looked into every one of her husband's shoes and pockets. She was methodical and careful. She searched all morning. But there was nothing in the bedroom. She began on the kitchen as she cooked her lunch, looking through packets and behind papers and inside the cupboards. There was nothing in the kitchen either. That left the hallway, with its hatch through the ceiling, and the front room, with its merchandise in sealed cardboard boxes. She searched the front room all afternoon, opening each box in turn, removing the contents, shaking out burqas, prising apart the battery packs of alarm clocks, unrolling prayer mats. She replaced each object, resealed each box and moved on to the next one. There was no mystery to be found in the front room. The impression it gave, of being a stockpile, was a true one. Nor did she find what she was looking for in the hallway. The hatch through the ceiling was sealed shut with paint, and she judged it had been that way for longer than she had been in England. But as she was climbing down from the chair, it came to her: the bathroom; specifically the boiler in the bathroom cupboard.

She felt behind the boiler with her hand. Dusty. Then, *something*. Her fingers found themselves clutching a slim paper packet. She pulled it out. Ripped it open. A slim paper envelope, with nothing in it but her passport.

TRANSLATOR: She steals her travel documents from her husband. This is not at all the right behaviour. Mrs Maher is getting herself into very big trouble.

By now it was dark outside, and Mariam was hungry. When she went downstairs to fetch vegetables from the shop, she almost tripped on the girl, who was sleeping sitting up. Mariam walked straight past without any comment. But when she came back carrying a plastic bag of onions and potatoes and ladies' fingers, the girl opened her eyes. *Tell me where he is,* she said. There was a small overnight bag on the ground at her feet. I've come from Bradford, she went on, her eyes following the direction of Mariam's. The girl was shivering. Please, when is he coming back? Mariam didn't answer. But she considered the fact that this girl had nowhere to sleep, that it would soon be night, and that her clothes were very flimsy. Her hair was terrible: thin, a nothing colour. Like a badly cooked chapati.

TRANSLATOR: She is kind to a British girl for no reason.
SOLICITOR: Paragraph 9.

Upstairs in the flat, the girl sat in the kitchen doing nothing to help as Mariam prepared the evening meal. You don't speak English? Even a little? she said. Mariam did, of course, a little. But she looked back at the girl blankly. The girl was so white, it was almost like she didn't exist. Oh that's bad, the girl said. She ate in silence, without complimenting Mariam's cooking, and refused a second helping. While Mariam was washing the plates, the girl went out onto the walkway to smoke. Afterwards, since it was late, and the bed was big, Mariam showed her the bedroom, expecting her to be grateful. Instead, the girl said, What, the two of us together? and made icky-sicky noises like a child. Feeling sick herself, Mariam gave the girl a blanket and a pillow and gestured to the front room, where she was welcome to make a bed for herself on the floor if she wanted, if she wasn't too scared, in amongst the boxes. Mariam and her lentil, exhausted by their searches, slept immediately.

In the middle of the night, the bedroom door opened. The girl had got cold lying by herself. Shivering, she got into bed. Mariam wrinkled her nose at the unladylike smell of cigarettes. Turning over, she went back to sleep, pleased despite everything by the warmth the girl gave out.

Just before dawn, Mariam awoke from a dream about home. Her aunt always rose before dawn for the first prayer of the day, and because Mariam had shared a bed with her almost all her life, she still woke at this hour, out of habit. She turned over in bed, and came face to face with the white girl, this ghost. Mariam had forgotten all about her. Nor had she ever been this close to a white person before. But now she remembered. The girl began to speak. She spoke of him. Mariam felt the insides of her body turning cold. One hand went down to her belly, to shield her baby lentil. The girl repeated: as his sister, she would know what a caring man he was? Even if she can't bloody well speak English? I miss him so much, the girl said. She'd come all this way to find him. I want him to be happy. Don't you understand? The girl's hand reached for her phone on the bedside table. She flicked through the pictures.

Him and the girl smiling,
Him and the girl almost naked on the beach,
Him and the girl in a restaurant with green shiny tables,
Him smiling in a way Mariam had never known.

TRANSLATOR: A bad mistake, to have let a stranger into her home without consulting her husband.
JUDGE: I think we might need to conclude today's session.

Father. Aunt. Aliya. Mariam thought of what each would tell her. She thought of the life she had, such a short one. She thought of her baby lentil. She didn't want it to know such a father. She thought of the sick-making English girl. She thought of the waters rising angrily and washing away everything she knew.

She got up from the bed, packed a small bag of clothes, her ornaments and passport, her father's bird stone, the photos of Aliya, and last night's dinner in a tiffin. The remainder of the money which her husband had left her came to almost £50, and this she put in the inside pocket of her handbag, next to her passport and the plastic card she wasn't supposed to use. She lifted her bags, to test their weight, and finally added three books: *A Textbook of Pakistan Studies, The Risalo of Shah Abdul—*

TRANSLATOR: Not a well-respected poet.
JUDGE: That's enough!

—Bhittai, which Father had bought her at the bookshop in Hyderabad, after she had seen for herself the ecstatic dancing at the urs, and her own *Notes on English Cities*. She wanted to take her auntie's quilt, each little square of cloth of which told a piece of her history. They told of her mother, who had died when Mariam was small: the pink one with yellow flowers was a suit she wore before she got married, the green paisley lawn was a present from her father, the blue swirls were cut from a bolt of suit material brought back from his posting in Pindi. Those sewn-together pieces of her mother's headscarves and shirts were all Mariam's memories of the woman who bore her. But she had left the quilt in the van, and her husband had parked the van with an acquaintance, and its location was unknown to her.

TRANSLATOR: I think— *No*— [*Shakes head*]
JUDGE: What has happened?
SOLICITOR: I'm not sure. [*To Translator*] Mr Khan, are you feeling unwell?

Before Mariam left, she woke the girl, showed her how to use the gas, the immersion heater, and where the clean sheets were kept. She handed over the only set of keys. Right at the end, as she was stepping out through the door, she gave the girl a piece of paper, on which she had written one word: *khula*.

TRANSLATOR: Unheard of! [*Thumps table*]
JUDGE: What *is* going on?

Also, she told her: *Go and see a doctor.*

It was still early in the morning when Mariam caught the train back to Hampstead. What am I doing, *Ma* and *Ri*? she asked them. But the two other parts of her chose not to answer.

Father?
Silence.
Aunt?
Silence.
Aliya?
Nothing.

SOLICITOR: I've just been told that [*consults colleague*], according to Islamqa.info, *khula* is woman's divorce.

There was nobody to answer; nobody to offer practical advice.

TRANSLATOR: She is actually walking out. [*Waves arms*] It is not possible in our culture.

On the path going down from the road to the hospital, as London's morning broke open all around her, Mariam sat on a bench and waited. When at last she saw the Sheedi lady doctor, she stood up, clutched her father's book tightly to her heart, and held up the V-stone—

JUDGE: Thank you. That will be all. The inquiry will close early today. I am relieved to report that the replacement translator will be here first thing in the morning.

The three men are definitely brothers. They look the same, for a start. Various categories of curly hair. Taller than the men Cwen was once familiar with. Her father, brothers. The others.

Instinctively, her sinews tighten. She tries to slow her breathing.

She is right to be wary. The men walk all over her island. They carry books, in which they make notes and sketches. They spend a long time at her hut, of which there is now almost no trace, except a low course or two of stones. Even so, they pace it out; wave their hands at the mound, gesture to her apple tree, the spring. They disagree about the spring. There is shouting. The sheep don't like them. They run to the far end of the island.

Although they don't come close to touching each other with their hands, Cwen feels the violence. She can see their silver pommelled swords. The daggers they carry in their belts. The ease with which those fists could smash a woman's nose, or penetrate an unwilling cunt. Cwen shudders.

At last they leave in their boat, and Cwen sniffs the air. Her island smells sullied.

She sighs, and feels Wind stir at the touch of her breath. It is that easy. Already, between Wind and her, they have the makings of a tempest, should she want it. She closes her eyes and listens to the noise the little storm makes; the waves, dashing on her beach, the clatter of pebbles and branches, the swirling of Wind as the sea is pounded.

Cwen, stop. If she let herself carry on, she could drown them all.

She opens her eyes again. The men have reached the island opposite.

Cwen thinks of the women she is drawing out. She knows they aren't ready. She knows they know nothing. Each time they come here, their feet touch the sand of her island – and they think they are safe. But an island this size never saved anyone in the long run. When the seas rise, you have to be ready; when the birds begin to die, you have to survive on roots. These women aren't prepared for any of that. If their boat broke and they were stuck here, they wouldn't last a week. They have no fish taboos, yet they don't know how to catch a fish. They have no wish to be attacked; but not one of them could lay a trap, or garrotte an invader, or staunch a bleeding wound – and there are several different ways: with a cloth, a piece of string, and either the birch polypore fungus or the giant puffball.

They *desire* it. They long to know everything she knows – about Wind and Moon and Sun; about the plants; about listening. And Cwen can do it. She can provide them with the knowledge. She can cause the puffballs to sprout, and the flint to break open its deadly milky sharpness, and crabs to land on the shore, and their eyes to open to each other. It's her island, she will do it if necessary. She will force the knowledge on them.

Cwen exhales deeply, ruffling the water between her and the people opposite. She pushes the rain clouds away to other people's islands.

The sky says it will be a fine day for weeping.

———

I ask for silence
to recount our history,
the first I remember...
I remember nine homes,
nine wooded rooms,
a wise bright tree...
There was no sand or sea,
no ice-cold waves.
There was no earth,
no sky;
but Sun shone from the south...
Sun knew not what temples she had,
Moon knew not his power,
The stars knew not their place...
Three women, all-powerful, came here...
They made laws,
selected life,
and children's destiny.
So I saw into all worlds
And described my vision.

Anon, *Völuspá: Seeress's Prophecy* (Old Norse), first written down in
Iceland or the Hebrides, AD 1220

7

Camille

The moment Eva vanished, that very instant almost, several other things became clear.

The headline discovery was that Seb's brothers had it in their hearts to shut Zoe out of the family.

Dr Camille Senghor, the woman Sebastian married, by contrast, revealed herself to be an ally.

She befriended Zoe.

The loss of Harcourt House – during the inquiry the value was put at £2 million, but that's not including the island of Cwen, the land in the north, nor the chattels – turned Eva's sons into enraged demons. To Camille, it was a relief.

JUDGE: I would like to thank you for taking the time and making the effort to appear before this inquiry. You have done so voluntarily. You have also provided a witness statement. Your perspectives are particularly helpful because you came to these islands as an outsider. You never had any financial or professional involvement with Eva's work, and yet you knew its ramifications and effects. Am I right?

CAMILLE: Yes.

JUDGE: What I would like to examine today is your submission that, contrary to the claims made by her sons—

CAMILLE: Her two elder sons, Henry and George.

JUDGE: That's right.

CAMILLE: Not Sebastian.

JUDGE: Exactly, her two elder sons, who have claimed that their mother, Eva, was exploited by a 'cabal of manipulative island women'. In paragraph 4, you state—

CAMILLE: Eva was motivated by her own opinions. She had beliefs about the world and its necessary direction which her sons may not have noticed. [*Pause*] I would like to add that, personally, I am so sad to have lost her.

Islanders are by and large not that familiar with people of colour. The odd mail-order bride from Thailand; the silent Pakistani waiters in the Indian restaurant in Ayrness; the occasional mixed-race cousin of somebody who visited for a weekend and then left again. Camille, glamorous and high-status, left them speechless. A tall, African-French woman with French- (not African-French) accented English, she was formidably dressed, in a trouser suit that was lush and green, and undoubtedly Parisian. Her hair, which she'd relaxed since moving back to France, illuminated her head like the halo of a saint in a Renaissance fresco. They were dazzled.

As a doctor of the hydra-headed disease of lust and passion (of genito-urinary medicine), Camille radiated efficiency and disapproval. Harry Harcourt-Vane, behind her in the painting, done in heavy oils, looked down with astonishment in his expression. She was the only woman to whom the judge listened without once interrupting.

JUDGE: You have stated that you were always an outsider in Britain; was it any different in the islands?

CAMILLE: Yes and no. As a doctor you are never an outsider. You are always immediately inside, looking at other people's bodies. Thus, Britain I know through its capital, its infections.

JUDGE: Doctors are impartial, you mean?

CAMILLE: No. Doctors deal in generalities, like everybody else.

The press liked her. They were warmer with her than they ever were with Inga, for example. Something about Inga brings out the worst in all those men with cameras.

CAMILLE: In Harlesden, where I worked on first arriving in London, I was told by my colleagues that our black male patients contracted gonorrhoea on trips to the Caribbean islands, which they then spread, with much swearing, through a concurrency of female partners.

JUDGE: [*Pause*] Typically racist? Or sexist? Or both?

CAMILLE: Both. But it's easy to come to these conclusions if you don't belong to the group with which you are dealing. For example, at St Mary's, Paddington, where the patients were Middle Eastern Muslims – it seemed to me that women walked through the door transfixed with guilt at the sexual act they had indulged in. At the Royal Free in Hampstead – largely white, quite teenage, fairly Jewish, with a median age of twenty-five, where seventy per cent of the HIV cases are homosexual – few of my patients considered sex and its outcomes taboo. No doubt I was wrong. The point is, everybody could do with some help understanding what it is like to belong to a different culture, black or white, man or woman. So, *do something about it*. That's what I told Eva. Specifically, Your islands are so white!

JUDGE: How could she do anything about that?

CAMILLE: In the 1960s, many small islands in Britain gave land away to applicants from the mainland – it was about counteracting depopulation. The selection process was always a bit oblique. So that's what Eva did. Her selection process was a bit oblique too.

JUDGE: Whom did she choose?

CAMILLE: Single mothers. Amrita Gill, who runs All Island Taxis, moved up about ten years ago. Her elder daughter studied with Jen. The younger one is the campaigner, Tara, Zoe's friend. Banu Yildiz, she came to Britain from Turkey aged twelve. Her elder son has moved away but Banu married an island man with whom she has a son, Raymond. Marigold Zhu. She runs the Golden Lotus.

JUDGE: Positive discrimination—

CAMILLE: Minority ethnic, yes. Black, no. As I said, these islands …

Speaking to the judge, Camille feels the irritating presence of those ghosts she isn't mentioning, hovering around her. *The men in her life*. She won't speak of them in public, but they are the ones who formed her.

Her father, who grew up in Dakar.

Her cousin, Basile, who thought Sebastian a real *tête de bite*, and told her so, in front of him, adding the Serer insult that he was a goat, a dog. (Sebastian, who understood neither language well, looked on, smiling.)

Her first significant lover, whose name she now never even uttered, who was born in the Parisian suburb of Saint-Denis, to north African Muslim parents. *His* family came from Algeria; *her* father was from Senegal; *she* was raised a Catholic; *he* a Muslim. While Camille didn't consider herself very dark – compared to her cousins in Dakar, for example; she was mixed-race, her mother was white – she was well aware that to the majority of the French people she met, she was black as night, ebony, deepest Africa. Certainly, she was the blackest student in medical college, and since he was the next-darkest in their year group, it was only because of this, she shouted at him later, that their friendship existed. But the truth is, for some reason she is unable to explain, he got deep inside her. She doesn't mean the sex. What she means is him and her, their closeness. And either (she jabbed the air as she spoke) that was forced on them by their skin-colour ghetto, or it was a rare unrepeatable marvel of two embracing souls.

He had a hardness in his heart about the women he slept with: she was warned of this in advance. With her he was different until they were lovers. Then the closeness of friendship vanished, leaving in its place the irritation of a man encumbered. And such an amount of pique and hurt, she felt she had absorbed it from all the women who had gone before: their accumulated rancour. He left her, as predicted. In shock at his coldness, Camille decided to finish her medical degree abroad. She applied for an elective in London.

She never told him, and for thirteen years they hadn't been in touch, so there was no way he could know. But she became a consultant in genito-urinary medicine and HIV because of his brother. He had an older brother whose escape from the *banlieue* took him as far as a hospital ward. He slept around; he shared – the thought makes Camille shudder – God knows countless needles; he contracted HIV. During her third year in medical college it developed into the condition known in France as *le syndrome d'immuno-déficience acquise*: SIDA. AIDS, as they call it in England.

Camille never met the older brother but she saw what it did to the younger, and during the six months she spent at St Mary's, the young Muslim men she treated made her think of her lover.

The second significant lover, the one who became her husband, found her at seven o'clock one Tuesday morning, in the Central Middlesex Hospital in Harlesden. He, tall and blonde with a white person's large, bouncy, care-free curls, was a parliamentary researcher with a then-and-now obscure British political party. He was almost thirty. She, a junior doctor, was twenty-five. Seb would normally have considered this hour of the morning too damn early for flirtation; but for Camille he made an exception. During the politicking hospital visit he asked for her number, and Camille, who hadn't yet been chatted up like this in Britain, found the brazenness a relief. All day long, he thought about the tall black lady doctor. He rang her that evening, and asked her to meet him for a drink. Hoping to impress her, he proposed the House of Commons Strangers' Bar. They ended up that night, back at the flat where Seb lived with his Great-Uncle Hubert in the top two floors of a building with very dirty windows in Covent Garden.

HENRY: Now that I think about it, Mother never spoke about Father, really, after his death. She didn't celebrate him as she ought to have done. We were young when he died, in our twenties. She didn't reach out to us, emotionally, at all.
JUDGE: I am sorry about that.

The old man Hubert had a thing for Frenchmen, which (Camille said) showed in his conversation. His speeches in that language were impeccable, the product of another age, *when people learned things lastingly in England*. He was an Anglican priest, who had recently retired from St Paul's. This was the church he still attended, and it was Camille – not Sebastian, nor his brothers, nor Eva – who was honoured with a tour of this peculiar breast-shaped English-British icon. Together, they stood beneath Wren's dome, as the old man pointed out what a travesty subsequent generations, especially the Victorians, had made of the interior. Against some black marble doors in the transept, on which had been inscribed in gold the names of viscounts, two angels slept as they leant on their large black swords. Beside them a brass plaque described a naval disaster: 'In Memory of the Officers, Seamen, Mariners & Boys.' Everywhere, the original had been graffitied over with memorials. Everywhere, she saw, were the names of men: lists of clerics, lists of deaths, lists of triumphs in battles, lists of male achievements.

(Zoe remembers Camille telling this story one evening at Her House; Eva loved it, of course; Sebastian tried to look amused, and the museum's *Quine* Commission followed not long after. The artist was a woman from Aberdeen; her work, 'Loons', a massive bronze sculpture on a plinth which, from a distance, looked familiar for being phallic. Up close it was composed of a jutting array of different fonts from the past three centuries, all copied from the islands' fifteen or so graveyards: the names of every woman buried in the archipelago.)

Camille could spend ages in Hubert's company, taking pleasure in the way he spoke, while Sebastian, who could not take part, exiled himself to the kitchen, to do the cooking. When the old man Hubert died, eight months after her wedding, Camille was distraught. He had shown her a straightforward affection which she missed, being away from her family, and making do instead with Seb's, which was wary of her, she thought, as if, being black, and a doctor of STDs, and French (those seemed to be the issues, in order of importance), she stood at a remove from their concerns. And although she liked the island house in which Seb had partly grown up, she didn't love it in the instinctive way with which she took to the eccentric flat in Covent Garden, with its shelves of eighteenth- and nineteenth-century French novels, and its row of tinned cassoulet in the kitchen, and its *papier d'arménie* in the bathroom. In the years after Hubert died, Camille would occasionally complain to Seb that it was actually the old, homosexual French-speaking priest who had wooed her; that Seb had merely stood by: handsome, silent and virile. But Seb always laughed when she told this story.

After a while you get used to human misery, to pain and suffering, as a doctor. And sexually transmitted disease, as a specialisation, is a better place to be than cancer or emergency trauma. At least, when you work in sexual health, your friends aren't constantly asking for free advice (imagine what it's like being a dermatologist). At least, by and large, the stigma has been diminished by education. At least, by and large, you can cure it. Still, the young ones – why are they so careless? She was often amazed by the teenage girls: their inept knowledge of their bodies, their completely medieval idea as to the location of their vital organs.

CAMILLE: One afternoon, a teenage girl appeared at my clinic.

Not a Londoner, not one of those sharp-tongued tirades of styled hair who liked to come in with six of her schoolfriends. No. This one was married already and newly pregnant. Camille, who had become adept at judging the inhabitants of this country at a glance—

CAMILLE: She was a Muslim, clearly. Dark-skinned. I guessed she was Somali. Turned out she was from Pakistan. An African in Pakistan. The eighteenth-century slave trade east out of Muscat.

Camille looked at the notes, and asked a few questions. Then she took the woman straight across the corridor to the examination room. She directed her to lie down on the bed, and to remove her loose cotton trousers. She drew the curtain around the bed and turned away – wishing, as always at this juncture, that she had a window. The smallest glimpse of sky would have been so nice; or a vista of Hampstead Heath. She pulled on a pair of gloves.

When she turned back again, the woman was lying, tense and ready. Camille could see in a glance. The sores were typical: there was no doubt at all.

'I'm going to take a sample for analysis just to be sure,' Camille said. 'It might hurt but not very much. OK?'

She bent over the woman's pubis. The sore had to be rubbed with a cotton swab; the woman flinched but didn't cry out. Camille would take it through to the lab at the back of the clinic. If it showed up under the microscope there was no need to send away a sample of blood.

'Do you work in Britain?' Camille asked, by way of small talk.

'Yes,' the woman said; and, after a pause, 'Teacher'.

'Marvellous,' said Camille, feeling proud, despite herself; it was so good when women from extra-disparaged minority ethnic groups got themselves employment. 'You can clothe yourself again,' she added, and returned to the desk to check the health questionnaire. *One sexual partner so far in her life.* It was completely unfair, as usual.

Ten minutes later, Camille called the woman through again. She had the injection ready, and also the tests for the other sexually transmitted infections. She would tell the woman to come back in a week for a check-up, and then in a month, and then in a further two months so they could be sure about the HIV. It was the husbands Camille feared in this scenario. Either the wives didn't tell them, or the husbands didn't listen; and so the women Camille had cleared of infection would go home to their partners to be infected all over again. She spoke in a voice practised to sound reassuring.

'It's syphilis. Good that we caught it at this early stage.'

She took out the syringe, pushed up the sleeve of the woman's long pink patterned shirt, and injected the penicillin into her arm. The HIV test, meanwhile, was so quick that nowadays patients barely had time to panic. The woman said nothing as Camille took her hands in hers, pricked her finger, and squeezed a drop of blood into the capsule.

'We'll just watch and see whether the dot ...'

The result was negative. Camille unwrapped a plaster and stuck it over the tiny puncture.

'And the blood tests.'

She drew off three bottles of blood.

'And the vaginal swab for chlamydia and gonorrhoea.'

There was silence as Camille directed the woman to the couch again. She unwrapped the kit, parted the woman's legs, inserted the swab into her vagina. She was so young and pretty – sweet smile, tiny in stature, nineteen years old. The beginning of her life.

Suddenly, the woman spoke.

'How I get it?'

Camille drew out the swab.

'It's a sexually transmitted disease,' she said. 'Passed between sexual partners.'

'My husband? To me? He got it from ... ?'

It was a hard thing to tell a woman about their spouse. Camille repeated what she always said: 'From someone else. There is no need to worry, now that you've taken the injection. But you must tell your husband to get treatment too, or he will reinfect you.'

She looked at the woman, whose eyes were huge and heavily-lined in black. 'You understand?'

The woman nodded.

'Is there anything else you would like to ask, Mrs Maher?'

The woman shook her head. Then she took a small white stone out of her handbag and kissed it.

CAMILLE: Eva's V-stone. She must have stolen it from me! I was absolutely shocked.

At thirty-nine, Camille was halfway through her life. The Senghors weren't that long-lived. Sometimes she wished she had taken more time off when her children were born. They were tiny and helpless and you thought they would be like that forever. So you went back to work and a nanny came in to do the daily looking after. You got on with your work – which anybody could have done – and, without your noticing it, your children grew up. The blissful moment you had for spending just with them had passed. Poof! Like that. You had all your life to work. Whereas children were a one-off creation.

Sometimes she felt the problem was with the work itself. Was the harsh truth that she was bored at the Royal Free? Was she really going to examine chlamydia swabs for the rest of her life? So much of who you were you learnt at school. In Camille's case: hard work; *swotting*, as the English said. The steady drip of adrenalin that came from succeeding. Deference to authority, a belief in what you were told. Your skin, which set you apart from your peers.

She thought of where she might be by now in France. Of who she might have been in Senegal. *Matrilinéaire.* The other lives she could have lived if only she didn't live in England.

CAMILLE: I had always been a man-pleaser, really. My father was so proud of me.

The most recent advantage of Camille's field of work, at her level, was the sympathetic hours. The clinic was open nine to five. Sometimes meetings went on until six – but not beyond. She would have liked to have been home in time for the children's *goûter*, as her mother always was. But then her mother worked next door. Camille always dropped her children to school in the morning, and always cooked their evening meal. She kept her phone on silent during office hours and, if there was an emergency, the school knew how to get hold of her. Sebastian worked awful hours and it was precisely those, he seemed to think, that gave his career its ennobling aspect. Was this what they called public service? – *really giving something back to society* – coming home after midnight, waking his wife as he crawled into bed, expecting that, less than seven hours later, she would know where the cleaner had hung his ironed shirts, presuming that, ten minutes after that, his hospital-bound wife and school-bound children would scoot out of the way in the bathroom, watch passively as he drank all the coffee and finished off the milk, risk being late for school and work as he rushed up and down three flights of stairs, looking for his phone—? And all for what? For the *Palace of Westminster*, that piety-bedecked gentleman's club. For his own glory and advancement.

Early on, she had thought she knew what lay in store for Seb and her. Like all politicians in his party, he had spoken in such high-minded terms of his righteous ambition and commitment to good and proper things, she reckoned they might survive together. Until she learnt that they all spoke like that; that it was a line they parroted, for good inner feeling and good external impact. Perhaps some of them believed it. Perhaps they all did. At one of those awkward London dinners which they used to attend before his party was in power, the man she was placed beside at table – a political journalist from a left-leaning paper – told her not to worry: Seb's party would never see power. All they were was a vote drain from the left. Good, Camille thought, we are safe then. But the journalist was mistaken.

Camille's problem was that she was used to being the busy one. It was she, in the past fifteen years, who'd had the important work life. After a stretch of years, you established a certain dynamic and rhythm as a couple. You came to an understanding of yourselves through certain things you did together, through ways of being which were insignificant in themselves, and yet which, over time, appeared – especially if they were taken away – to go to the heart of what kept you at peace. Until he became minister last year,

Seb had entertained the children all weekend; made their weekly night out together an institution; had time to concoct complicated bookings for unconventional holidays far away from Britain. Just thinking about the things which Sebastian and she no longer discussed made Camille feel exhausted. He had long since ceased to enquire about her work.

'Today I decided to take up sheep farming in France,' she said one evening in the kitchen.

'Did you, darling?' Sebastian said, looking up from his phone just long enough to give her the impression that he attended to her words; only realising she had uttered words which required his active consideration, from the flash of hatred on her face. And Camille's thoughts made her catch her breath. *Where had this bitterness come from?*

There were several possible sources. The fact that she hadn't taken her children to Senegal. (Unpardonable. Her fault, of course, for not insisting. Just because they lived in England: no direct flights from London.) The entitlement of the Harcourt-Vane gene pool. (His brothers and their offspring. Especially his brothers. How they talked to each other.) Zoe, Sebastian's daughter. (*Not Zoe herself: Sebastian's treatment of her.*) When Camille first met Sebastian, he had complained that his mother didn't appreciate how difficult it was for him to break through Zoe's barrier of shyness. In Camille's opinion, most of that was due to apathy on his part: he was simply too busy to get to know her. He ought to have invited her to London for the weekend. Or included her in family holidays to the South of France, or made a point of coming up to the islands to see her school plays and attend her Sports Day. But he didn't do these things. Instead, he chose to maintain a cordial distance.

At first he told himself that he was doing this for the sake of Camille, for the children. But Camille had always liked Zoe.

Camille could also see that Eva truly loved Sebastian's firstborn. That much was clear. It was *she* Eva spoke of always, when she rang. Zoe's getting into environmental issues, she would tell her son; next time you're up why don't you go and speak at her school? And Seb would shake his head at this folly of his mother's – she had no idea of the demands on his time.

The truth was, and Camille knew it, that since being promoted as minister in a surprise reshuffle, Seb was overworked and under-supported; he didn't have a mentor in Parliament; he didn't have a friend outside the House from whom to seek guidance; his wife hated his work; his children missed him. He missed them. But because he was a man, he couldn't admit this to anyone. Ministerial life was itself an assault on all the things he liked best about being an adult, all the simple *bon vivant* pleasures of dining, partying, boozing – cooking bouillabaisse for Camille, choosing the perfect dance tracks for parties, inventing new entertainments for his noisy group of friends from school and college. Nowadays he socialised non-stop – but in a debased, corrupted way. He had long ago perfected the art of small talk, and at first it had been exhilarating to exercise the skill in office. This was how the wheels of state were oiled: by parties such as those which Sebastian attended every night, instead of getting home to Highgate. He learnt to talk on the rosy side of the party line. To listen; look fascinated-sceptical about what he was being told, depending on who was doing the telling – and never to speak the truth unless truth was medically certified in advance as a pure undefiled country virgin. In which case you spoke about her all the time. You quoted her every word, you dragged her with you on constituency visits, during statements to the House, on to television for routine scraps and policy scuffles. You tried not to notice how weary Truth became after some weeks on the job; you squinted and ignored the bruises which appeared on her arms, the dark shadows which had begun to line her eyes, the less-than-respectful looks she gave you when she heard you speaking about her with a passion only just this side of decent. You tried not to envisage too closely the ramifications of the legislation you were drafting, which was surely going to de-virginate any Truth remaining. You tried to remember how Truth had appeared once, before you inveigled her; and not to see her as she was now, smoking on the pavement, her cheeks made pink with rouge; and once her dirty work was done, not to notice how peremptorily she was dispatched by your minion back to where she came from, with a pat on the bottom and some money for the fare.

JUDGE: Is it your opinion that Eva had a strong aversion to British political life?
CAMILLE: Absolutely. We both did.

Of course it was easier for Seb, entering politics in the wake of his father. Even though they belonged to different parties – and these days the parties weren't that far apart – Sebastian was familiar with the etiquette, which in Camille's opinion was largely what it came down to; and the expectations people had. People felt they knew him; he had a history there; he fitted in. She thought of the Machiavelli she had read at school: *for it is sufficient only not to transgress the customs of his ancestors, and to deal prudently with the circumstances as they arise, for a prince of average powers to maintain himself in his state.*

For Sebastian, as a child, observing his father, politics must have seemed a life of constant travel, sudden absence, and urgent conversations on the phone, away from the dinner table. Camille suspected that his father enjoyed every minute of it even as his wife had suffered.

JUDGE: But what she was building in the islands, wasn't it political too?
CAMILLE: Yes, but she was trying something new.

There were so many things Camille missed about home. The longer she spent in England, the longer the list grew. Most were so obvious you never thought you'd miss them.

– *Friends, former lovers, her family (an edited version).*
– *Her language.*
– *The proximity of warm southern climes (not misty northern ones).*
– *Sorry to say, but a certain way of dressing.*
– *Her ancestral culture.*

Camille's father had married the daughter of a village baker. Not in his native village, Ziguinchor, in Senegal, but N—, in southern France. A bakery that was run on the highest principles and visited by bread-eaters, biscuit-fanciers, from over twenty-five kilometres away. Camille's parents met at university in Grenoble. They finished their degrees, got pregnant immediately after, and were married in the town hall. He, who had studied engineering, once planned a productive career in bridges. Instead he moved to his wife's village (actually a small town with a weekly market and a museum of agricultural implements) where he joined his father-in-law at the bread oven. Even today, Camille's father still bakes everything he cooks with wood. As a result, Camille grew up with an understanding of the landscape's purpose. It was the chestnut forests beyond the town, which became the heat that cooked Grandpère's staple almond biscuits. The cows in the fields which provided the butter. Camille, sitting as a little girl by the window in the front of the shop, heard the pride in her mother's voice: The best ingredients, vanilla from Réunion, almonds from Spain, stone-ground French flour, butter from the farm shop. (Given this, it was hard for Camille not to disdain the bakery where Zoe's mother worked. She tried. She understood that the English didn't have high standards. She bought her children the disgusting English-British doughnuts.)

An only child, Camille was quiet, studious and uncomplaining – except, that is, when she was visiting her cousins in Senegal. Every summer, in August, when the bakery was closed, they flew to Dakar, where her cousins went to school, where her aunt and uncle worked, and the next day took the boat south to Casamance, where the family house was. Over the next month, Camille had her hair done in a ripple of plaits, and her father wore capacious, vibrant wax bazin suits. In the market she watched him haggle for vegetables and fish. She and her favourite cousin, Basile, walked into the forest with her aunt to collect madd fruit. For a whole month, Camille forgot about N—, about the bakery, about her schoolfriends, Marie-Claude and Anne-Marie. She cried when the month was up, and she had to go home again to France.

But back in the bakery with her parents, she soon grew accustomed to the familiar rhythm of her days, and Senegal became a flickering memory on the periphery of her attention.

The problem of who we might have been.

As a child one could move from one life to another without any issue. Then one grew up, and was forced to choose between them.

In England, Camille considered her children's chances; the quality, that is, of their English cousinships. There were several hard things about being Sebastian's wife, and one of them was his brothers and their offspring. Spoilt Jonah, from whom Melanie learnt to whine for treats. Polly and her brother, who watched too much television and at the weekend demanded outings to buy things. Sebastian's brothers; Sebastian's brothers' wives ...

The Harcourt-Vane gene pool made Camille anxious on behalf of her children.

CAMILLE: The colliding worlds of doctor and patient.

After how many meetings can you decide to trust a stranger? Aged eighteen with the first lover: it was instant. In her twenties, with Seb, it took a while, and even then it was the uncle who clinched it. With Eva, the trust and love grew with each encounter. But an unknown foreign woman with syphilis, without mutual friends or any common interests?

It began in the clinic with the V-stone.

As the Pakistani woman kissed it, Camille saw that it was the little stone carving that her six-year-old daughter had been lent by Eva.

Camille's mother-in-law often found something nice to give the children when they spent the weekend. But antiques! That was over the top. Seeing the smooth white stone, carved with a V, in her daughter's possession one Sunday evening as she packed her bag for school the next morning, Camille was annoyed with her mother-in-law. She picked up the carving: a rounded white stone which fitted nicely in the palm. How old was it? Altogether more like something from Senegal than Britain. This wasn't an object to give to a six-year-old child.

'Why is it in your school bag?' Camille asked her daughter, who began to cry. She had been planning to take it in for Monday morning Show & Tell. Camille put the stone in her pocket. She would ring her mother-in-law and find out whether or not the fact of it demanded retribution.

But Eva, when she answered the phone, laughed at Camille.

'I wanted her to see it. It's a V-stone: an ancient, Neolithic, symbol of woman. I took it out to show her, and then somebody arrived and I forgot to take it back. It's fine. Bring it next time.'

Camille made an impatient noise. 'This may not be till Christmas.'

'Come before that,' Eva said, even though they both knew that this was unlikely. The three wives of Eva's three sons, different though they were, felt as one in their lack of love for Harcourt House. Octavia, wife of George, found Eva irritatingly eccentric in her habits and opinions, and her house uncomfortable (the beds were icy; there was competition for hot baths at Christmas). Henry's wife, the timid, dark-haired Harriet, viewed both Eva and her dwelling as sources of potential hazard for her precious son Jonah – he had once got sick after eating Eva's home-made ice cream; he might fall into the pond; when he was three, Eva had given him nightmares by taking him to an inappropriate pantomime in Ayrness. For Camille, it was the aristocratic history of Harcourt House which raised her hackles. Christmas dinner often became a history lesson in Abolition. (One of the early Harcourts had made money from the sugar trade *aux Caraïbes*.) None of this upset Eva, who understood very well that each generation was disconcerted by the next, and vice versa; that a little disconcertment was better than outright war.

'Just keep the amulet safe for me,' she said.

A silence. Then:

'It's not *the* amulet? That V-stone is your *amulet*?'

'Yes, my amulet. That's it.'

'But the amulet is really precious, isn't it?'

'As a V-stone, it's become ever-more important,' Eva said, sounding annoyed now. 'But in and of itself it's probably not that valuable. I travelled around Yugoslavia with it in my bag, for God's sake.'

CAMILLE: Seb's father often told the story of the amulet. It's what first made him notice Eva – her independence. Eva's emphasis was slightly different.

Autumn 1967. Harry Harcourt-Vane is twenty-five years old, and working at chambers near Aldwych. He owns a small flat in Camden which only feels small, his architect suggests on the first site visit, because of the configuration of the internal walls.

'You see, the elevation is promising, and look how light comes in through these windows.'

On their second meeting, in the architect's office to discuss the plans, Harry notices the stone lying on the older man's desk. A paperweight? There is something mesmerising about it. He picks it up, examines the grooves carved in the stone, puts it down, and says, 'Where is that curious piece from?'

The architect glances over in surprise.

'Yugoslavia.'

The door opens and a young woman of about Harry's age appears with a tray of tea.

'Who was *that*?' Harry asks when she is gone, in a way which is awed but perhaps also a little leering. He guesses, from the girl's demeanour, that she is no office skivvy.

That was Eva. During the six months that it took for the work to be done on Harry's flat – for it to be transformed in the way Benjamin Levi had promised – Harry thought often, in ways more lascivious than leering, of the severe, pretty, slim, silent woman, dressed in a pair of men's trousers and a thick blue jumper. It was only when he went to the Hampstead office to hand over the final cheque, and remarked on the stone paperweight's absence from the desk, that he discovered the girl had gone too.

'Eva, my daughter, has it,' the architect said. 'I made her take it with her to Sarajevo.'

CAMILLE: It was probably exactly those qualities in Eva which Harry found most attractive, that he then set out to smother.

This was the stone that Camille had been carrying around in her bag – for weeks now. In fact, she had forgotten all about it, until she saw it in her patient's hands.

At first she was so shocked that she merely stared as the woman, Mrs Maher, turned over the small white stone then rocked back and forth, her eyes tightly closed.

She took it from my bag! – That was Camille's first thought.

Luckily, her second was: *Let me check, before I confront her.*

She unzipped the inside pocket of her handbag.

Eva's stone was still there. Camille took it out and held it up.

Identical in shape and size and colour to the one her patient was holding.

CAMILLE: I thought I was going mad, but when I asked Mariam Maher about it, she had very little to say. Her father had given it to her as a special souvenir from an outing they went on to the hills. But given that we had spoken about it, I wasn't so surprised when I arrived at work the next morning, and there she was, standing on the path by the hospital. Different headscarf, same sweet face, bag packed at her feet. And holding out, like a secret message, Eva's ancient V-stone, or one exactly like it.

JUDGE: You knew nothing of what Eva was up to in the islands?

CAMILLE: Not explicitly. Of course the institutions to which our lives were shackled, Seb's especially, are so outdated – *antique*, relics from an obsolete past – sometimes you get the feeling that nothing will change for another thousand years. Whereas in the islands, things are different. I had felt it for a while without being able or ready to articulate the difference. Women in charge of so many things; Zoe speaking in a way that was quite unusual, because of the schooling she was getting – no witchy Hansel and Gretel; every mention of a brilliant misogynist, Picasso, for example, coming with a tragic caveat. Eva's sons saw their mother as guardian of their ancestral home; they didn't appreciate that she was a force for transformation. She reminds me of the rip currents my parents used to warn me of in Senegal. An entire body of water, moving the other way from how it seems on the surface. That's what Eva was doing: carrying us far from where we had started. So when my patient appeared before me, I immediately thought of Eva. In London, somebody in this difficult position could easily get lost, could drown. Whereas Eva, I knew she would react with love. I rang her right away.

'Eva,' Camille said – making her mother-in-law's name sound like *Ever* – 'I have a patient, a Pakistani woman, Africa-descended, with a V-stone, just like yours.'

'Really?' said Eva. 'How amazing.' And she began to tell Camille how she had recently been thinking more and more, since their conversation, about the V-stone as an international symbol of ancient female wisdom, and the respect for it which had once prevailed in the world. She was working with this woman, Alice, on a compilation of women-centred epics, and the V-stone was the beginning of that; it fitted in so perfectly with the idea of these islands as a globally-significant catalyst. The V-stones were their talisman, part of the empowerment offered to women anciently and now—

'Can I send her to see you?' Camille said. 'She's a teacher.'

'A teacher?' said Eva.

'She's catching the afternoon flight,' Camille said. 'Can you meet it? If not I'll give her money for the taxi.'

'Is she staying a long time?'

'It's your choice,' Camille said, and sketched the details of her patient's situation. 'She could teach Zoe, no? That might please Red Ruth.'

This was their name for Zoe's other grandma.

'Oh, I see,' said Eva.

'Yes,' said Camille. 'It's like that. She's dressed in green and is carrying a small overnight bag.'

'Well, all right,' said Eva. 'And what about my stone, can you send it back with her?'

'No,' said Camille, 'I think not. Just in case she . . . you know, gets lost. But that refuge you've been talking about establishing—'

'Yes, indeed,' said Eva.

Everything about this exchange pleased me, Eva wrote in her notebook that night. She was pleased that at least one daughter-in-law felt comfortable enough to take liberties with her time and her house. She was pleased at the thought of employing the woman to teach Zoe about things she couldn't learn in the islands. She was happy that Camille understood her emotional need to be hospitable. It had once been in the British spirit to welcome strangers. And Camille, who had read *Beyond Illyria*, understood this instinct.

What kindness you were shown in Bosnia, her daughter-in-law had said once.

Mother is repaying a cosmic debt, remarked Sebastian.

Because her son hadn't read her book, Eva ignored him. But he was right: it *was* a debt. In Bosnia she had become indebted. Only Camille sympathised. Eva didn't know why all the things she loved about Camille also made her worry. Perhaps she sensed that Camille was strong-headed enough, free enough, to cut Sebastian loose if his behaviour ever warranted non-forgiveness.

As Eva drove to the airport to fetch Camille's patient, she rang Alice in London. 'I'm off to collect a Pakistani woman from the plane,' she shouted into her phone.

It scared Alice to think of Eva careering round those narrow island roads. They would take away her licence if she wasn't careful.

'Will you come up and meet her?' Eva went on. 'You can speak Urdu, can't you?'

'Well,' Alice said. 'I'm a bit rusty now.'

'Camille sent her,' Eva said, and spoke very fast about how offering women refuge was a central idea for her island community, the motiveless reaching out of one woman to another was, in its essence, the most ancient of all ancient ideas, it was what all the Neolithic temples—

'I'll try,' Alice said. 'I was planning to come up soon anyway. I've found an excellent Norse epic for you. And I'd like to speak Urdu to your friend. But I've got to go now, Eva.'

Eva had rung at six o'clock, even though she knew it was the witching hour for people with young children.

Later, Alice would also wonder about the things Eva didn't talk about. Mariam's husband, for example. At the time, Eva emphasised the fact that Mariam was convalescing, emotionally; that she had to be given space and time to leave her wounds alone, to lick them back to health, to rebuild her defences. By which Alice understood her to mean that the conspicuous absence of conversation around this subject was actually a strength. For sometimes, wasn't it better not to speak? People got so carried away when speaking. When often, the best approach was to say nothing. Or if one must speak, to speak of untroublesome things: the progress of a row of seedlings towards the light, of the sun across the heavens. Never the progress of a politician to the point of his undoing. Never a heroine to the plot's unknotting.

In her day, women often came over to seek her advice; but also to complain about this and that. Cwen always kept her own counsel. With the groups, she knew that silence had its own power, that brevity was better, and that elliptical phrases uttered in a high strained voice were the best revenue-earner when she was hungry. But when women came over on their own, all they wanted was to talk, and to be sure of someone listening. Cwen was excellent at that. She would sit, motionless, concentrating not so much on the words as the emotions. It was interesting, watching the emotions.

Being a healer, Cwen knew without compunction that there are certain rhythms which must be respected. *I am on good terms with Moon*, she would say. Moon controls the tides, which control all things. Moon is the greatest marker of passing time, up there in the sky. *And Sun:* Cwen is still, even now, delighted. Can you imagine life without her … ? No, it is unthinkable. *Wind, I like Wind too.* A big presence; hot-tempered, unpredictable; a bit like Cwen herself. She couldn't live without Wind, in the winter. The things that get blown here! A bird with deep-pink feathers. Black wings with a strap of white. A shivery little thing. A beautiful gift. *Then there is Spring* – by which she means the waters. *Spring is my friend.* Yes, the fact is Cwen is all these things – Moon, Sun, Wind, Spring – before she is a woman.

No one ever worshipped Cwen in the beginning. It was after she died that her popularity and fame grew beyond anything her father can have dreamt of. The women, in particular, continued to visit. But Cwen began to feel something disturbing: they were desperate for her attention. She didn't like it. She wasn't sure where the desperation came from.

The peak of desperation was followed by stillness. During that time, she allowed herself to soak into the earth of her island, to calcify into its very substance.

When at last she woke, therefore, it was with one clear piece of knowledge.

Cwen rises. She has that knowledge in her blood. She stretches. She looks out at the sea. Moon is up. The tide is in. It laps right up to the cliff where the peat is crumbling into the water. Cwen knows that the women are coming over tonight. She feels it. They will move over her, and around her, and through her, not seeing, but searching, not really knowing, but wanting. They have a song. It is a good one, from the histories, in which women lure men to their islands with apples. *Begin a voyage across the clear sea*, they sing. *Go and find the Islands of Women.* But this time, when the women arrive, Cwen will test them.

She doesn't hold her breath.

She blows on the waves, and a breaker sloshes over their boat. It's harmless – they get wet. Cwen waits to see what will happen. At least one of them cries. The rest of the women, drenched head to toe, move quickly. They carry their firewood up to the high part of the beach. They count each other, to be sure, and begin the slow process of lighting a fire.

As the sparks fly up into the night, the singing begins. They have lovely voices. Cwen watches the processing and the chanting. She watches them watching each other. They move over her, as the air has moved all this day with the birds; as plants have swayed with bees; as the waters have parted for the fish; as the earth has trembled with mice and rabbits. Now all these things are waiting. They are watching the women. They are waiting to see how Cwen will react.

Cwen thinks of Wind. Wind can help her.

With Wind in her hands, she moves through fire. The flames leap up towards the stars, and the women jump back. Cwen knows what the question is. It is not whether women can live with men – *they can, they always have done* – but whether they can live together;

and beyond themselves, with the things not like them, water, trees, worms. The women who survive will be those who can hear the whales singing, smell the butterflies coming before they see them, sense the rain in the air, as Cwen had done.

The women glance at each other across the licking, rampant flames. These questions are almost completely unknown, unthought, even. Alone, without the presence of a male god; alone with the bees and each other? Firelight lights up everyone's faces. Cwen thinks of how women think. All the time, they are comparing. *She used to be thinner. How can she have let herself go? I can see her tummy through that top. Ooh, she's got so thin and haggard.* She judges them harshly for it. Like every woman, Cwen was beautiful once, and young. She got over it long ago. About fourteen hundred years back.

Looking around the fire, Cwen sees equal quantities of terror and hope. *It is not enough.* She remembers sweating, skin on skin. She remembers the beat of another woman's heart; blood on blood; wrist pulse against temple. She remembers blood trust and skin promise in the passing on of knowledge.

She tells them, whispering it at first. Then she screams it.

It is the two young ones who react. They turn their hands to the flame, and their cheeks to the fire, and although they say nothing, they smile, emboldened.

Then, to Cwen's surprise, they begin to strip.

———

Then Albina said:
'This land to which we have come,
We do not know its name,
Nor if it ever had a lord.
Therefore, since I am the leader,
We will name it after me.
Albina is my name –
From which it will be called Albion,
And hence this country
Will remember us always.'

Anon, *On the Great Giants* (Anglo-Norman), c.1250–1333

POPE JOAN: . . . *in England, she was taken for a cleric by everyone and pursued the study of letters and of love . . . Thus, endowed with admirable knowledge, she left England and went to Rome . . . Since in addition to her scholarly knowledge she was very virtuous and saintly, everyone believed her to be a man . . . A woman, then, was the Vicar of Christ on earth. God from on high was merciful to His people and did not allow a woman to hold so lofty a place . . . And so she was thrown into a horrid dungeon by the cardinals, where this wretched woman died in the midst of her laments.*

Giovanni Boccaccio, *On Famous Women* (Latin), 1359

8

Lucija

LUCIJA: I never told her quite how well I knew her book. We read it at
   school, you see, and then during the siege, I hid it so they wouldn't
   use it as fuel. Also, I'm friends with Mevludin's grandson.

Sister Lucija looks out at the reporters with their notebooks.
Because she is a nun, she has been photographed more than most.
She will never forget the foreign journalists in Sarajevo during the
war, asking her questions, telling her things. They liked sound bites
from schoolgirls. The terrible stories from the capital, to match the
horrific stories from the east of the country.

She remembered what Alice had told her, that beyond the judge's
head was the sea. That she should find the sea, and focus on that if
she was nervous. Although Bosnia was almost completely landlocked,
when Lucija was growing up it was in the middle of Yugoslavia's
geographical grandeur, which stretched from the plains to the forests
and down to the coast. Even Sarajevo itself, with its river and mountains,
had let them feel nature's wildness. Here in the chilly archipelago there
was lots of wildness but it was wisest to forget about natural warmth.
The utter relaxation of summer on the Dalmatian coast. Those warm
evenings in Sarajevo's Spanish cemetery, where they congregated
with their bottles of beer, and greasy paper bags of pies, and their
music, on Friday and Saturday nights just above the graveyard gates.

As the judge asks Lucija a question, an image forms in her head of her schoolfriend, Omer Mevludin, meeting her cousin, Tanja, for the first time – *I had no idea what was about to happen*, Omer told Lucija later – *and then I knelt down and unbuttoned his fly*, Tanja said, as Lucija gasped in horror, *and he gasped out in amazement and fright and whaaoooo! he cried*— For very soon Tanja was drawing back to spit and grimace, and to take a swig from a bottle of beer, and Omer was staring up at the moon through the leaves of the trees. It was the most amazing thing that had ever happened. As it exploded, an image formed: three women, dressed up in high caps with huge fringed scarves enveloping their bodies from the crown of the heads down to their knees. *I puzzled about it*, Omer went on, *until the next morning I woke up and remembered: Grandpa's photograph from 1912.*

It was the first print to go missing from the collection. Omer's mother, crazy with grief and worry, took down the prints which hung in the dining room, and sold them while his father was out – she lived in fear of starving; the price of food on Sarajevo's black market.

LUCIJA: Sorry? Yes, it told me of what my country had been. That my memories weren't wrong. That the war was an aberration. That there is hope. I typed out an extract for you—
SOLICITOR: Thank you. Submission 21a.

From *Beyond Illyria* by Eva Levi [pub. 1969: pp. 72–3]

I had long known of Mevludin's work, of course, and since moving to Sarajevo, I had been coming across it continually. I saw his photographs in the Museum of Sarajevo down by the river. I noticed a beautiful print of the city taken from the hills to the south, which hangs in the atrium of the National Library. I saw them in private houses; people were always very glad to show off their Mevludins to strangers. Then, after a year of travel and research, I rang the photographer and made an appointment to see him.

When I arrived at the studio, the first thing he commented on was my name.

'So, you are Jewish.' He scrutinised me as if about to take my portrait. 'Sephardic like our Sarajevo Jews.'

'Am I?'

There was a young boy whom he employed to make coffee for him and to clean the studio while he worked, and this child – he was perhaps fourteen years old – had been preparing the coffee over the stove when I arrived, boiling it up and letting it cool again, boiling it up, letting it cool. The boy, who didn't say a word all the time I was visiting, handed me some coffee in a small cup and I took it from him and looked around the studio, as Mevludin continued talking. The photographer was speaking to me with his back turned as he searched for something in the shelves he had by the window – large wide shelves which held numerous black box files, each identified with a date and a few cryptic notes written in a mixture of alphabets: Cyrillic, Arabic, Roman. Mevludin opened one box file, then another, then another, all the time talking about the Sephardic family of his son's new wife. I was saying something in a vague and surprised and non-committal way about my own Abrahamic roots, when he turned to me with a print in his hands.

'It was one of the first photographs I took and the first I ever developed. I went out into the street on that first day after returning with my box from Vienna – and bam! These Jewess ladies. I had to persuade them to stand there, ten minutes, twenty minutes, thirty minutes, as I adjusted the shutter and the aperture and they adjusted their headscarves. I fed the little girl sweets and promised her an ice cream. And then, at the last minute, as everybody was losing patience with my new box, the sun went behind a cloud and the light was perfect. The three women stopped squinting and smiled, and I took the picture. In that moment I knew that I would become a photographer, the best one in the whole of Yugoslavia.'

That was how Mevludin talked. He could talk like this for hours – about the photographs he took, about members of his clan, about his country, about Tito, about things that never normally got said concerning socialism, for he was too old and too famous to fear reprisals from the authorities. That morning in his studio, he also talked about technology, technique, and the teleology of pictorial representations, in his part of the world. 'We are musical people. The Ottomans imported their own traditions to Bosnia. But the land is too hard for an art such as painting or sculpture, which requires such outlay from the artist. Only now, with the ease of producing these portraits, thanks to the industry and the economics of the Federation, is it possible for families of even modest means to own a picture of themselves.'

He was referring, of course, to his studio portraits. They were the money-spinners which allowed him to buy his flat on Ferhadija Street and to send his elder son away to be educated in Belgrade and the younger one in Paris. He showed me his backdrops: the Gazi Husrev-beg mosque, the Miljacka River running through the centre of the city, the bridge at Mostar, the walled city of Dubrovnik, the islands of the Adriatic rising up through those calm blue waters. In front of these scenes he had positioned and photographed countless families from Sarajevo, Travnik, Mostar.

He jabbed a finger at the photograph of the Sephardic Jewish women. 'But my art is the pictures I take in the street.'

He pulled out another picture from a box. A young woman: dark hair, dark eyes. 'My daughter-in-law,' he said. 'Spanish blood, like you. Her grandmother still speaks the old language.'

I shook my head; I looked nothing like his daughter-in-law.

JUDGE: How well known a photographer was Mevludin?

LUCIJA: Well known before the war outside our country. Famous, within Bosnia. Then came the war, and it inflated the value. By the time peace was declared, Mevludin's photographs were being bought for ready money by rich expatriate Yugoslavs and a clique of foreign collectors. His scenes of the countryside around Sarajevo, of the old quarters of the city, of the most beautiful daughters of Sarajevo without their headscarves; you could say it turned from an outdated craft, at the time of Mevludin's death, a forgotten trade packed away in a cupboard, to a hoard of gold later. But his grandson, Omer, even when he was a schoolboy planned on becoming the chronicler of his grandfather's career.

Lucija was homesick.

She had known this for sure, ever since she found herself singing Bosnian songs down the phone to her old schoolfriend, Omer. She would sign out of her internet account, pay for the hour she had used, and walk outside, into the sun, to sit on the harbour wall and sing. She sang Omer Bosnian *sevdah*, into his voicemail – the ones they'd both loved, which his grandfather Mevludin had loved before them, as made famous by the voices of Silvana and Himzo Polovina. The songs went into the air, and all the way to Sarajevo, where Omer was, accompanied by the sound of waves and seagulls.

LUCIJA: She wrote about the music, also. I copied that for you too.

SOLICITOR: Submission 21b.

JUDGE: Thank you, I will read it later. You knew of Eva Levi, of course, before meeting her?

LUCIJA: Yes, everybody mentioned her. *The woman who wrote about your country.* It didn't take long to work it out. And she knew about me. She was supporting our convent. She knew there was a nun from the former Yugoslavia.

Before long, Lucija's colleagues in the convent held a meeting amongst themselves and decided that it might do them all good if, in the short term, Sister Lucija managed the refuge set-up as well as convent-to-world communications, via trips by ferry into Ayrness. In the case of the convent, there were insuperable physical restraints, involving several fathoms of deep salty water, to the free-flow of internet connectivity.

'You ought to go and meet Eva Levi,' said Sister Geraldine. But Lucija didn't want to meet her. Supposing she wasn't as great as her book? Supposing she no longer cared about Bosnia?

She did want to travel off Papa Astrid, however. The moment she stepped from the convent's motorboat on to the island of Astrid and waited, with her rucksack on her back, for the ferry to Ayrness, she felt relief rushing through her. She waited there alongside the farmer with his truckload of sheep, and the man who fixed the wind turbines, and the young family who'd been visiting their grandparents, and the slim, blonde, businesslike woman who tapped away on her phone throughout the ensuing half-hour journey, and she breathed cold air into her lungs. She looked out at the islands lying one beyond the other. Sometimes, at the convent, when she walked out with her pail to the chickens, these very islands looked too much like diminishing hopes; but today they were beautiful, tranquil, soothing. They promised adventure.

Lucija really liked the other sisters but it was hard work sometimes, living together, day in, day out. She wasn't used to it yet. She wasn't even used to God, let alone Jesus. The idea of talking to them in prayers for the rest of her life sometimes made her weep. *Oh Mary, mother of God, pray for us. Saints Cwen, Brigid, Astrid, anciently of the islands, pray for us.*

179

For the first few months of her time in the islands, therefore, while sitting at an internet café in Ayrness Harbour, the sun streaming through the window and warming her cheek, Lucija dispensed with convent business as quickly as she could, and typed messages to her schoolfriends. One was in New Zealand, another in Canada. Her cousin Tanja was in Melbourne. Omer was at home in Sarajevo.

LUCIJA: I looked at videos on YouTube. I learnt the songs I didn't know, and sang them to Omer. I sang them to myself when I was walking around town. But it wasn't practical, having to go to Ayrness to type an email. So Sister Brigid sent me off to the smartphone shop in Berwick. I was on the 6.20 return boat, singing away, the phone in my bag, when I heard someone singing 'Kad ja pođoh na Bembašu', the love song with its Sephardic melody. I jumped to my feet.

Eyes full of tears: a woman, with silver snakes for hair, holding a briefcase. As the woman sang about the Bembasa lovers, Lucija began to speak to her, rapidly, in their language. But the old woman shook her head.

LUCIJA: I cried then. We both did. She hugged me.

(It was the first time Lucija had been hugged in years.)

LUCIJA: Sarajevo is not so big a city, but still, I was far from home and finally to meet the one person in the islands who knew Sarajevo well – who had known Mevludin! When it happened, it was great for me. I felt the world of home reaching out in a caress. I have been away from it for too too long.
JUDGE: How long had you been in the islands by then?
LUCIJA: Six months. But sixteen years away from Sarajevo.

The island the nuns had bought was small, one mile by two, and until they arrived there, only Sister Geraldine, who had been managing the nearby Archipelago Women's Club for a year by then, had seen it. The others had made do with the fourteen photos on the estate agent's website. As it turned out, yes, it was bleak; but it was lovely.

Really, everything they had hoped for. There was a farmhouse and outbuildings and fields for the chickens and cows that Sister Brigid intended to buy. Money had been set aside at Sister Geraldine's request for a greenhouse, though Sister Brigid quipped that keeping some for the litigation they might face would be useful. They had broken with Rome, and with Britain. The ancient Celtic Christians had had independent monasteries on islands; the fact that it was mostly men who lived there, so everybody said, meant nothing in this day and age. The Norsemen and women had known island independence too. *Papay* was the Norse name for those small islands; 'holy men'. Sister Brigid said *papay* meant 'paps' – breasts. Little breasts in the sea. Large ones, sometimes. Holy women, in other words. Sacred mammary glands afloat in the salt.

JUDGE: You were Eva's accountant for some years?

SIGRID [HENDERSON]: Correct.

JUDGE: Are you at liberty to elucidate on this matter of Eva's financial relationship with the convent?

SIGRID: The Convent of All Our Holy Mothers was a cause to which Eva regularly gave money, in a personal capacity. She contributed to the convent's start-up costs. She enlisted Sister Geraldine in the running of the Archipelago Women's Club, which was largely how the convent was financed. Eva was long of the opinion that the island of Papa Astrid, that is, the convent itself, would be the ideal location for the women's refuge. She wanted it to be there for a number of reasons. The nuns had brought in new staff at AWC; the running of the club was going so well. She thought they would do an even better job with the refuge. There was a farmhouse building which would be perfect as a place for women who had suffered during war, or from domestic abuse, to get away from things, to receive treatment, before rehabilitating back into mainstream life. Or, even better, helping them to realise that, actually, maybe mainstream life is part of the problem. There are other ways. She gave [*consults notes*] over £3,000, most recently, for that. Mariam Maher was the first woman but since then there have been many others.

They made a striking pair, as they walked off the boat: the nun in a green habit; Eva, in blue trousers, her rain cloud of hair. Eva had persuaded Lucija to come back to Harcourt House for supper – and, since that meant missing the last ferry home, to stay the night.

'I'll call the convent and let them know you're with me. You will want to see all my Bosnian things. I have a copper coffee pot, and coffee grinder, plus a Dalmatian silver filigree bangle—'

Lucija held her breath. She wasn't sure she could cope with this.

Eva said, 'I also have an early Mevludin. You know, the photographer?'

Lucija's eyes widened. 'Of course! I was at school in Sarajevo with Mevludin's grandson. The family owned a lot of his prints but during the siege they had to sell them out of the country.'

'Oh,' Eva said, 'how very sad that is.' She glanced quickly at Lucija and then back at the road. She drove quite fast. Lucija felt a bit sick.

Omer had replied to Lucija's voicemail with another song of Silvana's, but he had made no plans to come and see her.

When they arrived at the house, Eva led Lucija straight upstairs to her bedroom, pulled the curtains right back, twisted them out of the light, and beckoned her round to the wall between the windows. Both women were silent as they looked at the print. It was one of Eva's most precious things. Lucija stepped up close to the photograph, and put a finger on the glass. She traced her finger over the faces of the women. The women were standing near where the bread queue massacre had happened.

Lucija said, 'Many of the Austro-Hungarian buildings on that street were saved from destruction by all the socialist concrete they were clad in—'

She stopped talking only because Eva was crying. Lucija put an arm around her. Then she cried, too. She hadn't cried for years, either.

JUDGE: What did you think of Eva?

LUCIJA: She was very emotional. For me, with the life I had been living recently – the quiet and subdued nature of the convent – it was extraordinary. She never pretended not to feel what she was feeling. So when she met me, everything got stirred up. She actually hadn't been back to Bosnia since writing *Beyond Illyria*, you see. She went outside after showing me Mevludin's picture, and didn't reappear until hours later. She came in just as Mariam and I were finishing supper. All wet through, her hair bedraggled, as if she was the one who had been through a flood. She didn't want to eat. I'm going to take a bath, she said; and I didn't see her again until the morning. That was how I got to know Mariam.

Mariam was in the kitchen, grinding cardamom pods in the stone pestle and mortar. That she, too, was wearing a headscarf was the main thing Lucija noticed – a fellow nun – and, also, her sweet face. Skin the colour of Lucija's polished-wood rosary beads from Dubrovnik. The room, a steamy, eye-stinging cauldron of frying and spices. The wooden board on the table, beautiful with its cathedrals of finely sliced onions. In a metal bowl, red lentils were soaking lazily in murky water, like tourists floating in the Adriatic. Lucija stood by the table, smiling, while Mariam tipped spices into hot oil and stood over the stove, stirring. Mariam was busy; she didn't speak; but when at last she glanced at Lucija – oh! – Lucija saw she had big black eyes. Black lashes.

It was only when they started eating supper that they started talking about the places they came from. Mariam was homesick, too, a bit. Quite a lot. She wouldn't speak about the people she loved. Too many tears came into her eyes when Lucija asked about them. She spoke haltingly of the food she ate at home, listed all sorts of delicious things, and how to prepare them. It was hard to make the things she most craved, here in Britain. She had been trying really hard, since coming to Eva's house. Eva was pleased but – Mariam wrinkled her beautiful face, and held up a forkful of the spicy thing she had made with lamb mince and courgette. Something about it wasn't quite right.

'It's delicious,' said Lucija, feeling an all-over tingling that might have been the chilli.

They also talked about the things they had brought with them from their countries. Lucija had brought very little, other than her memories. But Mariam had her brightly coloured clothes, she had the book of poetry her father had given her, and shyly, very shyly, she fetched from her room a carved stone to show Lucija.

'A vagina stone!' Lucija exclaimed, for the pebble was deeply carved with the Neolithic V that Gimbutas had described in the woman-temples along the Danube. Lucija knew about vagina stones from Eva's book. She used to draw them, the Vs, on all her school textbooks.

Luckily, Mariam didn't know the word *vagina*. Instead, she mimed birds flying with her fingers. The birds flew across Eva's kitchen in the colours of Mariam's clothing, orange, and indigo. Suddenly Lucija felt breathless. She felt an electricity inside her.

Oh my God, she thought, help me.

'Yes?' Mariam asked.

'Birds, yes,' Lucija said. 'Maybe.'

'Maybe,' Mariam echoed.

LUCIJA: Eva had offered her a job, teaching her daughter. Mariam had told the doctor she was a teacher because it sounded good. But she wasn't a teacher. Nevertheless, she tried teaching the girl anyway.

ZOE: We had one or two lessons. She told me the four most important things about her country were: *1. Arabic letters are written opposite from English ones, right to left; 2. The Prophet of Islam (PBUH) loved poetry and women; 3. Pakistan's greatest poet is Shah Abdul Latif; 4. The quickest way for women to find freedom is to learn some English.*

MARIAM: Even then, it is not to be expected. And the actual best route to advancement is not to be black like I am. [*Laughs*]

LUCIJA: Soon enough the lessons were forgotten. But by then it was too late: the whole idea had driven Eva's sons crazy.

That night, Lucija took out her phone and typed a message to Omer:

There is a Mevludin in this house. I gazed at it. A Mevludin! It brought back all the things that for sixteen years I have tried to block out, that come back in dreams only, so that I wake in my British bed, with the cold moonlight seeping through the curtains, and turn my head into the pillow to cling on as hard as I can to the sunlight in my head.

She lay quite still in the dark for several hours. Then she wrote to him again:

Oh Omer, a woman has appeared out of the English mist who is unlike me, or any other woman I have known. This woman, there is something which makes me catch my breath. She has a pure soul. I know I can hear you laughing.

At last Lucija pushed back her heavy blankets and walked out on to the landing. Moonlight came through the library windows, and the stair windows, and through the windows along the front of the house. Lucija moved around the house, seeking out the moonlight as it fell on her skin, stopping only when she felt the moon upon her. In this way she felt herself into the other women's dreams, closing her eyes as she saw them, the visions, rising and mingling. The swoop of some beautiful, long-winged white birds; the clatter of cooking pots; the rush of water; the smile of a father. Tigers. A female Buddha. A runaway ship womaned by an all-Bosnian crew. And just once, around dawn, a young man, in a boat, far out at sea. Dreams which took only a few seconds to dream and yet felt like aeons. Long lives lived in seconds. She knew which dreams were which. It was her own dreams she could barely remember. Sometimes, when she woke, she recalled the tinge of things delicious and it scorched her. Kissing; soft skin; long fragrant hair. A love spasm. Inappropriate love for inappropriate people.

Lucija got up again when it was light. Eva, too, rose early. They met in the kitchen, where Eva made them both coffee, in the Bosnian way, in her long-handled copper coffee pot.

LUCIJA: We spoke that morning about Mevludin. You should invite his grandson over here, Lucija, she said to me. I nodded. I couldn't imagine Omer in the islands.
JUDGE: Did Omer come?
LUCIJA: No. I wish he could have met her. She meant nothing to him.

They talked about Mariam.
'She has a vagina stone,' Lucija said.

185

'Yes,' said Eva. 'Just like mine. My father gave me mine, over half a century ago, for safekeeping on my travels.'

'A Yugoslav stone?'

'I don't know. He told me he'd acquired it in Trieste, during National Service after the war. The man who sold it to him, by circular logic a refugee from Tito's new red Yugoslavia, told him it was Roman.'

Eva grew up with this story, as her sons had grown up with hers – the amulet stone lived on a shelf in her father's study in Hampstead – but the modern-day Yugoslavs she met thought it might be older than that. An Illyrian guardian deity, perhaps. A Scordisci demon. Gimbutas, who was working at a dig in Serbia at the time, told her it was Neolithic. There were other such carvings along the Danube, on rocks, and in the structures she called temples. Later, in motherhood, Eva showed it to a friend from university who had gone to work for the British Museum: Probably Roman, the man told her, just a number stone, for counting. Five. A price-tag maybe.

Eva said, 'It's amazing, isn't it, that ancient symbol, here, and in Pakistan, and in Yugoslavia.'

'A women's code,' Lucija said.

Eva glanced at her. 'Exactly. An international network of ideas. That's what we need. A movement that crosses languages and cultures.'

LUCIJA: I tried to tell Omer how wonderful she was to Mariam and me. *Wonderful.* How she was always doing everything at once. She would pull down Bosnian things to show me; start a conversation about Pakistani music, to include Mariam. She tried to include us all in what she was saying or doing, to make connections and make everyone feel at home. I didn't want to leave that morning and go back to the convent.

JUDGE: What about your religious beliefs?

LUCIJA: I always found her very open-minded. So, for example, she spoke to me about the female Pope, who she said was English. From the eighth century, I think. And even if this pope never existed, Eva said, it proved her point, that these islands of Britain have since ancient times been associated with sacred independent

186

women. Why? I don't know. Probably because, at one time, Britain really was at the edge of the known world, and that was the only place where such women could be thought of as existing. Eva and Alice were working on some kind of gynotopia anthology together.

Eva didn't ask Lucija why she had become a nun. She didn't say, was it because of the war? Obviously it was. The war had done strange things to all of their heads. Becoming a nun was the least extreme reaction to what had happened in certain parts of her country, with their now-tragic names.

LUCIJA: I believe I may have said this before but I really think it was her time in my country of Bosnia that gave her such a sharp understanding of how the politics of a place implicates its people, and vice versa. You follow? See, back then, my country wasn't so sad. Back then, my Yugoslavia was an independent republic wedged between Stalin's Soviet Union and the capitalist West, a state that was freer than the East European satellite states, whose citizens, Eva told me, were often better informed about the world than those she had encountered in France or England; a polity linked for geo-political-historical-cultural dimension with Nehru's India and Nasser's Egypt: a self-declared part of the non-aligned Third World. Yes. In my Yugoslavia, Eva saw clearly that politics is not just about economics but also about culture, and that culture isn't a vaguely determined thing: it is actually quite precise. It was this that she set out to prove with regard to her work, here in the islands. She posted an advert in the newspaper's listings column, something like: VOLUNTEERS REQUIRED FOR ARCHIPELAGO LIFE DOCUMENTATION PROJECT.
JUDGE: [*Sigh*] What was that?
LUCIJA: Sister Geraldine knows about it. She was one of the interviewees.

Eva worked with Jen on the Archipelago Life Documentation Project, or Impact Interviews, as she called them for short, throughout Zoe's childhood and adolescence. Every six months, one of them would borrow a camera from college, and tour the islands, interviewing their volunteers for around half an hour each. None of the volunteers ever met each other; none of them were ever told what the interviews were for, beyond the brief paragraph contained on the disclosure form that mentioned a sociological study of archipelago life conducted by the college and overseen by the Chair of Archipelago Women's Studies.

Island people come and go – especially those who move out here from the British mainland – and there are faces in the Impact Interviews which appear once or twice, and then disappear, never to be heard from again. A farmer from Eastray had a heart attack four interviews in; the lady from the delicatessen in Lerston is missing from several of the winter interviews because she liked to visit her sister in Bangalore during December. But there are about twelve regulars over a period of fifteen or so years – Eva's twelve disciples, Jen liked to call them – and the hours and hours of footage are an illuminating portrait of an archipelago changing under the guiding hand of Eva's group of women. The main thing they bring home is how quickly humans adapt; how little the majority of us question the way things are done, the things that are done to us. How necessary it therefore is that somebody, anybody, should ring the changes.

Along with Sister Geraldine, and Lucette, who founded the chocolate factory, there is the tenant farmer from Skellar whom Eva often interviewed during August, on the outlying island of Skalpay, as he sheared the tough breed of sheep he kept there. There's the young school-leaver from Astrid who begins by working in the crab factory, and eventually graduates to ferrywoman on the service between Lerston and Dounsay. There's the mackerel fisherman, happiest on his trawler (they'll be the ones catching fish next, he comments grumpily of women in general, after his niece becomes manager of Lerston Pelagic); the schoolteacher from remote and windy Tarn; the stay-at-home mother from Eastray; the woman who runs Dounsay Dairy; the hippy woman who set up the organic veg-box scheme at Tarbert; the woman from the post office; the Tarn boy who works on a North Sea oil rig and loves the big money he is getting just as much as he comes to hate being apart from his family; and Jonny Brant, originally of Clifton, Bristol, who moved up to Astrid as a boy with his parents when the council was giving away vacant plots of land for free in the 1960s.

Anyone who watches all two hundred or so hours of footage (the tapes are available for viewing at the Islands of Women Foundation Archive) will hear the pride in Eva's voice, as she talks to her interviewees. It is also *almost* possible to hear her shouting – for example, at the farmer from Skellar, who explains that his daughter has gone from an internship at *Archipelago Now* to a job with the *Scotsman* in Edinburgh, and yet, when pressed, puts these opportunities down to the increased amount of meat in the modern island diet – *We did it! We did!*

JUDGE: How did Eva's work change things for you on the islands?
JONNY: On Astrid? It didn't.
JUDGE: You got a community shop?
JONNY: That wasn't anything to do with Eva.
JUDGE: It was set up by—
JONNY: My wife and three other women set it up.
JUDGE: Did they get help? Seed funding, for example?
JONNY: Yes, from a fund called— Can't remember the name.
JUDGE: Archipelago Women in Work?
JONNY: Possibly.
JUDGE: Is the shop going well?
JONNY: Very.
JUDGE: What difference has it made to your life, directly?
JONNY: ... Er. Don't have to go to Aldi in Ayrness?
JUDGE: Who looks after the grand-kids while your wife is in the shop?
JONNY: I do. I do.

During all this time, Eva was scrupulous in keeping up appearances. That is, she remained, to the outside world, the same respectable-looking person as before; she had probably taught a quarter of the island's population by the time she gave up teaching to become deputy principal. Despite the power she wielded, nobody guessed what she was doing, least of all her sons. She remained, until the end, discreet, secretive – a tale that unfolds inwards.

LUCIJA: I believe she worked from behind the scenes. You have to understand this. That's why so many people are ignorant of the changes she helped bring about.

The question of how honourable it was to force through changes to a culture and society without that culture's explicit knowledge and consent has come up repeatedly at the inquiry. These questions have not yet been satisfactorily answered—

STELLA: Nor have the majority of people ever explicitly consented to the patriarchal status quo.

—because they have no satisfactory answer.

LUCIJA: From that first time, I could see that there were many pressures in her life.
JUDGE: What were the pressures?
LUCIJA: Her sons, for example. They rang, one by one, that morning. I had gone for a walk in the garden. Mariam had cooked lunch, it was all ready and prepared. I came into the kitchen. Eva was at the table, her back to me, kneading bread. The phone rang, and she answered it on loudspeaker. That was always how she spoke to people. She just had to press a button, with her hands covered in bread dough, or soap suds. She never sat down, except in her study. I waited at the door, for the conversation to finish, but then the phone rang again, and then a third time.

– Mother, Sebastian tells me you have a Pakistani refugee living with you at the moment.
– Oh, hello, Henry, said Eva. Yes that's right. And a nun, as of yesterday.
– A nun?
– Well, she stayed the night, she's from the convent on Papa Astrid. But I've given her an open invitation to return. She's from Bosnia.
– And the Pakistani?
– Yes?
– Is she a Muslim?

– I should think so, very likely.

– Mother! What are they all doing there all of a sudden? The Pakistani might be an illegal. The Bosnian might be.

– I don't think so. Almost every Bosnian who came here between '92 and '95 was given ILR.

– ILR?

– Indefinite Leave to Remain. You must know that.

(You had to remember, when arguing with your son who was a lawyer, that half of his genes were yours. You were capable of answering in kind.)

– Not my area of law, Mother.

– Well, they had a war on. And I liked her the moment I saw her. Sometimes you can tell how a person is just by looking at them. You can tell how interesting and empathetic they are before they've even opened their mouth.

– Can you? Useful when you don't share a mother tongue.

– Something about the eyes. You know what I'm talking about, Henry. You can *smell* it.

– But what is she doing in the house? Why here? Why Harcourt? Where's the Pakistani sleeping?

– Mariam? In the attic room.

– Sebastian's room?

– He hasn't slept there since he was a teenager, Henry.

– And the Bosnian? Are they both Muslim?

– You're being silly, Henry. Lucija's a nun.

– The Pakistani's a patient of Camille's, George tells me. She'll have an STI, Mother, you must be careful.

– Honestly, Henry. I'm not going to sleep with her.

– *What's she doing living with you?*

– Camille sent her up. I'm employing her to teach Zoe.

– Zoe? Well make sure Sebastian pays. There's no reason why you should.

– Don't be so mean, Henry.

– I'm serious. I absolutely insist.

JUDGE: Why did you and your brothers react so badly to the welcome your mother gave to outsiders?

HENRY: I don't think I reacted badly. My mother's lifestyle concerned

191

me. What we saw was her increasingly eccentric way of giving shelter to utterly random people – wanderers, really – people without responsibilities, without a regular income or home or career, who live on benefits and don't pay any tax.

The phone rang again.

– Mother. At last.

– Hello, George. Have you been trying to get hold of me?

– I've been trying to get hold of Seb and you. Has he spoken to you about Cwen? Your phone's always engaged.

– About Cwen? No.

– Cwen and Harcourt Wood. We're going to go for it. In short, Sebastian says they're changing the planning laws so that councils will be able to give the go-ahead to develop certain greenfield sites, if the council concerned can prove the need, et cetera.

– Is *that* what you were doing up here recently? Somebody told me they'd seen you out on the island.

– We've been thinking about it for a while, now, Mother, the three of us. Now's our moment. It's not yet public, but that's the gist. They're shaking up a lot of inconvenient legislation, cutting red tape, making Britain greener. So the place we could develop, very sensitively, would be just below the clifftop, to the east of the house. As well as Cwen. You wouldn't see either from the house, and we could apply for access over the western side of the hill. Four holiday villas. Cwen as a private island. It's something we haven't exploited at all, as a family. But we should. Seb says half the cabinet go on holiday to the Hebrides. Well, they should come here, instead. People pay for remote. We paid £10,000 a week for a hunting lodge in Scotland. We were fifteen people, but still.

– Absolutely not.

– Please think about it, Mother.

–

– Mother!

GEORGE: We associated everything about Harcourt House with our father, from the attic at the top where she put the Pakistani woman to stay, to the tower in the orchard.

JUDGE: Everything? Even though your mother had lived in the islands for years by then?

Sebastian and his brothers: sitting by the pond at Harcourt, late one night, drinking White Russians. They were drunk, but still. Camille, approaching through the dark. It made her sick, how they spoke to each other out of earshot of their wives.

'That tower, I love it almost more than the house,' Seb was saying. 'Typical, wonderful Dad, having it converted for us.'

'For you!' said Henry. 'He had it done for me.'

'No he *didn't*, Henry,' put in George. 'It was for all of us, our den.'

'Do you remember Seb trying to get in?' Henry said. 'Banging his little fists.'

'Banging girls there later,' said George.

'I was always so happy to be included, I always took the worst part. The Roundhead—'

'The Red Indian.'

'The girl.'

'They found it romantic,' Sebastian said wistfully. 'That tower, like an aphrodisiac. Kissing against the sunset, the view of the islands.'

'Lucky bugger,' said George.

'Is that how you won Camille?'

'Always worked for me until I met her. Quite frankly I think she finds this whole place an utter turn-off.'

'Maybe they don't go in for towers in the same way in France, or wherever.'

'She says not every woman finds phallic symbols liberating.' Sebastian sounded almost surprised as he said it.

'You've always been into quickies in public places, haven't you, Seb?' said George.

'Zoe *was* conceived in a car park,' said Henry.

'A playground,' said George.

JUDGE: Weren't you proud of what she had worked for?
HENRY: Here? In the middle of nowhere? In this nothing place? By definition, she did nothing important, except waste our money.

In Eva's kitchen, the phone rang a third time.

– Hello, Mother.

– Hello, Sebastian, said Eva. Speak of the devil.

– Me?

– George says the Cwen thing is your idea.

– What Cwen thing?

– George says that *this* government, *of which you are a part*, is changing the planning rules to make it easier—

– Mother, did he really say that? I told him, it's not even public yet, he needs to shut up. He'll get me in trouble.

– Well, I'm not developing Cwen or the wood.

– No, of course not, Mother. I know that.

– So. How are you, then? Why are you ringing? Is it about Mariam, Zoe's tutor?

– I wasn't ringing about that, though Henry has sent me at least five texts. He says I must pay for the tuition. How much do I owe you?

– I wasn't going to ask you for money, obviously.

– Henry's insisting. I'll get my secretary to set it up tomorrow. So, about my visit next week—

– You can't make it. Zoe will be so disappointed.

– I *can* make it. The thing is. I've been meaning to ask. It's a piece that one of the Sunday papers are doing; a feature on me in my childhood home. They want to take some photos. Nothing too intrusive, just a few—

– A bleak time in terms of flowers—

– A photographer and an assistant.

– In the garden, not in the house?

– A few internal shots too, I think. Next to some of the family pictures maybe. I'm wondering about the Burne-Jones. Father loved that picture, didn't he?

– *The Sea Nymphs*? Yes, of course. I've got to go now, Seb. Love to Camille and the children.

Eva turned the phone off with a knuckle. She hadn't thought of the Burne-Jones as an asset before. But there it was, hanging right under her nose. She had nothing against Burne-Jones himself but the painting was a bit depressing: three unhappy-looking young women hovering in a chilly-looking sea, clad only in their own long hair, with the island of Cwen in the background, like a seventh bosom. Apparently he'd used island schoolgirls as models, and paid them a pittance. Of course, Burne-Jones himself had been paid almost nothing for the picture; invited up as a young man, by Harry's great-great-grandfather. How much would *The Sea Nymphs* go for today? A million, two?

What Eva knew for a fact was that, even a year ago, Seb would never have agreed to be photographed at Harcourt. Five years ago, he would never have brought a journalist anywhere near his childhood home. In fact, for the majority of his working life, Sebastian had deliberately concealed aspects of who he was. Five years ago, he would have arranged to be interviewed, not in the islands, but in some socially-ambiguous London greasy spoon. It was only since being promoted as junior minister at Defra that a rural profile had become expedient, as it had been for his father before him.

Camille, to her credit, refused throughout to be photographed with Seb. She made this clear from the beginning and, in Eva's opinion, Seb only had himself to blame for presuming that a beautiful, independent-minded woman who happened to be in love with him would eventually bend to his will. Lesser women might have been swayed but Camille was very sure in her sense of her rights as a person. And all the time that Seb was trying to browbeat Camille into appearing with him in public, he was careful never to talk about his family – neither the island summers of his childhood, nor their antique island house, nor his father's time as a minister under Thatcher, nor his daughter Zoe. The only aspect of himself which Seb discussed was his rise within the party, from parliamentary researcher, secretary, backbench MP, to minister. That and a coy but pointed mention of his wife in repeated press interviews. Eva dreaded the impact on Seb's family of his political career. Especially the impact on Camille.

During the late 1980s, when Sebastian's father was heading up the Ministry of Defence, it was a young reporter who had hinted at Harry's fondness for working late into the night with only his parliamentary secretary for company, and also that he had been accompanied by his parliamentary secretary on an official visit to the Royal Ordnance Factory in Lancashire, and furthermore that the minister and his parliamentary secretary took the unusual decision to delay a return to London by staying overnight in Manchester, in order, his office clarified, to pay a personal visit to factory workers in their homes on Saturday morning. These were bitter things to read about one's husband on Sunday morning, alone in the islands – even if what was being implied was no revelation. This same husband had once spoken often of a young, sweet-mouthed breath of fresh air in his office (hair in Eva-imitation curls); until suddenly she was no longer mentioned; except by their pre-pubescent sons, who returned home from a visit to Westminster talking of a nice pretty lady who had bought them each a Sherbet Dip and allowed them to push each other around the office on a wheelie desk chair.

But it wasn't just that. It was also that they had tried, and failed – Jen and she – to make their mark on national politics. Currently, all of the islands' politicians – one from the Scottish constituency, one from the English, and one MSP – were men.

Eva also knew that it was partly cowardice, as well as pragmatism, which had made her efface herself as leader of her own political movement. All the scrutiny, when it came, would fall on Inga. Inga was the one they would shout at, when everything came out in the end, as it certainly would. At least Inga knew this, and understood the risks.

Getting up from the table, Eva saw Sister Lucija, standing in the doorway. She smiled at the nun, covered the bread with a cloth, and carried the bowl over to the sideboard by the sink, where she washed and dried her hands. The room smelt of cardamom and cinnamon; Mariam liked to keep a pot of chai on the hotplate. For Lucija, Eva had ground up some coffee beans extra fine. The house already smelt of Sindh; soon it would also smell of Sarajevo.

'Here,' Eva said to Lucija, taking down a green-and-pink-striped box from the shelf above the sink, and sitting back down at the table, 'you've got a sweet tooth. Lucette's sent me a tester pack of the latest things from the chocolate factory. Each one's imprinted with the face of an epoch-changing woman. They don't list who's who, you have to guess; they change weekly. They digital-print the moulds, and there's a local islands-wide competition. You can win a ... ' She studied the flap of the box. 'I don't know what you win. Mention on the next box maybe. There's obvious people like Virginia Woolf – she has such a good profile for chocolates, like a Roman emperor –' Eva picked Virginia out, and gave her to Lucija '– but also, apparently, locals like Inga, being head of the council.' She stared into the box. 'I'm not sure I'd recognise Inga, if I saw her on a chocolate. Inga, are you there?'

With relief, Lucija saw the quick return of Eva's smile.

'I'm happy with Virginia,' Lucija said. She nodded towards the kitchen window. 'Here comes Mariam.'

'She walks across the lawn and back, every morning,' Eva said, 'to check that the sea is still there, and the sky. I'll try ... oh yes, hello, Epona. The Celtic horse-goddess. Lucette has an equine interest. You know, stables out at her place. A horse called Monarch.' Eva put the pink chocolate in her mouth.

They ate their chocolates in silence, watching as Mariam approached the house.

'She's brave,' Eva said eventually. 'I think being outside actually scares her. But she makes herself do it.'

'She loves the moon,' Lucija said.

Eva's face brightened again. 'Yes, we share that love. She says the moon is on the Pakistani flag. She thinks it should be on ours. We gaze upon it, she and I, as avidly as lunatics.' From the first floor of Harcourt House it was possible to see across to Ayrness Bay, and on clear nights when the moon was full, it cast its light as brightly as a city.

Mariam's face, framed by her headscarf, was so beautiful, Lucija thought.

Cheshire cat-like, thought Eva: her smile, almost disembodied. It was nice having Mariam here with her in the house. When Eva saw Mariam looking out with fresh eyes at the sea, she felt the passing of time as heavily as if it had jumped on her back. She had had fresh eyes, once. Ah yes, all those journeys we make again and again through our minds, those repeated forays they call neural pathways, shadowing the real pathways, through our houses and streets and woods and coasts; the days and years that pass, seconds of opportunity and waste; how long life is, how needlessly expansive. How much Eva had lived before Zoe knew her, or Inga, or Sebastian, or Camille. In the Neolithic, they died at forty. And what they accomplished! And yet everything, almost all the sweetness in her life, had happened after that age. *This, her borrowed time.*

'An Arabian sea nymph,' Eva said to herself as Mariam entered the kitchen.

The young ones come over again, alone. It is daytime.

They approach her spring holding hands, as if they are scared.

Cwen nods. They are right to be scared, though it isn't she who will hurt them. In their free hands they are holding a stick, a wand of what? *Birch*? She laughs. Birch is for shape-shifting. Still. She watches as they circle her spring, and put their heads right in, and take three sacred sips.

Cwen thinks: *I am their forebear. How it is done now is how it will happen in the future.*

They throw sacred metalwork into Cwen's water as an offering: a ring from one finger, a bangle from another. Frowning, they undress.

When they open their hands again, Cwen sees that they have collected ochre from her headland. They have crumbled it into a gravelly powder which they mix with water from the spring. Between their palms, it is a vivid red. They smear each other's faces and bodies with the paste; shoulders and breasts, along ribcage, stomachs and bum cheeks, ulna and radius, tibia and fibulas, up to the ends of their toes and fingers.

It is an old ritual of landright and birthright but Cwen hasn't seen it done by women so young before. They are completely red now, like boiled lobsters. All their solemnity vanishes as they stand back to survey each other's work. They laugh and laugh at each other.

If seawater is her tears,
spring water the mucus of her nose, mouth and cunt,
– this ochre is her blood.

She feels their naked feet moving over her, as they set off for the beach. Two red blurs. They run into the water, knee deep, thigh deep, breast deep, neck deep. They have vanished. When they emerge again from the sea, the birthright colour is dripping off them. The cold water raises bumps on their skin—

She can see through their skin to their blood and their bones. Oh, she would protect them from harm, if she could. She watches as they lie on their backs on the sand, cleaned of ochre, side by side, squinting up at the sun. She whispers in their ears, to see if they can hear her, like the girl can.

Her breath ruffles their hair.

One of them puts her hand up to her cheek, as if to brush away a fly.

But of the words themselves, they hear nothing.

Fatigued, even angered, Cwen raises a tempest and calms it again in a beat. The girls, lying on the sand, haven't even noticed.

Cwen thinks of the child, now almost a woman. It is time to call her in.

So they rode tyll they com to a laake that was a fayre watir and brode. And in the myddis Arthure was ware of an arme clothed in whyght samyte, that helde a fayre swerde in that honde.

'Lo,' seyde Merlion, 'yondir ys the swerde that I spoke off.'
So with that they saw a damesell goynge uppon the laake.
'What damoysel is that?' said Arthur.
'That is the Lady of the Lake,' seyde Merlion. 'There ys a grete roche, and therein ys as fayre a paleyce as ony on erthe, and rychely besayne. And thys damesel woll com to you anone, and than speke ye fayre to hir, that she may gyff you that swerde.'

Thomas Malory, *Le Morte d'Arthur* (English), 1485

I don't know whose fault it was, mine, yours, or Raphael's, but we never thought of asking, and he never thought of telling us whereabouts in the New World Utopia is ... For one thing, it makes me feel rather a fool, after all I've written about the island, not to know what sea it is in. For another, there are one or two people in England who want to go there.

Thomas More, *Utopia* (Latin), 1516

9

Stella

The press fell in love with Stella and Tara during the inquiry.

JUDGE: Are you responsible for the website, PatriarchyPantsDown.com?
STELLA: No.
JUDGE: Are you aware of the website to which I refer?
STELLA: Yes.
JUDGE: The IP address is the server at Ayrness High School.
STELLA: Er, there are, like, seven hundred pupils at the school, and fifty members of staff?
JUDGE: What is your opinion of the site?
STELLA: [*Sighs*] Actually, we think this kind of stunt is of limited value, in the real world. We think there are other, more sympathetic ways for the sisterhood to address those kinds of troubles. [*Pause*] But at least the pictures were heavily pixellated.
JUDGE: This was the kind of ethos that was allowed to develop at school?
STELLA: No, I wouldn't say that.

Since the inquiry opened, a mainland company has begun selling T-shirts printed with Stella's vulva tattoo. When Tara announced that 'Climate Change is MAN-made', her statement was turned into a rap by an artist, DJV, which has had 609,785 views on

YouTube. Both young women have had several dozen men offer to rape them.

JUDGE: Can you elaborate, please, on the programme of feminist classes that was put in place while you were at the school?

STELLA: Well, apart from the Monday morning lectures for the boys, and the bonding sessions for the girls, everything else was strictly optional.

JUDGE: What were the options?

STELLA: Every Wednesday morning Inga Stenbridge came in to host a Female Power workshop—

(Eight a.m., the islands still dark, the trees dripping with mist, the schoolgirls chanting, *We women: beautiful women, strong women, hurt women, powerful women.*)

STELLA: —and during Thursday assemblies there were lectures. But no prescribed topics.

JUDGE: What might those topics have included?

STELLA: For example, Mx Thompson gave a very useful assembly on contraception.

JUDGE: You mean, the lecture called 'How to Pin it All on Women: The Sexist Basis of Western Contraception'?

STELLA: That's right. And on Fridays there was girls' kung fu.

SOLICITOR: [*Whispers*]

JUDGE: It has been brought to my attention, more than once, indeed there have also been online rumours, and some islanders have been telling members of the press that you were encouraged to hold ... Vulva Viewings?

STELLA: [*Laughs*] Men have been saying all kinds of things, recently. But, no. Not actual vulvas. Only my tattoo.

The day Stella got it done – the vulva tattooed in green between her shoulder blades – her father said to her, 'What's that triangle? A bird?'

'It's a vulva, Dad,' Stella explained. (Very patient daughter.)

Her father said: 'It looks like a child's drawing of a bird.' And warming to his theme: 'A bird shitting. That *other* thing, child, is down below; you think you're likely to forget?' And thinking he was really being witty now: 'Is that what this is, a reminder?'

'I don't need a reminder,' Stella said, squinting a little as she tried to look at her tattoo, which was effectively in her blindspot, and experiencing (it is true) the thrill of the novelty intermixed with an atavistic sense of horror. She was standing at the window of the flat; sunlight came in, warming, but only barely, her bare back. Down below, in the street, shoppers were passing by muffled in coats and hats and scarves; it was winter, after all. She saw the tall Bosnian nun, sweeping along in her bright green ankle-length tweed dress, and with her, another little dash of colour, pink and yellow amidst the British blue and grey, the Pakistani teenager.

'It's Neolithic,' Stella said, and pulled on the coat that was lying over the kitchen chair. 'The Neolithic people carved them on their altars.'

'Oh well, that's different,' her father said. 'I can see that has some validity. What are you getting at, though?'

'Don't you know yet?' Stella asked, and pranced out, leaving the conversation at that.

'Get us some vulva paper, I mean bog roll, while you're out,' her father shouted after her, just before she banged the front door, just to have the last word.

Stella lived on the main shopping street in Ayrness, a short walk from the tattoo parlour in one direction, and Rowan and Inga's in the other. Neither of them would have got a tattoo, even at her age. They were too wary of what the old guard thought. Only her generation was truly free. It was a new age; she was sure of it. Tara had had it done first, on her ankle. Hers looked a bit like the islands' flag. Tara's mother, Amrita, got the idea after going to the Archipelago Women's Club where Vs were part of the branding. Stella's V was both more Neolithic, being bigger, and more explicit, seeing as there was no mistaking it. It was not unlike those cowrie shells people wore which were only obviously vulvas if you were minded to be lewd. The 'thing' of seventeenth-century parlance, Mx Thompson said.

By the time she got down to the street, the nun and the Pakistani were standing outside M&Co. Skintight jeans were still in fashion, bejewelled with sparkling plastic blobs; rows and rows of them, down either leg. Neither the Bosnian nun nor the Pakistani teenager seemed like potential customers but they were enjoying the perusal, smiling as they gazed into the shop window, their glances meeting in their reflections. The yellow and pink fringe of Mariam's headscarf trembled as she laughed. The soft black shoe of the nun nudged the blue spotted welly-boot of the other; their fingers – *oh little silver darlings*, Stella thought, *they're holding hands.*

Stella was prepared for this meeting. In her coat pocket she had the texts, printed out double-sided on recycled paper. For Mariam, a series of points summarising the established academic theory that the rise of the worship of Allah had historically co-opted and suppressed the pre-existing matriarchal religion of the goddess Al-Lat. For the nun, edited extracts from various female mystics. Stella had given all the male pronouns new grandeur and meaning by the simple addition of an extra S. Plus bits from the Bible. She wasn't a Christian but she felt the need to defend this book for its rare moments of female solidarity. It was Stella's grandmother who had spoken to her of Ruth and Naomi: how, after Naomi's husband and sons died, her daughter-in-law Ruth stayed with her, and there was famine and they became gleaners. Stella had read out this passage at the last gathering on Cwen, to the surprise of the other women, who were totally allergic to patriarchal texts. *And Ruth said, Intreat me not to leave thee … for whither thou goest, I will go; and where thou lodgest, I will lodge: thy people shall be my people, and thy God my God: Where thou diest, I will die, and there will I be buried.*

This is our heritage, Stella had argued, we have to use it.

– And God to Jeremiah! How mystic was that? *Before I formed you in the womb, I knew you.* She would turn it into a song, before the winter was out.

She'd pasted the words from the Book of Ruth and Book of Jeremiah at the top of the papers she'd put together for Sister Lucija. She would offer to send somebody to pick them up; the meeting was tonight. She would warn them to dress warmly; the island got cold very quickly after dark. The mannequin's jeans, she saw as she approached, had little rips all the way up the thigh, on either side of the studs.

JUDGE: Did it work? Did they come?

STELLA: [*Scowls*] No. [*Pause*] I wanted to invite Zoe instead but Inga said, *Not yet.* Apparently she wasn't ready.

Zoe wasn't ready partly because she was struggling socially at school. Pauline and Kath, her best friends ever since Reception, felt jilted now that she'd joined the Green Club and consequently were being mean to her. Stella and Tara could see what was going on, and they did their best to compensate. Since Ravi seemed interested in educating Zoe in matters to do with the environment, Tara gave them the task of organising logistics for the Green Club camping trip. For a start, Barbara Anderson at the museum café, where Zoe worked weekends, would need to be told. Stella wanted them to think about how to recruit more young men to the cause. Pauline and Kath liked that even less.

'What about that Ravi, then?' said Pauline.

'What about him?'

They stared at her.

'It's not like *that*,' she said.

'What *is* it like, then?' asked Kath, her face hard.

'It's ...'

She went round to Ravi's after school. They got the bus out of Ayrness together, sitting side by side at the back. Unlike her, Ravi seemed completely at ease. 'Here, listen to this,' he said, and gave Zoe one of his earphones. 'She's Irish, Lisa O'Neill, it's a song about a man who murdered women, being murdered himself.' They listened to the silky deep of her voice – 'Along the North Strand' – the song's ancient thrill. 'Maybe you could sing it at one of the gatherings on Cwen.'

'I haven't been to any gatherings on Cwen,' Zoe said. 'What happens at them?'

'I haven't been either,' said Ravi. 'You'll have to ask S&T. They go.'

'What do they get up to?' This close she could smell him; sunshine and salt, Cwen's smell; the thrill of walking over that wild island.

'It's a secret,' Ravi said. 'I think they give each other support. Discuss things.'

The sun was setting and the ancient cairn, protected and cut off by the sea, was illuminated by the secret meaning it had guarded for so long; that tangible piece of human magic. Ravi took a picture of Zoe in profile looking out at Cwen, and sent it to her. Zoe felt shyer and more pleased than ever.

They got down at the bay, and Ravi led her along the coastal path to his family's plot. It was two caravans stuck together, with a huge oak tree overhead whose branches tapped against the fogged-up windows. He said, 'My mother's making chard-dolma again. I hope you like it. She grows the chard herself. She's got a space in the Ayrness allotment. She gathers all kinds of wild food too, sea beet and mussels and seaweed. Round here, they think she's a witch.'

Ravi's mother smiled at them when they came in. She'd tied her hair up in a flowered headscarf while doing the cooking. Who's your friend, Raymond? she asked him in Turkish. From Green Club, said Ravi. He showed Zoe where to leave her shoes. They sat side by side again in the cooking fug of his caravan kitchen, facing the big window with its steamed-up view out over the sea. We're working on the details of the camping trip, Ravi told his mum. His father came in, still in his fish-farm overalls, nodded to the kids, and went straight into the bathroom to shower off the fish stink. We're trying to work out how to recruit more young men, Ravi went on. In English, he added, 'We need a strategy. They want us to be educated into the kind of boys they want to be friends with.'

His mother said, Raymond, how old is she?

Almost sixteen, Ravi said.

'You're already a boy I want to be friends with,' said Zoe, without thinking. She blushed.

Ravi smiled at Zoe, pleased and amused. A big smile.

His mother said to him, No dick, you understand? Fingers and tongue only, until she comes of age.

He grimaced at her. Yes, mother, I know.

'Maybe we need an initiation ceremony,' Zoe was saying, her face still hot. She mimed slicing her arm with a knife. 'Some tribes in the desert cut their boys at puberty, so that they bleed, like girls, I learnt that in girls' assembly. Mx Thompson said so.'

'All the extra attention you get, as women,' said Ravi. 'Maybe boys need that.'

'What attention?' Zoe said. 'We don't get any attention.'

'Your periods,' said Ravi. 'We don't have a dramatic watershed moment. Maybe attention is the wrong word.'

Zoe felt all the blood that should have been draining from her womb, but wasn't, rushing to her face.

His face was mischievous and joyous.

Fingers and tongue only, Raymond, repeated his mother.

RAVI: I became friends with Stella and Tara because I didn't want to be a man like that.

JUDGE: Like what? Like Turkish men?

RAVI: I hardly know any Turkish men. Stell & T let me be myself. These men who've been going crazy; it's hard for them, giving up a power which they only just discovered isn't their god-given right.

'Have you got any selfies with you and that ... Ravi?' said Kath.

Zoe shook her head. She felt shy about showing them the picture Ravi had taken.

'God, you're useless,' said Kath.

'You've got Green Club today, haven't you? Get one then, OK?'

'OK,' said Zoe. But already she hated her friends for berating her.

Zoe looked out for Ravi in the school corridors, and in the yard, and in the streets around school.

'Hey, Zoe,' he said to her, as he passed.

'Hey, Ravi,' she said to him; as she wondered, with hot shame, what it would be like if they had sex.

CAMILLE: One night that autumn, sitting in the kitchen in London, the children in bed, Sebastian confided something in me. His brothers wanted to develop the island of Cwen.

'Under what law can they do that?' Camille said.

Sebastian poured a glass of wine. 'They wouldn't need to chop down the entire wood: some of the trees are an asset in property terms. But a lot of them would have to go.' He got up and began drying plates from the sink.

Then: 'I played in that wood as a child.'

'The one where we ... ?'

209

He nodded.

One of the al fresco fucks they used to favour was under an oak tree. There was silence, each thinking their own thoughts. It was quite corrupt, she felt, to cut down an old wood for profit, particularly when your job was lecturing other people – other countries even – on the importance of preserving forests. And there it was: the problem with the British. The British type of corruption was just more subtle than the rest. Their corruption had laws to uphold it. 'All the things you're saying about British colonialism, you could say for ancient Britain too,' Seb had said with his infuriating calm in the midst of one of their early discussions about Africa. 'Only, we don't complain about the Romans. Or the Vikings. Or the Normans.'

Camille looked out of the window into the street-lamp-lit London night, and saw the ghost of a Roman legion tramping across the lawn. She detested how flippant her husband could be.

Seb filled the empty pasta pot and began to scrub it.

Then:

'I think my brother George may have money problems.'

JUDGE: Please confirm your full name.

JIM: James Anthony Mills.

JUDGE: You taught geography at Ayrness High.

JIM: I'm asking for my job back, now that Miss Thompson has been suspended.

JUDGE: You recently gave an interview to BBC *Look North* complaining of the feminist agenda of some of the female teachers there. It's also something that you mention in your witness statement.

JIM: That's right. At the time I didn't know there was an actual agenda but I knew something was up. We were mistreated, the boys and I.

JUDGE: Can you detail some of the things you consider miscarriages of justice?

JIM: Our views were never listened to, in staff meetings. I don't think the things we said were ever written down. We were interrupted constantly. I've put in a Freedom of Information request because I think we were paid less than female members of staff of an equivalent pay grade. It happened with the collusion of the council.

JUDGE: The female staff who you say were paid more, did they have special skills?

JIM: I doubt it. I don't think so.

JUDGE: And amongst the students?

JIM: The female students tended to avoid me. Other male members of staff would say the same.

JUDGE: Did any male students come to you with complaints of mistreatment, discrimination?

JIM: No, but that's only because they didn't realise.

JUDGE: How would you describe the culture among female members of staff?

[*Pause*]

JIM: Yeasty.

PUBLIC GALLERY: [*Laughter*]

Zoe didn't tell her mum where the Green Club was camping. The original plan was up on the common overlooking Astrid, but that had been changed at the very last minute. Apparently there was a weather front coming in, and the common was too exposed. It was Ravi who'd suggested Harcourt Wood. I'm sure my grandmother won't mind, Zoe said, but I'll ask her just in case. And the others nodded.

In the end, the weather held, in a manner of speaking. No storms, although it rained on and off, as the wind moved the weather through. Enthusiastically, the Green Club explored the wood. They communed with the trees. The great old oak on the boundary with the North Field was centuries old, its wide, comfortable trunk covered with little twigs, like stubble on a scruffy man's chin, or hair on an emancipated woman's leg. Zoe pointed out rabbit holes to her friends, and gave them wood sorrel to taste, a tangy shot of lemon. They listened to the birds sing. For supper they ate sorrel with potatoes, which, since they had forgotten a knife, they cut into pieces with their teeth, then fried with eggs. 'Gross,' said Ravi, looking at the shreds of premasticated raw tattie. 'It'll be delicious,' said Stella, stirring it around in the pan with a stick. It was pretty good; and afterwards, as Stella played the fiddle, and the others washed up, they shared out Ravi's only packet of Minstrels.

The girls were camping in one tent, Ravi alone in another. Will you be OK? they asked him, mostly as a joke. You won't be scared? Or cold? By yourself? He scowled at them, and ducked inside his tent and that was the last they heard of him for the night.

In their tent, side by side in the dark, the girls talked about trees, about the things Mx Thompson had told them.

'How beautiful this wood is,' Stella said.

'The pride of the islands,' said Tara.

'My dad loves this wood,' said Zoe. This was a true fact because Eva had told her.

At the thought of her father, Zoe felt a familiar intermingling of anxiety and love. She had eavesdropped on more than one conversation between her father and her uncles. They had come up, the three of them, without warning Eva. Eva was at college when they got to Her House. But Zoe was there, always hanging on her relatives' words. George, who had visited earlier in the year too, spent another hour up at the wood, pacing around. And later that afternoon, as Zoe was finishing her essay on why George Eliot took a man's name, and only called one of her novels (the least popular) after a woman, she heard George's voice, and Henry's, clear and authoritative and bossy, and her father's, coming back muffled, the discomfort evident, below in the hall. Zoe, unseen at the table near the window, forever savouring her relatives' exotic worlds.

'When is he up next?' asked Tara.

'He's coming up to the islands soon,' Zoe said. 'The weekend after.'

'Is he?' said Tara.

'Are you sure?' said Stella.

'Pretty sure,' Zoe said.

JUDGE: What were you after?

STELLA: What else? Knowledge.

That night in the tent, Zoe asked through the dark, 'What do you two talk about in Female Bonding?' For she knew that Tara and Stella had paired up.

'It's private,' Stella said.

'Do you have boyfriends?'

'Boyfriends?' said Stella. 'Boyfriends? No, I don't *think* so.'

Zoe wondered, as she lay there, if she was supposed to know that Stella's sarcasm was because Tara and she were lesbians, as Pauline and Kath had said, or were ideologically opposed to boyfriends, as seemed likely, or too busy, which was plausible, or because they just had casual sex. She was still wondering these things when she woke in the morning to a bleep, a text from Ravi:

Awake?

She glanced round at the other two. Tara was snoring. Stella was asleep with her arms clutched around her pillow. Zoe unzipped the tent to let out their night-long breath, and to breathe in a stream of wintery fresh air, over her face, into her nostrils and lungs. The air told her how lovely the day already was, and the wood, and these islands, and her friends. Ravi's tent rustled open. When she looked up, blinking in the sunlight, she could see just the outline of him. He knelt down in a blur.

'Got to go and help my dad with the house. I left the papers they wanted, and the T-shirts. Blue rucksack, in my tent. I'll come back to pack up the tent later. OK?'

'OK,' Zoe said.

He frowned at her. 'Don't let them boss you, all right?' He lifted her hand to his lips.

Was that a kiss? As he walked away across the wood, getting smaller and smaller, she held the fingers he had touched up to her cheek – they felt hot. Too agitated to lie still any longer, she got out of her sleeping bag and stood barefoot in the wet grass between the tents, to salute the sun through the trees, as she had been taught at school. She flicked an ant off the half-remaining blueberry muffin from yesterday and ate it. She looked up through the leaves at the sun. Then she went to Ravi's tent. He had already put away his clothes and his sleeping bag. On the roll mat by the door was a bag. Inside was a stack of papers. There was a typed sheet, decorated with green star stickers. *This is the scandal of today: Coalition's Wanton Ecocidal Nonsense! CWEN! Consolidate Women's Environment Now! CWEN! Come Women Engage Now! CWEN!* Further down in the bag were some large folded sheets – banners. Zoe unfolded one. CWEN, it read, in big green, red and yellow letters—

JUDGE: You smuggled it all into the house that day?

STELLA: [*Smiles*] Operation CWEN. To begin with, yes, Zoe was partly a useful way to access her grandmother and her father; but she soon became one of us.

'Now,' said Stella, when she had woken up, peed, and forked the last of last night's baked beans into her mouth, 'before we get on to today's true business, I want you both to know that I'm going to apply for university after all, even though it's really mainland and corrupt. I think I'll be able to teach them something.'

'Of course you will,' said Tara.

'Let's go swimming to celebrate,' Zoe said. 'It's high tide, so it'll be full of seaweed—'

She could see the disbelief on their faces.

'You access the divine in cold seawater,' she said.

'Arguably not,' said Tara.

But Zoe led them down the steep path to the beach. The tide was in, as she had said it would be, and as soon as her feet touched the sand, she pulled off her pyjamas, tied her curly seaweed hair up in a band, and pushed herself out into the sea, through the fronds of brown bladderwrack, which tickled her skin as she swam through them.

The other two followed her with shrieks. Tara dipped her head below the water and came up bellowing. Stella swam towards Zoe. 'I love it,' she said happily, her eyes golden.

They ran up and down on the sand to get warm.

Back at their encampment, the girls packed everything up. Then they sat under the oak tree in the drizzle, looking out at the sea, where there was a rainbow over Cwen, as Tara rolled long joints, and Stella played them her new God-womb composition. They smoked the joints with a lot of giggling, letting Zoe have a little puff. She felt a pleasant drifting-apart of her body and her head.

'It's mandrake leaf,' Tara said. 'Ravi's mum gets it for us.'

'So,' Stella said, after a long, even more drifty silence, 'you said you wanted to introduce us to your grandmother.'

'Did I?' said Zoe. Had she? She didn't remember having said that. Maybe she had.

'After having camped on her land,' said Stella.

'Oh, yes.' Zoe tried to imagine how a meeting with Eva might go. It might go nicely.

'Can we please go there now?' said Tara.

Zoe didn't normally invite her secondary schoolfriends back to her grandmother's house. It was private, away from school, away from the other islanders she didn't quite belong to. On the other hand, it was eleven o'clock already. Saturday mornings were when women from the islands dropped in, to see Eva, which meant that she was always at home, but you never knew who else might be there, too.

'I don't know if she's in,' Zoe said.

'But it's open house on Saturdays,' Tara said.

'Not since Mariam arrived,' Zoe said. 'Mariam is from Pakistan and—'

'We know about Mariam,' said Stella.

'The floods there are happening because we are causing climate change here,' said Zoe.

'Very likely,' said Stella. 'Well, let's go and meet her.'

'Let's go right now,' said Tara.

'It's unpredictable,' said Zoe. 'She might be there, she might not—'

'We'll risk it,' said Stella.

They walked down through the wood towards the house. When they emerged from the trees, into the field, and saw the house below them, Stella and Tara both said, at the same moment, 'Wow.'

Zoe felt a thrill of pride but also embarrassment at the extravagance of this island mansion. She had a sudden vision of the house being rebuilt, stone by stone, by women.

'It's going to be such a great resource,' said Stella.

'My Granny Ruth doesn't like it,' Zoe said. 'She says it's over the top and exploitative.'

'She's probably right,' said Tara.

They walked across the field.

'She might be in her study,' Zoe said. 'Wait here, I'll find out.'

Zoe hardly ever entered Eva's study. Even Marcin, the cleaner, never touched the desk, or emptied the wastepaper bin. While Tara and Stella unburdened themselves of their rucksacks in the porch, Zoe tapped on the study door.

'Yes?'

'It's me, I'm here with my friends, Stella and Tara, they want to say—'

'Go through to the kitchen. I'll join you there. Zoe, will you make the tea? There are biscuits.'

In the kitchen, Zoe moved around the room she knew so well as slowly as if she was underwater. She lifted the kettle, filled it under the tap, washed the teapot, measured out the tea leaves, each movement self-conscious. She felt a bubble of excitement; Stella and Tara, at ease, were chatting to Eva about how great the camping was, and how kind it had been of Eva, and soon they were making her laugh with a tale of the horrendous food at Ayrness High.

'Of course, under the new regime Food Avoidance is totally taboo,' Tara said. 'So however bad the food is we're stuck with it? In case it looks like we're going anorexic which is what happens to schoolgirls where masculine culture is allowed to dominate? Over there, over the water, girls make themselves sick just because the porn-advertising-capitalist nexus has made them want to look different from how—'

'How's it all going at the school?' asked Eva.

'Mx Thompson has brought in some great new classes,' said Tara.

'What are your favourites?'

Stella and Tara listed them.

'That's marvellous,' said Eva. 'And the counselling?'

'I love it,' said Stella.

'Is an hour's session every term enough, though?' Eva asked.

'Just about,' said Tara. 'To establish the major themes of our personal epic.'

'I'm glad,' Eva said. 'And are they helping you decide what to study at university? That's important too, you know.'

Stella scowled. 'I looked up English literature courses at all these mainland universities and it's like, they're totally obsessed with Shakespeare? Er, haven't you noticed that unfortunately for the subsequent course of civilisation, he forgot to write good female parts? Mx Thompson says over there he's seen as the pinnacle of Western art! I actually *wept* upon making this discovery.' She flung her arms out. 'O, womankind! O, twenty-first century!'

Eva laughed. 'What's Rowan Thompson like, as a teacher?'

'I have counselling with them,' Tara said. 'We need to examine each day as it goes by, you know? And make sure we aren't letting things happen that shouldn't. The counselling is there to help us mediate that process.'

'Eva,' said Stella, 'we know that you want to keep it all quiet. But just to let you know that *we* want to make some things really clear, in our own way. We feel like, we just can't wait any longer.'

'I know,' Eva said. 'But just be patient. Nobody's going to want to hear that they're in the wrong, are they? Hearing you talk like that makes me scared.'

'So far it's just the parents at school,' said Stella. 'Some of the dads don't like it. Mx Thompson gets complaints.'

'Collateral damage,' said Tara, nonchalantly.

'Please, we must all be very careful,' said Eva. 'We've kept it quiet until now for a reason.'

JUDGE: She supported you. But she was nervous.
STELLA: She had done it secretly, all this time, I guess is why.

'Let's go out on the roof, shall we?' Tara said, after Eva had gone back to her study.

'The view must be amazing,' said Stella.

'It's winter!' said Zoe. She had been out on to the roof, once, with Eva, years ago, to clear the gutters. You had to climb through a hatch in the attic bedroom, crawl along the beams, unlatch a skylight, and push your way out on to the balustrade, without falling through the insulation to the bedrooms below. The house was three storeys high. From up there, the drop was dizzying. But suddenly Zoe felt like she could probably fly if she needed to.

'*Have* you been out on the roof?' asked Tara.

'Once,' Zoe said, doubtfully; but her friends were all delight.

'Let's do it.'

'I bet you can see Cwen from up there too.'

They waited impatiently as she put the ladder in position and pushed up the hatch. Zoe went first. She could feel the pulse of her blood through her arms and legs. There was a whispering in her ears which was probably the elevation. She called down to the others, 'Come on,' her voice sounding, even to her, very distant. She crept along the beam towards the skylight, and, when she pushed it open, found they were right in the middle of the roof. They crawled out and sat back against the tiles. The sun came out, lighting up the islands in the distance. The expanse of it was glorious.

'It's like being on a magic carpet,' said Stella. 'Look at the birds!'

'The sea, our islands,' said Tara. 'Here we are, above everything—'

'All-powerful,' said Stella.

'Poised in a moment of change,' said Tara.

'It's raining over there, now, look,' said Stella. Her nose stud flashed in the sunlight.

'Where's Cwen?' asked Tara.

'The other way,' Zoe said. 'You can see her if you stand. Hold on.'

She put out a hand and Tara held it as she reached up to look over the roof to the island.

'*No way,*' Tara said, as she sat down again. 'Our Cwen.'

The three of them sat with their eyes closed, feeling the sunshine and wind on their skin.

'*Mashallah,*' said Zoe, quoting Mariam.

'When does your father arrive again?' said Stella.

Zoe's eyes opened. 'Next weekend,' she said, and felt nervous, as she always did, when thinking of Sebastian. 'What are you planning?' she said. 'I saw the banners Ravi had.'

'We need to act,' Stella began.

'To protest,' added Tara.

'I know,' Zoe said, sadly. 'They're such dicks.'

She lay back against the roof and looked up at the clouds. *Cwen; Sebastian. Sebastian; Cwen.* She shut her eyes, and felt herself being lifted up on her thoughts, away from the wrangling of her uncles, as she swooped with feathered arms right up over the islands, gliding on the warm air currents. She could see Cwen's chambered cairn; the stone door had been propped open. Sunlight was flooding into that cold stone space. She swooped down into the chamber. On the back wall, in the darkest spot, where the sunlight hit, were the ancient carvings.

She wasn't sure how much time had passed when she opened her eyes again. She was lying in Tara's lap. Stella and Tara were staring down at her.

'You were singing,' Tara said.

Zoe closed her eyes again. She felt the shudder of the cairn's coldness, as her fingers traced the V-symbol.

'Cwen was telling me to go there.'

The fifteenth year. Cwen's doing.

They are coming over together, just the two of them. The woman, whose muscles are not as strong as they once were, is easily tired, and this time it is the girl who is rowing. How long has it been? she asks her grandmother, and the old woman looks worried. Too long, a year? Nine months?

Six, seven months, the girl says, we came at spring equinox, remember?

Why didn't you want the others to come? the old woman asks, and the girl shakes her head. Just you and me this time.

It has worked too well. Cwen stretches a little, feels them becoming each other, feels her becoming them. Who is who? Whose eye is this, whose hand, whose brain, whose voice? Between the three of them, things are blurring.

When they get to her island, they sit idly on the beach for a while, chatting. Cwen doesn't bother listening. It is love talk, mindless and relaxing. But after a while, the girl says something; and abruptly, the laughter stops. Her grandmother looks angry. She picks up sand in her hands, lets it fall through her fingers, gesticulates across the water to the great dark mass of the hill, and again, behind them, to Cwen's island. The girl nods. The woman hugs the girl to her. Cwen sees the woman's tears fall.

Eventually, they get to their feet; but slowly, as if they are weighed down by something. They walk up, hand in hand, to Cwen's spring. The woman is still upset by whatever the girl has told her. But they drink Cwen's waters from their metal cup, and smile at each other. We put that cup there, the girl says. Remember?

In the afternoon, they walk all over the headland, collecting ochre.

Cwen watches them as they gather the practical magic in baskets. Moved by their efforts, she leans over and kisses them both, wishing them courage. Only the girl feels her kiss.

She feels the girl's sharp intake of breath as they look at each other.

What are you doing? the woman asks, straightening up from her work, and catching sight of her grandchild standing upright in the gorse, still and tense as a deer, smelling the air. Graceful as the apple tree by the spring, she thinks.

The girl turns to her. Time to go back, she says.

———

The wandring Islands . . .
Where many Mermayds haunt, making false melodies . . .
There, whence that Musick seemed heard to bee,
Was the faire Witche her self now solacing,
With a new Lover, whom through sorceree
And witchcraft, she from farre did thither bring . . .
But all those pleasant bowres and Pallace brave,
Guyon *broke downe, with rigour pittilesse;*
Ne ought their goodly workmanship might save
Them from the tempest of his wrathfulnesse,
But that their blisse he turn'd to balefulnesse:
Their groves he feld, their gardins did deface . . .
And of the fairest late, now made the fowlest place.

Edmund Spenser, *The Faerie Queene*, London, 1590

His mother was a witch, and one so strong
That could control the moon, make flows and ebbs,
And deal in her command without her power . . .
You'd be king o'the isle, sirrah?

William Shakespeare, *The Tempest*, London, 1612

Though I be
A princess, and by that prerogative stand free . . .
Because no power above can examine me;
Yet . . . many wandering eyes upon my ways,
Being left alone a sea-mark, it behoves me
To use a little caution, and be circumspect.

John Fletcher, *The Island Princess*, London, c.1621

10

Nina

WOMEN: *Thank you, Nina. We really appreciate the effort you have made to get here this evening, to talk to us here on Cwen.*

NINA: *No problem.* [Pause] *It's a bit weird.* [Pause] *Can I smoke?*

WOMEN: *Yes, of course.*

[Nina takes out a cigarette]

WOMEN: *So, we wanted to ask you what you thought of Eva's work?*

NINA: [Click of lighter] *At the college?*

WOMEN: *Well, the effort she spent on securing female leadership.*

NINA: [Drag, exhale] *Sorry, what?*

WOMEN: [Sigh] *The women at the museum, the council. You know.*

NINA: [Drag, exhale. Smoke ring]

WOMEN: *She was fighting for a better world?*

NINA: [Tap, drag, exhale] *She was?*

WOMEN: *Because of Zoe, your daughter.*

NINA: *Because of Zoe?* [Stubs out the half-smoked cigarette on a rock; pockets butt] *Sorry – I'm trying to smoke less.*

WOMEN: *Well?*

NINA: *Er, no, I don't think so.*

Unusually, for an islander, Nina Brock had very little talent for gossip. Gossip washed back and forth across the islands as sure as the tide coming out and in; you could throw a plastic bottle of tittle-tattle overboard while crossing from Ayrness to Dounsay – *young Stella Armitage has got herself a feminist tattoo* – and be sure that, six days later, it would wash up in Lerston Sound (Stella's great-aunt, unfortunately informed of this violation by young Zoe Brock, the waitress, while enjoying her monthly outing to the Golden Oldies lunch club at the museum).

Nina had no online life; no smartphone, no Facebook. Of course, she heard things, while rolling out pastry in the production room, or serving customers in the shop, and sometimes those things did concern goings-on at Harcourt House, or the latest thing that Eva was up to in college. But Nina herself had no interest in matching names to faces; was not turned on by the excited pitch of other people's voices; had no taste for the power accrued by acquiring and disseminating slightly inaccurate, sensational information. And thus when Alice, Eva's amanuensis, came in that October to buy a dozen Halloween doughnuts, topped with a meringue ghost ('I've heard they've won awards,' she said brightly; adding, anxiety rolling in like fog, 'the meringue isn't made with raw eggs, is it?'; and of course it wasn't, and of course anybody else could've told at once that she was pregnant); or Barbara tripled the museum's order for bobbit (a fact worth immediately sharing with one's colleagues); or Jen Mackae, who never normally graced the premises (her husband, Alan, did the big weekly supermarket stint with the children), stopped by asking for some sourdough – 'Eva's getting into it,' she said with a roll of her eyes – Nina did nothing with the opportunities. She certainly had no more interest in *sourdough* than she had any notion of making social capital from random bits of island news. She would twist shut a bag of iced buns, and hand over the change, and turn with a polite nod to the next customer, her face not exactly placid as custard – custard-tart like, it intimated wrinkles of worry – but you could be sure she wasn't listening to the chat. Who knew what Nina was thinking? Zoe had no idea; nor did Ruth. It's probably fair to say that nobody else ever stopped to wonder. But Zoe loved her mother.

Cant pick u up today going to dock

OK, Mum. What's wrong?

Nofing. I watered yr basil it was really wilty

Thanks, what about the tomatoes?

Shore Im busy tonite will do it tomora

I'll help you.

Theyr green

Mum, when did you have your first boyfriend?

! Not tellin

I haven't had a boyfriend yet.

Yr to yung

I want one. Is it because I haven't grown up around men?

Its becos boys yr age are stoooopid and u r to great 4 them

Probably everyone on the islands owes Nina an apology. For ignoring her. For thinking she was dull. For not trying to find her interesting. For always remarking on her weight. It's not even feminist to be thin. (Some further guidance on this point might be necessary.) Also, so much has been written already about Zoe's father's side of the family; what about Nina's? The truth is, she was one of those many women who went through life in the islands without taking part in any meaningful woman-centred activity, without crossing Eva's women's radar (wide and generous though they thought it was); whose opinions were as harmless and unobtrusive as far-off clouds on a summer's day. That's what *anybody* would have said, had they been asked about her, without actually asking her first. After first, most likely, asking, *Who?*

Naturally, Nina herself considered her interior life every bit as rich and rewarding as the exterior part. For example, there were boyfriends, who came and went, generally causing more hassle in the end than they were worth, and normally running up against the exacting standards of Ruth before they became too entrenched. Were it not for the friends she had had since childhood, the romantic flux she experienced might have caused her more bother. But often, listening to Natalie, Emma and Lizzie complaining about their husbands and live-in boyfriends

225

in the pub, she felt relieved to be free of all that. The way they described it, these men were shockingly unhygienic. Once a year the friends went as a foursome to Glasgow or Newcastle, availing themselves of a midweek deal to stay in a hotel in the centre of town, shopping their way around Metrocentre or Princes Square in the morning and going to a Kylie concert in the evening. Nina didn't cultivate new friends in general; she had no need to. Her job was a bit boring, but really it was OK. The one person she had no time for in the islands was Eva.

JUDGE: Now that you know what you know—
NINA: I don't know anything. Never did.
JUDGE: Eva *was* Zoe's grandmother.
NINA: Not mine, though. What can I say? I didn't know anything about any of it.

The storms were coming in by the time Alice arrived in the islands for what she hoped was her last visit of the year. Eva and she were supposed to be finalising the collection of epics. In the early autumn Alice had collated a whole load of texts from the medieval period which she knew Eva would like; but now that she was early-days pregnant, the baby inside her was almost all she could think about. She didn't want to miscarry. On the plane, she looked again at the Chaucer she had added to their female epics edition, and then deleted at the last minute: 'Is it for ye wolde have my queynte allone?' 'Trewely, as myne housbondes tolde me, I hadde the beste quoniam myghte be.' 'By God, if wommen hadde writen stories … They wolde han writen of men moore wikkednesse, Than al the mark of Adam may redresse.' She shut her eyes as the plane came in to land – it was very windy and the aircraft shook like a tin can on a string – and thought of the Wife of Bath. 'I knowe yow for a trewe wyf, dame Alys.' She felt so sick; maybe she should suggest to Eva a kind of communal authorship, by all the women. They could choose a text each, or something. Like a cookbook. The thought of cookbooks made her want to retch.

It was stormy in the islands; Alice shivered as she took a taxi into town: the wind was bending people in half on the high street, sweeping sheets of seawater over the harbour wall. She went via the bakery at Lerston, even though it was well out of the way, for with the clean island air in her blood she was immediately craving fat and sugar; and by the time the taxi reached Harcourt House, and a dozen doughnuts became ten, the trees in the wood were pulsing and stretching like epic dancers, and she saw that a window on the first floor had blown open. The library window. Alice let herself in and walked upstairs. The house appeared to be empty. Eva had texted to say that somebody would be home, but Alice heard nothing. On the windowsill, Zoe's biology textbook was lying, soaking up the rain, acquiring new girth and dimension. A page stuck out as a bookmark to the chapter on human reproduction. Alice opened up the paper. It was waterlogged only along the edges. Zoe had drawn a diagram, in her neat, italic teenage writing, of what looked like a monthly chart of a woman's menstrual cycle. In five different-colour pens the girl had written out different phases: days of creativity ('spring') juxtaposed with days of internal self-examination ('winter'). Alice put the paper back on the desk. As far as she was concerned, her own menstrual cycle was a complete mystery; she had lived with it for over two decades now, without discerning any connection to the moon. She would've been useless as a hunter-gatherer (or 'gatherer-hunter', as a vegan friend had recently corrected her, the Mesolithic diet having been at least sixty per cent nuts and tofu). Thank goodness nobody ever asked her to navigate by the stars. But then: she had grown up with the menstrual cycle as a curse rather than a superpower. She picked the paper up again, and studied it. Next to bleeding, Zoe had written 'Monthly meditation; vision quest; deep listening to self; time out.' Outside, the wind was circling the house, faster and faster, pushing at the windows, probing the roof tiles. Alice remembered how much Eva loved the storms; they remind me why I live in the islands, she liked to say. To Alice, the islands felt strange, vulnerable, as if they were about to flood, as the whole world was, and the islands first, probably, inundated with salt and folly.

Alice loved coming here; but also, it felt a bit crazy. Like, something was bound to give. Everything Eva was doing was just too much, somehow.

She walked next door to the small bedroom that Eva had told her was hers for the week. She sniffed the pillows, and the duvet.

Yuk. When she was pregnant, everything smelt disgusting. Ancient bedding such as this seemed to reveal its ancestry; all the skin shed by the men and women who had used it, stretching back to Edwardian times, probably; Victorian times, maybe. How old did pillows get, in houses like this? She felt a wave of nausea; the bile rising in her throat.

A door opened at the other end of the passage. A mellifluosity of voices after the silence: the house wasn't empty after all. I'll show you where it is, said a girl's voice, Eva's granddaughter Zoe; and after her came the young Pakistani woman; and then a nun in one of those strange green habits which they wore in the islands. They failed to notice Alice – the passage was dark at that time of the afternoon – and, instead of going her way, turned as one, a murmuration, to descend the stairs. Alice heard them swooshing through the dining room below.

A text came in on Alice's phone from the childminder in London. Her heart gave a lurch but it was nothing, only a question about chocolate, was her daughter allowed it, as she claimed? *No*, she texted back. Then, *Yes, OK*. She turned her phone off and went downstairs to the empty kitchen. She would make them tea.

She had it ready for them when they came through, a swoop of birds. She'd enjoyed listening to them as they blew through the house, only the emotion in their voices reaching her ears through the intervening layers of stone and wood and mortar. She imagined them picking things up, pointing things out, not really commenting on the house itself but on themselves: their own relationships, through it, to each other. And when they entered the kitchen at last, it was like gannets, in a burst of noisy chatter. Alice greeted the Pakistani girl, a Sheedi, and said something to her in Urdu; shook hands, formally, with Zoe; kissed the tall nun (Slavic cheeks with bones so high that they hurt when you kiss them, just as Eva writes somewhere in her book). *Happy; they all seemed happy.*

The happy sense lasted all evening. When Eva got home from college, Alice felt it in the air again, undeniable. *Happiness had blown in from afar and taken roost in Harcourt House.* She could sense the displacement of the air as the happiness beat its wings, the sonorous invisible cooing as it made itself at home there.

JUDGE: Your daughter, Zoe, was happy with Eva?

NINA: Yes. Now that she is gone I can see it. Eva was a good grandmother to Zoe in general.

JUDGE: It was only that one issue with which you had a problem?

NINA: I had no real relationship with Eva. We didn't talk. She wasn't interested in me as a person.

JUDGE: Were you interested in her?

NINA: I found her ... I don't know what to say. I never gave her much thought.

JUDGE: Until Mariam arrived—

NINA: Yes, Mariam, the girl from Pakistan. Eva not telling me she'd arranged a teacher for Zoe: that really set me off. But also, those stuck-up teenagers from Green Club.

You could speak of the country's nuclear codes in the Lerston Bakery, in front of Nina Brock, and be sure not to hear them repeated for another century. Talk of Zoe was different, however. The first public chat that Nina heard, of the things Zoe was up to, was as she was tonging a custard slice into a paper bag for old Mrs Anderson from the museum. Barbara said, 'Zoe has really made friends with Eva's Muslim guest, hasn't she? That black, you know, Muslim, woman's come to the museum two weekends in a row for tea and bobbit, with that nun from Papa Astrid, and each time Zoe was chatting away, bright as a button. Apparently she's been teaching her about Muslim religion? Arabic and whatnot?'

Nina had no idea what Barbara was talking about.

She was almost on her period, so it only got worse when Pauline Parker's mother came in, in her usual harried rush, to buy her sliced wholemeal at twenty-five past five (she always arrived just before closing, on her way home from work, so that, technically, she was making Nina do overtime), and said, 'You're very brave, Nina, encouraging Zoe to get into environmentalism, just like her father, the Green Club, is it? Pauline's very impressed, and camping on Eva's land, so generous.'

Nina, who had crouched down to get the loaf of bread, paused for a moment on her knees, looking up at the harassed-looking woman with her green eyeshadow slightly awry, as the sun illuminated the smudgy fingerprints of all that day's children. She felt a flash of confusion so white-hot it may as well have been anger.

NINA: Zoe hadn't said they were camping at Harcourt, else I would've known. She had said they were camping on the common.

Because Alice was staying, as well as Mariam, and Lucija was coming back for the weekend, and Seb was due up soon for his magazine photoshoot, and Eva wanted Zoe to have a chance to see him, Eva emailed Jen and Inga to suggest postponing their meeting, which usually took place at Harcourt House on the last Friday evening of every month.

I disagree, Jen wrote back. *We've got a lot to discuss. We need to meet, now more than ever.*

So the troika met at eight, with wine, in the sitting room, with the fire lit and the door closed against the rest of the house. All three women knew that the house was overcrowded. It wasn't just the hectic variety of guests – Bosnian nun, anxious amanuensis, Pakistani girl, island teenager – but all the things, the ancestral things, the books, the elegant, aristocratic clutter that Inga found so irritating. Still, it was marginally better to meet here, in this space, than at Jen's house, with the children and husband's evening rewards of television, Xbox, music, devices. Nor at Inga's where Rowan – made up of pale pauses and even paler silence – sucked up a lot of mental space in that tidy flat. Even so, the growing inconveniences of Harcourt House were leading Inga to suspect that a more formal setting might be better.

'I'll take minutes,' said Jen soothingly. She was also well aware that the time had come for them to have some of those conversations that, until then, they had, by tacit mutual agreement, managed to put off. 'By the way,' she said, as if it were an afterthought. 'Before I forget: Ursula rang me to say that men are writing in to complain of female bias at the museum and the college.'

'Let them write,' said Inga, crossing her long legs so that the denim of her jeans rasped.

'And at school too—'

'The school project seems a total success,' Eva said, leaning forward to put another log on the fire, and noting, with a dash of regret, the beautiful lichen outbursts growing from the edges of its twigs. 'But I'm worried that those stars of ours are definitely up to something. I didn't ask what. Do either of you know?'

'I sometimes think they might be the most annoying teenagers in the world,' said Jen, thinking a little bitterly of the contrast with her own two layabouts.

'Finance is the first point on the agenda,' said Inga. 'We need to raise more money.'

'Agreed,' said Eva. 'I've been thinking about it too, and when it's the right time, we can make a big announcement. But I'm not ready yet.'

'It's almost impossible to raise funds when we can't tell funders what we're doing,' said Jen.

Inga said, 'We have some options. We could create an alternative finance industry here, for example.' There was a moment of silence, and then Jen and Eva spoke together.

'What do you mean?' (Eva's genuinely perplexed voice.)

'Who've you been hanging out with?' (Jen, a note of aggression.)

Inga took a sip of water and said, slowly, 'We need to find steady ways of making our archipelago self-sustaining. Islands such as Man, and those in the Channel, have focused on creating an environment conducive to the financial services industry. Jersey has made trust law a speciality and is recognised for this specialism in international finance circles—'

'Jesus, what you're describing is a tax haven,' said Jen. 'We're trying to create a new world here, haven't you noticed?'

'Exactly,' said Inga. Her voice was calm. 'What I was getting to saying is that we should do the opposite, we should set ourselves up in opposition to the kind of activities that these other islands offer. We could be a refuge—'

'Nobody makes money from offering refuge!'

'Crypto-currency. If we claimed some autonomy – our own virtual currency would be a start – we could finance all sorts of things as well as helping small businesses which at the moment are so unfairly penalised by large corporate tax evasion.'

'You sound a bit bananas, Inga,' Jen observed politely. 'Like, maybe you're living in cloud cuckoo land.'

'It's the basis of other islands' economies,' Inga said. 'It's what they do.'

'When we are ready,' Eva repeated, 'we can declare ourselves. I'm gathering names, I'll share them with you both. But if we bring attention to ourselves too early—'

'You'll ruin everything if you do anything too radical, Inga,' said Jen. 'Your position at the council isn't for life, you know. There are ambitious men who want your job. John Rendall, Damian Ellis, Matt Wilson. Colin Grieves is disgruntled. He may move against you. I don't think we'll be able to get you in again at the next election.'

'It's happening already,' Inga said. 'That's what I'm talking about. We need to move fast for that reason. What I worry is, we'll really screw it up with these administrative baby steps, these compromises. We've just been reacting; they have this, so we must have it too. They run that, so let's make sure our women are in place. We're just replicating the male universe in reverse. They've made us into little—'

'What's the other option?' said Jen.

Inga took a deep breath. 'For Eva to give us something. The house, for example.'

Both women looked at Eva.

'It is what you said would happen,' said Jen.

'My sons,' said Eva. 'It'll be so hard on them.'

'Have to tell them sometime, Eva,' said Jen.

'They'll go completely crazy. It can't be now. My life won't be worth living. It'll have to be after I'm dead.'

She added, 'There are other things. I could sell the Burne-Jones. It's probably worth more than the house.'

'Where is it?' said Inga.

'Just there,' said Eva, and pointed behind them.

They turned to look.

'*Nice*,' said Jen.

'They look absolutely miserable,' said Inga.

'How much is it worth?' asked Jen.

'Sotheby's estimate between four to six million. They've got a Pre-Raphaelite auction coming up.'

Inga actually rubbed her hands together. 'Just think what we could do with those cold white shoulders alone.'

'Those cherry-red nipples!' said Jen. 'A hundred k each?'

232

'Eva!'

The voice came from outside. Somebody was calling her, even though everybody knew that these meetings weren't to be interrupted.

'Eva,' said Inga. 'You've got to let these people give you some space.'

There was a tap on the door.

'Grandma?'

It was Zoe.

'I'm sorry,' Eva said to the other two. She went out into the hall.

'It's Mum,' Zoe whispered.

But Jen and Inga heard it all.

JEN: Nina. There was lots of shouting.

Eva walked across the hall. There she was: Nina, her face shiny and livid with exertion, standing in the open front door, the darkness and cold at her back.

'What the fuck, Eva? – This is my little girl we are talking about not some experiment who you can play around with any way you like – I let her come up here and now not only she's hanging out with Jen and Inga and their fancy ways of talking, speaking about women's power all the time, now it's about Islam too, and OK, whatever, but didn't it cross your mind even once to check with me that it was OK for this Mariam to give her lessons – like, maybe you could think to ask? It's my daughter, Eva, not yours, I gave birth to her and I am the one who looked after her, like, maybe you don't have any idea what it's like, raising a child alone. And I put up with it so long, the total neglect from her dad; and me doing all the hard work bringing her up, and none of you saying thank you, Nina, or well done, Nina, or isn't it nice, Nina, that Zoe's turned out so well, all clever and well balanced, and hasn't gone completely off the rails despite her dad ignoring her. And of course you get to do the fancy things, and take her to the fancy places, because you got the money, and maybe it's a shame that for just one second you hadn't thought to ask me what I think, or how I'm doing, just too busy to see beyond your own nose and your important issues – and now making her think like she's got to get into green issues just to be like him or get his attention – because when did he ever stop to take any notice of her for one single second? – and it's not like he's sincere about anything he's saying anyway, or gives a fuck about anyone but himself—'

JEN: She sounded crazy but what she said was true.

Zoe watched in horror as her mother stood in the porch, shrieking at Grandma Eva; and there was her beloved grandmother growing more and more upset – for what can you do when the zombie mother of your favourite grandchild rises up and demands retribution for years of condescension and neglect?

'Run upstairs, Zoe,' Eva said, cutting across Nina's high-pitched monologue about the danger the child's life had been in, as well as the insufferable conceit of Sebastian and his brothers.

'Don't you tell my daughter what to do,' Nina shouted but Zoe had already fled up the front stairs, to the landing outside her grandmother's bedroom, up the next flight, to the attic room where Mariam now lived.

Zoe lay on the bed in Mariam's room and put her fingers in her ears. Even from there she could feel the tremor of her mother's shouting. The words were indistinguishable but she sensed the disruption: to the stones of the house which shuddered in distaste, to the trembling glass of the windows, to the wood pigeons whose call from the branches of the oak tree outside was usually so soothing – even they seemed agitated this evening. She could detect the anxious scurrying of woodlice beneath the floorboards, the fluttering of moths behind the curtains and in the cupboards. She felt the thud of her own heart and the sound of her mother's anger vibrating through her to her. Even worse than the image of her was her tone of voice, which Zoe knew Stella would say was drawn from the soap operas her mother watched every night on television, and the tabloids she read during her tea breaks at work. And yet in everything her mother spoke there was a subsidiary sound, an undercurrent of something authentically Ninaesque. Zoe hated the house for disdaining her. Nobody should disdain Nina, not Eva, not Stella.

NINA: All that shouting. Didn't achieve anything. Just made me feel stupid. And Eva felt bad, I could see that. Kept apologising. Saying, Nina, I just want us to be friends. All right, Eva, I said. Let's just leave it, OK? And all the while those women of Eva's, looking on. They didn't like me. Looked down on me.

JUDGE: Did you like them?

NINA: I didn't interfere in their lives, did I? It was them who interfered in mine.

JUDGE: Then what happened?

NINA: I left, angry as anything, in my car before I could get even madder by being lectured to by Eva. Forgot all about Zoe—

JUDGE: *Was* she lecturing you?

NINA: If she was, I was too hopping mad to listen. So, I was driving back past the church when I see her come out of the churchyard gate. She fainted, like right there, on the path. I screeched to a halt.

JUDGE: Who fainted?

NINA: Mariam. You know, the black woman. The Pakistani girl. The Muslim.

Little lentil, Mariam whispered. She begged her little lentil not to leave her. Her little lentil was ten weeks old inside her. *Dark red blood clots.*

NINA: Seems like none of them knew she was pregnant. If Eva knew, she kept it from the rest of them.

They had all heard Mariam's voice, sweet and melancholy and lilting, drifting down the passage as she took a bath, or up the stairs as she cooked in the kitchen. They weren't to know it was lullabies she was singing; nor that she told her lentil long stories in Sindhi, as she walked about the house, or took her daily stroll outside to see the sea: stories of its grandfather, who had fought so bravely against the Indians, high up in the mountains where the ibex are, and who, had he been alive, would have taken her baby and its mother to see the red fort on the river, which the Mughals built and where he was once stationed; stories of Britain, too, eloquent descriptions in Sindhi or Urdu, of the strange things to be found there, of the flight into the islands – the plane which was so tiny, it

235

felt like flying in a rickshaw – the jagged coastline, the dark endless sea. *Nakedness*, she told her baby, *I saw the country naked. The sky*, she said, *about to swallow me up.* She said that in English, just to show off how good she was getting.

'Are you OK?' Nina touched her shoulder and Mariam moaned. 'Are you hurt?'

Mariam moaned. 'My baby.'

'Oh God, are you—? Oh my God. Let's get you in the car. I'll take you in.'

But the pain stopped suddenly as they arrived at hospital. It was as if a bubble inside her had been pricked; and when Nina opened the car door for her, and Mariam stood up, a warm liquid rushed out, down her legs.

After that, Mariam was wheeled from room to room, on her back on a trolley, her eyes half-closed against the ceiling lights. She held Nina's hand. Sometimes it was a man looking down on her and sometimes a woman. To her own surprise she felt no objection as they stripped her. *Little lentil, little lentil.* Their gentleness soothed her. She saw the face of Nina appear and disappear. *Thank you*, Mariam said, over and over again. *Thank you. Meherbani. Thank you. Shukriya.*

They pricked her arm with liquids, and the liquids made her disappear. She dreamt sweet dreams of home. Of Aliya, Faiz, and Fatima.

When she woke, her baby lentil had gone.

Nina brought Mariam home to Eva's house the following afternoon, alone without her lentil, her body flat.

'Thank you so much, Nina,' Eva said quietly to Nina; clearly trying to heal years of misunderstanding in one greeting. Nina shrugged. 'Poor thing.' However much she liked Mariam she wasn't ready for a heart-to-heart with Eva.

The whole household was waiting to welcome Mariam but she barely saw them. Eva and Alice were like clouds passing overhead, silent, unnoticed. Only Lucija, dressed in her fulsome nun's habit, caught her eye. Mariam put out a hand. Lucija led her upstairs, laid her down on the bed, sat beside her, stroking her hair, as the tears washed through her.

The tears did no good, however.

Mariam stayed in her attic room as people came and went in the house below; people arrived and were kept away, their voices in a different part of the town, the azan in the distance, the clatter of pots from another house as one of the wives or daughters did the dishes.

She imagined sending a text to her aunt:

I love Christmas in London! So sparkly!

And how her aunt might write back:

Our Prophet (PBUH) told his followers not to—

But Mariam had destroyed her phone's SIM. She heard a footstep on the stairs. It was Lucija, bringing up her food.

'Please get up now, Mariam,' said Lucija. But Mariam didn't want to get up.

'Please come and wash now, Mariam,' Lucija insisted. But Mariam didn't want to wash.

She waited until the house was asleep; then she took out the book of poetry her father had given her, and wrote him a message in Sindhi in the margin: *My baby died.* Writing made her cry again. She did something so wrong, she thought, that her baby left her.

She walked downstairs, creaking through the old house, in and out of the night-time shadows. She wrote messages to her little lentil in secret places: on the inside of the cupboard door in the bathroom, along the cardboard ridge of the icing-sugar packet which Eva brought home with her shopping, on the wall of the study behind the huge volume of the *Times Atlas. I am sorry – I will never not be sorry – that you left me.*

She remembered her Latif: she was Sassui, following her lover hopelessly through the desert; Sohni, swimming over the river faithfully and fatally to Mehar. Without her baby lentil to distract her, she looked with new eyes at this house where she had come to live and defend her child from its father. Such a strange place, now she thought of it. She told *Ma* and *Ri: Where we come from, the richer a person is, the further they live from their village; and the wiser they are, the more modern things and shops they put between themselves and the fields of sugar cane and wheat which bred them. But now here I am in a house all worn and old, stuck on a rock in the middle of the deep dark sea. The house itself, with its darkness and anarchy.*

Trodden all over by outdoor shoes.

She didn't tell *Ma* and *Ri* that all her worst fears of the English had been confirmed by a photograph Sister Lucija pointed out to her, trying to make her laugh. It was called *Our Honeymoon in France* and showed a young man and woman sitting on a stretch of yellow sand, the sea a blue haze behind them. He was dressed in tiny blue shorts, she in the tiniest of swimsuits. Everything was on display: their naked knees, the hair standing up on their legs, the deep curves of the woman's bosom (with a gasp Mariam realised it was Eva), the hair that grows upwards from between a man's legs sprouting out in tufty curls from the top of his shorts. Mariam felt *disgusted*. She did not want to see any more such pictures. She thought with something like nostalgia of the boxes of unsold burqas left behind in London.

She stood at the window looking at the sea, shining in the moonlight. At the trees creaking above her head. Blossoms in winter which she didn't know the names of. Sand on the beach, the sea which she was scared of. In a hundred years' time, she thought, some English people will stare at the writing on the study wall and wonder at the sorrow of a Sheedi girl alone in a stranger's house without her baby to keep her happy.

Eventually, she told *Ma* and *Ri* what had happened. *Ri* was the first to answer.

It happened to me too, she said.

Ma, who fell pregnant within months of getting married, who had recently been delivered of a baby boy, made a soothing, overly complacent noise.

Ri said, In Karachi I went to the shrine of Abdullah Shah Ghazi.

Ma, whom motherhood had made pious, emitted what sounded like a tut. Shrines are false worship, she said.

The other two ignored her.

Ri asked, Is there a shrine you can go to?

Mariam said, There is a church nearby.

A church? said *Ma*.

Good, said *Ri*. Although, if you ask me, a shrine would be better.

Following *Ri*'s advice, Mariam began to visit the church across the field. She sought out the Prophet Isa. She knew what *Ma* thought: that her baby lentil had died because she had run away, gone independent. But Mariam wanted the Prophet Isa, a baby himself, to tell her it wasn't so. She sat alone in the church, contemplating the baby in the painting, surrounded by other babies in the sky. The strangeness of it – a blue sky, with babies floating in it – made her feel unrooted. There was nothing to be scared of now, was there. Nothing in the islands. Nothing in the house. Only, perhaps, her husband. Only her own sad heart.

JUDGE: On page 12 of your witness statement you have written that everything changed for you in the islands. Would you like to explain?
MARIAM: My baby had run down my legs, oozing into my shoes—
TRANSLATOR: I am telling you exactly what she says. Should I carry on?
JUDGE: Please.
MARIAM: I thought about this baby, this product of myself and my husband. I thought of how it is written that, *We created you out of dust, then out of a sperm, then we fashioned you into something which clings into a chewed lump of flesh.* Imam Jaffar al-Sadiq writes that there is no life until the fourth month. My little lentil was just a chewed lump of flesh. I thought about my husband, who had made this baby with me. I had asked for *khula*, the woman-initiated divorce, and after that you must do *iddah*, the waiting time, three menstrual cycles must pass, or if you are pregnant the baby must be delivered, *for it is not lawful for them to hide what God has created in their wombs,* before divorce can be granted. You must do *iddah* and then decide.

Mariam's mind felt empty: she couldn't decide. She read the *Risalo*. *O full moon! Without my beloved I am in darkest night.* She shook her head. He had never been her beloved. She knew that.

MARIAM: So my time in Eva's house, that was *iddah* only. And then it was my time for deciding.

The day Sebastian Vane was due to arrive in the islands for his photoshoot, Lucija led Mariam down to the sitting room and showed her the piano. She was trying out many different ways of taking Mariam out of herself; she was getting desperate.

'I was always quite good at the piano,' Lucija said, a little boastfully. 'My mother insisted that I took lessons and, really, I wasn't bad. I used to play with Omer. Omer loves jazz. I always preferred Bach.'

Mariam didn't know what Lucija was talking about. She watched as Lucija opened the piano lid.

'After fifteen years, the notes will come out a bit rough, and raw,' Lucija said, and played a line from a Bach sonata, to demonstrate. She glanced round to see if Mariam was enjoying it. 'Have you ever seen a piano before, Mariam?' Mariam shook her head. So Lucija played to bring her back to life; to bring her back to a remembering of all the good things. She stumbled at first. Her fingers seemed heavy. The music was inside her, a dim memory, a bubble pushing its way through the murky depths of everything that had happened since. She played the tune that Eva had been singing on the boat.

For a while, Mariam listened, and forgot about her lentil and her husband. But then the music changed, grew dissonant, and she grew restless. She wanted to go back to the church; to speak with Isa. But the church was no good either. *Ri* was right. She needed a shrine, a saint.

Lucija stopped playing. Mariam wasn't listening.

Outside the window, in the epic island sky, the moon was up already. Lucija remembered something Sister Brigid had told her about getting beyond human grief by accessing another reality, the transcendental. 'Seeing the stars above,' Brigid said. Sister Brigid swore by psilocybin. It was one of the reasons she liked their islands. This autumn she had gathered and dried magic mushrooms from the chapel's burial ground and given some to Lucija.

Nina arranged to take a longer lunch break than usual; and drove over to Harcourt House. That same Nina, who never went out of her way to see Eva, who had survived in the islands by living in a calming bubble of ignorance of Eva's whereabouts, who had never once during all the span of Zoe's existence dropped by Harcourt House socially, actually just really wanted to know how Mariam was doing.

She took a bag of iced currant buns, and as she drove across the island, from one coast to another, she thought of Mariam's baby, squidged out of her like the jam from a doughnut, and of how Mariam had held so tight to her hand in the hospital.

When she got to Harcourt House, she parked and got out of her car, and there was Mariam herself, walking back across the church field dressed top to toe in material the colour of sunflowers, or egg yolks – her face a bright moon in the yellow. Honestly, she was as glorious as the JCB that had passed too near Nina's own small blue Peugeot this morning on the narrow road to Lerston. Didn't she look just like a pop star in a music video, or maybe more like a saint, walking on water? Nina waved, feeling pleased. At the same moment, there appeared in the doorway of the house the dark outline of a woman, Mariam's shadow. Nina knew she was a nun.

NINA: I was raised a Catholic. She was one of the new nuns, from Papa Astrid.

Nina and Mariam sat together on the bench under the crab-apple tree, facing the ocean. Nina handed over the buns. Mariam wasted no time. 'The Prophet was man,' she explained to Nina, holding the paper bag from the bakery neatly on her knees; 'Isa was *man*, half the world, *men*. He has put love and mercy between our hearts.'

'Oh yes,' said Nina.

Mariam pointed up into the sky. 'Look at *moon*,' she said. Nina looked and, indeed, the moon was out already, a pale crescent hanging above the sea. 'Moon says: we come from mother's womb, man's seed put baby there, God's womb makes world.'

Mariam turned her full-moon eyes upon her. Nina put a hand out and stroked Mariam's agitated forearm.

JUDGE: Had you come to a decision?

MARIAM: Not until then. It was exactly after that time with Nina and Lucija, dancing, that I came to realise: the baby had left and given me a chance.

The nun appeared before them, as if transported there by her own anxiety; Nina hadn't heard her approaching.

'Tea!' said Mariam.

'I made it specially for you,' the nun said, handing a cup to Mariam; who handed it on to Nina, who drank it down, in a gulp; she was thirsty.

'Oh,' said the nun.

Steam rose into the winter air. Nina only half-noticed the tea's sweet musty taste of earth and leaves. It was cold already. The clouds were racing across the sky in the bay, patterning the sea with their shadows as if an invisible hand was lazily trailing its fingers through the water; God, probably, filling people's wombs, and emptying them. Nina noticed her happy feelings rising into the air like steam. Her happy thoughts were mingling with the clouds. They were the clouds. Now Mariam was pointing at the sky. She began to sing, in a foreign language, and Nina, and also Lucija, listened and understood exactly what she was saying. Mariam was pointing out that they had each other, that they were lucky, that the world was a beautiful place, that Fatima and Ayesha and all the wives of the Prophet—

'Cwen,' said Lucija, 'Brigid.'

'Madonna,' said Nina.

—would look after them as they had looked after each other. As the clouds began swirling above them in an amazing multicoloured dance, and the starlings performed an extra pirouette in the sky, diving and rising and diving, the women took each other's hands, and got to their feet, and began to move across the lawn. It was so sensual. Normally Nina hated dancing. But today she was being led by Mariam, who was queen of them all – her movements so languid, she was golden treacle dripping upwards.

In the sky the starlings were turning, falling, climbing.

They heard a car but did not falter in their dance. The car was coming towards them down the drive. Still holding hands, they watched, entranced; trapped in the golden, translucent suspense of late afternoon, as the vehicle moved nearer and nearer. The car stopped. A man got out.

They had forgotten him completely—

—the minister, the son, Sebastian Vane.

The woman arrives on Cwen's island, alone. At a glance, Cwen can see that it will be the last time.

The woman is old now. She spends the afternoon by the spring. She sits by the spring, staring out to sea, barely moving, even when the flock of black sheep approach boldly and regard her from a distance. Cwen, too, watches the woman, as the hours pass. She has seen this sadness and resignation before, in others. It is not what Cwen wants. She doesn't want sadness; she wants transformation.

Before she has decided what the remedy will be, she hears noise from the island opposite. Her women are gathering. They are crossing over in two boats. Her gang of women is coming. Cwen can hear the excited pitch of their voices, as they approach. Something is happening.

And Cwen knows, without looking, that they are bringing the one they want to punish. They will make her cry as they enact her initiation.

The old woman has heard them, too. Together, they stand by the cairn, looking down at the group of women on the beach.

The women pull their boats up beyond the high-tide mark and light a fire – gorse branches, pine, sage. It crackles in the wind. White smoke drifts up towards the cairn.

Cwen doesn't like it. She raises her arms and is about to punish them in their turn, with rain and snow, or a plague of wasps, when the old woman steps forward. She begins to walk slowly down the hill. The full glory of the setting sun is in her face, and Cwen knows she is magnificent. The sun is her crown, as it was for the goddess Anu. The land is her body.

With Sun in both their faces, Cwen sees what she must do.

The group on the beach look up, startled, across the firesmoke. The woman they are initiating, face smeared in ochre, runs from them, over the bracken, straight up the hill, through the gorse, scratches on her legs, blood streaks on her arms, but she doesn't care, on up the hill and into the arms of their Anu. They soothe each other in a long embrace.

And now the granddaugther comes up the hill towards them, relief in her smile and every part of her. When she reaches her grandmother's side, she kisses her on the cheek. You are here, she says.

They love each other so much, Cwen can see that.

But Cwen knows now what she requires from this new Anu. She requires a sacrifice which the girl will not want her to make.

She watches them, awaiting her moment.

———

*The Scene is opened, and there is presented a Rock as in the Sea,
whereupon sits the Princess and the Lady* Happy . . .

L. Happy. *I feed the Sun, which gives them light,
And makes them shine in darkest night,
Moist vapour from my brest I give,
Which he sucks forth, and makes him live,
Or else his Fire would soon go out,
Grow dark, or burn the World throughout.*

Margaret Cavendish, *The Convent of Pleasure*, London, 1668

*You may admire that you see no men amongst us, the reason whereon I
shall tell you according to our tradition . . . they resolved to make a new
form of government . . . our people agreed not to let any men remain above
a month on the Isle, nor male child above four months, without absolute
necessity of special Licence . . . their Religeon consists in worshiping the
Moon according to the custom of the Ancient Brittains.*

Anon (John Shirley), *A Discovery of Fonseca in a Voyage to Surranam.
The Island so long sought for in the Western Ocean. Inhabited by Women
with the Account of their Habits, Customs and Religion*, Dublin, 1682

*The island of Handa is tenanted by twelve families . . . It is curious enough,
that they have established nothing less than Royalty amongst them, in the
person of the eldest widow on the island, who is designed Queen; and her
prerogative is recognized not only by the islanders, but by visitors from the
mainland.*

Reverend George Tulloch, 'Edderachillis', *New Statistical Account*,
Edinburgh, 1845

I will raise the hearth-fire
As Mary would.
The encirclement of Bride and Mary
On the fire, and on the floor,
And on the household all.

'Togail an Teine' / 'Kindling the Fire' (Gaelic), collected from the Hebrides, 1900

11

Tara

TARA: Almost all women benefit from initiation. Some say we were
a bit too rough in the beginning but I feel like our guidance has to
be strong and unambiguous. However, I really did appreciate the
surprise input from Mariam Maher.

The three men arrived at Harcourt House. The three women
continued dancing.

Nina could see that one of the men was Sebastian, but she
didn't want to interrupt her dance. Unlike Lucija, who stopped
and went over and introduced herself, Nina was trying to contain
her feelings about the universe, which had only just occurred to
her in their overwhelmingness. She knew that she ought to drive
back to work. Instead, she danced with Mariam around the garden.
There was such great joy to be had in dancing across the grass – *that
was what the grass was there for, exactly, to be danced on* – how strange
that no one had ever thought to put it to that use before. They
moved their bodies around each other like fish writhing through
underwater caverns; it was beautiful and amazing. They ignored
the polite laughs from the minister.

Meanwhile, the photoshoot began. The photographer and his
assistant, with at least two cameras each, were snapping, looking at
their screens, focusing, rewinding, camera lenses pointing this way

and that, before they were even halfway across the lawn. Mariam's dance was just reaching its apex when she was somewhat abruptly ushered over to the mahonia near the house, which was in *bloom*, it being winter, and being a mahonia its flowers were *yellow*, and *my God, that bright yellow trouser-dress you are wearing looks so good against the glossy, spiky green*, and Minister, if you stand a little to her left, and yes, yes, *perfect* – it wasn't anybody's fault that perhaps fifty photographs were taken before any of the women had a chance to object.

LUCIJA: Fifty photos? More like five hundred. This is the thing I am angry with myself for, and Eva. She should've said to those men, *You've got to leave Mariam alone.* She should've said to me, *They will arrive at this time, they will need to photograph this, and that, and go here, and there, and since I am busy as always and will not get back in time, and also, I hate this kind of thing, I will not be there to defend you – but anyway, you are free, there is nothing they can make you do.* But of course she didn't; and of course they could. Before we knew it, *snap snap snap*, Eva's son and Mariam, in a shot by those nice yellow flowers, ever so perfect, just one more, keep going, one more smile?

CAMILLE: To be fair to Sebastian, I don't think he knew she'd been in hospital. The photographer was there. Seb was making the most of a fine opportunity. That was all his training. To make the most. Maybe a little bit, or a lot, yes, he was also playing up for the cameras. He was probably thinking how very photogenic this all looked, here in this rural place. He had perfected his concerned face; knew it would come out looking good. The photographer didn't ask. He just snapped.

SEBASTIAN: Naturally, I felt really really annoyed with my mother. She was nowhere to be seen. Instead, there was Nina, and the Pakistani Muslim woman, and even a nun. Clearly, it was the Bosnian nun my brothers had been complaining about. Plus the Pakistani woman – she who was Zoe's so-called tutor. Immediately, the nun came over and started talking to me. She went on and on about a quince tree that grew near the grave of the photographer Mevludin in Sarajevo. Told me in a completely crazy way how Mevludin's daughter-in-law's visits to the Sarajevo cemetery would increase tenfold in the autumn when the tree was fruiting. She would return to their apartment on (*some unpronounceable Bosnian street*), her pockets bulging, and when the nun and her schoolfriend (*another unspellable Bosnian name*) got home from school, the whole flat, dining room, sitting room, his bedroom, kitchen, hallway, stairwell were all infused with the sweet smell of stewing fruit. I realised that my brothers had been right all along. Our mother must have become very eccentric to tolerate these people. When I told my brothers that night, they went apeshit. Said we should get her examined. But by then I was too busy with all the CWEN stuff to think about Mother.

Throughout this ordeal, with the nun, and the Muslim, and the mother of his firstborn, Sebastian remained his usual composed and gracious self. His good breeding was such that he displayed neither discomfort nor embarrassment. He did clock the arrival of the other car – wondered if it was his mother, at last – but instead it was a woman called Alice, who explained that Eva was busy but had asked her, Alice, to come to the house and make coffee for everyone? Having posed for several pictures in the garden, Seb said he would wait outside with Alice, while the photograper and his assistant had a quick look round the house. They wanted to set up three or four interior shots, at least, the centrepiece being in front of the Burne-Jones, as discussed. Sebastian looked from the women dancing to the crescent moon in the sky, and back at Alice, who was apparently the only sane one.

Alice went into the house and came out a short while later with a plate of biscuits. She said she was really enjoying the dancing on the lawn, which was getting even twirlier, now that Lucija had rejoined Mariam and Nina. It was hard to keep a straight face but Alice managed to smile warily at the minister – and make light of it. Island photoshoots: such cheerful and informal affairs! She went back inside to fetch the coffee, and when she returned, the minister and she stood on the front terrace in the winter sunshine, drinking coffee and eating the biscuits Mariam had made, as if it was totally normal to have a nun, a woman in a headscarf and the mother of the minister's child gambolling across the garden. The sky was suddenly ablaze with light. The photoshoot was going to be amazing.

Sebastian felt calmer as he talked to Alice. She was asking him all kinds of questions, and listening with great attention to his detailed answers. The more he talked, the calmer he felt. He liked talking; he liked being reminded of how good he was with women. Just last week at a biodiversity and business conference, a young girl had waylaid him like this. Not young in the sense of underage – she was probably in her mid-twenties. But young in comparison to how Sebastian felt. Young: sincere, earnest. She had green eyes and freckles scattered like delicate brown sugar crystals all down the sides of her long straight nose. Sebastian concentrated on the freckles as she was speaking, and took in not a single thing she was saying. He noticed her plain linen shift dress, the silver ring in her nose, the curling of her brownish hair, the human tang of which he could smell even from a distance, and which suggested, first that her hair was dirty, and secondly that the tidy dress she wore had probably been borrowed for the occasion. As a husband, one learnt to decode the secrets via which women prepared their bodies for scrutiny by the outside world. He guessed without listening to the girl what her words would be about: biodiversity, rising sea levels, dying butterfly species, endangered polar bears, methane gas seeping out of melting polar ice caps. But the reason the girl was speaking to *him* was because she liked him, he could see that. He was still, even now, a man whom women liked.

It reassured Seb; his brothers Henry and George, for example, supercilious though they were with him, were not, in the outside world, the intuitively-expert readers of women that he was. The nose-ring girl, for example, would not have bothered engaging either of them in conversation. It was Seb who had always charmed the ladies. Aged fourteen, you couldn't have guessed which of your classmates would thrive in the world beyond school. But you knew that the blessed one who, by the age of eleven, had fingered a girl, and slept with one by thirteen, and spent not a term thereafter without a girlfriend, would always get lucky, even as the years passed and the jowls lengthened and the disappointments of life accumulated. The infant stud never lost his winning ways. Sometimes, the male group even sacrificed individual desires for the sake of one lifelong charmer. Seb, for example, had thrived on his reputation at school; found it burnished by his friends during lull periods at college – they practically brought the girls to his door. He hoped that because he was a man, and not a youth-oppressed woman, he would age in a distinguished way. And yet, it was impossible to escape the truth: how old he felt now. That was another, unexpected side effect of being in power. He was still on the young side, of course, for a politician. He looked good on television, or when snapped in the papers, or even in the drab constituency literature. *Precocious* was one of the words used in the press after he was promoted to junior Defra minister. And yet more and more frequently, Seb caught an anxious glimpse of that not-far-enough-away time when the balance of yearning would no longer tilt forwards – old enough to vote, old enough to drive, old enough to establish a household and sire children and set out some viable political ambitions – but backwards: too old to take drugs, too old to wear his favourite denim jacket, too old to risk his muscles playing rugby—

Alice shouted, Look out!

Four banners had dropped from the roof. They had been flung down, rather.

Alice squinted up at the three black figures on the roof. They were silhouetted against the sky like the elegant and inscrutable titles of the Studio Ghibli film she had just been watching with her daughter. She saw to her amusement that the banners had each been stitched with the word CWEN in different colours, yellow, green and red. The fourth banner, in rainbow colours, read: *Climate Change is MAN-made.* The three black figures in balaclavas were waving.

Apparently, from up there, they got a really good shot. At any rate, it appeared on all the news-websites that night, and on the cover of some local and national newspapers the next morning: *Seb, looking upwards, startled, as the schoolgirls' message hit him in yellow, green, and red—*

TARA: Hit him metaphorically. We didn't actually cause him any harm.

JUDGE: 'CWEN' has kindly provided a witness statement, in which you explain that you are '*eco-feminists*'?

TARA: Correct. Each banner is an artistic, feminist, environmental statement. The green one stands for CLIMATE WILL EVISCERATE NAYSAYERS. The red one—

JUDGE: Thank you. You discovered something, that later became national news, about a tip-off Sebastian Vane gave his brother, a property developer.

TARA: Yes, George Harcourt-Vane had lodged an application with the council which was prepared in the knowledge that the government was soon to change planning regulations for greenfield sites.

JUDGE: Who helped you?

TARA: We had a source.

JUDGE: The photographs you published—

TARA: Got syndicated all over the world. I myself took the one of the banner falling.

JUDGE: And the minister in the garden, kissing—

TARA: That's completely different.

At the sight of the ninjas on the roof, Sebastian had shouted, 'No!' and ducked behind one of his mother's outsize terracotta plant pots, with herbs in.

An instant later, when he learnt that the ninjas were just island schoolgirls, he knew that he had embarrassed himself. Cunting cunts! Luckily, the photographer and his assistant had missed it all. The woman Alice was still standing by the table where she'd been serving coffee, biting her lips, and texting somebody. The nun and Nina and the black Muslim woman had danced away across the lawn and were now in the field.

Alice looked round. She said, to Sebastian, 'Yes, it's definitely your daughter, Zoe, and her schoolfriends. They have an environment group at school.'

Up on the roof the ninjas had taken off their balaclavas and were taking selfies. She was right, unfortunately. One of them was Zoe.

'I won't call the police, then,' he said.

He felt even angrier with his mother than before; really, it was hard to see the funny side, especially as he knew everyone was laughing at him. Fuck, these islands were annoying! Total chaos. Like the Third World on the edge of Britain.

'Is that one with short hair a boy or a girl?'

'A girl. Tara Gill,' said Alice.

Seb turned to her.

'You look familiar, do we know each other, actually?' (Which, it turned out later, was one of his lines.) But Alice, looking up from her phone, already knew the answer. 'You were two years ahead of me at college,' she said; and he looked as amused as he was gratified. He asked a few questions, with genuine interest behind them, 'Did our paths ever cross? Were you in any of the societies?' And Alice, putting the phone back in her pocket, said, 'No, not really, but I remember you from—'

He took her arm. 'Listen, while I'm waiting for the photographers to set up the inside shots, let me show you round the garden. Have you been into the Victorian tower? My great-great-grandfather built it as a kind of folly. From the top floor you can see all the way across the islands—'

Alice allowed him to lead her into the orchard, even though she had seen it all before with Eva.

JUDGE: Alice was a great help to Eva – Eva herself makes this claim in her notebooks. And yet you disapproved? You didn't like her?

TARA: Who, Alice? There's not much to say but, yes, I guess we were suspicious of her at first, another Eva hanger-on. I personally found it irritating how she was always asking questions about the islands. She was ignorant about some things, and over-informed about others. I felt at times like we were being studied.

JUDGE: But Eva wanted somebody to record everything you women had done together.

TARA: [*Frowns*] Of course, it's no big deal.

After the banners were dropped, Tara looked down at the garden, at the minister, Zoe's father, and Alice, and Nina and Mariam and Lucija. Even the amazing lawn dancing stopped for a moment. Her heart was thumping. *Zabardast*. They'd done it. Stella was practically jumping for joy – it had all been a success – the banners were fluttering from the roof as graciously as Tibetan prayer flags from a stupa. Tara glanced at Zoe. She had wanted to involve Zoe in the action, from the start, not just because it was convenient to, but because it was important for her to take part. Tara knew that Zoe could see the logic of this.

But still, it was *her* father they were attacking with their granite immovable principles.

'Well done, comrades,' Stella said to them both. Tara was happy to see her all abuzz. 'Hey, Zoe, wasn't it cool?' Stella said. 'We told you it was going to be great, didn't we? And now I'm going to ring Ravi, OK? To make sure he's on it with the tweets.'

The other two nodded.

'Look, your father's going into the orchard,' Tara said. 'Do you want to go and talk to him? Explain ourselves? See if we can get a good interview?'

They took off their black outfits, and got back into their jeans, and bundled everything into bags.

As they came downstairs, they saw the photographer and his assistant in the hall, looking puzzled. 'Guys, do you know where the Burne-Jones painting of the sea nymphs is? We're supposed to be photographing the minister in front of it.' Zoe and Tara shrugged. The men looked back down at their cameras and light meters. 'Well, can you tell the minister that we need him in about ten minutes?'

Zoe and Tara walked out into the porch, blinking in the sunlight.

Zoe said, 'He's so busy when he comes to the islands.' She thought of how it was; he would call out to her, and grab her in a hug, and explain loudly to friends, 'This is my daughter, Zoe, she lives here, in the archipelago. An indigenous island girl.' She thought she should get it tattooed on her forehead: *A totally indigenous island product.* – Then somebody would ask him something, or want to be shown something in the house or garden, and Seb would wince an apology to his daughter, and squeeze her hand, and, until now, that was the extent of their interaction. She was used to it. And *still* she waited around, as the sun moved across the sky, hoping for some contact with her father. Well, she'd had enough. She wanted their relationship to evolve on a new footing. She was no longer a little girl he could ignore.

'Let's go and see what he has to say,' she said.

As they walked across the lawn and into the orchard, Zoe imagined telling her father about the environment – her concerns about it – and discussing with him CWEN's slogan, *Climate Change is MAN-made*, in an open and honest way. Maybe he would listen to her and, in his position of power, *do something*.

They pushed their way through the gate in the hedge. Beyond was the orchard, where Eva's chickens lived, and the Victorian brick-tower folly that her father and his brothers had used as a playroom when they were younger.

'Oh my God,' said Tara suddenly. 'Sssh. Stop.'

She lifted her camera phone to eye level.

Over by the far orchard wall, standing below the tower, amidst the orchard's nettles and rotting apples, Zoe saw him. He was unmistakable, in his slick London suit, his over-the-top curly blonde hair, his extreme male handsomeness. *He had his hands on that woman, Alice.* He had stopped to face her. They watched as he pushed his face against hers, put his hand on her breast, and kissed her.

Who knows what might have happened thereafter had the voice of the photographer not penetrated the orchard: calling for Sebastian, bellowing for him, as he roamed towards them through the garden, 'Minister, the light's just right, we need you now, OK?'

Tara mimed silence to Zoe. The two of them waited, unseen, behind the thick box hedge on the edge of the orchard, as Tara saved the video file. They watched as the minister followed the photographer back to the house. Tara was thinking of all the noise this would make. However, she said nothing to anyone; she thought on her feet, continuing to improvise, by going to Alice's aid, and inviting her to the meeting on Cwen that night.

Zoe did as she was told, thinking—

ZOE: I was thinking of that quote Mx Thompson has up in their classroom. Power and domination as key elements of typical patriarchal sexual activity. Kate Millett.

JUDGE: Do you want to explain what happened in the garden?
ALICE: I – [*Stops*] It was a difficult time for me.

Sebastian's skin had smelt of aftershave; his mouth had tasted of coffee.

JUDGE: The video that was uploaded shows him kissing you.
ALICE: [*Clears throat*] Yes.

JUDGE: Were his advances unsolicited?

ALICE: Of course! I had morning sickness. When he kissed me I was in the middle of explaining to him what I had come up to the islands to discuss with Eva – but hadn't yet because she had been so busy – all the research I'd been doing on the late-medieval iteration of the islands of women. I'd read the whole of Malory's *Morte d'Arthur*, and other romance texts, such as *Silence*, about a girl who is brought up as a boy in order not to be disinherited. Malory's story is ostensibly set in Arthur's court, but interspersed throughout are tantalising mentions of a parallel island kingdom, run by women – the Lady of the Lake, whose name is Nyneve, and Arthur's magician sister, Morgan the fairy, and the Queen of the Wasteland. They are the ones who take Arthur away on the boat at the end, when he is dying. Anyway, then he kissed me, and I was immediately sick into the flower bed. It's horrible in the moment, and afterwards you feel better, normally. But not on this occasion. The women took me over to the island, to Cwen. For a ritual.

JUDGE: Can you describe the ritual?

ALICE: They didn't know, couldn't know – for I'd told nobody other than my husband – that I was pregnant. I was at the sick stage, when half the foodstuffs of the world become impossible to keep down. One minute it's chips I want to eat, next it's an entire plate of spinach; and smells become almost impossible to tolerate, coffee is absolutely disgusting, it's as if my body is rejecting anything that isn't of this land – turnips are fine, and cabbage. You will remember that I had spent the afternoon making and then serving coffee. Worse even than coffee is male perfume – there is one particularly repulsive form of quite popular aftershave, I have no idea of the name but it makes the London Underground a total nightmare; and Sebastian was an aftershave wearer. His tongue in my mouth was like a snake. Nothing was further from my mind than being kissed. On the island, the women surrounded me, and I felt them smearing my hair and cheeks and neck with something cold and sticky. They were circling around me, and the bonfire smoked and crackled with driftwood and seaweed, and the seaweed suddenly started burning weirdly bright, and the smoke was yellow and noxious – *I thought, kelp smoke is dangerous, in the eighteenth century it made limpets fall off rocks and island women miscarry* – and I was about to break free,

to run down to the beach and swim back to safety, even though I
didn't understand the tides, or the currents; but I didn't care, in that
moment I just wanted to be out of there, I had a baby inside me to
protect, and a child at home in London, and I knew that I could
outrun any of those women, it was what I had always been good
at. Then Tara shouted, CWEN! And each woman whispered, *Cwen
will heal you*, and in their eyes I saw what the women had done to
me: my face, my eyes, my nose, my cheeks, my hair, my neck were
streaked and matted with blood. *Cwen gives you her wisdom*, they
sang. *Her womb wisdom*. They had covered me with their period
blood. I was sick again, on the sand.

JUDGE: It doesn't sound very nice.

ALICE: One of those classical authors, Strabo I think, compared a
British island to the Greek island of Samothrace. We know that
there was a female-worship-centred mystery cult on Samothrace,
based around worship of the Great Mother. But you weren't
allowed to say the gods' names, even. Alexander the Great's parents
belonged, and Lysander, and Herodotus, but also many normal
Greeks. Unlike other mystery cults, it was inclusive: freewomen and
men, children and slaves. That's all I can say about the Cwen rituals.
Do you know what a vision quest is? Well, it was a bit like that. At
least there wasn't animal sacrifice. There were no blood libations.

TARA: It's actually been really upsetting to hear her talk about the
Cwen rituals like that? Though it's not surprising. I was trying to
let her know that she'd been seen, and would be heard. It was
supposed to be a healing process for her. It was supposed to be an
honour. But with her patriarchal mindset, she assumed she was
being taken to the island to be punished, as men like to punish
women. That wasn't the case. Punish her for what? Women feel so
guilty all the time for no reason. We rowed her across to the island,
led her around the sacred fire, and smeared her with Cwen's own
island ochre. Just like the ancients used in the very first markings
that became art.

ALICE: The tide was in. The waters were purple, gleaming in the setting
sun. Seaweed had floated to the surface of the water, twists of it,
turmeric yellow, caper-sized beads, ruched tendrils, Tudor ruffs. My

eyes began watering with the sage smoke – these people are obsessed with sage – and I thought I was about to go out of my mind when, over the hill, Eva appeared. I ran to her, up the hill. She held me in her arms. I was sobbing but I knew I was safe now. *Sssssh*, she told me. All the chanting stopped. Somebody kicked the smoking branches out of the fire. Eva looked down at the group of women on the beach but said nothing. Instead, she led me back up the hill to Cwen's own spring, and there she washed my face with spring water. I was still crying as she and Zoe cleaned me. They dried me, and dressed me again. And for a while, all the voices went quiet in my head. I thought of what Thomas More was doing, taking all those prior stories and enfolding them into his radical island republic. That was Eva's role, too, I'm convinced of it.

TARA: The thing that saved it all was Mariam Maher. While Zoe and Eva and Alice were up by the spring, we were standing there watching, kind of aghast – our collectiveness might have been shattered, forever, maybe. Until I noticed that Mariam and the nun, and Nina, Zoe's mum, had all begun dancing. Right there, on the beach. *Amazing*, that young Pakistani woman, sweet face, tidy headscarf, what was she doing? Swaying to some beat, and she held out her hands to Nina and the nun, and it was like there was some trance music in their heads, I could see it, and the sweat on their faces, and Stella and I looked at each other, and we were like, *this is it*. This is what we need. We didn't think twice, we ran to join Mariam and her friends, and we danced together, honouring the saint of the island, and whoever Mariam's saints were, and our mothers and sisters and grandmothers, and all those other women who we absolutely need to honour more than we do already. We danced and danced, all of us. Nina looked amazing, like a goddess. My whole body was running with sweat. We were laughing and we were crying. Honestly, it was epic.

JUDGE: You are saying you got it wrong, earlier, the initiation you planned?

TARA: Only briefly. After that we got it so so right.

CWEN, it turned out, was quite an organised little outfit. On Sunday night, as Sebastian was making his way back to London,

CWEN released a series of statements, tweets and press releases:

Help stop our ancient islands being rampaged upon by business interests, for private profit;

Climate Change Denial is the Biggest Threat to World Peace;

Cos of Nonsense men, our precious ecosystem is changing forever.

And the next day, when Sebastian allowed his office to put out a statement graciously declining to press charges (trespass) and pointing out that schoolchildren were right to take up environmental causes, CWEN immediately retaliated by issuing video footage of their second stunt, a performance, really, at the centre of the islands, where the sixteen Neolithic standing stones are lit up by the sky at sunrise. The YouTube video is well worth watching; three figures dressed all in black, wearing balaclavas, and doing to the stones what to viewers – and passers-by the next morning – must have seemed like a catastrophic act of vandalism: each Neolithic standing stone daubed with red letters, inside and out:

CWEN WILL YOU ACT?

Numerous outraged photographs were uploaded, and posted online, with predictable comments about the desecration of ancient heritage. All of which helped CWEN to make their ensuing point more forcefully: that there is damage which is erasable – and there is damage which is permanent. They posted a time-lapse video, only two minutes long, of the three of them washing the stones clean of ochre. *Voiceover:* teenage rant.

TARA: I think we made a really fair point, you know? Maybe, that was what these standing stones were actually *for*, in the Neolithic? Kind of like giant blackboards? Televisions? Maybe they had messages inscribed on them daily, hourly, in chalk or ochre? All this modern social media: now I think, this thing in us is really ancient.

CWEN's third action was staged on the island itself. The video, filmed by Ravi, shows Tara and Stella standing astride the chambered cairn, demanding the return of their saint:

We want Cwen, our island-healer, back. Our saint was taken away almost a century ago to Oxford University, where her sex was mis-assigned on account of a gendered reading of the healer's personal accoutrements, a dagger, some metal divining rods, and a gospel book which was not even found on the body, but in a side chamber. We will reclaim her.

Submission 13a: CWEN media coverage

<u>Sunday</u>
Twitter: #CWEN: Schoolkids on roof of Defra minister Vane's island house protest threat to ancient British woodland from government's changes to greenfield regs

<u>Monday</u>
GreenWatch.co.uk: Schoolgirls yesterday staged a protest on the roof of Defra junior minister Sebastian Vane's childhood home. The three schoolgirls tweeted photographs of the stunt and also released a statement protesting against the government's proposed changes to the status of greenfield sites. The schoolgirls claim that the government intends to push through new legislation to free up many greenfield sites for planning, including the wood which backs on to Mr Vane's own home and a nearby island. There was as yet no comment from Defra this morning. A spokeswoman for the prime minister's office issued a statement deploring the illegal invasion of government ministers' homes and calling Greenpeace and other environmental protest organisations irresponsible for encouraging copycat actions.

<u>Tuesday</u>
Greenpeace press website: . . . and while Greenpeace UK does not encourage schoolchildren to stage dangerous and illegal protests, we acknowledge that the larger issues raised by the islands' school group, CWEN, are valid. Greenpeace will continue to work with governments and environmental groups to protect ancient woodland both here and abroad.

<u>Wednesday</u>
Guardian.co.uk/environment: The three schoolchildren involved in the illegal action last Sunday afternoon also appear to have leaked details of the government's controversial proposed changes to planning regulation. All the members of the group CWEN, 'Championing Women's Engagement with Nature', attend Ayrness High School in the remote North Sea archipelago.

<u>Thursday</u>
Ayrness High Governors' Board: ... and in the light of the actions of
'CWEN', we have asked Miss Thompson to stand down with immediate
effect ...

TARA: Their dismissal was its own patriarchal scandal. It shows how
   prejudiced many people are, especially towards eco-oriented change,
   you know? The employment tribunal will find in Mx Thompson's
   favour, if the world is fair.

By the time the newspaper interview with Sebastian was published
the following weekend, things were a little tense in the minister's office.
   It was Jen who woke Eva, by ringing on the house phone.
   'Have you seen them?'
   'What?'
   'The papers. Oh, Eva.'
   'What?'
   'I'll read you the worst bit ... *Vane, who speaks with pride of his
mother's travels through the former Yugoslavia, described multiculturalism
as* ... blah blah ... *As for the Pakistani tutor who teaches his daughter
(fifteen-year-old Zoe Brock, born of a former liaison while Mr Vane was a
student)* – There's even a photograph.'
   'Of Zoe?'
   'Of Mariam.'
   'Mariam? I told him she came here for refuge. He knew she'd fled
her husband—'
   Eva hung up, and went downstairs to collect the Sunday papers
from the porch. She hated the proliferation of reading material, the
cooking supplements, the trees that were killed to inform people
about the good places to travel and the right books to read. The
glossy magazines were the worst. She ripped this one out of its
polythene sheath.
   The first thing she noticed was how lovely the house looked
in winter, with the low afternoon sunshine lighting up the warm
yellow stone. The second thing which caught her eye was the
garden: the herbaceous borders all weeded and mulched and
pruned. The third thing she saw was Mariam.
   For the main spread, the photographer had captured Sebastian

standing in front of the house, his hands thrust awkwardly into his pockets, in a pose which was uncharacteristic of him, but which she recognised as borrowed from a recent prime minister. It was a wide-angled shot, taking in the entire façade of Harcourt House. There in the corner, by the mahonia, standing absolutely still, bolt upright, face front – *her* pose characteristic of Bosnian peasants in the 1960s – was a woman in a headscarf. Eva read the caption: *Mariam Maher, a recent immigrant to Britain from Pakistan, lives at the house, and works as a tutor for Sebastian Vane's eldest daughter, Zoe.*

Eva walked through to the kitchen and, with trembling hands, dialled her son's number.

'Mariam's in the magazine.'

'Mum,' said Sebastian. He sounded upbeat. 'The guys liked her. Thought she would add some local—'

'She's staying with me because she's run away from her husband. She's in hiding.'

'Oh come on, Mum.'

'Camille must have told you. Sebastian, what were you—'

'Stop being so anxious.'

'She came to me for refuge.'

'It looks great. It's a great interview. It shows your hospitality and ours. It's like a symbol of Britain—'

Eva put down the phone. She was shaking. She walked over to the window and pushed it open. Despite the cold, she stood there for a long time, looking up at the sky, feeling the anger she had been trying to contain almost her entire life, fly upwards, turning and wheeling and cawing. It was no good trusting any more that everything would come right on its own; such optimism was foolish.

She emailed her solicitor that moment, standing right there, tapping into her phone: telling him she would be in the following morning, first thing, to make an important change to her will.

The next morning – which was Monday – at around 8.20 a.m., while Sebastian was being asked, on the *Today* programme, by the by, whether the tutor employed to teach his daughter had the right to work in this country: and of course he said, Yes, well, by taught I don't mean a formal system of education, my daughter goes to Ayrness High School, but yes, of course naturally Mrs, er, the woman has the right to teach my daughter – which was an unfortunate claim because, actually, this turned out to be very much a matter for debate, Mariam's spouse visa depending on her staying at the side of her unfaithful husband, and giving her no right whatsoever to work in Britain once she'd divorced him (which she hadn't yet, not technically, only semi-Islamically); and thus by the time Sebastian's office had put out a statement in the afternoon, clarifying that in fact the Pakistani woman wasn't his daughter's tutor, the *Daily Mail* had already discovered that he was wrong about the rights he had quoted her as having, while the *Sun*, upon its arrival in the islands, learnt that Mariam always wore a headscarf, and prayed many times daily; and later that day, Sebastian, while being grilled yet again, revealed that Mariam had been his wife's patient; after which, the *Daily Mail*, in Hampstead, discovered, without too much difficulty, that she'd visited the sexual health clinic there; and soon right-wing chatter on the internet was calling Sebastian *slapdash*, and Zoe *illegitimate*, and Mariam *syphilitic*; while also pointing out that, thanks to the Home Secretary's new minimum income requirement, in the future, penniless immigrants like Mariam Maher would be kept out of the country – Eva drove into Ayrness.

She waited for a moment outside the solicitor's office, sitting in her car, her phone switched off, her stomach empty, her mind racing, reminding herself of exactly what she was here for. Then she got out, strode up to the building, and pushed her way through the door. Of course, even then, even later – especially over the ensuing week, as she endured, from afar, the public shaming of her son – she suffered qualms of conscience; knew that all three of her sons loved Harcourt House, just as they loved their father's art collection. Or rather, that they thought of both as integral to their self-image. She knew that what she was doing would give them a terrible shock. But as Eva wrote in her notebook, Mariam and Lucija and Camille had each borne exile from their culture – as had she, in a way; it was often good for individuals to start afresh. That was the whole point of myths of exile, such as the one about Albina. Her sons had such good lives already, and a large unwieldy house like Harcourt would just be a burden to them, as it had, in part, been to her, as well as a source of unnecessary conflict. Well, from now on it would be different. Christians jeered at Hindus and Buddhists for their belief in reincarnation but that was what a house like this did to a family: it enforced repetition of habits, status, character, not to mention misogyny. And having rehearsed the arguments she had been through many times already, Eva felt strangely calm and light-headed.

Then she flew down to London.

JUDGE: She never stopped feeling like she was stealing from them, really, did she?
JEN: Not really, no. It wasn't an easy decision.

In London, Camille had been working late, finishing reports, trying to make Sebastian notice her absence. The only people who noticed were her children. The children: confused. Camille: unhappy. Sebastian: absorbed by this media furore.

It had been like this for a while: the harder Seb worked, the less time he had to spend with her, the more infrequent their love-making, the more her eye wandered. She had had her children; her body was her own again; her breasts were no longer being sucked by needy infants, her vagina would never again function as a birth canal. So she found herself being looked at by other men; she who had passed coldly through England's flaccid pit of male snakes, now found their thrusting and writhing arousing. Stupid, crass men excited her at the most inelegant moments. Standing in a lift, walking to the Tube, crossing Hampstead Heath, she wanted to be taken away by the men she saw, and ravished.

Worse, in the meantime, deep inside, she felt a pathetic yearning for a world in which everything was clear. For a higher authority than herself; for a system in which the Book – *whichever Book* – was still revered for the wisdom of the elders. Of course she knew that her thoughts on this subject were irrational; that the yearning she felt came down to familiarity, to the so-oft-repeated poetry contained in the Book of her childhood devotions. Which was bad luck, because, despite the architecture of the French cathedrals, baroque music from Spain, the Madonnas of the Italian Renaissance, weighed in the balance, none of this was worth it, if the wisdom of the elders damaged her daughter's sense of herself as a woman. Did it, or didn't it? What she also knew, instinctively, was that a life without a Book was a life of indolence and corruption, of lust but not love, of anger and greed and envy, a life of not caring.

CAMILLE: Then suddenly our house was being doorstepped. They'd warned me about this but Seb worked for Defra. Nothing he'd done so far in his career had warranted doorstepping. Thank God for Eva.

Eva arrived in warrior mode. It was she who dealt with the journalists and photographers on the doorstep – the flash of cameras, the thrust of recording devices: the ridiculous onslaught which went on, day after day. Seb was no help. Possibly he was even enjoying it. That would have made Eva angry, had she had a moment to think about it, but – she hadn't come down to help Seb. She was in London to lend support to her daughter-in-law and the grandchildren during her son's ignominious hour in the media glare. Unfortunately, she could remember exactly what it was like.

Eva rang home every evening to check up on Mariam; spoke to Lucija; told Jen, and texted Ruth, to keep an eye out for journalists insinuating themselves with island locals. To her surprise, Nina rang and left a long message, explaining that Mariam's interview had gone really well, and wasn't it good that Mariam had *found her voice*, even if some of the things she was putting out there were hard to hear. Eva listened to it twice, without understanding.

She ignored texts from George:

Zoe was involved in this CWEN stuff?

And from Henry:

Seb mentioned he was supposed to be photographed in front of the Burne-Jones? Is it on loan to an exhibition somewhere?

With the help of Nina, whose idea it was, and Lucija, who typed the email, Mariam Maher sent a message to the London reporter for *Dawn*, the Pakistani newspaper, offering to give an interview.

The woman, Shahzadi Siddiqui, couldn't believe her luck. The fate of Mariam Maher had made the national news back home; *Dawn* was doing occasional features on immigrants to Britain following the Home Secretary's prejudiced minimum income requirement. But Shahzadi herself had barely been outside London since arriving in the UK six months before, and she was a bit challenged by the idea of putting such a distance between herself and the city; clad in a fleece jacket and rubber boots from M&S, moreover, *ghastly*. But of course Shahzadi was totally prepared to suffer for her art, even if it meant getting muddy. And so Mariam and she met one day later, exactly as Mariam proposed, in the island's bakery at a windswept place called Lerston, where they spoke in Sindhi over tea and a rather strange cheesecake which tasted faintly of cherry yoghurt. (Sister Lucija sat on a nearby table. Nina was watching from behind the counter.) It was a stormy day and Shahzadi found the entire expedition a strain on her resources – but as soon as she met Mariam, she knew it was worth it. What a woman. A little downtrodden Sheedi girl from the nowhere town of Mirpur Khas, becoming famous all over the world, for being a feminist.

'I hate this man,' Mariam said.

'You mean your husband?' Shahzadi asked.

'No, not him!' Mariam replied. 'This big politician, who took my picture.'

'Sebastian Vane?'

'Yes, him. He is very bad at looking after his mother, leaving her alone in the islands like this. So cold here, you wouldn't guess how much it rains. All his family money comes from the former colonies, they had sugar plantations and slaves in the Africas.'

'The Caribbean?'

'And nowadays a jet-set lifestyle that's contributing to the heating of the world and the melting of the glaciers. He is a greedy man looking for money and fame, just as bad as the men at home. We should be rebelling. This is unequal distribution of resources. And these British people dare to quibble about my legal status in this country; what about what they have done to mine?'

'What do you want to happen now?' Shahzadi asked.

'I want a divorce,' Mariam said. 'I want residency in Britain, and when all that is regularised, I want to go home and see my family.'

Shahzadi, careful not to mention the exact location, described Mariam as living in 'some remote islands off the east coast of Britain'. Nevertheless, thanks to Seb's prior exposure, any irate husband/father/brother could have found her.

The interview was syndicated across the world.

Shahzadi's editor in Karachi was so pleased, he went round to her mother's house in Zamzama, with a bottle of whisky.

Submission 13b: Media coverage

Monday
Daily Telegraph: Doubts were already being raised over the good judgement of Sebastian Vane, junior minister at Defra, after his mother's house was invaded last weekend by young protesters complaining about Defra's proposed changes to planning regulations. In a separate blow to the minister's reputation, it was discovered that Mariam Maher, the immigrant Pakistani he employs as tutor for his daughter, has left her husband. UK Visas and Immigration (formerly the UK Border Agency) stated that Mrs Maher does not have the right to stay in this country if she divorces her husband. It was also discovered that, contrary to previous claims by Vane's office, the Pakistani woman does not possess any teaching qualifications either here or in Pakistan. Shadow minister for Defra, Celine Roberts, claimed last night that 'this shoddy behaviour illustrates the government's arrogance and double standards, with one rule for the people and another for themselves'.

Tuesday
Daily Mail: Defra junior minister Sebastian Vane, at the centre of the sordid TUTORGATE scandal, has admitted to paying an illegal immigrant from Pakistan cash to teach his illegitimate teenage daughter about Islam. Neighbours in Ayrness, the quiet harbour town where Mr Vane's daughter lives, fear that England's ancient Christian past is under siege. 'It's not just the cities,' one anxious local woman told us. 'It's happening in the rural areas too. Mrs Maher wears a headscarf when out shopping and just think of the message that sends. Our islands are being taken over by Islamic missionaries.'

Wednesday
Guardian: Sebastian Vane, Defra's beleaguered junior minister, was last night refusing to quit after it emerged that his elder brother, George Harcourt-Vane, a property developer, may have benefited from Defra tip-offs in his business dealings with island bureaucrats. Papers lodged with the council offices in Ayrness show that George Harcourt-Vane

put in a bid to develop some ancient woodland and a nearby island for housing as early as November. Vane, facing renewed calls for his resignation, refused to answer questions from journalists last night about his future in the government. Dr Quinn, professor of media at City University, observed, 'This new accusation may stick, if it is proved that information benefiting Mr George Harcourt-Vane in his business affairs did indeed come from the minister, his brother.'

Thursday
Sothebys.com: Edward Burne-Jones / *The Sea Nymphs*
Estimate: 4,000,000–6,000,000 GBP
Lot sold: 27 bids, reserve met
8,215,000 GBP
Bidding is closed.

The day the sale went through, Eva rang the house, as usual, and nobody answered. She found herself unable to reach either Lucija or Mariam on their mobiles. She rang and rang, and nobody picked up. She rang Jen; but Jen was out of signal. She tried Marcin, her cleaner, but he was in Berwick. So finally she rang Inga. 'Eva,' Inga said, when she answered. 'I've been wanting to talk to you – your son George. He's been getting a little bit . . . over-eager with some of my officials on the council. A holiday housing scheme? On Cwen?' 'Inga, please,' Eva said, 'I can't get through to Lucija and Mariam. Can you go up to my house and find out what's going on?' 'Sure,' said Inga. 'We'll talk about the other thing later.'

An hour later, at four o'clock, Inga rang back to say that the house was locked, and in darkness.

So Eva caught a flight up to the islands.

As she arrived in Ayrness, she got a text from her son Henry, asking again about the Burne-Jones.

Then another, saying that he was driving up that afternoon, and would meet her at the house.

Then a third: he was on the last boat.

But he was coming too late. She had already transferred the money.

268

The boat was halfway across to the island before Cwen realised what she had to do. She had become more powerful in death. In life, she was only a healer. In death, she became a saint.

Of course, life was the precious thing. Life was blood and love. Life was tears. Death was none of these things, and life was what mattered. But death had qualities, too, the first of which was that it was everlasting. And moreover, sometimes, through death, new ideas were born and new lives spawned. Sometimes, of a person's two eras, it was death that took over.

She saw the figures on the headland first. She recognised the man: one of those brothers.

The wind was coming from the north-east, and after that it was obvious. It was the end, and the beginning. It was the agony, and the transformation. It was the hearth-fire and the Queen widow; it was Bride and Mary.

But it took a huge effort to lift her arms, and drag the waves, and drag them again, and again, and again. There was a pounding in her head and the rain felt like hail on her face. Her hair was wet and her dress was soaked. She ripped it from her and stood there by her cairn, her face tipped up to the sky. Wind roared around her island, as Cwen called the woman to her.

———

12

Ruth

By chance, Ruth saw Eva coming out of the airport on the evening she got in from London. Everybody in the islands knew why she had gone – no islander ever went willingly to the capital.

Eva looked exhausted.

JUDGE: How well did you know Eva Harcourt-Vane?
RUTH: Not well at all, really. It's a shame. [*Sniffs*] What a waste. While she was in London we were texting each other every day. I told her: It's all right, pet. Zoe's OK. The journalists went home and Zoe's life, at least, went back to normal. Momentarily. For Eva, Zoe was always the most important thing.

At least sixty per cent of people on island flights tend to know each other, more or less; and normally there would have been at least five people keen to talk to Eva. On a normal day Eva would have stood there, chatting in the warmth of the terminal building, or suggested that they fetch a cup of tea and cake from the café and sit for a moment by the big window overlooking the runway. But that evening she merely nodded and walked quickly out of the building and across the wet tarmac of the car park. It was so windy the plane almost hadn't made it. Ruth could see, from where she was standing, that when Eva opened the car, the wind almost tore the door off.

RUTH: I thought about waving hello – but I was on duty. That was the last time I saw her.

It wasn't until Eva drove out of Ayrness, and along the coast, and the hill of Harcourt loomed up before her, darkly – a layer of ancient black overlaid upon the other layers of darkness – that her fingers finally unclenched themselves from the steering wheel. She had hated being in London. She had hated how Seb was oblivious to the damage he was doing, how much he liked the media attention. How he thought Camille and the children would get over it. She had given up feeling distressed by George. She pushed all thoughts of Henry out of her mind. Right now, he was irrelevant.

She drew up at the front of the house. Normally it would have been golden with lamplight at this time of night. But it was in darkness, as Inga had said.

Her phone blinked with a voicemail. She began listening to it: something very complicated from Alice about how, in the Renaissance, male writers couldn't help writing about sexy island women, and at the same time couldn't stop destroying them either, if you just think about Spenser with Acrasia and Phaedria, and Shakespeare with Sycorax, whom Prospero basically—

Eva got out of the car. As she walked round the front towards the kitchen door, she saw one of the kitchen windows flapping in the wind; the glass had been smashed, and still lay where it had fallen. She peered through the broken window. In the thin light of her phone she saw a vase of the mahonia which Mariam liked to pick for the house on the kitchen table: the wind had blown it over. The puddle of water had spread along the table and over a piece of white paper that was held there by her heavy stone mortar.

Reception was often terrible on this side of the house but there was just enough coverage for the call to go through to the police. Eva was still speaking to the operator as she entered the kitchen. She flicked on the light and stood looking down at the note on the table. She recognised Sister Lucija's handwriting but whatever it was that the nun had wanted to communicate was lost. She could just make out the words 'Papa Astrid'.

Eva distinctly remembered the operator, somebody in the police call centre, telling her to leave the premises, even as she

274

left the kitchen and turned towards the back stairs. The rest of the house was silent, as well as darker and colder than she remembered it being for a long time. She switched on lights as she went: up the stairs, along the passage to the landing outside her bedroom, on up the stairs to the attic. As she walked, she called for them – *Mariam! Lucija!* On the top floor, she opened the door of the room where Mariam slept. The covers were pushed back from the mattress on the floor. There was a knight's helmet on the chair. One of Mariam's pretty colourful shirts was hanging over the window. There were a few books on the shelf – a school textbook about Pakistan, some poetry. Words in Sindhi, the language Mariam spoke, maybe; or Urdu? She wasn't sure. What else? She looked around her. What on earth had happened?

She went downstairs again.

The first thing she saw, when she entered her bedroom, was its absence on her wall. For many decades now, her eyes had sought that street scene, her photograph from Sarajevo, taking comfort in those Jewish women and their child, who had lived with her in the islands, helping her look with strength and equanimity at the fields and trees and sea outside her window.

She found the picture frame on the floor and, when she bent down to pick it up, glass fell onto the carpet. The print had gone. She looked between the smashed glass at her feet and the blank space on the wall, and still failed to understand what had happened.

Among the glass was a small snapshot. She knew immediately what it was. She had put it in with Mevludin's print when she had it framed in London, years ago. By then she had known she wasn't going back to Sarajevo.

She picked it up, and looked at it. It was a black and white photograph, taken in Sarajevo by one of her friends. Eva as a young woman, sitting at a café table, hunched forward, happy. Sitting with her, their shoulders touching, was Daris. He was happy, too. She turned the photograph over. Faded handwriting in brown ink. *Daris with Eva, 1965.*

Mariam! Mariam!

It was a man's voice, coming from downstairs. Eva propped the picture up on her bedside table and hurried out of her bedroom, and down the front stairs, turning on lights as she went. The voice was coming from the cellar, the door to which appeared to be bolted from the outside.

Mariam, Mariam, Mariam.

Eva walked down the first few steps towards the cellar door. 'Who's that?' she called, and the voice shouted back, 'I have come to help Mariam, I am her husband, my name is Amjad Maher.'

'You!' Eva said. Then she hesitated. 'Yes, Mariam told us about you.'

'What? What did she tell you?' said the voice. He sounded distant and intimate at the same time; talking to him through that thick oak door was like discussing rail travel across Britain with an Indian girl who said her name was Lucy and yet was probably called Parvati; *Where are you, Bangalore, Gurgaon?*, Eva usually ended up asking; and her susceptibility to these long-distance, cross-cultural exchanges had almost had her scammed before, by young women with faint Indian accents who called up asking to fix her computer, to increase her broadband, please could she turn her computer on, and tell her the password?, and yes, being Eva, she almost fell for it. Everybody in the islands had that exploitable weakness: wanting faster broadband.

'She ran away from you,' Eva said.

The man began muttering to himself. He might have been swearing.

'Because of your girlfriend?' Eva said.

And then the explanations came, in English; he liked the girlfriend very much but she wasn't suitable for marrying, not the right match at all, it had to be a girl from his culture; so many expectations to get married and become the family man, to continue the family name and the business, and all. He is an educated man, and Mariam and he share a country and a religion. How clever Mariam was – how important to the business; how quickly she had adapted to the selling side; how good she was at it. He was lost without her. He came home to find the girlfriend – *very cross former girlfriend* – where he had been expecting a loving wife. Since they were living in London – where their marital home was – he had hoped for some modern marriage set-up, some go-ahead wife, not a harried daughter-in-law being bossed around by his mother. Amjad and Mariam's chances were all the better because Amjad's mother, God rest her soul, was dead, and his aunt was far away in Bradford. His mother had not been a restful woman! Just one visit to his aunt in Manningham was enough to remind him that. Of course, both his mother and his wife were very good cooks. His life got so much better after Mariam came to England. It was a big shock finding she had gone.

'She thinks your business is irreligious,' Eva said.

Amjad protested at this insult. Of course, most of the alarm clocks and prayer mats and so on were made in China, which wasn't completely Islamic, but that was the nature of the modern world. Mariam had a very active imagination; too many Indian films in her childhood—

'You gave her syphilis,' Eva said.

There was silence for a moment behind the door. When Amjad spoke again, he sounded sorrowful and bitter, though about what, Eva wasn't sure. 'How can I explain. Such pressure in my culture, to conform. And of course I wanted to, very much, marry somebody who would understand me and all ...' He sighed. 'Karen is better off without me, really. She's starting college soon.' He sighed again. 'Mariam is so far from home. It is right that she should be with people of her own kind.' Another pause. '*I am sorry*,' Amjad Maher said. And indeed, he did manage to sound genuinely remorseful. A little more chipper, after a moment: 'It happens sometimes like that, na? But things can get better.'

'Can they?' said Eva.

He laughed again, possibly apologetically. And then he said, unexpectedly, '*Ai, I really love her*'; and despite herself, Eva heard, in his voice, something she had not allowed herself to hear for a long time – the tenderness that can also exist in a man. Something blossomed in her briefly. She saw flowers in a wood, anemones, bluebells.

'What do you want?' she said.

'To see my Mariam again,' he answered. 'Where is she?'

'You tell me,' Eva said.

'I saw her, and then I was knocked to the ground and dragged in here.'

'By whom?' said Eva.

'By a man all dressed in flowing green,' said Amjad. 'Like the Pakistan cricket team.'

There was silence while Eva considered this.

'I miss her so much,' Amjad said.

'I think I know where she might be,' Eva said.

'We must go there at once!' said Amjad.

'You committed trespass. Lucija acted in self-defence. I won't press charges if you don't. But now you have to let Mariam alone to come to her own decisions. It would be best if you can remain married to her for now. I know where she is. She is safe. She is being looked after by our island saint. If you leave her be, I will help you. I will also take you to meet the saint.'

She tapped into her phone.

'I will transfer some money to you now, to defray income lost through Mariam's decision to relocate. I have written to my solicitor, asking him to transfer you further funds every quarter for as long as Mariam remains in the islands.'

At that moment, a text flashed up on Eva's phone. It was from Henry:

Driving to the house from ferry. Are you there?

Eva said, 'Wait while I unbolt the door.'

The door, which is very heavy and quite stiff, took a good deal of effort to open, even the small distance she pulled it. Light from the hall fell through the two-inch gap, illuminating a slight figure and releasing a waft of greasy air, the smell of chips, and then underneath it, something more rancid, human defecation. How long had he been in here? Eva squinted, as she pulled the door wider, and found herself looking at a young man with tousled dark hair and big scared eyes. He did not look in the least bit like a match for Mariam. His shirt was crumpled.

No, Amjad told the detective later, he didn't know where the woman was planning on taking him. All he knew was that he wanted to see his wife.

RUTH: The line cut out as she went down the remaining steps to unbolt the door. That's all we know. And that Amjad was scared of the police.

That night, under questioning, Amjad Maher admitted to having entered Harcourt House at 7.40 a.m. through the kitchen door. The first thing he saw, upon entering the house, was his wife's orange headscarf, which he had gifted to her, on top of a pile of washing. He put it round his neck and went to find her, climbing the back stairs and proceeding along the first-floor passage. Winter mornings are dark in the islands. When he reached the landing, where the front staircase curves upwards to the attic, his way was lit by the light coming from under Mariam's door. *Like a runway,* he told the police, *taking me back to her.* His wife was sitting up in bed, reading a book of poetry.

Mariam! he exclaimed.

Naturally, she screamed.

Amjad Maher had ascertained, from exterior surveillance of the house the previous evening, that his wife was sleeping at the top of the house. He saw her going up to bed that night; he watched her ascend. There are no curtains over the long stair windows.

The mistake Amjad Maher made was to have assumed that Mariam was alone in the house. But Sister Lucija was also staying. It was she who ran upstairs, knocked Amjad Maher over the head with the helmet from the medieval suit of armour in the hall, wrestled him to the floor and, with Mariam's help, dragged him down two flights of stairs to the cellar, which they bolted from the outside. Then the two of them fled.

The police were not alerted to the intruder/victim until that night, when Eva returned to the house. She stayed on the phone to the police as she walked upstairs, and everything until the moment when she walked down to the cellar door was recorded on the call. By then the police were on their way. They arrived in time to see Eva Levi and Amjad Maher hurrying out of the house, and up through the wood. Because of the emergency call, and the break-in, and the fact that Amjad's van with Islamic writing on the outside had been spotted in the Aldi car park, the police followed them, their torches shaking.

RUTH: I arrived in the second dispatch car just after Eva's son Henry. I wasn't in time to see the boat.

LUCIJA: I saw it. I had come back, having put Mariam on Papa Astrid, to let her husband out of his hole. He must've been scared. There was apple juice and wine and pickles. But still.

279

There was a full moon, and very little cover in the wood, so the police never lost sight of her. They continued right up to the top of the hill in a straight line, until they reached the cliff path, where they came face to face with the precipitous descent to the vast churning sea below, which, dark and shining in the moonlight, was already pitted with rain. The tide was in, lapping up against the seaweed straggle of the high-tide mark.

LUCIJA: I ran down the cliff path. I could see that Eva was halfway across to the island already. The man, Mariam's ex-husband, was standing on the beach. He shouted that he had wanted to go with her in the boat, but she hadn't waited.

The policewoman could see that the wind was getting up. It was madness. The flock of sheep on the island was running back and forth, spooked by something. She rang the coastguard, while her colleague made his way down to the beach, after Lucija. The policewoman heard a shout. Another man had reached the clifftop – Henry Harcourt-Vane, Eva's eldest son. More police were running up through the woods behind him. All watched as the boat seemed to lurch to starboard in a wave. Eva lifted her hands in the air, as if in benediction, and the wind scooped up objects from the boat and scattered them on the waters. Some papers, a piece of fabric which turned out to be her woollen scarf; it twirled up into the sky, a beautiful, exotic seabird, and down into the oily, seething sea. It was difficult to see much else.

The coastguards were on their way; Eva had almost got the boat as far as Cwen. When suddenly, a wave, or a current, span the boat round. It was carried down the south side of Cwen, and out of sight.

ALICE: I knew it had happened before I heard. I knew something awful—

There was a scream from the beach. The nun, Sister Lucija, ran out into the sea. The policeman was forced to wade in after her, and haul her, wet and salty, weeping and cussing, back to safety.

Eva had gone.

The coastguards were out all night, looking. The storm made things very difficult for them. The wind raged until the following morning, at which point all the local fishermen and women went out; a police helicopter; and islanders on both coasts, walking up and down the islands. It was late in the year; too cold, in those seas, for anyone to have—

ZOE: I can still recall the smell of her. It is so familiar.

That night, in her bed in Oaklands Close, Zoe was woken by the thunder. She shuddered each time the lightning cracked in the sky like a giant breaking bones. When she eventually slept, her dreams were of Eva. She dreamt that Eva and she were in a motorboat, hunched against the rain. The rain splashed across the windscreen and sloshed against the doors. The windscreen wipers lolloped back and forth across the glass.

It is lighter there in the summer, Grandma Eva said, and darker in the winter.

Where? Zoe said.

Where we are going, said Eva.

Where are we going? said Zoe.

Away, said Grandma E. This entire country might lift off and float away, she added.

The islands are like blobs of meringue floating in a bowl of custard, Zoe said.

No they are not, said her grandmother.

That birch tree with the yellow leaves is like a thousand puppets dancing to the same tune, Zoe said.

I don't think so, said Eva.

What is it like, then? Zoe asked.

I think it is like itself.

I am like you, Zoe said.

How so?

But she wasn't sure.

ZOE: When I woke up, my grandmother Ruth was sitting on the end of the bed. My mother Nina was crouched by my pillow.

281

Zoe cried out.

LUCIJA: Given how little they want you to come to their country in the first place, leaving it is harder than you might think. After we had locked Amjad Maher in the cellar, I sat in the kitchen and thought: we have maybe eighteen hours before anyone notices our absence and alerts the authorities. I thought: we have to get out of the islands before that. I thought: let Mariam go up to collect the things we need, passports, money, clothes, while I sit here in the kitchen and think. I thought: if we get to an airport, and take a flight out, to Sarajevo, Zagreb, we can get away, make a new life, leave her crazy past behind us. There are cheap flights to Croatia. Just then Mariam returned with her passport. Mine was burgundy. Why was hers green? I took it from her and had a look. Of course I didn't know the half of it: immigrant teenager on a spouse visa, Pakistani passport, fleeing from her husband. *Plan B*: drive all the way to Sarajevo. At checkpoints between countries, Mariam could hide under the seat. That was how many people I knew had got out of the disintegrating Yugoslavia in the first place. But we were on an island. I couldn't get a car on to the ferry without somebody asking who it belonged to. I thought: why are some lives lived in the extreme? And others wholly placid? *Plan C*: Papa Astrid. We nuns have declared the convent a law unto itself, outwith the writ of any nation-state's jurisdiction. As spiritual force fields go it's quite potent.

JUDGE: Did you plan to steal her Mevludin print from the beginning?

LUCIJA: I didn't steal it. I took it with me as I left because that was my instinct. My country lost its best things during the war. I knew she would have understood. I never had a chance to discuss it with her but in that moment I knew it was the right thing to do. Eva was a very generous and understanding person. Afterwards, I was proved right by the will. She had already thought to leave it to me. She knew it had value to me because of Bosnia, and my friendship with Mevludin's family, far beyond any monetary value. Of all the possessions she could have given me, this one is legitimately mine. A repatriation of culture. A rematriation, rather.

JUDGE: You were lucky, too.

RUTH: We let them both go. He admitted to entering the house. She admitted to acting in self-defence, and using civilian powers of arrest. They had both seen Eva taken away in front of their eyes. An understanding had passed between them. The money aspect – Eva was improvising. He never got the money, nor did he ask for it.

ALICE: After I heard that Eva was missing, presumed dead, my dreams got quite intense. I heard her talking to me, calling to me. I knew only too well what Pomponius Mela had written, about some islands near Britain where some female oracles lived, who could stir up the wind and the waves. My dreams were full of rising seas and totally unseasonable weather events. I felt that Eva was in control of it, in a wild way. She kept telling me things, sometimes she was shouting at me, sometimes she was recounting long ancient stories – all the work we'd been doing together – sometimes she was scolding me for not writing fast enough. She shouted about the wind and the rain, how she would stir it all up and make the seas rise and drown us if we didn't wake from our indolence. It was an invasion of my personal space. [*Blows nose*] I got into such a state that my husband didn't want me to go back to the islands ever again. He was worried for the effect on my mental health – what had Eva done to my head? I was beside myself with worry – Eva was missing. Why? What did it mean? Which legend was it?—

JUDGE: Thank you—

ALICE: And weeks later, when I finally unpacked my small travelling bag, from that last trip, in the seams were little runnels of archipelago sand, mud and grit. It was as if Eva had sent me a message, saying, *I made you promise, and now, whatever happens, however difficult it becomes, I want you never to forget.* [*Weeps*]

By mid-December in the islands, the sun is low on the horizon, its light in islanders' eyes, ears, on their skin and tongue. The strong winter winds, which strip the silver birch trees of their little dancing leaves in seconds, blow the leaves out to sea, blurring the boundaries between earth and water. The sea rises. Everything empties. Only the trees stand out on the horizon, tall and black and spare. And so the sun comes in, resplendent.

In Her House, the sun was flowing in from the garden, filling the house with its colour. Zoe's feet crunched in the broken glass at the bottom of her grandmother's bed. There was a photograph of young-Eva that she hadn't seen before. Somebody, a ghost, had placed it on the bedside table. She opened the window to let the wind waft in the smell of earth and sea. The heartless, ever-restless, elsewhere-bound sea. Then she lay on her grandmother's bed, tears running down her cheeks. She lay there, listening to the wind. She could feel it, all around her, rattling the window, bringing in its sea breath. The wind and the sun, speeding Eva away on her migration.

NINA: She might've sat there forever if we hadn't gone to get her.

The correct thing would have been to have laid out the body in her best dress, with white quartz pebbles over her eyes, because quartz is the stone of second sight; and her ears stopped with beeswax, in case the spirits took her on a tour of hell; and a crab apple in her mouth, for nourishment on her journey – crab being the most fertile of fruit trees, and its fruit the most long-lasting. (The goddess Anu eats the crab when she wades at dawn through the Moon-drawn waters.) The dress should have been of undyed hemp or linen, the weave of kindness and compassion, with a belt incorporating one strand coloured with woad, to signify the Isles of the Blessed and the waters of these islands. And in her hands they should have placed a wand of hazel, for divination, and around her hair a thong of birch and mistletoe, for shape-shifting, and twisted around the second finger of her left hand, a ring of amber, showing her wisdom. And her grave should have been orientated to the rising winter solstice sun, and her bier scattered with hazelnut shells, because the nut of that tree is so plentiful and tasty, even a small child will eat it. And the mound covering the grave should have been so huge that every passing boat would have known that a great woman lay there, and hence to feel fear and respect, as well as great sorrow. And her followers should have been allowed over the water to pray at her grave, once the mound had been raised, and to remember her with songs and weeping. Yes, all that Cwen would have done.

Instead, she lays her out in the underwater cave beneath the island. With her own hands she chooses limpet shells to trace the pattern of her bones. Scallops to emerge from her scalp like curls. Mussel shells over her eyes. Cowries on each of her fingers and toes. A grey pebble with a white streak of sky over her nipples. An oyster, rainbow-sheened inside, its hard grey barnacle ridges the whorl of her pudenda.

In this way, shell by shell, stone by stone, she becomes her.

NANA PEAZANT: *The ancestors and the womb, they one, they're the same. We carry these memories inside of we . . . Let them old souls come into your heart . . . let them touch you with the hands of time. Let them feed your head with wisdom that ain't from this day and time. Cause when you leave this island, Eli Peazant, you ain't going to no land of milk and honey.*

Julie Dash, *Daughters of the Dust*, 1991

No woman is an island-ess.

Chris Kraus, *I Love Dick*, Los Angeles, 1997

13

Women

ZOE: [*Weeps*]

Nobody knows who placed the first shell. It may have been Stella – she has a good eye for a symbol. The day after Eva disappeared, women began arriving at the Islands of Women Study Centre, with their vulva-shaped offerings in the vagina-shaped harbour, where the air has the reassuring rank tang of dead fish and seaweed. They brought fingerprint-pressed cowries, lapis-streaked mussels, yellow ridged limpets, and left them in her honour. Not, as the council tried to claim later, to the detriment of public health (*littering of highway*).

JEN: I would go past in the evening, and tidy up the shells. Some people were treading on them, perhaps on purpose; it was making a mess . . . and I didn't like to think of Eva's memory being trampled on. It was chaos. Eva missing. We were waiting for the coroner's report.

Since it was cold at that time of year, and in order to encourage people to linger – *it was really important to do that* – the women began giving out soup and tea, chocolates and cake; miniature bottles of whisky, donated by the Archipelago Women's Whisky Distillery. They set up a book of remembrances under a shelter.

JEN: The sons wanted a memorial service; and for the estate's affairs to be settled. They still had no idea, at that stage. Then there was Zoe.

Zoe went looking for her, after the storm. She walked up and down the beach, regardless of the tide, the waves breaking over her, feet slipping on seaweed, face cold with tears.

She stood looking out at the island of Cwen. She knew that Cwen knew.

NINA: Mum said, she needs to go and see a therapist. My doc in Ayrness referred her to a guy – a man. Zoe's friends said it was outrageous but still. That's who was available in Ayrness at short notice.

His office had a window which gave on to a car park, behind which was the cinema, a building that, until comparatively recently, had represented the very pinnacle of adulthood for Kath, Pauline and Zoe on the nights when they managed to get into 18s. Beyond the cinema was the main road, and on the other side of that was the hospital where Zoe was born.

Concentrate on the good things, the man said, the first time, and so Zoe pressed her fingers into the blue settee, with its rough fabric pattern like corrugated cardboard, and tried to think. What were the good things? She didn't want to be talking to this man. She wanted to be back on the beach, walking and looking.

The air in the therapist's room smelt faintly of the breath of people who ate curry last night for tea. The man sat looking at her. What would he do, if she told him the good things? She hadn't said anything yet. He continued to wait. He was young but not handsome and was dressed like a teacher.

Try and recall the last pleasant thing you did together, the man said. Zoe watched a white van with blue lettering on its side draw into the car park and cruise around twice, looking for a space. She glanced back at the man, who was looking at her with a little frown between his eyes. Obediently, to show that she was taking his words seriously, she shifted on the settee, turning her body away from the window. She looked at the man's desk, which was fake wood with one locking drawer on the left like the teachers' desks at school, but with nothing on it.

Can you think of one nice thing you did together? said the man, looking at her with his blinky-blue eyes. There were only nice things. And she didn't want to think of them because from now on—

RUTH: She began going out, to parties. A bit defiant.

The day the new mural of Eva was defaced, Zoe went to Tommy Marsden's party at his house in Ayrness. His parents had gone to Berwick for the weekend. She hated the whispers, the boys asking if you were OK, the girls who stopped talking when you walked by. But if she stayed home she would sleep, and if she slept, she would dream, and then when she woke—

At Tommy's house there were vodka bottles, whisky, beer and cider. Zoe drank several quite evil cocktails very fast and was sick for what seemed like hours into Tommy Marsden's parents' bathroom toilet, with its pine-scented blue ball of toilet cleaner under the rim. She wiped her mouth on the pale pink towelling toilet-seat lid before lifting it again and heaving out more vomit. She remembered kissing Benny Shearer and, before he could get excited, being sick on his new Nike trainers. She didn't even like Benny Shearer.

NINA: She began screaming in her sleep.

Zoe would wake to the sound of Nina sleeping on the floor by her bed: snoring because there was a draught and she didn't have a pillow.

'You're seeing your therapist again today, aren't you?' Nina asked.

Zoe groaned. The groan made her feel strange in her body, and pained in her head. *Maybe she was going to die, too.* 'Maybe I'm going to die,' she said, out loud. Nina jumped up. 'Zoe! Into the bathroom. I'm going to ring that therapist and ask him to see you every day. Once a week isn't enough. Into the shower, dressed, out.' She called down the passage: 'Mum, will you come and help?'

Ruth came rushing from her bedroom, in her dressing gown, hair sticking up. 'Out of bed, pet,' said Ruth.

Zoe squeezed her eyes shut.

'Right then,' said Nina.

'Ready?' said Ruth.

They pulled back Zoe's bedcovers and heaved her upwards.

'*Oh,*' Nina said.

'What?' Zoe asked.

'*Oh,*' said Ruth.

It was the first time Zoe had seen Ruth cry up close.

She looked down. There was blood on the bedsheet and her old Minnie Mouse cover.

'Oh,' Zoe said.

With a finger, she touched the red, and drew it in a streak across the sheet.

She felt arms around her shoulders, wet kisses on her cheeks, and – as she closed her eyes in amazement that the moment had finally come – the cold whisper of something else passed through her: not just the screaming of the wind the night her grandmother left, but a warm breath on her face, the sharp scent of island salt, a thing with a womb and two breasts, who was and wasn't a woman.

RUTH: She was changing too much. Before our eyes.

Nina dropped Zoe at the therapist's office on the way to work.

What is your earliest memory – The therapist was wearing pale blue trousers. Really ugly. The frown between his eyes was more like a bulge. He wasn't young after all. Probably he was really old, like in his thirties – *of your grandmother?*

All Mx Thompson's talk in assembly was of intergenerational sharing in Native American menstruation circles and modern-day 'red tents' – but her grandmother was gone from her. The flow between generations had been staunched, in Zoe's case. She felt a wave of self-pity. Water welled up. Tears and snot. Hot face, pain behind the eyes. Zoe clenched her fists. She felt angry with this man. Stupid, ugly man. She didn't want to cry. The memory came to her of walking along the beach at Cwen, holding some cowries in her fist, and Eva bending down, kissing her on her head, and the happy feeling inside, the certainty of being loved. Zoe wailed.

Ah good, said this most annoying man.

After the session, Zoe walked outside into the cold tangy air. Her face felt all blotchy. But as she stood in the street, and the wind pummelled her face and whipped her hair around her head as if it were alive and trying to tell her something, she found that she didn't need any help understanding. She no longer cared about her father's neglect. She no longer cared about her stupid uncles. She no longer cared about Pauline and Kath and how mean they could be. She would be happy regardless of whether Ravi was just a friend. She felt all these thoughts flowing out of her with the blood itself. She watched the boats in the harbour, then she took out her phone and walked to the porch of the Islands of Women Study Centre to be out of the wind. She rang her mum, who wouldn't be able to pick up, because she was at work. But Nina answered immediately. 'I love you, Mum,' Zoe said. 'Of course you do,' said Nina. They talked about Mariam, who was still on Papa Astrid. The nuns were in communication with her husband, who hadn't been charged with trespass, but was still hoping not to divorce her. Mariam really wanted her quilt back from him. But Sister Geraldine said that the people she needed to talk to were immigration lawyers. 'Meanwhile, I'm thinking of a change of career,' Nina said. Now that Zoe was almost grown-up, she wanted to do something really meaningful, to her personally, and what she had really really loved, she missed it so much, was the baby-toddler stage, the warmth and the cuddles. So, she was thinking of setting up as a childminder. She could do it from home, and childminders were in short supply in the islands. You'd be brilliant at that, Zoe said. They were still speaking, when a call came in from Sebastian.

'It's Sebastian calling,' Zoe said.

This never happened.

'Is it?' said Nina. 'Well hang up, then, see what he wants.'

Zoe heard *heaving noises*, as if Sebastian was practising breath meditation, or yoga, or was having sex. Zoe had heard two of her classmates having sex in Tommy Marsden's parents' bedroom while locked in their toilet. Her father sounded like one of them. Then Zoe realised he was crying.

JUDGE: In what spirit did you release the video of Sebastian Vane in the orchard?

TARA: In the spirit of anger and disappointment and frustration. Of course, I was wrong to do that. I see that now. In doing so, I behaved like them. But we had tried the political angle first – the insider dealing, we published copies of the application George Harcourt-Vane had submitted to the Islands' Council – but somehow, although it gained traction, it didn't stick. He hung on. It was the sex angle, finally, that did it.

CAMILLE: I was at work when it happened.

All morning Camille had been troubled by a test result. All the doctors in genito-urinary had them done, every year. Obviously, for the past twenty years, they'd come back normal. This time she had chlamydia. She was just absorbing the possible implications of this when somebody knocked on the café window.

CAMILLE: It was my lunch break. I was eating my sandwich in a café on the corner of South End Green. A number of things too personal to go into contributed to this moment, but when I looked up from my coffee and sandwich, and through the window, and saw a photographer standing in the street, pointing a lens at my face, I knew that my life in England was over. There was a click from the other side of the glass and I ducked, spilling coffee on to my lap. As I stared down at my shoes, and felt hot coffee soaking through my skirt and trickling down my leg, I thought: I have eaten lunch on this street every weekday for the past eight years. I thought: That's it, I'm moving back to France.

She thought: I don't care whether or not he comes with me.

Afterwards, she wished, in particular, that she hadn't taken out her mobile, dialled her husband's number, her head still ducked below the table, and in a *shocked hiss* told him that she had had enough, that his nation was small, his ethnicity corrupt, that she despised his brothers, that it was time for her to move away with the children – to Senegal. This last bit was a mistake. Because, although she might have felt, in that moment, like removing the children as far as possible from their paternal culture, she wasn't going to move to Senegal, just like that; which made her sound irrational (hysterical), and she was a woman who had spent her entire life making sure the opposite sex couldn't find any fault with her like that. She had no point to prove. Had she been able to grasp the scale of his crime against herself, she may well have acted differently. May not have acted at all. May have sat still and thought. May have sat still and weighed her love in the balance: its long history, its great early passion, the feel of him, the smell of his hair (animal), the tone of his voice (she liked it), the things he said, the ways he touched her. And if Seb was now in tears, and if it was, indeed, taking him a little while to realise what she was talking about, this only illustrated how annoying men were, how predominantly deaf always, when women spoke. Whereas, when she spoke, she seemed to feel the soft warm French-then-Senegalese breeze passing over her skin, in counterpoint to the cold English rage she was experiencing. She knew, even as she was speaking, that a stronger rhetorician than she would have left the argument at that. But she had months, if not years, of suppressed anguish to air. And so out came the things she had been thinking about Britain and her British life, into the startled air of the still-below-the-table phone conversation. She had tried to make her home among these people and these places but the task was too enormous and she now felt defeated. She felt betrayed by the politicians who were introducing structural financing which was taking the NHS to which she had devoted twelve years of her career down the route of part-privatisation, and this crisis was made exponentially more disastrous by the fact that it was her husband who was a part of that political process. There was a silliness to England that she found infuriating. A lack of seriousness! You still have a queen! Even your revolution, your civil war, whatever you call it, was a failure! Your women are so self-deprecating! Why was she often the only black person at parties, at the events they went to? Had her blackness been an asset to him in his political progress? Is that why he had wanted

295

her to appear beside him in public? Was it? Had he no shame? She was a person with a life to lead, and British politics and British cultural life were making her life a farce. It was a colonised mentality; you people never have recovered from being a distant, unimportant colony of Rome. Did he know that there were at least two female rulers in Britain when Rome invaded – he hadn't known that, had he? Celtic women owned property and land; they had professions. Unlike the women of the empire. And you British, without questioning whether what you had was actually better, allowed those Roman values to prevail; for they, with their anti-female mentality, made you feel like barbarians. *You never got over it.* Worse, you took that Roman woman-oppression and exported it around the world.

At this point, Camille got out from under the table – mobile phone still pressed to her ear – and walked towards the door, not caring about the photographer any more – indeed, she had forgotten all about him. Thus, she was momentarily unprepared for the dazzling cacophony of shutters clicking, for the ten reporters who held up their recording devices and screamed over each other. She froze, still unsure what was happening. Until one voice – a voice that she would never forget as long as she lived, for it was the voice that made everything clear, a posh, Oxbridge-educated, youthful voice, belonging to a woman – said,

'Are you going to leave him, Mrs Vane?'

CAMILLE: I never mentioned Eva to him. I felt sorry for that later. Because what I was busy feeling was this huge relief. I was thinking: I'm going home.

The island gossip made Zoe cry, for Camille and the children. Alice wasn't the only one he had propositioned, apparently; other women had come forward, or were rumoured to have done, one by one, in pairs, in threesomes.

NINA: Really, that man.

ZOE: I guess he was ringing to tell me. To alert me. All the journalists. That was good of him, I suppose.

JUDGE: Maybe he realised—
ZOE: Maybe.

STELLA: Like father, like son.

NINA: It was too much, after Eva's disappearance.

RUTH: Once the coroner's report was released, the solicitor was able to begin settling the estate. In the meantime, the family arranged Eva's memorial service. By then I was really worried about Zoe.

The rain rattled down on the roof of the church, causing the vicar to clear her voice, and the sons, who were doing most of the readings, to speak even louder than normal. The women scattered themselves throughout the church, Jen and Inga near the front, Zoe's schoolfriends and teachers and colleagues from the museum café dotted here and there, Ravi (honorary schoolgirl) near the font, Zoe herself sitting with Nina (new haircut) and Ruth (in her uniform) in the pew behind Sebastian and his children, his brothers and their offspring, all dressed in smart black coats from Paris or New York or London. It was – Camille said later – a severely buttoned-up affair, literally, figuratively. Who cried? she said. Zoe. Zoe wept noisily, in gulps, her judders audible to everyone, even to Stella and Tara, twenty pews behind. She wept and wept so that her nose streamed and her hanky turned to mush and Nina and Ruth took it in turns to hold her and soothe her.

CAMILLE: The church was packed like that because people loved her.
INGA: Because of the mystery.
JEN: People were shocked. There were rumours that she'd been seen. There were theories about how she might have survived. Some hero-types went and searched the English skerries, even, which are uninhabited. But most people respected her and, whatever the outcome, they wanted to show that. All the good work she did, it went beyond the college, the Archipelago Women's—
RUTH: Island people turn out for each other, we're good that way.
LUCIJA: She touched many lives, as the phrase goes.
NINA: The service was *properly big*.

STELLA: This was the moment we realised – because of the numbers of women who attended – there were crowds of people in the churchyard. We saw how her work had become bigger than herself.

TARA: It transcended her. It was awesome.

Lucija, too, was in tears as she sat in the church. She was there with the other nuns, but she was also representing Mariam Maher, who couldn't be present until her legal situation was regularised. Lucija was there for herself, also. These past few weeks, watching Mariam pray in her bedroom at the convent, with her hands and face and feet clean, and her hair tucked away in a headscarf, Lucija admired but was unable to take part in the purity of this solo act of worship. The concentration, the hallowed whispered words, the bending and prostrating and lifting and kneeling and standing. Mariam had promised she would pray like this for Eva, while the service was going on at Harcourt. Lucija wished she could do the same, sitting here in the church. But it was impossible to pray now that Eva was gone.

It is true that Eva's disappearance, plus the son's political–sexual scandal, and all the gory details in the tabloids, had drawn people out of their winter lethargy and into the pond-stillness of the old island church. It was her they had come for, of course, but there was something else. Before the inquiry was announced, and islanders were invaded and scrutinised by the mainland, there was a moment of gradual, dawning collective knowledge. Islanders felt that Eva – who was theirs – should be recognised for all the good she did. Her service to the college. Her support for the paper (Ursula King had published a gushing editorial). Her success on Skellar, with the Archipelago Women's Club, which drew in tourists from as far away as London.

And also to defend what she stood for from her sons – mainland men.

Islanders who might not normally have considered squeezing themselves into their black funeral suit with its old-fashioned bum flaps, and ironing a bright white cotton shirt – such as Eva's dentist, for example – or brushing the dust off a heavy tweed overcoat which smelt strongly of mothballs, and removing from the buttonhole this November's poppy – such as the head of Ayrness High's Board of Governors – for a person with whom they weren't exactly on dining, let alone regular-telephoning terms, nevertheless made this effort. Women who, during Eva's life, had not counted themselves her friends, felt moved by the articles they read in the paper. They recalled chance meetings with tenderness. The statements put out by Inga at the council, the discussions on the radio, the usual internet community chatter, all testified to Eva's general goodness. When a call went out from somewhere to bring shells to the church, as a symbol of how Eva was lost to the sea, and to whom she belonged, every mourner who knew held a shell in their hands to leave at the foot of the altar.

The most surprising people found themselves depositing a shell. The dean of the abbey. The headmistress of Ayrness High. Barbara Anderson from the museum. Nothing had prepared the sons for this spontaneous symbolic act. It was an upsurge of island unity. Nobody had told them to bring shells. There they stood, empty-handed, out of touch.

For even though she was Jewish, it was the dominant local cult that claimed her. Her children had been christened in that church, her husband buried in the churchyard, and it was in this church with its paintings of Isa on the wall, that her sons chose to stage her farewell. Octavia, Eva's daughter-in-law, chose the hymns and the readings, in consultation with Henry and George, and ordered flowers and food for the wake with the help of Harriet. Seb was not consulted – because nobody was speaking to him, and both brothers and both their wives were glad that Camille, despite having come to the islands for the service, had not come up to the house beforehand, or after. Firstly, it gave them an excuse to cut her out. Secondly, it was Camille who had sent her syphilitic patient to Harcourt House. Thirdly, it was Seb who had brought Harcourt to the attention of that patient's crazy Islamist husband. Fourthly, it was Camille who was leaving Seb, when she ought to stand by him – *they could work through this, that's what everybody did* – but basically, yes, they were both totally toxic, and the sooner she cleared out, the better. Fifthly, it was almost Christmas. They would get the memorial done, and then they would go home to London, and try to take the grandchildren's mind off it, with lots of presents, and a stint somewhere foreign. It was freezing up in the islands.

CAMILLE: I saw it all before it happened, the bickering and squabbling—

RUTH: The assassinations of character when the substance of the will was revealed. I just wanted to get Zoe out of there. I feared for her. Not for her life but for her well-being.

INGA: How the sons reacted to her work presaged all the rest.

Camille said afterwards that all the unsayable things that were uttered, the horrible tones of voice, the nasty accusations – could actually be seen, months, even years in advance: waves of discord scurrying across the bay, silent crests appearing out of nowhere, luscious spillages of familial rifts borne thither by the tides. Camille, especially, understood how the little things had always irked her brothers-in-law – the way in which their mother doted on Seb, her baby; how Seb's wife had been given Harry's mother's pearl earrings (by Eva; I hated them, said Camille), and Henry's wife Harriet was given the emerald ones (by Harry), but Octavia, George felt, had always been undervalued by his parents for reasons he didn't understand at all (But she got the ruby necklace! Harriet cried). These disputes were inflated beyond their individual worth, until they bounced around the house like children's balloons at a party, innocent of the explosion that would occur when the women noticed the missing diamonds. Worse, all the prejudices and attitudes which Henry and Harriet, Octavia and George, had harboured for so long, and had suppressed more or less during Eva's lifetime and throughout Camille's marriage, now began seeping to the surface. Their thoughts were oil spills on water, heavy, polluting liquids which sloshed again and again against the smooth plaster façade of their voices and expressions, until the derangement began to show – an angry red pustule appearing in the middle of Octavia's immaculately made-up cheek (*She wouldn't know, being French, or wherever she is from*); a mottled streak across Harriet's forehead (*I can't believe the pearl set is going out of the country!*); a whitehead glowing from George's nose (*But your children can't be considered true Harcourt-Vanes, not in the spirit of the past generations. Not if they don't grow up here*).

300

It was for all these reasons – and because she couldn't yet, if ever, face whichever other women were involved in Seb's misdeeds – that Camille left the islands immediately after the service. She wanted to honour Eva in this public way, but she did not want to go to the wake. She, alone of the Harcourt-Vane sons and their wives, kissed a shell and added it to the pile in the church. Then she booked a taxi, flight, and train south. So that, two days later, by the time Seb returned to London, she had taken all her personal possessions out of the house in Highgate, and written a list of what she would like to claim from their marriage, to be trucked to France, Paris, Saint-Germain. It was precisely to that elegant *quartier*, where she had studied once, almost penniless, that she would return, penniful now, with her children. To inhabit the city differently – herself, too – in her new bare knowledge.

JUDGE: You are Zoe's stepmother. What was your feeling at this moment, as you left?

CAMILLE: Of course I worried, still worry, about leaving her alone in the islands. But she is a strong young woman. She has Nina and Ruth. And yes, she grew during that time, into her female power. I feel that, as a woman but also as a doctor.

Islanders outnumbered the incomers by ten to one at the wake, which was held at Harcourt House. Because, whatever the sons intended, it was a proper island shindig. There were lots of mainlanders: acquaintances and family and friends from what, after all, had been a long life, much of it lived elsewhere; tall men with thick grey hair and red noses; old women with powder on their cheeks and pearls around their necks; middle-aged men with dandruff on their collars and mud on their shoes; fabulous-looking teenagers, arrogant and overdressed, up from London; children with haughty expressions and mobile phones, which they played games on, sitting on the stairs. But there were many more people from the islands.

Inside the house, Lucija was helping Nina hand out the filled rolls, cakes and slices which the bakery at Lerston had spontaneously donated. Which was lucky, because Eva's daughters-in-law, on their special diets, really had no idea *how much* islanders like to eat, at wakes especially. As it was, the wine was in danger of running out, and they hadn't thought to get in any beer or whisky. Nina licked sugar off her finger and had a teary moment, thinking of Eva turning up so happy and eager in the hospital when Zoe was born. She'd sat there all night, waiting for a glimpse of the baby, and Nina hadn't even let her hold her.

Outside in the garden, the after-rain glow had evaporated from Eva's plants and shrubs and everything looked naked and shivery and bereft. Zoe was sitting on the bench under the crab-apple tree, looking out to sea. Only a few friends had seen her since the night Eva went. Ruth had become extremely fierce, in the process of recalibrating her own, and other people's, attitudes to Eva. The dead and the still-living; Tara said she gave mother-bears a bad name. The result was that those who had wanted to go round to Oaklands Close, and take Zoe into their arms and weep, hadn't been free to.

As the women gathered around her, Zoe glanced up. How are you coping? somebody asked. Zoe plucked at her plain black jersey dress with her fingers. 'I should've worn something of Eva's; I wished I'd worn one of her dark blue jerseys and her dark blue cords.' 'Why didn't you?' asked Stella. 'Because I came up to the house last night, after the family arrived, and they didn't invite me in.' '*What?*' So Zoe explained how she'd heard Sebastian, but didn't see him, shouting at someone in the study, and that someone turned out to be both of his brothers (as she saw when she tiptoed back through the front door and past the windows); and then she learnt that Camille wasn't staying at the house, that Sebastian almost hadn't made it in, because of the weather; and in the kitchen were her young cousins Polly and Jonah and baby George eating their dinner at the long kitchen table while their mothers, Harriet and Octavia, tried to control the shrieks and stop the cross-table launching of clods of food. 'Not a good time, Zoe,' Octavia said, damp-of-face, one hand held out in warning, as she came through the kitchen door. 'Polly, get your hands out of Jonah's mashed potato!'

Not a good time! Not a good time for her, Zoe, who was used to dropping in whenever she felt like it! Not a good time for Zoe, who for years had kept her schoolbooks and personal things on the desk next to the window in the library! Not a good time for Zoe, who had half-grown up there!

'What did you do?'

'Went home,' she said with a sad smile.

'Oh Zoe!'

'There was still so much that she wanted to achieve, wasn't there.'

'Those sons of hers—'

'*Please.*'

'Not the publicity she wanted, it is true.'

'Not exactly.'

'It's such a tragedy.'

'You need to be radical if you want any change to happen.'

'Eva held a lot of tensions in check. There are people on the warpath already and talk like this will just—'

'During the service they didn't even mention any of her wor—'

'Not even the Islands of Women Study Centre—'

'Or the Archipelago Women's Club.'

'The homily was a travesty.'

'Who cares about that? We own Eva's legacy now. Have some pride.'

'Did you see how many women came?'

'Her sons have no idea. There's no competition.'

'What's going to happen to it next? To the house and everything?'

'I just don't believe that Eva was unprepared. I'm not sure, but for now let's just trust that she knew what she was doing, you know?'

Zoe spoke up, low but clear. 'She said that you had to deal with it all comprehensively, and in detail. It's taken generations to get this far, a slow and gradual shift. You have to give people time to adapt, she said; and when the time does come you have to act quickly. She said that the most important thing is for us all to work together.'

'Hello,' said a male voice.

It was Ravi.

'Oh,' said Zoe. She got to her feet, pleasure radiating upwards.

'I've uploaded a new playlist for you,' he said. 'And I've got Lisa O'Neill on CD, for your mum to play in her car. Where is she?'

'I think she's indoors,' said Zoe, 'I'll take you.'

And she led him away across the grass, into the house.

The women she had left behind all began speaking at once—
'Who on earth is he?'
'Very nice.'
'Are they ... you know?...'
'His mother is Banu Yildiz from the—'
'We supported her green housing initiative? I hear she's very enlightened, in her own way.'
'Married one of the men from the fish farm.'
'Can't hold that against her. The boy's a total dreamboat.'
'If only I'd had a boyfriend like that when I was fifteen.'
Tara and Stella, sitting where Zoe had, under the crab-apple tree, looked stoically out to sea.
'I used to think,' Tara said to Stella, 'That *we* made him, you and I. Through our intellect, out of desperation.'
Stella sighed.
'But actually he's a collective fantasy, the projection of all our unmet longings.'

JUDGE: Did she ever talk to you of the man she loved in Sarajevo?
ZOE: Daris? No.

During the wake, and before the house was locked up (illegally) by her sons, Jen took down from the attic bedroom the portrait of Eva as a young mother that Harry had commissioned after she gave birth to George: ugly thick daubs of oil, with Eva looking awkward, dressed up in pearls, done by the same artist as the one of Harry in the college library. Propped up in the window of the Islands of Women Study Centre, and garlanded in marigolds and seaweed, the portrait took on a different aspect: mysterious, compassionate, knowing. (When her sons saw it there they accused the Foundation of theft but were ignored.)

Meanwhile, the line of shells grew longer. The cowries, pressed into putty on the wall; mussels and limpets: prostrating pilgrims. The greater threat was from boot heels and anger, but soon Inga kept two women sitting there at all times, under the shelter, with soup and cake and sweeties. To everyone's surprise, the most unexpected women came forward as volunteers. Pauline Parker and Kath Kidman. Their mothers. Then others, and still more.

By the time the shell line stretched around the corner of the building, the schoolchildren had begun painting the mural of Eva on the wall that faces the sea. (It's still there today, minus the offending graffiti.) When arriving from Astrid or Dounsay, it's the first thing the eye alights on. Unlike the oil painting of the woman as young mother, the mural of Eva as crone captures her vitality. She looks happy: in her essence. They did her in black and white, with rainbows coming out of her fingertips and mingling with her hair. Behind her is the island of Cwen.

At the time of Eva's disappearance, the house was still owned by her outright; and it was reckoned by Inga and Jen (a little defensively, it is true) that had she intended to leave it to her sons, and should they have wished to keep it, they would have found it hard to raise the money from their existing assets to pay the monumental death duties. They would have complained about having to sell the house, of course, and would have used their mother's inaction over the issue of inheritance tax – she should have given it to them years ago, that was the correct and proper process – as a scapegoat. But in reality they would have been as glad of the money as they were happy to imply that their hands were tied. For times had changed. Their wives had more than full-time jobs, their children were at school in the south, and since they were all wedded to the south now, they would have put Harcourt House on the market, and with the proceeds bought a holiday house in Italy (Harriet); a gold-trimmed handbag (Octavia); a piece of land in Casamance (Camille). And Zoe would have become the only Harcourt-Vane left in the islands.

But that is not what happened. Instead, Eva left the house to the Islands of Women Foundation, a registered charity, which didn't have to pay inheritance tax and therefore, as the press release put it, 'is extremely privileged to keep this fantastic asset for the future of all women and the world'.

SEBASTIAN: George was in debt. Problems with his business. Well, what can I say. If our mother had acted correctly, it would've sorted him out.

HENRY: I could see the Burne-Jones had gone. But nobody knew where. Then came her last will and testament, revealing the extent of the damage.

JUDGE: You and your brother immediately took action to dispute it.

HENRY: She was overly-emotional. Had Father known how emotional she was, how easily she was swayed—

GEORGE: We couldn't believe it.

ANNE: Their own mother, the poor boys, it was such a shock. Once after my brother Harry died, Eva asked me if I felt like a victim of primogeniture! [*Raised eyebrows*] I didn't think about what it meant, at the time; it was simply too embarrassing. She wasn't from the same milieu, so she didn't understand.

SEBASTIAN: The solicitor explained that my mother had made several changes to her will, in the weeks before her presumed death. There was no doubt, he said, that Eva Harcourt-Vane remained, until that time, in sound mind and body.

HENRY: We dispute that, of course. It began with small things: the photographic print by Mevludin, the photographer from Sarajevo, which was being left to Sister Lucija from the Papa Astrid convent. I collect photography. Mother knew that.

CAMILLE: I was in Paris. The children asleep in bed. Sebastian rang me in a state. He was babbling. He thought I knew. The Burne-Jones – Eva had sold it for eight million! He said: Do you know what she's done with it all, everything our father collected, and his father and father before him? I didn't know. I had no idea. It turned out that she'd gifted it to a feminist foundation. I felt a complete and total thunderbolt of pride. Wow! She did it. *Bravo, Eva.* And the rest? Sebastian took a deep breath. I could hear him trying to control himself. *Everything* else, her share in the Archipelago Women's Club on Skellar, her father's Hampstead flat, her shares in this and that, the newspaper and other things, she'd left to Zoe. *Formidable!* He said, I think the Hampstead flat is probably worth more than Harcourt House. I laughed, Well, that was hers, outright. I asked him: What did she leave you? He said: She's left us a few things. I asked: The furniture, you mean? The carpets? He said: Henry got the Isfahan carpet. I got the walnut cabinet and the table inlaid with tortoiseshell. George got— I interrupted: She's given you the love-things. What does the money mean to you? You have plenty of money. [*Pause*] I added: And the other thing, she's made it so that Zoe is formally recognised as part of the family. *Enfin! Félicitations, Eva.* And it's true! You know what? For the first time in his life, Eva had focused his attention.

The Islands of Women Foundation, with Jen at its head, took control of the house. The items of furniture that Eva had bequeathed to her sons (for she was sensitive on that point, whatever they claimed) were picked up by courier and taken south. Alice had been appointed executor, but she didn't return anybody's calls – it was said that she was ill. So Zoe took it upon herself to catalogue Eva's literary archive: every book, every physical piece of writing, every letter that Eva had saved, the folders of Harcourt House history and business, the files about the Islands of Women Study Centre, the notebooks, chequebooks, letters and papers. It took up most of the study: Eva's literary output. Zoe went through it all, notating every item. It was tedious but it was also an act of love.

Jen encouraged Zoe to pick out small items of little monetary value but great emotional worth, while the estate was being settled. Nobody would notice if she took Eva's blue Guernsey, her last packet of wine gums, the collection of Bosnian things, the coffee pot, a bracelet which Lucija said came from Dubrovnik. Zoe did so in silence. She was often quiet in those days.

The one thing the women couldn't access was Eva's computer. That was really frustrating. Nobody could find where she had written down the password. Why hadn't Eva thought of that? There was a computer expert in Berwick but he was a man.

WOMEN: *We have come together here tonight on Cwen to give each succour in this difficult time of Eva's passing. We should also take a moment to find compassion in our hearts for Eva's sons, who had no idea that their mother would act as she did, and cannot consequently understand it. To them, no mother or wife ever acted in this way, from the beginning of the world. We should have compassion for them in their moment of confusion.*

On the Friday night before the winter solstice, Zoe went to Lorraine Henderson's Christmas party in the Hendersons' barn out beyond Lerston. Everyone in her class was going. She went in her clear-eyed state, even though she hardly ever spoke to Lorraine, who had been going out with Finn Thompson for almost the whole year and lived with him in a hermetically sealed love-unit. There was a long table of cider and beer bottles in the barn and they'd somehow put up disco lights and even a strobe. Lorraine's older brother was DJ-ing. As Zoe watched her schoolfriends dancing in their jerky inert ways, she felt another flood of lucidity. There were some things that mattered; but there were many things that didn't. She waved kindly at Pauline and Kath, who were dancing on the edge of the group, dressed in what looked like brand-new ruched velvet bodycon dresses; they must have gone to Berwick specially. With Pauline in red and Kath in green, they looked like demented Christmas elves. The shimmering velvet created an impressive dancefloor phosphorescence. Zoe admired the effect from afar. But she didn't want to talk to them yet.

Outside, it was a clear night. Zoe tipped her head back and stared up at the Milky Way. Oh, the stars were amazing. You could wander into fabulous intricate thoughtscapes just thinking about the distance, the time, the infinite space. She heard a voice and turned. It was Ravi.

'Hello, Zoetrope,' he said.

Zoe didn't even blush as she said, 'My bleeding began.'

He held out his hand. 'Open it.'

She prised apart his fingers and there in the palm of his hand was a little glass bottle with a pipette labelled *Drink me*. 'My mother makes it from herbs and roots to relax in the evenings but if you drink a whole pipetteful you can hear the music of the spheres.'

He squeezed some liquid into her mouth, then his. They looked at each other. 'Can you hear it yet?' The stars were reaching down and stroking her on the skin and hair. 'It's the stars, I can feel,' she said. She reached up, sensing in her fingertips the stardust she was made of. She reached out for Ravi.

There was a copse of silver birch beyond the barn. When they lay down in the dry leaves, she saw Cassiopeia above their heads, dancing and laughing. Go on, Cassiopeia was saying, don't be shy. The ghostly white trees were beginning to sway and dance; she knew they were watching, she could see their eyes and lips and vulvas, opening and closing. A thousand eyes. She heard the leaves beneath her and felt Cassiopeia's laughter as their bodies touched. His mouth was on her skin. She felt his fingers undoing buttons and pulling away clothing. It was freezing; her skin tingled at his warmth. Where his fingers were, she felt a whispering. She arched her body back; saw beneath his skin, as the hot blood circulated around her body, and her voice dissolved into the saltwaters of Cwen's island, and the moon tides surged through her, and the waves rippled to the ends of her limbs. Her voice rose into the darkness, as the stars laughed with pleasure, and the waters of the island mingled with hers. Zoe's body shuddered in Ravi's hands. The darkness wrapped around her.

Well done, my girl, Cassiopeia said.

JUDGE: During this time between Eva's death and the announcement of the inquiry, did you foresee the problems you would face?

JEN: Not on that scale, no. At the college we were concerned with processing the work that Eva had done, and consolidating her reputation as an educator and thought-leader. By then Inga was facing insurrection at the council. There were reports of male groups coming to the islands, so we were prepared for that, or, at least, alerted to it. Of course, it also took a bit of time for Eva's sons to figure out exactly what had happened. But they immediately began to enquire into the nature of the Foundation, who ran it, how, what its founding principles were; whether there were any chinks there that they could exploit in its charitable status. Eva had been very careful, of course; she'd followed all the best advice. It was a steep learning curve for the sons. Eventually one of them spoke to Colin Grieves, who had worked at the paper; and Dr Finlay, Eva's old boss at the college. They reached certain surmises; feelers were put out on social media. They gradually built a case. I tried not to panic.

RUTH: It began with the flag-burning. Men burning the islands' flag. They piled them up and burnt them in the middle of the street in Ayrness. That was when I really began to worry.

That night, Zoe and Ravi broke into Harcourt House. She had been visiting every now and then, even though it was locked and off-limits. She knew the secret ways in – the window of the downstairs bathroom, for example, the catch of which came loose with a bit of rattling. Once inside, she would run to the alarm by the back door, and press in her date of birth – which was the code Eva had set – before the police were called out. It was worth it, for even weeks later, the house still smelt of Eva: in the kitchen; on the landing outside her bedroom; in the bathroom; in the bedroom itself. Most of Eva's things were there still. Which meant that part of Eva was there, too. So Zoe went to breathe in what was left of her. She would sit in the library, ostensibly leafing through a book, but in reality waiting for the tiniest thing – a gust of air wafting Eva's scent, the way the light fell through a doorway, the worn middle of the stair carpet up to the attic, the creak of the hall door – to trigger the grief she came for. She walked round the house, seeking it out, and when it hit, she'd curl up where she was. The howls, the gasping for air; all this drama telling you, merely, in the end, that you were the alive one. Grief doing for you nothing more noble or glorious than that.

She didn't want to sleep in any of the bedrooms, so they made a bed for themselves at the top of the stairs outside her grandmother's bedroom, using blankets from the attic that had been Mariam's. With his arms wrapped around her, she slept. Again she travelled back, beyond Eva, beyond Eva's ancestors, beyond anybody who bore Eva's name, or Ruth's, to the time when Cwen reigned resplendent on her island. She saw Cwen in the distance, waiting for her. Zoe stepped on to the sand, and Cwen came down to meet her. In one hand she carried an apple and in the other a smooth grey wave-worn stone. The stone was carved with a V. Cwen put the apple to Zoe's lips. Cwen smiled.

When Zoe opened her eyes again, the house was flooded with sunlight. Ravi was still asleep. The landing was echoing with a noise that seemed familiar. Zoe looked around in surprise.

There it was. Eva's house phone on the table in the landing. Zoe got to her feet. With exaggerated care she picked up the receiver.

'Zoe?' said a voice. 'I've been trying to get hold of you for weeks.'

'Hello?' said Zoe.

'It's Parvati,' said the woman. 'I'm calling from India on behalf of your late grandmother Eva. Do you mind if I ask, did you answer the phone in the study? No? Then I need you to put down this handset and pick up the one in there.'

The study. Eva had worked there alone. Zoe knew that it would feel strange, even upsetting, to sit at Eva's desk, the place where she had done so much of her thinking, at her computer, from which she'd managed so much of her campaigning. But it was also true that Zoe had been to almost every other place in the house. She was wearing those places out. Where else was Eva now? Perhaps in the study. So she did as Parvati asked.

'Are you there yet? Excellent. Well done, Zoe. Now, sit down, and place your finger on the keyboard. Perfect, yes, like that. Is the screen changing colour?'

Zoe knew that they'd been trying to unlock Eva's computer. Back before they stopped trying, Jen had called Zoe up, and asked her for some suggestions: different names, addresses, dates of birth. The computer remained impervious.

Zoe touched a finger to the keyboard. Immediately the inert black screen dissolved into green, then yellow, then pink.

'Excellent,' said Parvati.

'There's a text box,' Zoe said.

'Type in your full name, please,' Parvati said.

Zoe typed in her name, and immediately her face appeared on the screen. She jumped. She had a spot on her chin.

'Just a minute,' said Parvati. 'I'm scanning you.'

The screen went black. Then it made a contented-sounding noise, and another box appeared.

'What does it say?' Parvati asked.

'It says, *Ring Alice.*'

'Oh,' said Parvati, sounding surprised for the first time. 'Well, I don't have her number. Can you get it for me?'

'Give me a minute,' Zoe said to Parvati. She sent Jen a text: *ALICE'S NUMBER? URGENT. HER HOUSE. NOW.*

'Here it is,' Zoe said, after a moment. 'Do I need to do anything else?'

'Yes please. Just stay by the phone. I'll speak to Alice and ring you right back.'

JUDGE: Did you finish your edition of female epics?
ALICE: What? Oh, that. No, not yet. Kids—

JUDGE: I see.
ALICE: I did collate some quotations from them.
SOLICITOR: Submission 1a.

JEN: Alice is very modest, but you know, one day I think we will do
something with all her hard work on the epics. For example, as part
of Eva's legacy, we're thinking of setting up a publication wing of the
Foundation. And really, I do love how she shows the development of
thinking about these island women, the ancient obsession with it, the
destructive instinct during the Renaissance, the gradual acceptance
filtering through which you see – you know, from men like Graves
and Deleuze. Yes, Deleuze – of course, I can take him or leave
him – but what I adore about his writing on desert islands is that
he produces this piece for a French fashion magazine in the 1950s,
Nouveau Femina, and they don't publish it! It's further proof; positive
mention of Circe and Calypso is just too scorching. So yes, I love how
Alice proved the persistence of this idea.

Jen had arrived at the house, and was drinking the cup of tea Ravi
had made her, by the time Parvati called back, forty minutes later.
　'Well that was very complicated,' Parvati said. 'Alice was very
hard to deal with, even worse than you. First she was feeding
her daughter lunch. Then the baby started crying – I told her,
go ahead and feed her, I am breast-milk friendly, and anyway, I
can't see what you're doing. Then the toddler wanted ice cream. I
could hear Alice saying, But you haven't had your pasta yet, and
so the toddler began crying too – and I said, Arre, why don't you
just give her ice cream on this one occasion? In India we really
like to indulge our children; what else is childhood for? At this,
Alice herself started to cry. She told me she's been ill. Anyway,
eventually I got her to calm down, and once the baby was drinking
milk, and the toddler had her ice cream, Alice sat down in front
of her computer and pulled up the files that Eva and she had got
ready. She told me all about this really interesting theory she'd
come across recently in an academic paper, very densely written
but she wished she could tell Eva, about how, although most
words for *queen* in Indo-European are derived from the word for
king – you know, like *rajan* and *rajni* in Sanskrit – in fact, originally,

312

back in the ancient days of sacral kingship, when the goddess reigned supreme, in the earliest Sanskrit texts, the Rig Veda for example, it was the female word for strength, *raj* in Sanskrit, that gave rise to the word for king! "The early Indo-Europeans had no kings." Cute, no? Here in India we just celebrated the festival of Dussehra, which I guess is all about the annual death of the king, and the total triumph of the goddess. We call her Durga. So, you should be getting the draft email soon. I hope it's not too late. Alice said, if you can just wait until eight or so tonight, after her children are asleep, she can discuss the final wording with you.'

INGA: The first I knew of it was the email, sent at 8.40 p.m., apparently from Eva, or from the *office of Eva Levi*, asking the recipient to be ready for a global gathering, all expenses paid, in the islands. A claim form was attached.

The phone rang. It was a woman from Edinburgh, from a women's group, saying, *Thank you for the important email invitation*, and, *Of course they would love to accept*, and, *Yes, the time had come*, and, *Did they have any dates in mind*, and, *But of course, they were ready to be actioned whenever the moment came*. The phone calls continued all that evening and into the next day. Some of the women said they'd called before. The ones who'd called during the memorial service, and had got the daughters-in-law, had had the phone put down on them. (Women with accents they didn't recognise and didn't respect.) Others had been calling while the house was closed. Now that it was open again, the phone never stopped ringing. From the grave – or so it seemed – Eva had called up her people.

Zoe was sitting in the kitchen at Harcourt, munching toast, when two texts came in on her phone at once. She read the one from Camille first. *Come and see us. We are waiting for you.* The other was from Tara. *Meet harbour bus stop @8. Party clothes.*

She texted back: *Ravi too?*

Tara: *Ravishing in a dress.*

When Zoe and Ravi reached the harbour it was already deserted. They'd considered a clothes swap but since what Zoe wore wasn't dressy enough, for Ravi, she'd rung up Pauline, who lived in Ayrness, and borrowed her mother's 1960s kaftan for him.

It was in the kids' dressing-up box anyway. This is Raymond, she told Pauline; she wanted to be kind. And now, she said, once he was in the kaftan, which had blue and silver stripes, This is Ravi. I need some eyeliner, Ravi said; and Pauline did it for him.

They waited at the bus stop, holding hands shyly (at least *all* of the passers-by undoubtedly knew who she was and were bound to tell on her to Ruth), and didn't hear the small car pull up. It honked; a door opened and Tara stepped out. She enfolded Zoe in a giant hug; Zoe smelt sandalwood and oranges and coffee. 'Where are we going?' Zoe asked.

'You'll see,' called Stella, who was sitting in the front, wrapped up in a gigantic green and blue tartan blanket, and smelling, as usual, kind of smoky. She was wearing bright pink lipstick which shimmered on her face like a diesel rainbow in the harbour. 'I've brought you a warm coat. Happy winter solstice, both. Get in the back.'

As Tara drove out along the coast road, Stella talked non-stop: about school, and a trip she was making to London in the spring, and the university she wanted to go to. They turned right, down a bumpy single-track road. It was a cloudy night, the darkness textured and grainy. But behind them came a pinprick of light. When Zoe turned to look, she saw a line of cars, the beam of their headlights, revealing and then reclothing the shoreline as they passed. She watched the waves, silent in the moonlight—

They turned a corner, and there was the curved outline of Cwen.

Somebody had lit a fire on the island. The jagged towering flames loomed up through the night.

'The boats have arrived,' Stella said. 'Here are our masks. I got you a peacock feather one, Zoe. Ravi, this is for you.' She handed him a plain black mask and, when he put it on, Zoe laughed. 'With your kaftan you look like Batman as a hippy.'

Zoe pulled the feathered mask over her face, feeling it tickle her arms as she bent her head to get out of the car. 'You look like the Queen of Sheba,' he said.

She wrapped herself in Stella's big coat and allowed Tara to take her hand as they made their way down to the beach, where a woman was standing on the shore, holding up a flare. Some women were already sitting in the boat, their hands on the oars. Another boat, also lit by a flare, was returning across the water. Zoe had made this journey so often with Eva, she didn't feel scared; but it felt strange and solemn to be rowing through Eva's last journey, in silence, in darkness, into the fire, the oars rising from the water and plunging in again, the waves hitting the bow.

They walked along the beach to join the circle of figures moving slowly around the fire. Zoe remembered the last time she was here with Eva, and the loss lashed out at her. She noticed that the turf had been cut away neatly for the fire pit. With one hand in Ravi's, and the other in Tara's, she joined the people processing around the fire, circling silently, one cheek warm from the flames, the other chilled by the cold. There were probably fifty in the circle; Stella later claimed a hundred. Not being able to see the faces, Zoe found herself focusing on the bodies; *were* they all women, apart from Ravi? She felt a frisson of excitement, and laughter. It was impossible to tell.

A call went up. *We have come here to honour you tonight, women of the islands! We have joined you to celebrate our newest figurehead, Eva Levi, and to ask protection for her work, as it encounters its gravest threat.*

'It's for her, isn't it,' Ravi whispered. 'To keep her with us.'

'Everybody's scared without her,' Zoe said, 'aren't they?'

Before Ravi could answer, Zoe found herself encircled by women. They were spiralling back and forth, reaching out and touching her cheeks, streaking her with something wet and soft, singing and crying, *Aei-ou-aeeeii-ou*, as if she was being preened and rubbed by a colony of seabirds. The circle broke up, and the masked figures began gyrating and dancing. The fire grew higher, the fiddle music started, and some women began to pull off their dark outer garments. Zoe glimpsed sequinned sheaths, bespangled bodysuits, bluish breasts, torsos clad in streaks of colour and iridescent feathers. She recognised the tune Stella had written, wreathing through the bodies with the firesmoke. Another fiddle picked it up, and another; somebody began singing; and the music was all around them.

Tara and Stella appeared beside her. They reached their arms around her, and swayed her body in rhythm with theirs. Above their heads, the clouds cleared, revealing the stars.

'When you eventually see Mariam, tell her we love what she's done for us,' said Tara.

'Make her promise, Tara!' Stella said.

'I promise I'll tell her,' said Zoe.

'Not that,' Stella said. 'Look up at the stars.'

'You must swear on Cassiopeia you won't leave her up there in the sky, unavenged,' said Tara. 'Promise you'll find the strength. Even though Eva has gone you mustn't give up. Now is the time. This is just the beginning.'

JUDGE: Was there anything illegal about these meetings on Cwen?
RUTH: No. I was angry with Tara and Stella for getting Zoe to go too, but then again, she came back so happy ... Even her mother has started going to the daily meetings that have been held during this inquiry.
JUDGE: Have you ever been?
RUTH: I have, yes.
JUDGE: Is it an ongoing process? When are you going next?
RUTH: [*Pause*] Tonight.
JUDGE: Why are you doing that?
RUTH: Eva thought it was important to connect women to the world around them. In the islands, most women know a fair bit about nature. But Eva stressed the things beyond our planet; the stars, for example, like Cassiopeia. Like most constellations, Cassiopeia itself means nothing out there in the solar system. How we see it, spread out against the sky, is not how it is in three dimensions.
JUDGE: And your point is?
RUTH: [*Pause*] You have to understand that, with men in charge, naturally the messages that the women here are spreading can seem a bit challenging. I understand that, of course. I'm a practical woman. But then, as a *police*woman, I have begun to ask myself, isn't this what the law is for?

Zoe danced until the fire died down. At midnight, the boats took everyone home, Ravi and the rest. But Zoe, Stella and Tara stayed behind. They had sleeping bags. They filled their water bottles from Cwen's spring, and pushed open the stone door of the cairn, and crawled down the entrance passage to the chamber. They slept there, the three of them, their heads towards the birthing passage, their feet high up in the womb, *Cwen's triplets*.

They left the door open, so that the next morning, when the solstice sun rose over the islands, it would shine straight down the entrance tunnel, and into the chamber where they lay.

Cwen opens her eyes and shuts them again. Sun. She is here, at last. She is bathing Cwen's eyelids, cleaning her forehead, touching her cheeks, dousing her throat, filling her stomach, aerating her heart, touching her here, there and everywhere, as she always does, at this time of year.

Now Cwen moves with Sun along the entrance passage. As Sun sweeps slowly over the three sleeping girls, Cwen lies down next to them. As Sun kisses their lips, caresses their necks, strokes their collarbones, warms their breasts, Cwen takes the hand of the seaweed-haired girl in her own.

Sun traverses their bodies, infusing them with her power.

By the time the seaweed girl opens her eyes, Sun has rebirthed her entirely.

Between the two of them, Cwen and Sun have made her ready.

———

A Minister may cause an inquiry to be held under this Act in relation to a case where it appears to him that –

*a) particular events have caused, or are capable of causing, public concern, or
b) there is public concern that particular events may have occurred.*

legislation.gov.uk, *Inquiries Act,* 2005

Three local women were disciplined, with one suspended from 'sealing ordinance', meaning she's banned from taking sacraments. The 'disciplinary action' was believed to involve admonishing and rebuking the women at the Kirk session.

The inquiry was carried out by the all-male panel, comprising ministers and elders, following strict rules laid out in the Book of Church Order of the Free Church – dubbed the Blue Book.

'Isle of Lewis church bosses apologise to widow of love-rat minister', *Scottish Sun,* Glasgow, 2018

Judge: Concluding Statements

JUDGE: Thank you all for assembling here today, for the close of the
     public inquiry into Unfair Female Advantage in the Islands.

The judge did not say, *Each time I utter the title of this inquiry, I tingle all
over with excitement.* She wouldn't have been able to, naturally; but
that is what every woman felt when the inquiry opened; and that
is what she seemed to be saying, as she stood up that first day, some
nine months after Eva's disappearance.

It had taken the inquiry three tries before a suitable chairman
could be found. The first ministerial appointee, a QC specialising
in financial fraud, had backed out pleading personal connections
to the inquiry (she had visited the islands as a child; she had once
given legal advice to Harry Harcourt-Vane about an investment
he had made overseas). The second, Judge Stephenson, a Northern
Irishman, felt moved to resign the post after making a preliminary
tour. Online reports that he was targeted by female activists
upon arriving at Lerston Harbour are completely fabricated. The
third, Judge Buxton, had built up a career in trust law, a branch
of commercial law which suggested somebody pragmatic and
sensible rather than an idealist. Of course, she immediately came
under attack, pre-emptively, for being biased on various accounts,
including but not limited to having been born (and continuing

to live) as a woman. Her birthplace itself, in Slovenia, a country about which she had said nothing in public, except once joking to the Bar Council, during her delivery of the Annual Law Reform lecture, that it was so relaxing to have moved across Europe to make her home in a country ironic enough to have St George as a national icon, caused various male commentators to speculate that she probably had a cultural bias in favour of Eva on account of the latter's written work. (Slovenia was the first part of the former Yugoslavia to claim independence.) Somebody anonymous even tried to prove that Judge Buxton and Eva Harcourt-Vane had met once. Mostly, however, the attacks focused on her femaleness, as might be expected.

It was this aspect of herself that the judge chose to address, head-on, in her opening remarks, and the corollary examples she gave, of bias in the other direction, men against women, a bias thoroughly proven by centuries of recent human history, and tempered only partially by her own work history – the cases she had worked on, the judgements she had given, resulting, when analysed by statisticians, in figures quite usual for the profession: where female defendants in magistrate courts are *fined* slightly more often than men (for mild crimes) and *sentenced* significantly less (for severe ones), with a similar pattern emerging in Crown courts; contributing factors being that men represent a far greater proportion of arrests, sentencing and incarceration, with female criminality hovering at around the quarter mark of the total. This line of debate provoked an interesting public discussion, without resulting in a winning personal attack; and indeed, the more everything the judge had ever done was trawled through, probed and tickled for proof of gender bias, conscious or unconscious, in either direction, the more biases pro and against were duly discovered by opposing camps according to their particular agenda, the more rapidly that line of questioning, the one about her being a woman, exhausted itself as efficiently as a gannet regurgitating oily fish into its baby's mouth.

The judge was a tall woman, with – indeed – one of those outrageously coloured, cropped, tousled, product-heavy heads of hair that women in public life sometimes assume in middle age. Not *red* exactly but magenta crossed with poppy interbred with letter-box maternal ancestry and a grandfather who was once a cherry. During the course of the inquiry, people grew to love – not just her flamboyant red hair – but also her deep, growly voice with its faint accent of an upbringing in a place far away. She expressed sense; vocalised calm; was the solid thrum of the double bass, toiling away amidst the hectic street traffic that is the rest of the orchestra. She commanded attention amidst the all-male clamour. But more and more often, as the inquiry went on, she was forced to ask for *quiet*, to demand in particular that the public respect the safety of her witnesses, some of whom had come from outside the islands to talk about their connection to Eva's work, and all of whom were speaking in public at great personal expense. It isn't nice to be made to stand up and position yourself publicly on an issue which probably goes to the heart of your private self as a woman, or a man, the judge said; I wouldn't like it either.

After she had listened to everything that anybody wanted to say, she went on, she would return home, to write her report, which she would deliver in a few months' time. In the meantime, thank you for your time and attention, and in particular for your respect of other people's points of view, many of which are bound to differ from those you yourself hold dear. You may well find discussion of such views upsetting. Please be prepared for a fairly sustained level of public trauma during the course of this inquiry.

And then she began questioning her witnesses, one by one.

The inquiry itself heralded the first outbreak of violence. The protests began the day it officially opened but nobody looked upon them as anything serious: *grumpy men*, out there on the streets, *disgruntled, mildly surprised, taken-aback men.*

It was Inga's evidence, two weeks later, which brought out the gropers and the vandals: the public face of the digital outrage that had flowed back and forth across the water, between the mainland and the islands, ever since Eva's disappearance. Of course, by then the women were used to a few island-born or -resident men protesting outside the library – staff from the high school, some schoolboys, friends of Colin Grieves. They shouted things; held up banners. Occasionally there was a bit of jostling; but nothing overly concerning. It was laughable.

Things got worse when the outsiders arrived. The ferrylubbers. Those from over the water. They were the ones who came over on the boat for a bit of a jolly – and then, when they got there, went on the rampage.

Already, since the inquiry opened, Inga had received more than the usual amount of aggression. She was used to it; she put on a bravado act. She relished men exposing themselves in broad daylight. Later it was claimed by some that she acted as agent provocateur; but she was as surprised as anyone. Nor did the men there need any fake encouragement.

The inquiry's final witness was DCI Ruth Brock. Early that morning, Inga convened a brief women's hearing at the harbour. Anybody watching as they came in by ferry might have thought that the thirty women were praying. The ferry from Berwick arrived at 9.30 a.m. Because the inquiry began at ten, and the women were on foot, they had set off by the time the boat docked in the harbour. Even if they'd seen the cars driving up the ramp and into town, nothing could have told them that that particular configuration of vehicles was special. Some vans; a lorry; the usual air-polluting cars. Inga marched in front. When they passed the Islands of Women Study Centre, the women saluted the mural of Eva and laid down a shell. Then they carried on up the hill and through town to the library, oblivious to what they were about to find when they rounded the corner of College Road.

The crowd was huge. Inga was used to being greeted antagonistically by a small group of men; but this one was massive. Instinctively, the women reached for each other. Inga's voice carried, 'Walk fast, don't stop.' But there were more men than women. Some women hadn't been tested like this, on their principles; they began whimpering a little. They couldn't help glancing at the men as they passed: a boy in a green-striped hoodie; a forehead with pimples; a ginger beard; a red baseball cap; a knuckleduster? (*no, a signet ring*). Trickles of sweat ran down the women's bodies; the body of men parted as they approached; and now they were walking in amongst them, single file or two by two; the men were all around them. The women could smell them – cigarettes, aftershave, laundry powder, sweat, deodorant, alcohol. They could feel their breath. They could hear them breathing. Stella put out a hand. 'Give us some space, please,' she said; and one of the men reached out to shove her. Like her, he was red-haired, pale, he could have been her brother.

324

She stumbled, the women moved to shield her, as Inga, turning to see what was happening, began to shout, 'Get back!' Somebody threw a stone. It hit Inga on the cheek. Hands reached in, some rough; some, sickeningly, stroking, touching, probing. The women screamed. Tara knew how to fight; kung fu at school was part of it, but she looked like she'd been ready for this all her life. Tara was shouting; then Stella scrambled to her feet, had pepper-sprayed four or five men before they even knew what was happening. One guy was bent over clutching his face where she'd smashed the butt of the can into his eye socket. Ravi, who had been waiting at the library doors, began moving down the steps. There was fear on his face. 'Ravi, run and get help,' shouted Stella; 'You, fuck off,' said a big man in a cap, turning to shove Ravi in the chest. From the library steps came shouts of 'Police! Police!', as Ruth – off-duty because she was about to give evidence – ran towards the crowd. 'Police, police, step back, fall back!' In the distance, the sound of sirens; here, in slow motion, Ruth, hitting out with her fists; Stella, now dispensing well-aimed kicks at assailants with her lace-up boots and screaming at the men, *I'll fucking kill you*; Ravi, standing up, blood streaming from his nose. At the sound of the approaching police cars, the men began shouting to each other to scarper. Stella was crying; she was lifted and half-carried up the library steps to where the judge was standing.

The judge had seen it all.

This was the damage: graffiti (*CUNTS*) on the pavement; a mother pushing a pram, surrounded and briefly terrified; a visiting tourist from Norway, groped. But as the men moved away from the library, on through town to the abbey, they grew bolder, encouraging each other all over again with their chanting and shouting. At the abbey, one man climbed on to the shoulders of another; they were all having fun; the top man pulled out his spray can and Barbara Anderson, who just happened to be walking her dog through the graveyard on the way to the newsagent to pick up the papers for the museum café, called out, horrified, 'Get down from there! Get down, you vandals!' The men turned to look at her. The man with the spray can jumped off his friend's shoulders. Within seconds Barbara was surrounded; pushed against the wall of the abbey, her dog yapping as hands reached in. Ruth saw it all:

the knot of men getting tighter, Barbara's voice rising in disbelief.

And yet not disbelief either; not completely. Because deep in their hearts everyone knows how fragile the civilised veneer is; how easy to smash to pieces.

RUTH: I wanted to arrest every man who had threatened my women.

Ruth could do very little; the crime rate is negligible in the islands, and as a result there's a low ratio of police per head of population, compared with other parts of the country. So although she ran at the men with two of her colleagues and got them away from Barbara, and arrested the most obvious perpetrators, the vast majority of the men weren't even cautioned. Nor did the men stop. They continued on through town. Shop windows were smashed. They tried to set fire to the Islands of Women Study Centre. The fire service was called out. Immediately, the council (controlled, more or less, by Colin Grieves) issued a statement urging the women of the archipelago to keep a low profile until peace had been restored. Ruth, while giving evidence that day, raised the question of official collusion with the rioters. At the end of the day, the judge intervened in person – issuing an injunction to the effect that, until the inquiry had concluded, no visiting men would be allowed to the islands unless they could prove prior residence or legitimate, prearranged reasons for travel. Those moving into the islands to be with family and friends were required to report twice daily to Ayrness police station. Social media accounts of troublemakers were being monitored; trolling would be strictly prosecuted. She would present her preliminary conclusions the following Monday; the report itself would be typed up and delivered in due course, but that might take months. In the meantime, there were a few unambiguous statements which needed to be made.

REPORTER: Is this what you expected?
INGA: The inquiry has acted like a lightning rod. A call to arms.
    Solidarity. Any woman who feels this way too should come to the
    islands and join us. We welcome you. For now, male supporters will
    have to cheer from the mainland.

The Sea Nymphs paid for them to come. The emails went out, spinning across the globe, passed from hand to hand, like Mariam and Eva's V-stones. Eva, as she had predicted, drew women in from all over the world.

During the run-up, Zoe barely had time to worry; but in small, snatched moments of repose, she was nervous. Would those other women, the ones they wanted, show their faces? Not the initiated; the others. They were the ones who would make the difference.

In Her House, the women lit the fires, so that Eva's home grew warm again, and familiar, and expansive. As women poured in from all over the country, and beyond, in a great glorious river, they lit fires, and invited them to arrange the little they had brought with them here and there in those large empty rooms. Inga, Jen and Zoe picked leaves and grasses and the occasional winter flower from the garden and deposited them, in jam jars, on every windowsill. They relit the Aga; flicked lighters and made the blue gas dance on the hob; loaded both stoves with Eva's huge saucepans and cooked up a feast. Inga took charge in the kitchen. Nobody could ever remember eating a meal she had cooked but it turned out that Eva had taught her minestrone, and Stella and Tara, after looking longingly through Eva's chest freezer in the shed, pulled out ice-cream tubs filled with summer fruit – last year's blackcurrants, gooseberries and raspberries – and baked a giant cake. There was also wine in the cellar, the distillery sent two cases of whisky, and Lucette Smith herself dropped off boxes of chocolate, daily. Nina drove over with trays of cake, and loaves of bread. Puffed; and when she got her breath back, chatty.

The women kept arriving. Thanks to *The Sea Nymphs*, the Islands of Women Study Centre had booked out all hotel and B&B accommodation throughout the islands for any visiting woman who needed it; but some, the younger ones, especially, wanted to stay in the house. The doors were opened wide, and in they came, with their sleeping bags, and scents, their chatter and their candles. (Absolutely no candles! Jen kept saying.) The house filled with the steam of baths, the smell of coffee, erupting on the stove, the odour of face creams and perfumes, of female sweat, the iron tang of menstrual blood. Voices grew louder, music more raucous; and Zoe, who found that she believed in the unplanned effect, let it all happen.

JUDGE: I have heard what you have to say, and now the time has come for me to offer my preliminary conclusions.

Only very late that Sunday night, once the household had finally fallen asleep, did the nuns arrive. Quietly, they circled the house, slowing as they passed each room, the ground-floor sitting room, study, kitchen; looking up at the darkened windows of the library, bathrooms, bedrooms. They closed their eyes and felt the dreams rising and mingling; from the sleeping forms in the attic, on the landing, in the airing cupboard outside the bathroom, where Stella had made her bed in the warmth given out by the boiler. They allowed the dreams to flicker through them: the modern Kurdish women's army, the fifteenth-century BC female pharaoh, the under-acknowledged Sheban queen, the sex dreams in which the gender of the figures was difficult to discern, the domestic scenes of washing up, hoovering, wiping down of surfaces and children's faces, the elaborate and extravagant finding of beautiful clothes in the local charity shop, the waves of happiness, the peaks of orgasm. Solemnly, they reassembled in the porch. It was cold; the wind was getting up. They joined palms. For a moment there was silence; above the wind, they could barely hear their breath. Then Sister Lucija spoke.

'It is enough. The hour has come.'

In London, Alice sat bolt upright in bed.

JUDGE: I believe that Eva Harcourt-Vane dreamt of what her death might bring, and tried to prepare you for it.

They were listening to her speak from one of the three overflow rooms where the Brighton Women's Tech Group had put up screens. Outside, two women's singing circles, from Southwark and Southall, were feeding the camerawomen and reporters vegetable samosas – they'd set up a street stall with a pan of boiling oil, and a tent behind, where a woman was rolling out dough and stuffing it with spiced potato, pinching it closed in a few neat movements. Because of the judge's injunction, only women had been allowed into the islands these past five days. The local media had covered it for weeks. But for the summing up, there were journalists – women only – from all over Britain and beyond. The London Women's Orchestra had sent a string quartet, who'd been giving free concerts throughout that week in the abbey (Mira Bai, Hildegard von Bingen, Meredith Monk). Through the doorway of the media tent, Zoe contemplated the new mural of Eva that had gone up overnight, on the wall of the library, painted by a street-art collective from Bristol. Eva looked even more messianic than usual, with her arms outstretched, and coloured birds flying up from her breast. Zoe thought of the real Eva, the one with cool palms caressing her cheeks, skin which smelt of cinnamon, the balled-up tissue, pen and packet of wine gums in every pocket of her coat. She felt a flutter of loss. Eva was everyone's; every woman in the islands had a licence to quote her and eulogise her, and to speak of Eva as if they'd loved her, as if she'd loved them.

Eva the icon, Eva who had catalysed this movement, was still here. But the Eva Zoe loved was gone.

JUDGE: She hoped to inspire other people to make the very difficult break with the patriarchal line – through their marriages, jobs, and choices. She knew that something would manifest, and she had prepared for that. It is my belief that, legally, Eva Harcourt-Vane was justified in acting as she did. She believed that what needed to happen was the healing of *all* our ancestral lines. What's at stake is our very existence as humans on this beautiful planet.

There was a gasp from the women around her. The judge was raising her voice as she spoke, over the muttering from the public gallery, and the small guttural sounds of wonder.

JUDGE: Furthermore, I would like to state, categorically, that I have found no wrong-doing with regard to the work Eva did, funded and encouraged others to do, here in the islands. Rather, although this inquiry was called to challenge her 'matriarchy', what it has opened my own eyes to is the need for a thoroughgoing overhaul of the 'patriarchy' in all its forms, invisible though they remain to many. The illegality of the male-dominated cultural construct has been made manifest to me here, as has the danger which it poses to women and other non-human species, in the form of man-made climate change, and other avoidable catastrophes. I now believe, perhaps belatedly – and I do hope that it is not too late – that there is a strong case for challenging it, legally, in all its forms, both here and internationally.

Outside in the yard, from the screen, from the library, began the shouting and cheering, the ecstatic swearing, the hugging and kissing, the jumping up and down, the standing stock-still and staring. The Hand Bells Women's Group from Frome, the Feminist Brass Band of Glasgow, the Edinburgh pop group V were clanging and hooting and singing. The five women from the Mirpur Khas Women's Welfare Organisation left the chai stand they had been running all week, when not leading participants in dancing the *leva* after Maghrib prayers, and whirled together around their Mugarman drum, arms raised to heaven. Zoe didn't move from her seat. Around her, people were on their feet, whooping, weeping. She tried to focus on one clear memory of her grandmother; but already the images were slipping away. The sensation of Eva's cheek against hers. Her hair, like a cloud. She tasted salty tears in her mouth. It wasn't any of these things. It was something else. Her way of being. Her looking after. Her love. *Her love.*

It was here, and it was gone.

It was real, and it was all in her head.

Zoe got to her feet. There was no going back now. She had already become what Eva intended.

Out on her island, Cwen feels the spirits of the dead stirring beneath her. Eva is among them.

The islanders opposite used to whisper that Cwen was guarding a giant's hoard of gold in that mound of hers; that one day they would come over and fight her for it. But Cwen knows what it contains – all the songs these people ever sang, the words of love they whispered, the caresses they gave each other, the stroke of a mother's hand on her daughter's hair, the hope that still exists for this species. She is as sure of it as she is sure of anything. Which is nothing. All the rest – the martial shrieks, children's whines, gods' names taken in vain, cries of humans in their death throes – all that floats upwards with the firesmoke. When it returns to earth, it does so harmlessly transfigured, as the rain itself, or snow, or small, hard balls of hail.

Sitting with her back against the door-stone, Cwen hears the women's shouts. She feels their power. On good days, when the sun falls full on her face, warming her after the cold nights, she can hear the histories, whispering to her. She knows what they are whispering: It will start from here.

Here in her island's fastness, with the sun on her face and the birds overhead and the sea below as defence and larder, Cwen feels the strength of her body and her mind. She feels the strength of Eva. They are mingling into one. Anu, Eva, her.

Here alone they are Cwen.

But out beyond their island, they have gathered their forces.

cwēn *old English*

queen *modern English*

quine *Doric*

Note on Sources

Page 5: I have adapted the words I quote from Strabo's *Geographica* using Horace Leonard Jones' translation in *Strabo: Geography, Books 3–5*, Loeb Classical Library edition, 1923.

Page 19: For Pomponius Mela's *Chorographia* I have adapted F. E. Romer's translation in *Pomponius Mela's Description of the World*, University of Michigan Press, 1998.

Page 39: The quotation from *Agricola* is taken from Cornelius Tacitus, *The Complete Works of Tacitus*, translated by Alfred John Church and William Jackson Brodribb, edited by Moses Hadas, The Modern Library, 1942 (1876). The quotation from the *Annals* is taken from Tacitus, *Annals: Books 13–16*, translated by John Jackson, Loeb Classical Library, 1937.

Page 61: The words I quote from Dionysius Periegetes are inspired by J. L. Lightfoot's translation in *Dionysius Periegetes: Description of the Known World with Introduction, Text, Translation, and Commentary*, Oxford, 2014.

Page 81: The quotation from Procopius is taken from H. B. Dewing's *Procopius with an English translation*, in seven volumes: *History of the Wars*, Books VII (continued) and VIII, Vol 5, London/New York, 1928.

Page 111: The quotation from *Voyage of Bran* (*Immram Brain*) is from Kenneth Jackson, *A Celtic Miscellany*, Penguin, 1951 (1971). The quotation from *The Adventures of Connla the Fair* (*Echtra Condla*) is from the translation by Tom P. Cross & Clark Harris Slover in *Lebor na hUidre*, Henry Holt & Co, 1936.

Page 125: The quotation from Geoffrey of Monmouth's *Life of Merlin* (*Vita Merlini*) is from the translation by John Jay Parry, University of Illinois Press, 1925.

Page 147: I have adapted the quotation from *Völuspá* (*Seeress's Prophecy*) using *The Elder Eddas of Saemund Sigfusson*, translated from the original Old Norse text into English by Benjamin Thorpe, London/Stockholm/Copenhagen/Berlin/New York, 1906, and Henry Adams Bellows's translation in *The Poetic Edda: translated from the Icelandic with an Introduction and Notes*, American-Scandinavian Foundation, 1926 (1923).

Page 172: My translation of the lines from *On the Great Giants* (*Des Grantz Geanz*) is inspired by Lesley Johnson's essay 'Return to Albion' in *Arthurian Literature 13*, Boydell & Brewer, 1995. The quotation from Boccaccio is taken from the translation by Guido A. Guarino, *On Famous Women* (*De Claris Mulieribus*), Rutgers, The State University of New Jersey, 1963.

Page 201: The quotation from Malory is taken from Eugène Vinaver, *Malory Works*, Oxford University Press, 1954/1971. The quotation from Thomas More's *Utopia* is from the translation by Paul Turner, Penguin, 1965.

Page 221: I quote from A. C. Hamilton's edition of Edmund Spenser's *The Faerie Queene*, Longman, 1977; Stanley Wells and Gary Taylor's edition of William Shakespeare's *The Complete Works*, Oxford University Press, 1988; and the RSC edition of John Fletcher's *The Island Princess*, Nick Hern Books, 2002.

Page 245: When quoting from Margaret Cavendish's *The Convent of Pleasure*, London, 1668, I used Anne Shaver's edition published by John Hopkins University Press in 1999. *A Discovery of Fonseca in a Voyage to Surranam. The Island so long sought for in the Western Ocean.*

Inhabited by Women with the Account of their Habits, Customs and Religion. And the Exact Longitude and Latitude of the Place taken from the Mouth of a Person cast away on the Place in an Hurricane with the Account of their being Cast away, Dublin, 1682, is included in Gregory Claeys' *Restoration and Augustan British Utopias*, Syracuse University Press, 2000, along with the speculation that it was written by John Shirley. Reverend George Tulloch's 1845 account of the island of Handa is from *The Statistical Accounts of Scotland 1971–1845*, 'Edderachillis', County of Sutherland, Vol. XV, p. 132. 'Togail an Teine' is taken from Alexander Carmichael's *Carmina Gadelica: Hymns and Incantations, with illustrative notes on words, rites, and customs, dying and obsolete, orally collected in the Highlands and Islands of Scotland and translated into English*, Edinburgh, 1900.

Page 271: Excerpt from Robert Graves, *The White Goddess*, Faber and Faber, 1948 (1961), pp. 67–68, reproduced with permission from the Robert Graves Copyright Trust. Thanks to the University of Chicago Press for permission to quote from Carl Darling Buck's *A Dictionary of Selected Synonyms in the Principal European Languages*. Copyright 1949 by the University of Chicago. Many thanks to Semiotext(e) for permission to quote from Gilles Deleuze's 'Desert Islands' in *Desert Islands and Other Texts 1953–1974*, translated by Michael Taormina, Semiotext(e), 2004.

Page 287: Many thanks to Julie Dash for permission to quote from her film *Daughters of the Dust*, New York, 1991. Thank you to Serpent's Tail for permission to quote from Chris Kraus, *I Love Dick*, 1997.

Page 319: Extracts quoted from https://www.legislation.gov.uk/ukpga/2005/12/section/1, and Simon Houston in the *Scottish Sun*, 2018.

Elsewhere in the book, Alice paraphrases Jeffrey Jerome Cohen's *Of Giants: Sex, Monsters, and the Middle Ages*, University of Minnesota Press, 1999, and quotes *The Riverside Chaucer*, edited by Larry D. Benson, Oxford University Press, 1988. Some of the words Colin speaks are adapted from a BBC Frontline Scotland documentary,

The Witch Hunt. Where Mariam quotes from the *Risalo* by Shah Abdul Latif, I have adapted Elsa Kazi's translation (Hyderabad, Sindh, 1965; http://apnaorg.com/books/english/shah-jo-risalo/book. php?fldr=book). Parvati quotes Prof Kim McCone's essay, '"King" and "Queen" in Celtic and Indo-European', *Ériu*, vol. 49, Royal Irish Academy, 1998, pp. 1–12.

I first heard Lisa O'Neill's rendition of an Irish traveller song from the Cassidy family on Radio 3's *Late Junction*, a show which I have loved from the beginning. (I can still remember the thrill of it; standing in my kitchen in Orkney and looking out at the night, as that voice sang of murder and revenge.) Lisa's version, which she calls 'Along the North Strand', was released in 2018, just after the years in which the book is set; but maybe it toured presciently to my islands before that. If not, then it definitely arrived with Sam Lee, who recorded a beautiful version, 'Northlands', in 2012. Of all the other wonderful music I listened to while writing this book, Björk's *Utopia* was particularly apposite; in particular track four.

Acknowledgements

If *Cwen* has an editorial apotheosis, I found her in Helen Conford, with whom it was a joy to work. I am very thankful for the care taken by Sarah Chalfant, Alba Ziegler-Bailey and all at the Wylie Agency. It has been a pleasure entrusting this book to the fabulous team at Profile: Andrew Franklin, Hannah Westland, Niamh Murray, Anna-Marie Fitzgerald, Valentina Zanca and Sarah-Jane Forder. In particular I would like to thank my Highland managing editor Lottie Fyfe for her great fortitude and forbearance. Thank you to the directors of Arcola Theatre in Hackney for my desk; to Santa Maddalena Foundation; to Hawthornden Castle Writers' Retreat; to Arts Council England for supporting the related art film and project about islands of women (https://www.alicealbinia. co.uk/cwen-islands-of-women-film); and to the Royal Literary Fund, a utopia for its writers during lockdown.

Goddess-armed Rebecca Carter, who read an early draft of the book, was wonderfully kind and astute as always. Tristram Stuart (Cwen when dress-ed) was a paragon of patience and a creative force. Arthur Jafa was a proper deus ex machina. Thank you to friends who read early and late drafts, especially John-Henry Butterworth, Clare Carlisle, Amy Cooper, Millie Darling, Jonny Davies, Rose Gibbs, Ruby Hamid, Léonie Hampton, Caroline Martin, Flora Pethybridge and Laura Yates; and to those who shared invaluable thoughts and criticism during the editing: Rowan Boyson, Lily Cole, Taran Khan, Rubina Greenwood, Ivana Ivičić, Alba Gibbs Joffe, Ralph Mathers, and the metaphor-defying Shan Vahidy.

While I was writing this book, my mother, siblings, in-laws, housemates, husband and friends all looked after my children, and by extension, me. I am so grateful – especially to said daughters. This is for you, interlaced with love, transcendent memories of grandmothers past, present and future – and the happy spirit of my father, whom alas (like your father's father), you never got to meet.